Andrew Smith knew ever since his days as an editor of his
high school newspaper that he wanted to be a writer.
He is the author of the highly acclaimed and Carnegie-nominated
Grasshopper Jungle and the much anticipated *The Alex Crow*.
He lives in rural Southern California with his family.

GRASSHOPPER JUNGLE

ANDREW SMITH

For Michael Bourret,
who would not allow me to quit.

First published in the USA in 2014 by Dutton Books,
a division of the Penguin Group (USA) Inc.,
375 Hudson Street, New York, New York 10014, USA

First published in Great Britain in 2014
This edition published 2015 by Electric Monkey – an imprint of Egmont UK Limited
The Yellow Building, 1 Nicholas Road, London W11 4AN

Text copyright © 2014 Andrew Smith
The moral rights of the author have been asserted

ISBN 978 1 4052 7810 2

58010/5

www.egmont.co.uk

A CIP catalogue record for this title is available from the British Library
Printed and bound in Great Britain by CPI Group

Ealing, Iowa, is a fictional town. None of the characters and places in this book actually exist. Any similarities between events and characters to actual history only occur in the true portions of this book, which aren't that many.

PART ONE: EALING

PART TWO: WATERLOO CORNFIELD

PART THREE: THE SILO

PART FOUR: THE END OF THE WORLD

EPILOGUE: LUCKY, A CIGARETTE RUN, AND THE BISON

PART 1: EALING

I READ SOMEWHERE that human beings are genetically predisposed to record history.

We believe it will prevent us from doing stupid things in the future.

But even though we dutifully archived elaborate records of everything we've ever done, we also managed to keep on doing dumber and dumber shit.

This is my history.

There are things in here: babies with two heads, insects as big as refrigerators, God, the devil, limbless warriors, rocket ships, sex, diving bells, theft, wars, monsters, internal combustion engines, love, cigarettes, joy, bomb shelters, pizza, and cruelty.

Just like it's always been.

KIMBER DRIVE

ROBBY BREES AND I made the road the Ealing Mall is built on.

Before we outgrew our devotion to BMX bicycles, the constant back-and-forth ruts we cut through the field we named *Grasshopper*

Jungle became the natural sweep of Kimber Drive, as though the dirt graders and street engineers who paved it couldn't help but follow the tracks Robby and I had laid.

Robby and I were the gods of concrete rivers, and history does prove to us that wherever boys ride bicycles, paved roadways ribbon along afterward like intestinal tapeworms.

So the mall went up—built like a row of happy lower teeth—grinned for a while, and then about a year ago some of the shops there began shutting down, blackening out like cavities when people left our town for other, better places.

BMX riding was for middle-school kids.

We still had our bikes, and I believe that there were times Robby and I thought about digging them out from the cobwebbed corners of our families' garages. But now that we were in high school—or at least in high school *classes*, because we'd attended Curtis Crane Lutheran Academy since kindergarten—we rode skateboards, and also managed to sneak away in Robby's old car.

We were in tenth grade, and Robby could drive, which was very convenient for me and my girlfriend, Shann Collins.

We could always depend on Robby. And I counted on the hope—the erotic plan I fantasized over—that one night he'd drive us out along the needle-straight roads cutting through the seas of cornfields surrounding Ealing, and Robby wouldn't say anything at all as I climbed on top of Shann and had sex with her right there on the piles of Robby's laundry that always seemed to lie scattered and unwashed in the dirty old Ford Explorer his dad left behind.

———

FIXING FEET

ON THE FRIDAY that ended our painfully slow first week after spring break, Robby and I took our boards and skated through the filthy back alley of Grasshopper Jungle.

Nobody cared about skaters anymore.

Well, at least nobody cared among the four remaining businesses that managed to stay open in the Ealing Mall after the McKeon plant closed down: The laundromat Robby never quite made it to, *The Pancake House*, and the liquor and thrift stores owned by Shann's stepdad.

So we could skate there, and did pretty much whatever we wanted to do.

Judging from the empty beer cans, the mysterious floral sleeper sofa we were certain was infested with pubic lice, and the pungent smell of piss in the alley, it was clear everyone else in Ealing was similarly okay with the no-limits code of conduct in Grasshopper Jungle, too.

And that proved to be an unfortunate fact for me and Robby on that Friday.

We had built ramps from sagging flaps of plywood that we laid across a flight of concrete steps behind a vacant unit that used to be a foot doctor's office.

"Bad business plan," Robby said.

"What?"

"Fixing people's feet in a town everyone's dying to run away from."

Robby was so smart it hurt my head to think about how sad he could be sometimes.

"We should go into business," I said.

"Want to have a fag?"

Robby liked calling cigarettes *fags*.

"Okay."

There was no way we'd ever sit down on that couch. We upended blue plastic milk crates and sat with forearms resting across our knees while we propped our feet on our boards and rocked them back and forth like we floated over invisible and soothing waves.

Robby was a better smoker. He could inhale thick, deep clouds of cigarette smoke and blow life-sized ghost models of both of us when he'd casually lean back and exhale.

I liked cigarettes, but I'd never smoke if Robby didn't.

"What kind of business?" Robby said.

"I don't know. I could write stuff. Maybe comic books."

"And you could draw me." Robby took a big drag from his cigarette. "I'd be like your spokesmodel or something."

I have to explain.

I have that obsession with history, too.

In one corner of my closet, stacked from the floor to the middle of my thigh, sits a pile of notebooks and composition binders filled with all the dumb shit I've ever done. My hope was that, one day, my dumb history would serve as the source for countless fictional accounts of, well, shit.

And I drew, too. There were thousands of sketches of me, of Shann and Robby, in those books.

I consider it my job to tell the truth.

"What, exactly, does a *spokesmodel* do?"

"We speak. And look good at the same time. It's a tough job, so I'd expect to make decent money."

"Multitasking."

"The *shit out of it*, Porcupine."

Robby called me *Porcupine* because of how I wore my hair. I didn't mind. Everyone else called me Austin.

Austin Szerba.

It is Polish.

Sometimes, in wonder, I can marvel at the connections that spiderweb through time and place; how a dying bull in Tsarist Russia may have been responsible for the end of the world in Ealing, Iowa.

It is the truth.

When he was a young man, Andrzej Szczerba, who was my great-great-great-grandfather, was exiled from his home in a small farming village called Kowale. Andrzej Szczerba had been involved in a radical movement to resist the imposition of Russian language and culture on Poles. Andrzej, like many Polish boys, hoped that one day his country, which had been treated like a sausage between the dog jaws of selfish neighboring empires, would be able to stand on its own.

It was a good idea, but it was not going to happen in Andrzej's lifetime.

So Andrzej was forced to leave Kowale—and travel to Siberia.

He did not get very far.

The train carrying the exiled Andrzej derailed when it struck a dying bull that had collapsed on the tracks. It was a terrible accident. Andrzej was left, presumed dead, abandoned in the middle of a snowy field.

Andrzej Szczerba wore a silver medallion with an image of Saint Casimir, who was the patron saint of Poland, on a chain around his neck. He believed Saint Casimir had saved his life in the train wreck, and every day for the rest of his life, Andrzej would kiss the medal and say a prayer, thanking Saint Casimir.

It was a fortunate thing for me that Andrzej Szczerba did not die in that snowy field. Wounded, he walked for two days until he came to the town of Hrodna, where he hid from the Russians and ultimately married a Polish girl named Aniela Masulka, who was my great-great-great-grandmother.

Andrzej's healthy Polish semen made four Catholic children with Aniela—two boys and two girls.

Only one of them, his youngest son, Krzys, would ever end up near Ealing, Iowa.

This is my history.

LOUIS ASKS A RHETORICAL QUESTION

WE LEANED OUR backs against the cinder-block wall, smoking in the cut of shade from a green rolling dumpster, and at just about the same time I talked Robby into taking his car to drive us over to Shann Collin's new old house, I looked up and noticed the population of Grasshopper Jungle had increased uncomfortably.

Four boys from Herbert Hoover High, the public school, had been watching us while they leaned against the galvanized steel railing along the edge of the stairway we had been using for a ramp.

"Candy Cane faggots, getting ready to make out with each other in Piss Alley."

The *Candy Cane* thing—that was what Hoover Boys enjoyed calling boys from Curtis Crane Lutheran Academy. Not just because it kind of rhymed. We had to wear ties to school. Whoever invented the uniform could have planned better to avoid the striped red-and-white design of them. Because when we'd wear our ties, white shirts, and blue sweaters with the little embroidered crosses inside bloodred hearts, you couldn't help but think we looked like, well, patriotic, Christian-boy candy canes.

But Robby and I weren't big enough losers to still be wearing our uniforms while skating.

Well, we weren't so much skating as smoking cigarettes, actually.

Robby wore a Hormel Spam T-shirt and baggy jeans with holes in them he sagged so low you could see half his citrus-motif boxers. They had oranges and lemons on them.

Citrus does not grow in Iowa.

I wore yellow-and-green basketball shorts and a black Orwells tee. So we didn't *look* like candy cane boys.

The Orwells are a punk band from Illinois.

The other part—the *faggot* part—well, let's just say Robby got picked on.

A lot.

I only knew one of the boys: Grant Wallace. It's hard not to know pretty much every kid in a town the size of Ealing, even if you didn't pay too much attention to people as a rule.

However, I did know this: Grant and his friends were there for no other reason than to start crap.

It was bound to be historic, too.

And two 140-pound *Candy Cane faggot* sophomores with cigarettes and skateboards were not likely to stop anything four bored and corn-fed twelfth-graders from Hoover had in mind.

Robby just sat back casually against the wall, puffing away on his cigarette.

I couldn't help but think he looked like a guy in one of those old black-and-white movies about firing squads and blindfolds and the Foreign Legion and shit like that.

One of Grant's friends, a pudgy guy with a face full of whiteheads and only one eyebrow, took his cell phone out from his pocket and began recording video of us.

Consult history: Nothing good ever happens when cell phones are used to record video.

And I guess that was as good as Grant's directorial cue to begin.

"Let me and Tyler borrow you guys' skateboards for a few minutes. We'll bring them back."

Tyler must have been the mule-faced kid on Grant's right, because he nodded, all excited, an encouragement for us to be cooperative *Candy Cane faggots*.

But Robby said no before the question was entirely out of Grant's mouth.

The truth is—and history will back me up on this, too—that when kids like Grant ask kids like me and Robby if they can borrow stuff like skateboards, the boards are either going to get stolen, or the kids like me and Robby are going to be beaten up and *then* the boards are going to get stolen.

The way kids like me and Robby get beaten up first is when one of them says no.

History class is over for today.

We got beaten up by Grant Wallace, Tyler, and some other kid who smelled like he had barf on his sleeves, while the fourth kid filmed it with his cell phone.

Oh, and extra credit in history: You should never wear loose mesh basketball shorts and boxer underwear if you're going to get kneed in the balls. Just so you know for the future.

I don't even think either one of us made it all the way to his feet before the kicks and punches started. Robby got a bloody nose.

Grant took our boards and chucked them up onto the roof of *The Pancake House*.

Then the four Hoover Boys took our shoes off and threw them on the roof, too.

And if the boards didn't make such a racket when they landed, Grant and his friends would have taken Robby's and my pants and sent them up to shoe-and-skateboard heaven, too. But the Chinese guy named Louis who worked in the kitchen of *The Pancake House* stuck his face out the back door, and asked, politely, what we thought we were doing.

I do not know what I thought I was doing.

But that question, in itself, when asked by a Chinese pancake chef named Louis, was enough to make Grant and his friends call an end to their diversion.

I was curled up on my side, cupping my nuts, while the sleeve of my black Orwells T-shirt adhered to some gooey piss stain on Grasshopper Jungle's asphalt.

Grant and the Hoover Boys left, and Louis, apparently satisfied with the lack of an answer to his rhetorical question about what we boys thought we were doing, shut the door.

For a moment, I found myself wondering, too, why guys like Grant Wallace, who called guys like me and Robby Brees *faggots*, always seemed to take pleasure in removing the trousers of littler guys.

That would be a good question for the books, I thought.

THERE'S BLOOD ON YOUR SPAM

"ARE YOU HURT?"

"Balls. Knee. Boxers."

"Oh. Um."

"There's blood on your Spam."

"Shit."

GRANT WALLACE MURDERED ME

ROBBY FELT BAD, not because of his bloody nose. Because he blamed himself when things like this happened. He cried a little, and that made me sad.

We recovered.

History shows, after things like that, you either get up and have a cigarette, in your socks, with your bloody friend, or you don't.

Since it wasn't time for Robby and me to die, we decided to have a smoke.

I believe Andrzej Szczerba would have wanted a smoke when he pulled himself, bloodied, up from the wreckage in that snowy field in Poland.

There are as many theories on how to deal with a bloody nose as there are ears of corn in all the combined silos of Iowa.

Robby's approach was artistic.

Propping himself dog-like on his hands and knees, he hung his head down, depositing thick crimson coins of blood from his nostrils and simultaneously puffing a cigarette, while he *drip-drip-dripped* a pointillist message on the blacktop: *GRANT WALLACE MURDERED ME*

I watched and smoked and wondered how our shoes and skateboards were getting along, up there on the roof.

Unfortunately, as funny as it was to both of us, Robby stopped bleeding after forming the second A, so he only got as far as GRANT WA

"Nobody's going to know what that means," I said.

"I should have used lowercase."

"Lowercase does use less blood. And a smaller font. Everyone knows that."

"Maybe you should punch me again."

I realized I'd never punched anyone in my life.

"I don't think so, Robby. You got any quarters on you?"

"Why?"

"Let's go throw our shirts in the laundry place. You need to learn how to use those things anyway."

So Robby and I limped around to the front of the mall and went inside Ealing Coin Wash Launderette, where, maximizing the return on our investment, we not only washed our T-shirts, but the socks we had on as well.

"This is boring," Robby observed while we waited for the fifth dime we slotted into the dryer to magically warm the dampness and detergent from our clothes. "No wonder I never come here."

"Doesn't your apartment building have a laundry room?"

"It's nasty."

"Worse than this?"

"This? This is like Hawaii, Porcupine. Sitting here with you, barefoot, with no shirts on, watching socks and shit go around."

Robby lived alone with his mom in a tiny two-bedroom at a place called the Del Vista Arms, a cheap stucco apartment building only three blocks from Grasshopper Jungle. We walked there, in our damp laundered socks and T-shirts.

Two of the apartments on Robby's floor had Pay or Quit notices taped to their doors.

"Wait here," he said, and he quietly snuck inside.

It meant his mother was home. Robby usually didn't like people to come over when his mom was there. I knew that. He was just going to get the keys to the Ford and take me for a ride, anyway.

So I waited.

"The blood didn't come out of your Spam shirt," I said.

We drove west, down Mercantile Street toward my house, and I noticed the diffused brown splotches of post-laundered blood that dotted Robby's chest. And he was still in his socks, too.

"I'll loan you a pair of shoes when we get to my house," I offered. "Then let's go get Shann and do something."

I glanced over my shoulder and checked out the backseat.

I wondered if I would ever not be horny, or confused about my horniness, or confused about why I got horny at stuff I wasn't supposed to get horny at.

As history is my judge, probably not.

"I think we should go up on the roof and get our shit back. Tonight, when no one will see us. Those were my best shoes."

Actually, those were Robby's only non-Lutheran-boy school shoes.

I was willing.

"I bet there's some cool shit up on that roof," I said.

"Oh yeah. No doubt everyone in Ealing hides their cool shit up on the roof of The Pancake House."

"Or maybe not."

WHAT MADE THIS COUNTRY GREAT

ROBBY HAD AN older sister named Sheila.

Sheila was married and lived with her husband and Robby's six-year-old nephew in Cedar Falls.

I had a brother named Eric.

Eric was in Afghanistan, shooting at people and shit like that.

As bad as Cedar Falls is, even the Del Vista Arms for that matter, Eric could have gone somewhere better than Afghanistan.

Both our moms took little blue pills to make them feel not so anxious. My mom took them because of Eric, and Robby's mom needed pills because when we were in seventh grade, Robby's dad left and didn't come back. My dad was a history teacher at Curtis Crane Lutheran Academy, and my mom was a bookkeeper at the Hy-Vee, so we had a house and a dog, and shit like that.

Hy-Vee sells groceries and shit.

My parents were predictable and ominous. They also weren't home yet when Robby and I got there in our still-wet socks and T-shirts.

"Watch out for dog shit," I said as we walked across the yard.

"Austin, you should mow your lawn."

"Then it would make the dog shit too easy to see and my dad would tell me to pick it up. So I'd have to mow the lawn *and* pick up dog shit."

"It's thinking like that that made this country great," Robby said. "You know, if they ever gave a Nobel Prize for avoiding work, every year some white guy in Iowa would get a million bucks and a trip to Sweden."

Thinking about me and Robby going to Sweden made me horny.

SHANN'S NEW OLD HOUSE

FIRST THING, NATURALLY: We got food from the kitchen.

We also made dirt tracks on the floor because socks are notoriously effective when it comes to redistributing filth from sidewalks, lawns, the Del Vista Arms, and Robby's untidy old Ford Explorer.

I boiled water, and we took Cups-O-Noodles and Doritos into my room.

Robby sat on my bed and ate, waiting patiently while I recorded the last little bit of the day's history in my notebook.

"Here." I tossed my cell phone over to the bed. "Call Shann."

"Have you ever *smelled* a *Dorito*?"

"Mmmm . . ." I had to think about it. I wrote. "Probably not."

"Just checking," he said, "'Cause they smell like my nephew's feet."

"Why did you smell a six-year-old kid's feet?"

"Good question."

As usual, Shann got mad because I had Robby call her using my phone, and when she answered, she thought it was me. This, quite naturally, made me horny. But Robby explained to her I was writing, and he told her that something terrible had happened to us. He asked if it would be okay that we came over to her new old house as soon as we finished eating.

Robby was such a suave communicator when it came to relaying messages to Shann. In fact, I believed it was the biggest component of why she was so much in love with me. Sometimes, I wished I could cut off Robby's head and attach it to my body, but there were more than a couple things wrong with that idea: First, uncomfortably enough, it kind of made me horny to think about a hybridized Robby/Austin having sex with Shann; and, second, decapitation was a sensitive topic in Ealing.

Well, anywhere, really. But, in Ealing during the late 1960s there was this weird string of serial murders that went unsolved. And they all involved headlessness.

History is full of decapitations, and Iowa is no exception.

So, after we finished eating, I outfitted Robby with some clean socks, a Titus Andronicus T-shirt (I changed into an Animal Collective shirt—all my tees are bands), and gave him my nicest pair of Adidas.

And both of us tried to pretend we didn't notice my dad's truck pulling up the drive just as we took off for Shann's.

"Perfect timing," I said.

Robby answered by pushing in the dashboard cigarette lighter.

Besides all the head-cutting-off shit that went on fifty years ago, Ealing was also known for Dr. Grady McKeon, founder of McKeon Industries, which, up until about six months ago, employed over half the town's labor force. Grady McKeon was some kind of scientist, and he made a fortune from defense programs during the Cold War. When the fight against Communism went south on McKeon, the factory retooled and started manufacturing sonic-pulse shower-heads and toothbrushes, which ultimately became far more profitable when made in Malaysia or somewhere like that. So the factory shut down, and that's also why most of the Ealing strip mall was deserted, and why every time I visited Robby at the Del Vista Arms, there were more and more Pay or Quit notices hanging on doors.

And that's a half century of an Iowa town's history in four sentences.

Grady McKeon was gone, but his much younger brother still lived and ran businesses in Ealing. Johnny McKeon owned *Tipsy Cricket Liquors* and the *From Attic to Seller* thrift store, both of which were big crowd-pleasers at the strip mall.

Johnny, who was responsible for thinking up the names of those two establishments entirely on his own, was also Shann's stepfather.

And Shannon Collins, whom Robby and I called Shann, her mother (the relatively brand-new Mrs. McKeon), and Johnny had just taken ownership of the McKeon House, a decrepit old wooden monstrosity that was on the registry of historic homes in Ealing.

Well, actually, it was the *only* historic home in Ealing.

It took Robby and me two cigarettes to get to Shann's new old house.

It had already been a rough day.

We were going to need another pack.

————

GOING SOMEWHERE YOU SHOULDN'T GO

SHANNON KISSED ME on the lips at the door of her new old house.

She kissed Robby on the lips, too.

Shann always kissed Robby on the mouth after she kissed me.

It made me horny.

I wondered what she would say if I asked her to have a three-some with us in her new old, unfurnished bedroom.

I knew what Robby would say.

Duh.

I wondered if it made me homosexual to even think about having a threesome with Robby and Shann. And I hated knowing that it would be easier for me to ask Robby to do it than to ask my own girlfriend.

I felt myself turning red and starting to sweat uncomfortably in my Animal Collective shirt.

And I realized that for a good three and a half minutes, I stood there at the doorway to a big empty house that smelled like old people's skin, thinking about three-ways involving my friends.

So I wondered if that meant I was gay.

I hadn't been listening to anything Shann and Robby were talking about, and while I was pondering my sexuality, they were probably thinking about how I was an idiot.

I might just as well have been a blowup doll.

These are the things I don't write down in the history books, but probably should.

I don't think any historians ever wrote shit like that.

"You have to excuse him. He got kneed in the balls."

"Huh?"

Robby nudged me with his shoulder and said it again, louder, because idiots always understand English when you yell it at them: "YOU HAVE TO EXCUSE HIM. HE GOT KNEED IN THE BALLS."

Shann put her hand flat on the side of my face, the way that real moms, who don't take lots of drugs every day, do to little boys they think might be sick. Real moms have sensors or some kind of shit like that in their hands.

Shann's mom, Mrs. McKeon, was a real mom. She also used to be a nurse, before she married Johnny McKeon.

"Are you okay, Austin?"

"Huh? Yeah. Oh. I'm sorry, Shann. I was kind of tripping out about something."

Having a three-way in Sweden with Robby and her was what I was tripping out about.

But I didn't tell her.

Shann's room *was* empty.

The entire house was mostly empty, so our footsteps and voices echoed like sound effects in horror films about three kids who are going somewhere they shouldn't go.

Thinking about things like that definitely did not make me horny.

In fact, just about the only things I noticed in that musty mausoleum of a house were unopened boxes—brand-new ones—containing McKeon Pulse-O-Matic® showerheads and toothbrushes.

"The moving van's going to be here this afternoon. They just finished at the house," Shann explained as the three of us stood awkwardly in her empty, echoey room.

Because, in an empty bedroom with creaky old wood floors, it is a natural human response to just stand there and shift your weight from foot to foot, and think about sex.

———

ROBBY'S VOLCANO

SHANN AND I started going out with each other in seventh grade.

When I think about it, a lot of stuff happened to us that year.

There are nine filled, double-sided-paged volumes of *Austin Szerba's Unexpurgated History of Ealing, Iowa* for that year alone.

That year, Eric went into the Marines and left me at home, brotherless, with our dog named Ingrid, a rusty golden retriever with a real dynamo of an excretory tract.

People in Ealing use expressions like *real dynamo* whenever something moves fast-er than a growing stalk of corn.

It was also the same year Robby's dad went to Guatemala to film a documentary about a volcanic eruption. Lots of stuff erupted that year, because Mr. Brees met a woman, got her pregnant, and expatriated to Guatemala.

And, just like a lot of boys in seventh grade, I started erupting quite frequently then, too.

A real dynamo.

And, that year Shannon Collins's mom moved to Ealing, enrolled her daughter at Curtis Crane Lutheran Academy (where we were all good, non-smoking, non-erupting Christians), and married Johnny McKeon, the owner of *From Attic to Seller*

Consignment Store and *Tipsy Cricket Liquors.*

And I fell in love with Shann Collins.

It was a very confusing time. I didn't realize then, in seventh grade as I was, that the time, and the eruptions, and everything else that happened to me would only keep getting more and more confusing through grades 8, 9, and 10.

I will tell you how it was I managed to get Shann Collins to fall in love with me, too: My best friend, Robby Brees, taught me how to dance.

I was infatuated with Shann from the moment I saw her. But, being the new kid at school, and new in Ealing, Shann kept pretty much to herself, especially when it came to such things as eruptive, real dynamo, horny thirteen-year-old boys.

Robby noticed how deeply smitten I was by Shann, so he selflessly taught me how to dance, just in time for the *Curtis Crane Lutheran Academy End-of-Year Mixed-Gender Mixer.* Normally, genders were not something that were permitted to mix at Curtis Crane Lutheran Academy.

So I went over to Robby's apartment every night for two and a half weeks, and we played vinyl records in his room and he taught me how to dance. This was just after Robby and his mother had to move out of their house and into the Del Vista Arms.

Robby was always the best dancer of any guy I ever knew, and girls like Shann love boys who can dance.

History does show that boys who dance are far more likely to pass along their genes than boys who don't.

Boys who dance are genetic volcanoes.

It made me feel confused, though, dancing alone with Robby in his bedroom, because it was kind of, well, fun and exceptional, in the same way that smoking cigarettes made me feel horny.

Seventh grade was also when Robby and I stole a pack of

cigarettes from Robby's mom. By the time we got into tenth grade, Robby's mom started buying them for us. She might take drugs and not have one of those sensor things in the palm of her hand like real moms do, but Mrs. Brees doesn't mind when teenage boys smoke cigarettes in her house and dance with each other, alone in the bedroom, and that's saying something.

That year, at the end of seventh grade, Robby confessed that he'd rather dance with me than with any girl. He didn't just mean *dance*. It was very confusing to me. It made me wonder more about myself, whom I doubted, than about Robby, whom I suppose I love.

At first, I thought Robby would grow out of it—you know, start erupting like everyone else.

But there was nothing wrong with Robby's volcano, and he never did grow out of it.

So it was at the *Curtis Crane Lutheran Academy End-of-Year Mixed-Gender Mixer* that Robby casually and bravely walked up to the new girl, Shann Collins, and announced to her:

"My friend Austin Szerba is shy. That's him over there. He is good-looking, don't you think? He's also a nice guy, he writes poetry, he's a really fantastic dancer. He would like very much if you would agree to dance with him."

And everything, confusing as it was, worked out beautifully for me and Shann and Robby after that.

DOORS THAT GO SOMEWHERE; DOORS THAT GO NOWHERE

"OKAY. SO, BASICALLY this house is, like, infested with demons or something," Shann told us.

Demonic infestations have a way of making guys feel not so horny.

"It's in the *Ealing Registry of Historical Homes*," I pointed out.

"People died here."

"You should get that kind of air freshener shit that you plug into outlets so it masks the scent of death and decay with springtime potpourri," Robby offered.

"Look at this," she said. "There are doors that go nowhere, and I swear I heard something ticking and rattling inside my wall a moment ago."

Shann used words like *moment*.

She wasn't from Ealing.

One of the walls in her creaky room had two doors set into it. The wall itself was kind of creepy. It had wallpaper with flowers that seemed to float like stemless clones between wide red stripes. If I pictured a room where I was going to murder someone, aside from the instruments of torture and shit like that, it would have this wallpaper. If I was on death row, awaiting electrocution, I'd be wearing pajamas with the same pattern on them.

Shann went to the door on the left and pulled it open.

When she opened it, there was only the jamb and frame of the door, and then a wall of bricks behind it.

"See?"

I could only imagine what was on the other side of the bricks.

Robby, naturally, felt compelled to say something less than comforting.

"I suggest you don't liberate whatever's imprisoned back there," he said.

Shann was getting angry. I knew I should intervene, but I didn't know what to say.

"Nowadays, people spend a lot of money for distressed bricks like those," I said.

It was probably for the best that Shann wasn't paying attention to me.

"And look at this," she said.

When she opened the second door, a long, narrow stairway extended down into darkness on the other side. The chasm was at least twenty feet deep, but it dead-ended at another distressed brick wall, and there were no other doorways leading off in any direction that I could see.

"What can you expect from a house this old?" I asked.

It was a good question.

Ghosts and shit like that, was what I was thinking, though. You wouldn't expect miniature ponies and trained talking peacocks that dispensed Sugar Babies and gumballs from their asses, would you?

"I don't want to stay in this room by myself," Shann said.

And that made me very horny again.

I also wanted candy.

Shann, obviously stressed, looked at Robby, then at me.

"I need to talk to you, Austin," she said, and motioned for me to go with her down the candyless staircase of death and decay.

Robby took the hint. "Uh. I need to go to the bathroom. Maybe Pulse-O-Matic® my teeth. Or take a shower. Or something."

He made a tentative, weight-shifting creak onto one leg and I followed Shann behind door number two.

We sat beside each other on the staircase.

Our bare legs touched.

Shann had a perfect body, a Friday-after-school body that was mostly visible because she was barefoot, and wore tight, cuffed shorts with a cantaloupe-colored halter top. A boy could go insane, I thought, just being this close to Shann's uncovered shoulders, wheat hair, and heavy breasts.

This staircase to nothing was a fitting dungeon for constantly erupting, real-dynamo sixteen-year-old boys like me.

"Why is Robby wearing your clothes, and what happened to you and him?"

While we sat there, three important things struck me about Shann: First, I realized that, like most girls I knew, Shann could ask questions in machine-gun bursts that peppered the male brain with entirely unrelated projectiles of interrogation. Second, it was often unstated, but clear by her tone, that Shann was jealous of Robby, possibly to the point of being a little curious about my sexuality. I know, maybe that was also my confusion, as well. Because, third, what was most troubling to me, was that despite all the fantasies, all the intricately structured if/then scenarios I concocted involving Shann Collins and me, whenever an opportunity to take action presented itself—like being alone with her in a nearly sealed dungeon—I became timid and restrained.

I couldn't understand it at all.

History chews up sexually uncertain boys, and spits us out as recycled, generic greeting cards for lonely old men.

Dr. Grady McKeon was a lonely old man. I can only conclude he must have also at one time been a sexually confused, unexplainably horny teenage boy who erupted all over everything at the least opportune times. He was twenty-five years old, and well on his way to building an empire of profits when his younger brother, Johnny, was born. I once heard a tobacco-chewing hog farmer say that, in Iowa, folks liked to spread out their children like dog shit on a dance floor.

Dr. Grady McKeon would be Shann's stepuncle, if there is such a thing, and if he weren't dead. He was the last person to live in the historic McKeon house. He died when his private jet went down in the Gulf of Mexico. Its engines choked to death on ash from Mount Huacamochtli, the same erupting volcano in Guatemala that Robert

Brees Sr. was filming a documentary on. And it also happened the same year Robby Brees and I smoked our first cigarette, danced together, and I fell in love with Shannon Collins.

Johnny McKeon never wanted to live in his dead brother's old house. It took Shann's mother about four years of badgering to get him to finally break down and take the place out of mothballs.

I held Shann's hand, and we sat there in the dungeon with our legs pressed together, and I was so frustrated I felt like I could explode. But I concentrated, and methodically went through the entire account of what happened to me and Robby at Grasshopper Jungle. I told her about our plan to climb up onto the roof of the Ealing Mall to get our stuff back.

"I'm coming with you," she decided.

"Not up on the roof," I said, so authoritatively my voice lowered an octave.

Sounding father-like to Shann in the echoing darkness of the staircase that led nowhere made me feel horny, demons or not. I scooted closer and put my arm around her so that my fingers relaxed and splayed across the little swath of exposed skin above the waist of her shorts.

"I'll wait in Robby's car. I'll be your lookout."

"Shann?" I said.

I almost had myself convinced to ask her if didn't she think it was time we had sex, and the thought made me feel dizzy. I would force myself to no longer have any doubt or confusion, to not wind up recycled by history.

"What?"

"This staircase really *is* creepy."

And just as I pushed her firmly against the distressed brick wall and put my open mouth over hers, Robby swung the door wide above us and said, "The moving van's here."

CURFEW

WHILE SHANN'S MOM, the movers, and Johnny McKeon worked at unloading and organizing the houseful of furniture they'd shipped over from their old-but-much-newer house, the three of us stole away in Robby's Ford Explorer on our mission to reclaim our shoes and skateboards.

Friday nights in Ealing, Iowa, rarely got more thrilling than climbing up on the roof of a three-quarters abandoned mall, and we were up for the excitement.

On Fridays, my curfew came at midnight, which meant that if I was quiet enough I could stay out until just before my mother served breakfast on Saturday morning.

I had to check in with my dad and mom, so they'd know I was still alive.

I told them I was going out for pizza with Robby and Shann.

It wasn't a lie; it was an abbreviation.

I was not concerned about going to hell.

Nobody who was born and raised in Ealing, Iowa, was afraid of hell, or Afghanistan, or living at the Del Vista Arms.

Checking in for Robby meant swinging by his two-bedroom deluxe apartment at the Del Vista Arms and asking his mom for five dollars and a fresh pack of cigarettes, while Shann and I waited in the parking lot.

Shann did not smoke.

She was smarter than Robby and me, but she didn't complain about our habit.

STUPID PEOPLE SHOULD NEVER READ BOOKS

IT TOOK ME a very long time to work up the nerve to kiss Shann Collins, who was the first and only girl I had ever kissed.

There was a possibility that I'd never have kissed her, too, because she was the one who actually initiated the kiss.

It happened nearly one full year after the *Curtis Crane Lutheran Academy End-of-Year Mixed-Gender Mixer*.

Like Robby explained to her: I was shy.

I was on the conveyor belt toward the paper shredder of history with countless scores of other sexually confused boys.

After the *Curtis Crane Lutheran Academy End-of-Year Mixed-Gender Mixer*, I tried to get Shann to pay more serious attention to me.

I tried any reasonable method I could think of. I joined the archery club when I found out she was a member, and I offered multiple times to do homework with her. Sadly, nothing seemed to result in serious progress.

At last, all I could do was let Shann Collins know that I would be there for her if she ever needed a friend or a favor. I do not believe I had any ulterior motives in telling her such a thing. Well, to be honest, I probably did.

I'd leave notes for Shann tucked inside her schoolbooks; I would compliment her on her outfit. She laughed at such things. Shann knew it was a ridiculous thing to write, since all the girls at Curtis Crane Lutheran Academy dressed exactly the same way. Still, history will show that patient boys with a sense of humor, who can also dance, tend to have more opportunities to participate in the evolution of the species than boys who give up and mope quietly on the sidelines.

But I began to worry. Rumors were spreading around Curtis Crane Lutheran Academy about me and Robby, even though I never heard anything directly.

Then, in the second semester of eighth grade, I was called in to the headmaster's office for something I wrote in a book report. Even though the book I read was in Curtis Crane's library, as well as the Ealing Public Library, apparently nobody other than kids had bothered to read the book until I wrote my report on it.

The book was called *The Chocolate War*, and the copy I read belonged to my brother, Eric. Mrs. Edith Mitchell, who was the eighth-grade English teacher, assumed the book was about a candy kingdom or something. She probably thought there were magical talking peacocks in the book that shot gumballs and Sugar Babies out of their asses.

But there were teenage boys in the book—Catholic boys—who masturbated.

Boys who attend Curtis Crane Lutheran Academy are not allowed to masturbate.

My father nearly lost his job because I wrote a report on a book that had Catholic boys and masturbation in it.

Pastor Roland Duff, the headmaster at Curtis Crane Lutheran Academy, was very distraught.

He had the school's only copy of *The Chocolate War* resting on his desk when I came to his office.

There, he counseled me about masturbation and Catholicism.

"My fear is that when boys read books such as this," he said, "they will assume there is nothing at all wrong with masturbation, and may, out of curiosity, attempt to masturbate. In fact, Austin, it is true that masturbation has serious harmful effects. It makes boys spiritually and physically weak."

The headmaster patted his forehead, which was damp, with a

handkerchief that had the Curtis Crane Lutheran Academy logo—
a black cross surrounded by a bloodred heart—embroidered on its
corner. I wondered if they had prepared him in his religious training
for giving teenage boys talks about masturbating.

He went on, "In history, entire armies have been defeated
because their soldiers masturbated too frequently. It happened to
the Italians in Ethiopia."

When he said the words *too frequently*, I wondered if there was
some number higher than once or twice per day that would get me
off the hook to hell and military failure.

In any event, I hoped he was right. I hoped the bad guys in
Afghanistan—where my brother, Eric, whose book got me into
trouble, was fighting—were also excessive masturbators like the
Italians.

Pastor Roland Duff continued, "Masturbation can also turn
boys into *homosexuals*."

When he said *homosexuals*, he waved his hands emphatically
like he was shaping a big blob of dough into a *homosexual* so I could
see what he was talking about.

That frightened me, and made me feel ashamed and confused.

Then he called my mother into the office and he talked to her
about masturbation, too.

Up until that day, I was certain my mother didn't know there
was such a thing as masturbation.

As I stood there, shifting my weight awkwardly from one foot
to the other, Pastor Roland Duff told my mother about the *Warning Signs of Masturbation*, so she could keep a better watch over me.

Then he sent me home with my mother and suspended me
from classes for one day.

When I came back to school, Mrs. Edith Mitchell made all the
girls leave the classroom while Pastor Roland Duff explained the

guidelines for books we boys were not allowed to read at Curtis Crane Lutheran Academy. We were no longer permitted to read any books that had masturbation, Catholics, or penises in them. Pastor Roland Duff gave the entire class of boys the same speech he'd given me about masturbation, weakness, and homosexuality.

Once again, he blamed masturbation for Italy losing wars.

That kind of shit never made it into history books, either.

Sometimes, during his speech, he would remark, "As I was explaining to Austin Szerba . . ."

And he would wave his hands as though he were shaping a doughy Austin Szerba in the air, so all the other boys could see what a boy who wrote a book report about masturbation and Catholics looked like.

Then he led the boys in prayer and excused us so Mrs. Edith Mitchell could have a similar talk with the girls.

Robby and I whispered outside that after all that masturbation talk, a cigarette would be nice.

It was the worst day of my life since Eric left home.

Everyone knew that I was the one to blame for all the trouble about masturbating. At Curtis Crane Lutheran Academy, you couldn't hear the name Austin Szerba and not think about masturbating.

I didn't speak in class again for the rest of the year.

Robby thought it was funny and told me I was brave.

Best friends do that kind of stuff.

When the boys were taken out of the room, I wondered if Mrs. Edith Mitchell was telling the girls about Austin Szerba, and how teenage boys masturbate, or if maybe she had found a book with girls who masturbated in it. Thinking about a book like that made me very horny.

The library was quieter and emptier than usual for a long time after that day.

But when the boys came back into the classroom, Shann deftly slipped a note onto my lap beneath our desks. I thought she was going to tease me about masturbating, but the note said this:

Okay, I'll admit it, Austin Szerba, you have finally won me over. I read The Chocolate War, *too. I love that book. This school is full of shit. Let's go get a Coke after class and hang out. By the way, I like what you're wearing today.*

I was dressed exactly like every other boy at Curtis Crane Lutheran Academy.

Later that day, Shann Collins and I kissed for the first time.

It happened right after I said to her, "Stupid people should never read books."

THE DEATH-RAY GUN

AT ONE HOUR before midnight, Shann and I waited inside an old Ford Explorer parked behind the Del Vista Arms. Robby Brees, dressed in a pair of my clean white socks, best Adidas skate shoes, and Titus Andronicus T-shirt, dashed into his apartment to get us more cigarettes and wave, in passing, at his mother.

Events that night were going to set in motion a disaster that would probably wipe out human life on the planet. That night, I was going to say something to Shann I had never said to anyone. I was going to do something I'd never done, and see things I could not understand and never believed existed.

This is history, and it is also the truth.

I sat in the front seat.

Robby refused to chauffeur us around like he was some kind of limo driver, he said, so either Shann or I always had to sit up front with him. This rule increased the degree of difficulty in actually fulfilling my fantasy regarding Shann Collins and Robby's backseat.

But now, Robby was gone.

"What are you doing?" Shann said as I shimmied my way between the front seats, over the center console where there was still an assortment of cassette tapes that had belonged to Robby's dad.

I thought what I was doing was obvious enough, so I said, "I'm looking for my death-ray gun."

"Well, if your ray gun doesn't look like a pair of Robby's underwear or socks, it isn't back here."

Robby needed to stop accumulating so much laundry this way, but it did keep the floor of his room tidy.

My foot got stuck between the passenger seat and console. My shoe came off. I left it there.

"I'm coming back there with you till Robby comes out."

"Robby came out in the seventh grade," Shann said.

A lot of things happened in seventh grade.

"There." I said, "I've never been back here alone with you, Shann. It's rather sexy."

I thought using the word *rather* would make me seem mature and like I was not from Ealing.

"I've never heard you say anything like that before, Austin," she said.

"*Rather?*"

"No. *Sexy*," Shann explained. And she was right about that. I never had spoken about sex with Shann. I was too afraid to.

"Well, it is sexy," I said. I kicked off my other shoe and scooted myself against her.

I put my arms around Shann. I leaned into her and brought my feet up onto the bench seat. I put my lips on her neck and licked her. She gasped.

"Shann, I want to tell you that I'm in love with you. I love you, Shann."

I had never said that before, either.

"Oh, Austin. I love you."

It was the first time Shann said it, too.

Then the dome light in the Explorer blinked on. Robby opened the driver's door.

"You are *not* having sex in my car—on top of my clothes!" Robby said.

I don't remember exactly how it happened, but the basketball shorts I'd been wearing that day were halfway down to my knees.

"Um. No. Robby. No."

Shann coughed nervously and straightened up, while I pulled my shorts back over my hips.

"One of you," Robby said sternly, "up front now. Let's go get our shit."

I squeezed my way back into the front seat.

Robby gave me an intense, scolding stare.

He shook his head and laughed at me. Robby wasn't angry. Robby was as shocked as I was. He and I both knew what probably would have happened if he had waited about one more minute before coming back to the car.

I extracted my shoe from the center console. Somehow my socks had come off, too. I tried to find them. Clothing has a way of abandoning ship sometimes.

Then Robby dropped a pack of cigarettes in my lap and pushed in the dashboard lighter.

He started the car.

"Light one for me, Porcupine," he said.

ROBBY COULD HAVE BEEN A PREACHER

WE CASED THE Ealing Mall.

We sat across the street at *Stan's Pizza*, where we ate and watched through the window.

Stan's closed at midnight. Stan was visibly angry that we came in and ordered. There was nobody in the place, and Stan wanted to go home.

I ordered a large Stan-preme in an attempt to cheer Stan up.

"We'll have a large *Stanpreme*, please. For here," I said.

In the same way that Johnny McKeon was proud for coming up with the names *Tipsy Cricket Liquors* and *From Attic to Seller Consignment Store* entirely on his own, and just as Dr. Grady McKeon was considered a genius for inventing the brand Pulse-O-Matic®, Stan must have been very pleased with himself for creating the concept of the *Stanpreme*.

People from Ealing were very creative.

We didn't know for certain that Stan's real name was Stan. We never asked him.

Stan was Mexican, so probably not.

We sat, ate, and watched.

Stan watched us.

Everything was dark at the Ealing Mall across the street, except the sign over the *Ealing Coin Wash Launderette*. The launderette never closed. There was no need to. Between the hours of 2:00 and 6:00 a.m., it was more of a public bathroom, a hash den, or a place to have sex than a launderette, though.

Thinking about having sex on the floor of the *Ealing Coin Wash Launderette* suddenly made me horny.

Nobody was out there.

This was Ealing at nighttime.

Nobody ever had any reason to be out, unless they were standing on the curb watching their house burn down.

I wondered if Ollie Jungfrau had gone home. Ollie worked at Johnny McKeon's liquor store. *Tipsy Cricket* closed at midnight, too, but it was already completely dark by the time Stan scooted the tin pizza disk containing his eponymous creation down on our table by the window.

That was the first time in history anyone from Ealing, Iowa, used the word *eponymous*. You could get beaten up in Ealing for using words like that.

Just like Robby and I got beaten up for sitting there smoking cigarettes and being queers. But I don't know if I'm really queer. Just some people think so.

We ate.

Robby asked Stan for three ice waters, please.

Stan was not a happy man.

We couldn't finish the *Stanpreme*. It was too big. Stan brought us a box for the three slices we had left on his tin disk.

"Do you think we should make a plan or something?" I asked.

Robby said, "This is Ealing. There's some kind of prohibition against making plans."

If we didn't hate being Lutherans so much, Robby could easily have been a preacher.

NEVER NAME A PIZZA JOINT STAN'S

ROBBY PARKED THE Explorer at the end of Grasshopper Jungle.

He positioned the vehicle facing Kimber Drive, so we could make a quick getaway if we had to.

Like real dynamos.

The pretense of doing something daring and wrong made the rescue of our shoes and skateboards a more thrilling mission to us. Nobody, ultimately, would give a shit about two teenage boys who'd been embarrassed and beaten up by some assholes from Hoover, who climbed up on an insignificant strip mall to get their shoes back.

Shann waited in the backseat.

When we were about ten feet from the car, Robby got an idea.

"Wait," he said. "We should leave our shoes in the Explorer."

It made sense, like most of the shit Robby told me. Once we got up on the roof, it would be easier if we didn't have to carry so much stuff back down. We could wear our roof shoes to make our descent.

It was really good that Grant Wallace and those dipshits didn't throw our pants up there, too, I thought.

We went back to the car.

Shann was already asleep on top of Robby's underwear and shit.

We took off our shoes and left them on the front seat.

Robby grabbed his pack of cigarettes and a book of matches and said, "Now we can do this."

A narrow steel ladder hung about six feet down from the roof's edge. It was impossible to reach the bottom of it, so Robby and I rolled the heavy green dumpster across the alley and lined it up below the ladder.

Then we climbed on top of the dumpster in our socks.

I didn't believe the garbage collectors ever emptied the thing anymore. The dumpster was sticky, and leaked a trail of dribbling fluid that smelled like piss and vomit when we rolled it away from the cinder-block wall beside the pubic-lice-infested couch.

From the top of the dumpster, we could barely reach the lowest rung on the ladder. I gave Robby a boost. His socks, which were actually my socks, felt wet and gooey in the stirrup of my palms.

I felt especially virile doing a pull-up to get myself onto the ladder after him.

Soon, we were up on the roof, where we could stand and look down at the dismal, cancerous sprawl of Ealing.

We lit cigarettes.

Robby said, "You should never name a pizza joint *Stan's*."

We stood, looking directly across Kimber Drive at the yellowed plastic lens that fronted the long fluorescent tubes illuminating the lettered sign for Stan's Pizza.

Someone had painted an *A* between the *S* and *T*, so the sign read: *Satan's Pizza*

People were always doing that to Stan.

They did it so many times that Stan simply gave up on cleaning the paint, and allowed the sign to say what the good people of Ealing wanted it to say:

Satan's Pizza

People from Ealing had a good sense of humor, too.

"I have seen Pastor Roland Duff eating there," I said.

"Did he order a *Satanpreme*?"

It was difficult to find our shoes and skateboards up on the roof at night. As I had originally theorized, there was plenty of cool shit up there, so Robby and I kept getting distracted. It didn't matter much, since Shann had fallen asleep, anyway.

We found a plastic flamingo with a long metal spike descending from its ass, so you could stick it in your lawn and fool passersby into thinking that flamingos were indigenous to Iowa.

Robby discovered two bottles of screw-top wine, full and sealed, and he placed them on the roof beside the top of the ladder.

We theorized that maybe back in the days when Ollie was thinner, he may have climbed up here to get drunk and talk to the flamingo. Ollie Jungfrau weighed more than four hundred pounds now.

Satan's delivered to *Tipsy Cricket Liquors.*

"Have you ever been drunk, Porcupine?" Robby said.

"No."

"One of these days, let's get drunk together."

"Okay," I said.

Like considering most things that were against some well-intended list of rules, thinking about getting drunk for the first time with Robby made me feel horny.

We found two round aluminum canisters that had reels of 16 mm film in them. Nobody watched 16 mm movies anymore. There was an old projector at Curtis Crane Lutheran Academy, but we decided not to take the films, just in case they were pornos or something.

We did want to take the flamingo, though.

Robby placed the plastic pink flamingo next to the bottles of wine.

"One of us can climb down first, then the other can toss down the bird and the wine," Robby said.

Robby also found a Halloween mask. It was covered in fur and looked like the face of a grimacing lemur. It was the face a lemur in an electric chair would make. That had to come home with us, too, we decided.

"If you ever want to get shot in Ealing, walk through someone's backyard at night with a lemur mask on," Robby said.

IF YOU EVER WANT TO GET SHOT IN EALING

WE FINALLY FOUND our shoes and put them on.

I was embarrassed to admit it, but it was kind of emotional for us being reunited with our stuff after that very long day.

I could see how Robby felt the same.

We put our skateboards down with the rest of the things we'd gathered, and then we sat beside the rooftop air ventilation unit to relax and have another cigarette.

"It feels good to have my shoes back," Robby said.

"If we didn't find them, I was going to let you have those Adidas of mine."

"Thanks."

We both exhaled smoke at the same time.

"Austin?"

"What?"

"Do you realize that today we got beaten up for being queers?"

"I know."

"But you're not a queer," Robby offered.

"I don't think so."

"Well, I apologize."

"You didn't do anything, Rob."

Sometimes, I called him Rob.

"I've never done anything," he said. "I've never even been kissed or anything, but I still get beaten up."

"Shann kisses you all the time."

"That isn't what I mean."

"I know."

"Well, if I'm going to get beat up for being queer, at least I'd like to know one time what it feels like to be kissed."

"Um. I guess you deserve that. You know. Everyone deserves to not feel alone."

"Can I kiss you, Austin?"

The air suddenly became unbreathably thin.

I thought about it. I shook my head.

"That would be too weird."

"Sorry."

"Don't be."

We sat there, smoking.

Everything was shitty and confusing.

Robby felt terrible.

I said, "I guess I would kiss you, Robby."

"Don't feel like you *have* to."

"I don't feel that way."

So Robby Brees, my best friend, and the guy who taught me how to dance so I could set into motion Shann Collins's falling in love with me, scooted around with his shoulders turned toward mine.

He was nervous.

I was terrified.

I watched him swallow a couple times.

Then Robby placed his cigarette carefully down on the gravel beside his foot. He put his hand behind my neck and kissed me.

He kissed me the way I kiss Shann, but it felt different, intense, scary.

Robby's tongue tasted like cigarettes when he slid it inside my mouth. I liked the taste, but it made me more confused. Our teeth bumped together. It made a sound like chimes in my head. I never bumped teeth with Shann when I kissed her.

When we finished kissing, Robby pulled his face away and I watched him lick his lips and swallow.

Robby's eyes were wet, like he was going to cry or something. He looked away and wiped his eyes.

Robby said, "I'm sorry."

"No. It's okay. I said you could. I said let's do it."

"Is it okay?"

"I said so, Robby. It was weird. Really. Are you okay?"

"I think that was the best moment of time in my entire life, Austin." Robby wiped his eyes and said, "Thank you. I've wanted to ask you to do that forever."

"You could have asked me."

"I didn't want you to hate me."

"How could I hate you?"

"For wanting to do that to you."

"Oh. Well. I am sorry if it was clumsy. I didn't know if I was supposed to act like the man or the woman."

Robby picked up his cigarette.

"You weren't supposed to *act* at all."

"Good. Because I'm pretty sure I was just being . . . um . . . Porcupine."

Robby puffed.

"You know what, Robby?"

"What?"

"If you ever want to get shot in Ealing, do *that* in someone's yard at night."

THE TRAPDOOR

WE SAT THERE without saying anything else until we'd smoked our cigarettes down.

I tried not to think about what Robby and I did.

What Robby and I just did was the only thing I *could* think about.

If I was confused and torn before going up on the roof with Robby, I was pulp, ready to be spit out by history, after we spent a few minutes there.

I tried to think like we didn't actually do it, but I could still taste Robby's mouth in mine. I tried to listen for Shann moving around below us in Grasshopper Jungle, so I wouldn't hear my mind telling me how it would be all right if Robby asked if he could kiss me again sometime.

It would be thrilling and daring.

After midnight, Ealing is quieter than a stone coffin.

Robby could tell I was confused—tripping out, we would say.

"Are you mad at me?" he said.

"Shit. I'm not mad."

"Okay. Look."

I hadn't been looking at Robby. Until he'd said that, I didn't even notice that I was staring at my shoelaces, tracing the zigzag path of them up, down, back, forth with the tip of my finger, like a train on a white switchback track, from one shoe to the other, over and over.

Around the loop, crossover, back and forth.

I raised my eyes.

Robby scooted through the gravel away from me.

He had lifted a square metal door in the roof, propped it open. I hadn't even realized it was there.

"Roof access ladder," Robby said. "It goes down into the secondhand store."

"It was left unlocked?" I said.

"Nobody ever comes up here."

"*Up here* has a watch-flamingo, and a lemur head."

"No one wants to mess with shit like that."

Robby lowered his face down below the rim of the trapdoor.

He said, "Do you want to go down there?"

I had already done something with Robby I never believed I would do. Climbing down inside Johnny McKeon's secondhand store in the middle of the night was meaningless shit in comparison.

I said, "That would be cool."

When I stood up, I was dizzy.

I was like the tip of my finger, zigging and zagging from eye to eye, following a string, making history.

Robby watched me get up. I caught his eyes looking at me. I knew we'd never look at each other the same, and I didn't know how I felt about that. I caught him trying to see if I had an erection. I tried to pull my T-shirt down to cover it.

The basketball shorts and boxers I'd been wearing that day revealed yet another strategic flaw for the history books.

History shows that erections happen at the worst possible times, and they stick around until someone else notices them. Often, it is either a librarian or an English teacher, like Mrs. Edith Mitchell.

I went to the edge of the roof, to the top of the small ladder we'd used to get up there.

"Shann," I said. "I just want to make sure she's okay."

Robby didn't answer.

Words like *okay* can mean all kinds of things.

Robby knew enough that saying anything might nail down a definition of *okay* that wasn't what either one of us wanted to hear.

The Explorer was dark and quiet.

Shann was still asleep.

We hadn't been gone for more than twenty minutes, even if time seemed to slow to a crawl now.

Across the street, *Satan's Pizza* winked. The fluorescent tubes inside the sign made an audible hiss like a dying wasp when it went dark.

Robby climbed down the trapdoor.

I followed him.

HUNGRY JACK

ON WEEKENDS AND over the summers I earned money doing jobs for Johnny McKeon at his *From Attic to Seller Consignment Store*. Johnny felt obligated to me because I was Shann's boyfriend.

Usually, the jobs required cleaning the store.

Secondhand stores are like vacuum cleaners to the world: They suck in everybody's shit.

History shows that, like Ealing, when towns are dying, the last things to catch the plague are the secondhand and liquor stores.

Johnny McKeon was on top of the world.

Sometimes, Johnny would receive new consignments out in Grasshopper Jungle, and then leave me to go through and sort boxes, unroll and sweep off rugs, and clean out the drawers in dressers and nightstands.

I found a lot of condoms and Bibles in them.

Johnny told me I could do whatever I wanted with those things.

I threw the Bibles in the dumpster.

Robby and I climbed down the ladder. It deposited us, like visiting aliens, into a common back room that connected *Tipsy Cricket Liquors* with *From Attic to Seller*.

The ladder was attached by metal brackets to a plasterboard wall where the electrical panel box for the store was located. I'd seen the ladder there plenty of times. I had even noticed the Roof Access↑

sign posted on the wall with an arrow pointing up, as though you might not know where a roof could be, direction-wise.

I never thought about going up on the roof of the mall before I went there with Robby.

On the other side of the wall was the shop's toilet. It was such a small space that you would be looking straight across at your own face in the mirror, and could reach the soap and paper towel dispensers and wash your hands in the sink while you were sitting on the toilet.

Ollie Jungfrau could never take a shit in there.

There was a sign on the door that said: *No Public Restroom*

Everyone knew the public restroom was at the launderette, or between the dumpster and the couch in Grasshopper Jungle if you couldn't hold it that far.

There was a homeless guy who'd come riding through on his rickety old bicycle about once per week or so. His bicycle was always teetering, precisely and ridiculously balanced with huge bundles and bags strapped to any available rusted crossbar. Robby and I called him Hungry Jack, but we never asked him his name.

Hungry Jack didn't have any front teeth.

Hungry Jack fought in Vietnam.

When he came through, Hungry Jack would stop and climb into the dumpster, dig around for things.

Robby and I caught him taking a shit one time, between the dumpster and the couch.

I have read that the human memory for smells is one of the most powerful bits of data that can be etched into our brains. Although it seemed so foreign to me, being inside *From Attic to Seller* in the middle of the night, the smell of the place was entirely familiar. The shop had this constant, perfumed odor of sorrow, death, abandonment, condoms, and Bible verses; that was like nothing I'd ever smelled anywhere else.

I felt as at home there as you'd have to feel, lying in your own coffin.

JOHNNY'S THINGS

"*THIS WAY*," I whispered.

Robby had never set foot inside the secondhand store until that night. I'd told him about it enough times.

"This is rather scary," Robby said.

Now Robby was speaking like a non-Ealingite.

"Do you want to get out?"

"No."

Robby put his hand on my shoulder so he wouldn't trip on anything. I led him out around the back counter, which was a rectangular glass case where Johnny McKeon displayed watches, jewelry, cameras, guns, and three framed insect collections.

There were only a few things in *From Attic to Seller* that I favored. The insects were among my most appreciated abandoned items.

One of the frames contained only butterflies. For some reason, I always found the butterflies to be boring. But the other two frames were wonders: One displayed forty-one beetles. I counted them. There were all kinds of oddities in the frame, including beetles with horns, and some nearly as large as my clenched fist. The beetles in the center were posed so their shells were open and their glassine wings spread wide.

The last frame had fifteen bugs in it. An enormous centipede curled around the bend at one corner, and a glossy black scorpion raised its stinging tail in the other. Centered against the white backing board was a vampire bat with little beaded eyes, frozen with its mouth snarled open.

"Isn't that the coolest shit?" I asked.

Robby said, "No."

Robby remained attached to my shoulder and I took him along the circular path around the main floor of the store.

Johnny McKeon arranged *From Attic to Seller Consignment Store* so that shoppers, or even people coming in to inquire about using the toilet, would have to walk a serpentine path from the front door to the back counter. His path led past every stack of clutter Johnny offered up for sale. *Tipsy Cricket* was different. At the liquor store, the counter was right up front, a deterrent to booze and cigarette thieves.

Johnny McKeon was a good marketer.

"I've never seen so much shit in my life," Robby said.

There were nightstands on top of end tables stacked perilously on dinner tables. And every flat surface of every item of furniture was covered in figurines, place settings, ashtrays, silverware, toys, picture frames, clocks, crucifixes, candles, rock collections, pocket-knives, and too many other things for me to list.

I put the price tags on almost every one of them for Johnny, too.

Johnny McKeon made a lot of money.

As soon as one corner of the shop would empty out, it quickly filled back up again. A lot of the things came from realtors and loan agents. Some people in Ealing left behind what they couldn't fit in the trunks and backseats of their cars when the banks took their homes.

Abandoned stuff from defeated Iowans had a way of migrating into Johnny McKeon's hands.

Robby's hand slipped from my shoulder.

He said, "Oops."

Objects clinked together in the dark. Figurines fell.

"Be careful," I said.

"Where are we going?"

"I want to see what Johnny's hiding," I said.

That scared Robby.

Robby grabbed my hand.

"Don't be such a baby," I said. "You wanted to come down here. I know where I'm going."

Robby started to let go of my hand.

"It's okay," I said. I pulled Robby along by the hand like a little kid.

Johnny McKeon kept things in his private office. He never let me go in there. Johnny never let anyone go in there.

There were things Johnny wouldn't sell. One of them was a sealed glass globe he kept on a shelf beside the office door. I was fascinated by the globe. It had been made by some of the scientists in the lab at McKeon Industries, and contained a perfectly balanced universe.

There was water, land, plants, bacteria, a species of tiny shrimp, worms, and even some translucent fish in there.

It was perfect.

It was sealed and self-sustaining.

Nothing got in and nothing got out.

My hand was wet and hot.

"You're sweating all over me," I said to Robby.

"Sorry."

I turned the knob to Johnny's office.

Of course, it was locked.

Robby bumped into me. He wasn't paying attention and he pinned me flat against the office door with his chest.

"No go," Robby said. "I guess we should get out of here."

"I know where Johnny keeps the key. It isn't very smart," I said.

Despite his creativity at naming businesses, and his eye for marketing strategies, Johnny McKeon wasn't that careful when it came to trusting teenage boys.

History lesson: Teenage boys watch you, even when they pretend they don't give a shit about your life.

Johnny kept the key resting flat on the lip of the molding at the top of the door.

I pulled it down and unlocked our way into Johnny McKeon's office, where he kept his secrets.

Robby said, "I really need a cigarette."

TWO-HEADED BOY

WE STOOD INSIDE Johnny McKeon's private office.

There were no windows. It was impossible to see anything in the dark.

Robby threw the switch for the office lights. I jumped when they came on.

You don't expect things to get all bright on you when you're nervous about doing something you're not supposed to be doing.

Robby shrugged apologetically.

He said, "We may as well turn on the light in here. Nobody can see us."

My heart raced, but Robby was right: Nobody could see us.

Robby shut the door to the office, which closed us in with Johnny's things.

Johnny McKeon's real-life horror show.

Johnny McKeon's office smelled the same as the rest of the shop, but wasn't nearly as cluttered. In fact, the office was rather tidy.

Rather.

I said it again.

The three walls boxing the office behind the door were lined with dark wooden shelves. Johnny had salvaged the shelves from the Ealing Public Library when it was remodeled three years before: the year we were in seventh grade.

"Holy shit," Robby said.

Here's why he said it: Johnny McKeon's shelves were full of horrible, grotesque things. They were the kinds of things that no sixteen-year-old boy could tear his eyes from. And there were four sixteen-year-old-boy eyes in Johnny's office.

One of the cases displayed another of the McKeon sealed glass globes, but this was different from the peaceful and pleasant nature-ball Johnny kept outside in the shop. The globe was about the size of a basketball, and it was propped steady atop a black lacquered stand with a brass plaque on front, as though it was some kind of trophy or shit like that. But this could not have been a trophy.

The plaque read:

MCKEON INDUSTRIES 1969
CONTAINED MI PLAGUE STRAIN 412E

Inside the globe was a festering universe.

The globe Robby and I studied held something resembling a black, folded, and coiled brain. The thing clearly was not a brain, but the wrinkled patterns on its surface made me think of one.

"This has to be like some kind of movie prop or something," Robby said.

"Look around, Rob. All the shit in here looks real," I said.

In fact, everything inside Johnny's office was real, we came to find out later. It didn't matter. Neither of us actually believed Johnny McKeon was hiding away props for horror films.

The black thing inside the globe pulsed and twitched like a beating heart. It seemed to become more animated the longer we stared at it. It was almost like a gelatinous cauliflower. Here and there on its velvet surface, a mound would rise up, like a mosquito bite, a black pimple, and then burst open at its peak.

Little volcanoes erupting.

When the pimples burst open, strands of oval globules, pale yellow pearls, coiled and twisted over the surface of the blob, then turned black and sprouted velvet hairs, dissolving back into the surface of the brain thing.

Where the glass globe with the fish, shrimp, plants, and worms outside in Johnny McKeon's shop emanated a placid, almost hopeful aura, this thing whispered of rot and death, disease.

Robby and I could have stared at Johnny's secret collection of things all night.

On another case was an assortment of large specimen jars.

All of them had a common etched label:

MCKEON INDUSTRIES 1969
HUMAN REPLICATION STRAND 4-VG-03

One of them contained a human head. It was a man's head. His eyes were squinted, half open, and although they were clouded, his pupils and irises were plainly visible. He had pale blue eyes. I could even see small blood vessels in the whites of his eyes. He had a mustache. His lips were tightly pursed and frowning.

"He doesn't look too happy," I said.

"This has to be fake," Robby said. "Who would keep shit like this?"

"Johnny McKeon would," I answered. "He probably found it when the plant shut down and thought it was cool."

"He could charge admission," Robby said.

Another jar on the rack held a pair of human hands.

The palms were pressed together. It reminded me of the trite framed artwork depicting disembodied praying hands that hung at teenager eye level above the long urinal in the boys' toilet at Curtis Crane Lutheran Academy.

The pictures were there to remind us what good teenage boys do with their hands.

The jar beside the hands contained a penis and testicles.

The position of the jars made an artistic statement about what happened to boys who masturbate.

"That guy probably went to Curtis Crane," Robby said.

His voice shook with nervousness.

There is nothing more deeply frightening to a sixteen-year-old boy than confronting the possibility of losing his penis.

We had to leave, but we were mesmerized.

But the thing on that particular rack that was most compelling was the jar containing a two-headed boy. It was a whole fetus, bluish in color and clay-like, tiny but fully developed.

Robby reached up and spun the jar around, making the boy pirouette for us as he floated in the zero gravity of his vacuum jar. His little legs were bowed and folded beneath him. A knotted umbilical strand corkscrewed from his round belly. One hand, its fingers so perfect, rested opened, palm up in front of the knob of his penis. The other hand was clenched in a defiant fist beside his hip. And from the boy's shoulders sprouted two perfect heads, one tilted to the side, resting. Both mouths were open, small black caverns that exposed the ridge of gums and the small rounded mounds of the boy's tongues. The eyes were open and hollow. Each plum-sized head was rimmed with a floating tuft of iron-colored hair.

There was something overwhelmingly sad about the boy.

I couldn't identify what it was.

Robby said, "This isn't right."

I said, "I think I know exactly what it would be like to have two heads like that."

The last wall contained specimens of bugs. But these weren't any bugs I'd ever seen. They also floated inside sealed rectangular glass cases filled with preserving fluid. They looked almost like aquariums with alien creatures in them.

Some of the bugs in the tanks were as big as middle-school kids.

They looked like praying mantises, or grasshoppers maybe.

The larger tanks only contained parts of bugs: heads, appendages, thoraxes.

The heads were as large as mine and Robby's.

The tanks were also labeled:

MCKEON INDUSTRIES 1969
UNSTOPPABLE SOLDIER—STRAND 4-VG-12

"We need to get out of here," Robby said.

I agreed.

It was too late, though. Robby and I were trapped in Johnny McKeon's office. Somebody was outside, in the main room of the shop.

They weren't making any attempt to be quiet, either.

BLUE LIGHT

"OH, SHIT, AUSTIN."

"Get the light," I whispered.

Robby flicked the switch, but Johnny McKeon's office didn't go dark.

The glass globe with the pulsating black shit in it wriggled and burned with a blue light. It was like writhing cobalt embers trapped inside the sphere of the glass. The thing in the sphere, whatever it was, obviously responded to light.

Hiding was our only option, but there was no place inside Johnny's office that was very suitable. Robby pointed at the desk. We pulled Johnny's chair out and huddled together, hugging each other in the small rectangular space below the desk.

We were just like that poor two-headed boy floating in fluid in the jar.

We didn't even think to lock Johnny's office door behind us.

Why would anyone have thought to do such a thing?

Because it would have been smart, I told myself.

The knob on the door squeaked and turned. There were footsteps. Someone came into the office. I put my face down on the floor and looked from under the desk. There were several sets of feet there.

Someone said, "What the crap is that?"

The shoes were positioned so whoever was inside with me and Robby was looking at the mysterious globe.

"It's alive," another voice concluded.

"People always said Johnny McKeon kept weird shit in here. Maybe it's an alien or something."

Robby's fingers squeezed around my arm. We both knew the voice. It was Grant Wallace. He and his boys had somehow gotten into *From Attic to Seller*.

"Let's take that shit," the kid named Tyler said.

"You're carrying it. It looks heavy," Grant said. "I don't want that shit. I came for the booze. Let's go."

The Hoover Boys apparently found their way into the back room connecting *Tipsy Cricket* with the secondhand store. They probably broke into the abandoned foot doctor's office to do it.

It was a simple matter.

For all anyone knew, Grant and his boys may have been planning their theft from *Tipsy Cricket* for a long time. It probably had everything to do with why we ran into them in Grasshopper Jungle earlier that day.

Technically, our encounter with Grant Wallace happened the day before, since it was solidly past midnight in our time zone, which was located under the desk in Johnny McKeon's office.

"Is that a dick?" one of the boys asked.

"It's a dick," another concluded.

"Johnny Mack has a dick in a bottle in his office," Grant affirmed.

"Maybe it's his," one of Grant's friends said.

"Let's take it," another of them said.

"I'm not touching it. It's a jar with a dick in it." I think Tyler said that.

"Oh yeah," someone else said. "And balls, too."

"That's sick. I'm not touching it. Hang on. I'm going to take a picture of that dick in a jar with my phone," the videographer decided.

"Text it to me." One of the Hoover Boys laughed.

I desperately wished they'd stop talking about the penis in the jar, but Grant and his friends were like lonely parakeets in front of a mirror.

Finally, after they'd exhausted all speculation and conversational rhetoric on the topic of penises in jars, the boys stood there numbly for a moment, apparently unable to detach their eyes. I heard the sound of something heavy and solid sliding on one of the shelves.

The blue shadows in the room swirled.

Tyler had lifted the globe.

It was not a good idea.

"Let's go. I'm thirsty," he said.

They left the door to Johnny's office standing open.

The blue light danced away into the darkness of the back room, and then faded entirely.

I grabbed Robby's wrist and pulled him out from our hiding place. Then I led him back through the shop and up the ladder to the roof.

PRIORITIES

ROBBY BREES AND I had our priorities.

As soon as we closed the hatch and were outside on the roof again, we lit cigarettes.

Smoking dynamos.

"Shit," Robby said.

"Shit," I agreed.

Shit, like the word *okay*, can mean any number of things. In fact, in the history I recorded in my book for that one Friday in Ealing, Iowa, I believe I used the word *shit* in every possible context.

I will have to go back through the history and check.

Robby and I said *shit*—nothing else—approximately eleven more times as we smoked our cigarettes up on the roof.

"What do you think that shit in the ball was?" Robby said.

"I don't know. You read the nameplate on it. It said *Contained Plague*."

"Nothing good is ever called *Plague*," Robby said.

"Maybe it was just some glow-in-the-dark experimental stuff," I said.

"I've done an experiment. We made a battery out of a lemon. Remember that?" Robby asked.

"Yes. It was a good experiment," I agreed. I nodded like a scientist would. "We knew what was supposed to happen before we even started it. And it worked."

"But I don't think things called *Plague* are the subject of the kinds of experiments we do in the lab at Curtis Crane," Robby said.

That's what it was—what Robby and I had done up there on the roof at Grasshopper Jungle—I thought.

An experiment.

It is perfectly normal for boys to *experiment*. I read it somewhere that was definitely not in a book at Curtis Crane Lutheran Academy. Or if it was in a book, it would certainly no longer be part of Curtis Crane Lutheran Academy's library collection. Not after the shit I did in eighth grade.

Maybe I heard some psychologist who specialized in *Teen Sexuality* say shit about things like *Boys experimenting* on one of those afternoon talk shows that are only on television for the fulfillment of depressed and lonely women.

Depressed and lonely women need to know about *Teen Sexuality* and how it's normal for boys to experiment. Normal. That's what the psychologist would say. The psychologist also would have been a slim woman with nicely trimmed hair, a sincere and calming smile, and modest jewelry.

That was bullshit.

History shows that real experiments, like the one we did with the lemon, always involve some reasonable expectation ahead of time about the outcome. About how things will work out.

Robby slid the pack of cigarettes into the back pocket on his sagging jeans and we gathered up our flamingo, wine, grimacing lemur, and skateboards. We made our way down the ladder and onto the dumpster we'd rolled across Grasshopper Jungle.

"Don't say anything to Shann," I cautioned.

I didn't need to tell Robby that. It was just one of those things boys do sometimes to confirm that there are secrets that shall be protected.

Robby said, "You mean about what we saw in her stepdad's office, or what we did up on the roof?"

I said, "Shit."

I imagined I had two arguing and confused heads sprouting up from my shoulders.

I felt sadness for that other boy inside the jar in Johnny McKeon's office.

HELL BREAKS LOOSE

SHANN WAS SLEEPING soundly in the backseat of Robby's Ford Explorer when we came back to the car. She stretched out comfortably, with her head lying on some crumpled socks and a pair of Robby's boxers that had fire trucks and Dalmatians on them.

Watching Shann sleep made me horny.

I was all messed up.

I thought I probably needed to talk to someone about how

sexually confused I felt. I couldn't talk to Robby about it, not after what we did on the roof. I thought, but only for half a second, about talking to Pastor Roland Duff. But I already felt guilty as it was.

I thought I could talk to my father.

It scared me to think about doing that, but my father would know what to tell me. He could help me sort things out. I just needed to work up the courage to start the conversation. Then everything would fall into place.

Everything always falls into place that way.

"Shann?" I whispered.

I ran my hand up her leg to wake her.

Shann opened her eyes slowly. She smiled at me.

I felt guilty and sad.

"Did you and Robby already go?" she asked.

I said yes, but didn't tell her we'd been gone for over an hour. It was nearly 2:00 a.m.

Robby opened the Explorer's rear gate and deposited our flamingo, the grimacing lemur head, skateboards, and wine bottles.

He already held an unlit cigarette in his mouth when he got behind the wheel.

Robby passed the pack to me and started the engine. We lit both our cigarettes on the same orange coiled moon burning at the end of the car's lighter. Our faces were so close our cheeks touched. I looked Robby straight in the eye as we leaned in to get the cigarettes going. It was awkward. I felt sad for Robby.

I turned around and reached back between the seats. I held Shann's hand.

Behind her, I saw a glowing blue ball floating down the steps in back of the vacant podiatrist's office. Grant and the Hoover Boys were coming out from the mall.

I glanced at Robby.

I was certain he saw the same thing in the rearview mirror. We both knew better than to say anything and have Shann turn around. She would only start asking questions. Maybe she'd want to confront those punks.

In a lot of ways, Shann was tougher than Robby and me.

Maybe the boys were already drunk. I can't be certain of it. But something happened to cause Tyler to let go of the glass globe. I watched the circle of blue light drop like a falling moon.

Robby coughed.

Back in Grasshopper Jungle, blue light splattered everywhere.

"I'm ready to go home," I said.

"Um. Yeah," Robby agreed.

Robby's hands gripped the wheel, but his eyes were pinned to the rearview mirror.

Grant and his friends were the first victims of *Contained MI Plague Strain 412E.*

Nobody knew anything about it.

Travis Pope and his wife, Eileen, had been hired by the association management of the Ealing Mall to clean the common areas every week. They drove through the lot Saturday mornings before sunrise, rarely doing anything about the debris that accumulated in the back alley of a soon-to-be abandoned mall.

That Saturday, Travis and Eileen stopped in Grasshopper Jungle and picked up large chunks of broken glass from the alley. Travis Pope tossed the shards into the dumpster somebody had pushed against the rear wall of *The Pancake House.* Travis cursed the winos and delinquent kids in the town for getting drunk and fucking in public.

Travis and Eileen Pope were the fifth and sixth victims of *Contained MI Plague Strain 412E.*

Nobody knew anything about it.

And later that morning, an old man Robby Brees and I called Hungry Jack, who was missing his front teeth and had served in the United States Army in Vietnam, climbed into the dumpster we rolled across Grasshopper Jungle. The dumpster had pieces of Johnny McKeon's sick broken universe inside it.

Hungry Jack became the seventh victim of *Contained MI Plague Strain 412E.*

All hell had broken loose. It splattered across the piss-soaked pavement of Grasshopper Jungle.

Nobody knew anything about it.

HISTORY IS FULL OF SHIT

EVERY DAY I wrote in my books.

I drew pictures, too.

That night, I drew a plastic flamingo with a spike coming out of its ass, a grimacing lemur, bottles of wine, and a picture of me with my shorts pulled down around my knees. In my drawing, I was in the backseat of Robby's Ford Explorer, lying on Shann Collins and some socks and a pair of my best friend's boxers that were printed with red fire trucks and spotted Dalmatian dogs.

I drew a two-headed baby boy trapped inside a pickle jar.

That night, I sat at my desk until the sky outside began to get light.

I took off my shoes and socks, and my Orwells T-shirt, too. I always write more accurate accounts of history when wearing as little as possible.

It's difficult to avoid the truth when you're undressed.

My armpits reeked. I had serious B.O.

That was also true.

Ingrid, my golden retriever, was in my bedroom. She liked to lie down beneath my desk so I could keep my bare feet in her fur. Ingrid, although she could shit better than any dog I knew—a real dynamo—never barked. When she was a puppy, she had a tumor on her neck. It made it so she couldn't bark, which helped me sneak into the house past curfew countless times.

Our house got robbed twice, too.

"You're a good dog, Ingrid," I said. I wriggled my toes in her fur. I wrote.

Even when I tried to tell everything that happened, I knew my accounts were ultimately nothing more than an abbreviation. It's not that I neglected to write details—I told the truth about Shann's room, the staircase leading down to nothing, what the main ingredients of a *Stanpreme* pizza are. I wrote what it felt like to have my bare penis pressing upward against the cool skin of Shann Collins's thigh.

That was also true.

I told about Robby kissing me. I described it in detail, down to the taste and feel of his tongue. I kept accurate count of the cigarettes we smoked, and described the things trapped inside the jars we found locked up in Johnny McKeon's office.

But no historian could ever put *everything* that happened in a book.

The book would be as big as the universe, and it would take multiple countless lifetimes to read.

History necessarily *had* to be an abbreviation.

Even those first men—obsessed with recording their history—who painted on cave walls in Lascaux and Altamira, only put the important details down.

We killed this big hairy thing and that big hairy thing. And that was our day. You know what I mean.

My name is an abbreviation.

Three grandfathers back, a man named Krzys Szczerba came to the United States from Poland.

People in America did not know what to do with all those consonants and shit in Krzys Szczerba's name. They decided to swap some out for vowels, and to take others away from Krzys Szczerba, so my three-grandfathers-back grandfather became Christopher Szerba.

I imagined. Sometimes I drew this picture: An official stone building, a repository for all the consonants and shit taken from refugees' names when they arrived on the doorstep of the United States of America. It is piled high everywhere with the letters we don't find useful: *C*s and *Z*s in great heaping mounds that looked so much like the black-and-white photographs of luggage or shoes from World War 2.

Krzys Szczerba.

History, and the United States of America, can call him Chris.

History is full of shit like that.

Krzys Szczerba came to America when he was seventeen years old.

In 1905, being seventeen years old made you a man. In 1969, when Hungry Jack fought in Vietnam, seventeen years old was a man. Now, I wasn't so sure. My brother, Eric, who was somewhere in Afghanistan, was twenty-two.

Krzys Szczerba came across the Atlantic with his father. They planned on working and earning enough money so Krzys's mother, brother, and two sisters could come to the United States, too. People who did that were called *Bread Polacks*. They came here to make money.

Krzys Szczerba's father died on the boat in the middle of the ocean.

His body was sent down naked into the water with prayers and a medallion of Saint Casimir.

Krzys Szczerba's family never came to their son.

Chris Szerba ended up in southern Minnesota, where he met a grocer's daughter named Eva Nightingale. Eva had breasts like frosted cupcakes and skin the color of homemade peach ice cream. Her body was a soft and generous pillow of endless desserts. Chris Szerba's semen found its way into Eva Nightingale's tummy, where it produced a good, cigarette-smoking, Catholic Polish boy named Andrzej.

Sometimes when I wrote my history, I would slip in pages I drew about Krzys Szczerba and his lonely and sad life in the United States.

It was hard for me, at times, to separate out the connections that crisscrossed like intersecting highways through and around my life in Ealing.

It was the truth, and I had to get it down.

And that was our day. You know what I mean.

I took off my boxers and went to bed.

It was 6:01 a.m.

The end of the world was about four hours old. Just a baby.

Johnny McKeon was picking up two dozen donuts at that moment.

Ollie Jungfrau was waking up, trying to decide if he should masturbate or not.

It was just after three in the afternoon in Afghanistan.

Louis, the Chinese cook at *The Pancake House*, whose real name was Ah Wong Sing, was taking a shit in the public restroom at the *Ealing Coin Wash Launderette*.

History never tells about people taking shits. I can't for a moment believe that guys like Theodore Roosevelt or Winston

Churchill never took a shit. History always abbreviates out the shit-taking and excess consonants.

In about a week, the pieces started coming together.

In a week, we figured out history.

Eventually, we would learn this:

The thing inside the globe, the *Contained MI Plague Strain 412E*, wasn't anything remarkable unless it came into contact with human blood.

Contained MI Plague Strain 412E really *was* contained and harmless inside Johnny McKeon's glass universe.

Tyler dropped that universe directly onto the spot where earlier that day Robby Brees began spelling out *GRANT WALLACE MURDERED ME* in his own blood.

The *Contained MI Plague Strain 412E* was happy to meet Robby Brees's blood.

Robby Brees was my best friend. He taught me how to dance. We smoked cigarettes. He kissed me. To be honest, I kissed him back. Robby was homosexual. I didn't know if I was anything.

I wondered what I was. None of that mattered. Nobody knew anything about it except for me and Robby.

The man whose scientific company invented the *Contained MI Plague Strain 412E* died when his plane crashed into the ocean. The plane's engines were destroyed by billowing plumes of caustic ash. The ash came from a volcano in Guatemala. It was called Huacamochtli. Robby Brees's dad was filming the Huacamochtli eruption at precisely the same moment that Dr. Grady McKeon's jet disintegrated on impact with the surface of the Gulf of Mexico.

Water is unyielding when you're moving at 500 mph.

We were in seventh grade then. My brother, Eric Christopher Szerba, joined the United States Marines that year. At the same moment Huacamochtli was being filmed by Robby's father and Dr.

Grady McKeon's body was being torn apart by the force of impact, my brother, Eric, was on his way to boot camp. Robby Brees's dad never came back to Ealing, Iowa. He didn't want to see Robby's mom ever again.

We found this out later:

The *Contained MI Plague Strain 412E* said hello to Robby Brees's blood on the asphalt in Grasshopper Jungle.

And the end of the world began at about 2:00 a.m., around three and a half feet away from a discarded floral-print sleeper sofa infested with pubic lice in Ealing, Iowa. One time, Travis Pope unfolded the sofa and fucked his wife, Eileen, on it.

Both of them had pubic lice.

It didn't matter.

History is my compulsion.

I see the connections.

PART 2: WATERLOO CORNFIELD

PALINDROMES

KRZYS SZCZERBA WAS Catholic.

He smoked cigarettes.

Christopher Szerba was Catholic.

He did not give up smoking cigarettes when he gave up the excess consonants.

All the Szerba boys were cigarette-smoking Catholics until my father fell in love with my mother and married her. He quit smoking, converted, and as a result, his semen created two strong Lutheran sons inside her body.

Their names were Eric Christopher and Austin Andrzej Szerba.

My dad picked up some discarded consonants from the waste-pile of history.

It is pronounced *Uhnn-zhay*.

Don't ask me why. It's Polish and shit.

I smoke cigarettes. I hate church. But one day, after I talk to my father about my confusing sexual impulses, I will change my name back to *Szczerba*.

My father's name was Eric Andrew Szerba. My mother was Connie Kenney before she married him.

People from Iowa like vowels and rhymes.

Lutherans in Iowa like John Deere tractors and big breakfasts on Saturdays.

Usually, my dad would only have to stand outside my door and speak my name to get me out of bed for our Saturday breakfast. That morning, the morning after Robby and I went up on the roof of the Ealing Mall to find some shit, my father had to come into my room and shake my shoulder.

"You stink, Austin," my father, whose name was Eric, told me.

"I have B.O.," I agreed.

"Ingrid needs to shit," my father said.

That was how we told each other good morning that day.

I sat up.

I would have gotten out of bed, but I realized I was naked under the sheet. I'd taken everything off when I finished writing, when I went to bed.

No sixteen-year-old boy wants to stand up naked in front of his father.

I thought about my decision to talk to him. I wanted to ask him if maybe he was confused about sexual attraction when he was my age. Or if maybe he was still confused about sexual attraction. Experimenting. Things falling into place. Where else would things fall, if not a place? It's not like things are just going to float away. Gravity works. Dr. Grady McKeon certainly knew that when he was watching the Gulf of Mexico get closer and closer and closer.

Maybe the guys who painted the caves in Lascaux and Altamira were sexually confused, too.

I could not bring myself to talk to my father about sexuality while I was naked.

I decided it could wait.

Things would have to float a little while longer.

My father could tell I was naked. He watched me, like he was testing to see if I would get out from under the sheet.

But I was naked. I wasn't going anywhere.

We watched each other, both of us caught up in eyeballing the palindrome of each other's lives.

My mother took an antianxiety drug called *Xanax*. It was a little blue pill that looked like a tiny kayak. Robbie's mother took it, too. Our moms were like Xanax sisters, except they didn't know much more about each other than first names, who their baby boys' best friends were, and Ealing gossip.

Kayak and *Xanax* are palindromes.

Robby's mother was named Connie, too.

It was always fascinating to me how perfect things could be if you just let all the connections happen. My history showed how everything connected in Ealing, Iowa.

You could never get *everything* in a book.

Good books are always about everything.

My mother would take her antianxiety drug when she felt stress or panic setting in. Saturday mornings usually meant no drugs. She took her drugs in the afternoons, on holidays, and whenever we had visiting human beings at the house.

"Um. Dad?"

"Yes, Austin?"

"Would you please let Ingrid outside for me so she can shit?"

"No problem, son."

I got out of bed and pulled on some shorts.

I stunk.

My phone was lying on the floor, under the rumpled boxers I wore the day before. No fire trucks and dogs. They were blue plaid. Iowa was blue plaid. That is the truth.

The battery in my phone was nearly dead.

At 3:45 a.m. I received a text message from Robby. It said:

I'm sorry, Austin.

Robby and I always used punctuation and spelling in text messages.

We both despised abbreviations.

I sent him a message in reply:

Don't be dumb, Robby.

I was certain Robby was asleep at that precise moment. I felt bad for calling him dumb, like maybe he would take it the wrong way and not know if I meant dumb for asking to kiss me or dumb for being sorry, which is what I meant.

So I sent him another message:

You shouldn't worry about me, Rob. Let's talk and have a fag later. Ha-ha. Now relax, and come meet me at SATAN'S after I get off at 5. Bring boards.

I was so confused.

That was true.

A BATH, A SHAVE, AND MODESTY

I AM POLISH.

My hair is the color of potato peels and I have skin the shade of boxed oatmeal.

Food descriptions work well in Iowa.

Polish kids have natural and persistent bags under their eyes. I think we evolved through a lot of sleepless nights or shit like that. If you read the history of Poland, which I have done, you'd probably just shake your head and say, *That is full of shit*.

I am Krzys Szczerba's great-great-grandson.

That is the only thing I know about myself with absolute certainty.

I think I would like to smoke a cigarette with him. I have a feeling Krzys Szczerba could cuss, had hair the color of russet potatoes, and Quaker Oats skin, just like me. I feel like I could ask him anything. He would tell me what to do.

He came to America when Theodore Roosevelt, a man who apparently never took a shit in his life, was president.

Connie, my mother, drove me to work at Johnny McKeon's *From Attic to Seller Consignment Store* that morning.

I did not have a big Lutheran Saturday breakfast with my mother and father because I needed a bath more.

On Saturdays I shave.

I did not actually *need* to shave. It was something that boys in Iowa start doing when they are sixteen, regardless of necessity. I ran the tip of my finger around my lips before applying the shaving cream. Robby's lips had some spiny little whiskers around them. I felt them when we kissed. I found the feeling to be a little unexpected. Also, his lips were thinner, not as heavy, as Shann's. I never thought about it before, how maybe Shann felt spiny little whiskers around my thin, un-meaty lips when we kissed.

I was disgusted with myself.

I called Shann while the bathtub was filling and I sat on the toilet, locked inside the bathroom. My mother and father ate their big Lutheran Saturday breakfast downstairs.

I told Shann I loved her.

She said she loved me.

I was naked, so I knew I was telling the truth.

Also, Shann did not say I love you, too.

Everyone knows *I love you, too* does not mean *I love you.*

The *too* makes it a concession, a gesture, an instinct of politeness.

History lesson for the morning.

I turned the water off and slid into the tub. My face began to sweat.

"I am in the bathtub, Shann," I said.

"Are you naked?" she asked.

"Well, I would be normally," I said, "but since I knew I would be talking to you, I went out and slipped into a modest bathing suit."

She knew I was kidding. It made me very horny to admit to her that I was, indeed, fully naked.

"I am totally naked," I admitted.

Shann told me that she slept well, that she was not scared in her new old bedroom as she thought she would be. But, she said, at exactly 6:00 a.m. there came a ticking sound from inside her wall. Shann explained that it sounded like a typewriter.

Nobody uses typewriters anymore, I told her.

At exactly 6:01 a.m. I was taking off all my clothes and going to bed.

Johnny McKeon was buying donuts.

The *Contained MI Plague Strain 412E* was dying off, but managed to wriggle around on three slices of *Stanpreme* pizza we threw in the dumpster, where it wormed its way down the esophagus of its last initial carrier, a homeless man named Hungry Jack, who participated in the killing of an entire village of women, elderly people, and children in Vietnam.

Ollie Jungfrau was probably masturbating.

Ah Wong Sing was taking a shit.

Something was ticking inside Shann Collins's wall.

She said the ticking stopped after a moment. Shann used words like *moment*. The way she talked made me horny. I told her if the ticking came again, maybe she could record it on her phone because I'd like to hear it.

She told me she would do that.

I shaved.

"*The Pancake House* is busy this morning," my mother said when she pulled into the front lot of the Ealing Mall. Then she said, "We should eat breakfast there sometime."

"Okay, Mom," I said. "If you want a donut, Johnny always brings coffee and donuts in for me and Ollie Jungfrau on Saturdays."

"Johnny McKeon is such a nice man," my mother said.

"Yes," I agreed, "Johnny takes good care of us."

She parked almost as far away from the secondhand store as you could get and still be on Kimber Drive. My mother was not very steady-handed at squeezing our Chevrolet between slotted cars in parking lots.

I wore a Modest Mouse T-shirt, the shoes we salvaged from the roof of the mall the night before, clean boxers—Iowa plaid—and loose 501s with a belt. I smelled good. My hair was still wet from the bath I took. I did not like my jeans to droop like Robby did. Boys at Curtis Crane Lutheran Academy were required to wear belts and matching socks. We would be called in to Pastor Roland Duff's office if our underwear showed.

Lutherans in Iowa are very modest.

"What is a *Modest Mouse*?" my mother asked.

She had a stretchy thing on her hair. It was green and looked like the waistband from a pair of fat guy's underwear. I didn't know what those things were called. You know, women from Iowa wear them. In their hair. Her nails needed a new coat of paint. They were chipped or grown out around the edges. Apparently, my mother's nails grew much faster than mine did. Real dynamos. She wore a green velour tracksuit with a zip-up top. I guessed it would be called a tracksuit. I'd never seen my mother run one time in my life. Who wants to run when you can kayak everywhere?

"Nothing," I said. "I don't know."

She parked the Suburban facing out toward the street, directly across from *Satan's Pizza*.

My mother was very calm that morning.

Maybe all I needed was a tiny blue kayak, to get things to fall into place for me.

I decided I would ask Robby if he'd ever gone kayaking on one of his mother's Xanax before. Probably not. Like me, Robby never even got drunk before.

But we could smoke cigarettes like real dynamos.

"Do you need one of us to come pick you up, Sweetie?" she asked.

My mother called me *Sweetie* when she was calm.

When she said *one of us*, it meant that she anticipated being drugged out by five, and my dad could come get me.

History does show that more of what we actually say is not contained in words, anyway. It's why those cave guys simply stuck to the pictures of big hairy things and shit like that.

"Robby and I are going skating," I said. "I'll call if I'm going to be late for dinner."

My mother leaned over and kissed me.

JOHNNY AND OLLIE

IT'S ABOUT TIME you met these two:

Ollie Jungfrau lifted half a maple bar to me when I walked through the door to *From Attic to Seller Consignment Store*. It was the kind of gesture drunken soldiers at a bar would make when weary battlefield comrades came in from the war looking for a drink.

But it was with half a donut.

"Hey, Dynamo," Ollie said, winking at me.

Ollie Jungfrau called me *Dynamo*. The first time he said it, I had to look it up. Who says *Dynamo*? People in Ealing, Iowa, do, that's who.

That's another word I'm going to try to erase from history, never say it again. But it is a challenging redirection. I'm from Ealing, Iowa, after all.

I rather wished Robby was there, so we could go have a cigarette.

"Hey, Ollie," I said.

Ollie panted contemplatively between bites of his donut. He had red stuff on his chin. The front lines of jelly donuts had already been decimated by the panzer division of Ollie's appetite.

"Coffee." Ollie waved his hand gracefully between a tall paper cup and me, as though he were introducing blind dates at a barn dance.

"Thanks," I said, appreciative of my date's quiet demeanor.

Coffee is a girl who never tells boys no. The idea of such a compliant partner normally would have made me horny, but I was too hungry, still sleepy, and I was also watching Ollie Jungfrau eat a donut at the exact moment sexual thoughts involving a quiet girl at an Iowa barn dance occurred to me.

I liked coffee. And cigarettes. Neither of these truths were welcome at my home. I did not like jelly donuts, however. All the more for Ollie and the customers. Jelly only belongs in one place. Two, if you have decent toast, I suppose.

History.

"*John-nnnny!*" Ollie called out in the direction of Johnny McKeon's office, "The kid's here!"

I heard Johnny moving things around in the back of the shop. I had already confirmed to myself that I did not feel guilty about being in the shop at night. I was an employee. Robby and I didn't do anything wrong. Well, we didn't do anything wrong *inside* the store, at least. What Grant Wallace and those other boys did would have happened whether or not Robby and I were there to see it.

So I did not feel guilty about the below-the-roof part of the night.

I sat down across the display counter from Ollie and selected a white-frosted cake donut with blue and yellow Iowa plaid sprinkles that scattered a candy galaxy over its surface.

Ollie nodded. He had an expression on his face like a saint receiving a vision of a bloodied Jesus. Ollie Jungfrau would have been the patron saint of donuts. Not that I'm allowed to believe in saints.

I did not believe in Jesus, either, even if he was good at picking donuts. I was not allowed to say that, either.

I might not put that shit down in the book.

"Good choice," Ollie said.

"It was calling my name, Ollie," I said.

"A voice like an angel."

Ollie took his donuts seriously.

Johnny McKeon looked agitated. He stood beside Ollie at the counter, with his palms flat on the glass and his elbows locked straight. Johnny was a giraffe of a man, and his hands looked like twin octopi. I had never seen anyone with fingers as long as Johnny McKeon's.

If Johnny McKeon ever gave you the thumb-and-index-finger international gesture for *OK*, trained poodles could jump through it.

Maybe even dolphins.

I looked past his fingers at the vampire bat and bugs in the collections below our donuts. Most people would probably not want to eat donuts here.

"Good morning, Johnny," I said. Sometimes I would say something corny, like "Hey-ho, Johnny."

But not today.

Johnny McKeon said, "Is it still morning?"

That was what Johnny always said to me.

Johnny McKeon was a mover. He was out of bed every day by five. He got things done. I liked him very much, and he knew that. Johnny was aware I smoked cigarettes, too. He'd get mad at me for it, but he'd also sometimes give me free smokes when he broke up vendor multi-pack specials at *Tipsy Cricket*.

"If your dad or mom tells me anything about this, I'm saying you stole them," is what he always said to me, too.

That morning, Johnny McKeon said to me:

"I'm going to leave you in charge of the store this morning, Austin. You can handle it. I need to run in to Waterloo and pick up some plywood and stuff. Some a-hole broke in through the podiatrist's last night."

Johnny never cussed. He had to be pretty mad to say something as daring as *a-hole*.

"Someone broke in?" I echoed.

"Yeah," Johnny said. "Right through the dang wall."

I looked at Ollie Jungfrau. He was eating a glazed bow tie and nodding. Apparently, he knew all the details. Naturally he would. It was Saturday, donut day, and Ollie always showed up first, before *Tipsy Cricket* was supposed to open.

"Sign of the times," Ollie analyzed, shaking his head in a grim I-saw-this-coming rhythm.

"Did you call the police?" I asked. My heartbeat accelerated. The coffee made me sweat. Under my armpits, the chemical beads of my deodorant stick began to erupt like miniature laboratory volcanoes. Outside in Grasshopper Jungle, the *Contained MI Plague Strain 412E* was now completely dead, having moved into the bodies of seven hosts. Robby Brees was asleep in his bed at the Del Vista Arms. Ingrid was taking a shit.

"They were here all morning. What can you do?" Johnny said. "'*You should have a video system. You should have an alarm,*' they said. But this is Ealing."

There never was anything worth filming in Ealing, unless you were one of Grant Wallace's buddies watching him kick the shit out of a couple *Candy Cane faggots.*

In Iowa, there are cameras trained on cornfields. So you can watch corn grow.

"My house has been robbed," I said. "Because my dog can't bark. I should teach her to shit on people."

Ollie chewed thoughtfully. "My uncle has a German shepherd who will do that. He only takes commands in German. *Scheiß, Dieter, scheiß!* And he'll toast a brownie on the spot."

Ollie Jungfrau was full of *Scheiße*.

"Did they take anything?" I asked.

Johnny said, "A case of Gilbey's Gin. And the sons of guns got into my office, too. They took a display I had in there."

I sipped my coffee and looked at the candy galaxy on my donut. It hovered on a perfect plane of glass above a rhinoceros beetle.

Johnny went on without any prodding, "I had one of those glass globes the scientists at M.I. made. It had this photoluminescent mold sealed up inside it. I really liked that thing. It made the nicest blue glow if I'd turn the lights on it at nighttime."

"Whoa, whoa, whoa," Ollie objected. "*What* kind of mold?"

"Photoluminescent," Johnny repeated.

Ollie took a bite of donut and shook his head rapidly. "Nope. No such word," he decided.

Ollie graduated from Herbert Hoover High School, third in his class.

Ollie Jungfrau was a tool.

"I think it means glow in the dark," I said.

Ollie unrolled his glazed fingers. He was counting something. "Then why wouldn't you just say *glow in the dark*, Johnny? It has less syllables."

"Was it . . . um . . . valuable?" I asked.

"Nah," Johnny said. "I don't think so. How would I know? It was just part of the crazy stuff from boxes that got delivered to me after M.I. shut down. I don't know anything about it."

Johnny reached below the counter and found a metal-cased Stanley tape measure. He placed this and a pencil on top of a pad of lined paper and slid the pile across the display case toward my cup of coffee.

Johnny said, "Bring this stuff, Austin. I need you to come back and help me take measurements so I can fix the danged wall. So they won't ever do something like that again."

They weren't ever going to do it again, plywood or not.

Nobody knew that, either.

THE PATCH JOB

THIS IS HOW history works: It is omniscient.

Everyone trusts history.

Think about it—when we read history books—nobody ever asks, *How did you find this out if it happened before you were born?*

History is unimpeachable, sublime.

It is my job.

I can tell you things that nobody could possibly know because I am the *recorder*. I found out everything in time, but I'm abbreviating. Cutting out the shit.

You have to trust me.

This is history.

You know what I mean.

Why wouldn't you trust me? I admitted everything. Think of how embarrassing these truths are to me.

Most of what I found out came to me much later, after the end of the world, when Robby and I would go out on cigarette runs. You will see. I did the work of history, what I am supposed to do. I found clues and artifacts everywhere, put them together. And I found out exactly what happened.

This is why you can trust me.

I couldn't begin to explain *why* things happened. *Why* isn't my job.

I would love to talk to Krzys Szczerba, or even my own father. They might know. They could tell me *why* I am the way I am.

All I can do is keep my lists of *what* happened.

That's what I do.

And that was our day. You know what I mean.

I considered telling Johnny McKeon about Grant Wallace and the Hoover Boys. It scared me to imagine what could possibly happen.

Nothing good might come of it, I thought. Shann would ask why Robby and I didn't say anything to her when we left Grasshopper Jungle. She would know something was wrong with me. I would spill my guts. Spilling my guts is how history gets recorded. Shann would find shit out.

When I thought about bad things happening between me and Robby and Shann, I could feel my balls shriveling up inside my body.

That's the truth.

History lesson for the day: My balls are barometers to emotional storms.

So I helped Johnny McKeon measure the wall at the spot the Hoover Boys dug through so they could get inside the back room. I held the zero end of the measure and Johnny pulled out the tape and called off numbers to me, which I recorded in pencil on my pad of paper. Like cave painters in France.

"What kind of crazy stuff?" I asked.

I suppose I'd been having an imaginary conversation in my head.

Johnny said, "What?"

"I mean, what kind of crazy stuff came in the boxes from M.I. after they closed down?"

"Oh." Johnny made another mark on the wall. "I can't believe they actually knocked out a stud just to get to some cheap gin. It was mostly things from experiments they were doing, I guess, from my brother's storage unit. It was a bunch of junk of his I inherited, I guess, but never looked at until the place got all packed up. To be honest, I didn't know what to do with the stuff. There was so much of it, I threw some away. I put stuff in the office. I even put some of it on the roof. I don't know what I was thinking, but it was my brother's, you know? Go figure. So. Eh."

"Oh." I said, "Um. I. Um . . . like experiments. Do you think I could see them sometime?"

I felt like asking Johnny McKeon how the little boy with two heads was getting on.

Johnny shrugged. "Eh. Maybe sometime, Austin. It's kind of . . . well . . . morbid stuff, if you ask me."

"Sounds like it could be cool," I said.

"Eh," Johnny said.

We measured. Johnny recited numbers and items, like *half-inch plywood*, *studs*, *drywall mud*, and *tape*, and shit like that. It sounded incredibly manly. My balls felt bigger just writing that shit down.

I printed in uppercase. It was manly.

"Hey, Johnny." I said, "Tonight, I'd like to take Shann out to dinner and a movie. Maybe to Waterloo. Would that be okay?"

"What are you? Asking permission to take your girlfriend on a date?" Johnny said.

"No. I'm asking for a ride. Do you think you could give us a ride?"

"Do I get to go to the show, too? I could sit in the middle," Johnny said.

He was teasing.

"Um."

"Don't you think it's about time you get your driver's license?"

I turned sixteen in February. It was a week until the beginning of May.

"My mom and dad don't want me to drive yet."

"That should do it," Johnny said, and rolled up the tape measure. "Sure. I'll take you kids. Only not too late. I don't want to have to come pick you up in Waterloo after midnight."

"I'll be at your house around six." I said, "Thanks, Johnny."

SAY PLEASE

WATERLOO, IOWA, SPRAWLED along the Cedar River, twenty miles away from Ealing.

Johnny McKeon took my notes and the shopping list he'd dictated and put me in charge of *From Attic to Seller*.

It made me feel like something—something with big balls—to know that Johnny trusted me, even if I did intend to go back and see if he still kept his office key on the trim molding above the door.

I was also planning on smoking at least one cigarette, too.

I rarely smoked alone, but I needed one.

In truth, until that day, I never smoked alone.

I'd just have to toughen up and go buy a pack from the tool in the liquor store.

Ollie Jungfrau left when it was time to open *Tipsy Cricket*, which didn't have a fixed schedule. Opening the liquor store happened once there were two or three people waiting outside the door. Usually, they'd tap on the glass with quarters or car keys to let Ollie and Johnny know there were thirsty Iowans with money who needed to spend it on alcohol.

The secondhand store, as always, smelled like insecticide, condoms, and despair, with a little sweet hint of unanswered prayers, formaldehyde, cardboard donut boxes, and chicory, all mixed in. I waited a few minutes, just to be sure Johnny wouldn't double back after something he'd forgotten, then I slipped through the back room to the pale green linoleum and fluorescent lights of *Tipsy Cricket Liquors*.

I made plenty of noise tracking my way through the back room.

I did not want to startle Ollie Jungfrau, or catch him looking at computer porn or masturbating behind the counter.

Making noise was the polite thing to do.

"Scared to be alone, Dynamo?" Ollie grinned at me sympathetically when he saw my intentionally clumsy entrance near the beer cooler in back.

"No," I said, with efficient curtness.

I was all business and could not waste time. I did not want to let Johnny down.

Ollie Jungfrau played games on a laptop computer tapped in to the wireless network from Johnny's office. He played all day long while he sat behind the counter at *Tipsy Cricket*. I did not see the allure of that particular pastime. But for a guy like Ollie, having his ego sucked into the fantasy of being a muscular soldier in tight clothing, trapped aboard a space station infested by aliens, was preferable to rooting his identity in the here and now.

Ollie Jungfrau killed thousands of aliens, every day.

It made him horny.

"By the way," Ollie said, "I looked up *photoluminescent* on the computer. It means glow in the dark."

"Okay," I agreed.

"That's stupid," Ollie decided.

Ollie Jungfrau never took his eyes from his laptop screen while we talked. He shot something with a spastic swipe at the space bar, or some shit like that. The thing on Ollie's screen howled in pain. Its leg came off.

Ollie laughed and put his game on pause.

He was sweating.

"I came over to buy some cigarettes," I said.

"For whom?" Ollie asked.

"Me."

"I think it's *I*."

"Me."

"What would your parents say?"

That was a pointless question, I thought. Why would Ollie Jungfrau ever want to insinuate himself into a conversation between me and my parents regarding cigarettes?

So I said, "They would tell I to say *please*."

A SNAPSHOT

OLLIE SOLD ME the cigarettes I asked for. I wanted to show Robby how brave and independent I could be. I bought two packs and a disposable lighter, then went back to the shop.

My balls were big.

I called Shann minutes before noon.

I asked her if she'd like to see a movie and have dinner with me in Waterloo that night.

"What about Robby?" she asked.

"Robby's fine," I answered. "Um. And how's your mom?"

"Fine," Shann said. "What are you talking about?"

"I thought you were just making small talk about other townsfolk we know," I said.

"No. I mean, are we all *three* hanging out tonight?"

"This isn't about Robby. I was planning on just me and you having a date, Shann," I said. "Johnny told me he'd drive us and everything."

Johnny McKeon wouldn't mind if Shann and I sat together in the backseat for the drive. It was a long, straight road to Waterloo.

The thought of having sex with Shann in the car while her stepfather drove us to Waterloo made me very horny.

Then the shop's front door opened. A family of tourists—a man, woman, and their identically clothed, identical twin boys who looked to be about six years old and undoubtedly had identically stinky feet, as Robby would confirm—came in and began their family expedition along Johnny's path of wonder and despair.

They marched through the maze in parade fashion. The mother, up front, regulated the speed. She stopped from time to time to admire a cow creamer or an iron trivet shaped like a squashed rooster. She pulled out drawers on dressers and nightstands.

She wasn't going to find any condoms.

A couple drawers still had Bibles in them.

The twin boys followed, shoulder to shoulder, holding hands. If they got a little closer to each other, they would look just like the boy in the jar Johnny McKeon kept inside the office. The father held up the rear of the parade. He had a canvas satchel, a man-purse, Robby and I called them, strapped diagonally across his shoulders.

They definitely were not from Iowa, I thought.

Maybe Minneapolis.

It wasn't unusual for tourists to stop at *From Attic to Seller* on Saturdays.

This family was probably on their way to the ocean, and found themselves trapped in the center of an enormous continent. They may have been looking for postcards so they could mail out desperate messages like:

Send help now! And that was our day. You know what I mean.

But Johnny McKeon did not sell postcards at *From Attic to Seller Consignment Store*. He did, however, sell condoms at *Tipsy Cricket Liquors*. I think most of the condoms he sold ended up stuck to the floor of the *Ealing Coin Wash Launderette*, or in dresser drawers and nightstands that I cleaned out when their owners lost homes and hope.

And that is an economic snapshot of the United States of America, and a dying Iowa town.

"It would be so nice to go out on a date, just you and me, Austin," Shann said.

"It's not like we never do that, Shann," I explained.

The family snaked their way closer to me at the counter. Along the way, the mother had picked up some objects.

"I know," Shann said, "but it's . . . well . . . different now, don't you think?"

My heart beat faster.

"Oh," I said. "Yes."

I didn't know what she meant. I suddenly felt guilty again, like Shann knew everything.

"I love you, Austin," Shann said.

Then I got it. I understood.

I was relieved and stupid at the same time.

"I love you, Shann." I did not say *too*. But I was fully clothed, anyway. "Did I tell you I am alone at the shop? Johnny needed to go to Waterloo to pick up some things. There are customers here."

I eyeballed the two packs of cigarettes I stacked on the glass case above my favorite insect collection.

"Austin?"

"What?"

"That ticking noise is happening again," she said. She sounded a little frightened.

It was exactly noon.

"Let me hear it."

Shann held her phone up to her wall. She had described the sound perfectly—typing. There was nothing else I could think of when I heard it. But the typing noise stopped in a matter of seconds.

It was exactly noon.

Ten hours in to the end of the world.

Nobody knew anything about it.

HAGGLED

"**I WILL PAY** five dollars for the snow globe from Iowa City, this corkscrew, *and* the porcelain corncobs salt-and-pepper shakers."

Mom, the drum major at the head of the tourist parade, placed her spoils on top of the counter beside my cigarettes. The two-headed boy with four arms and legs pressed its noses against the face of the glass case and left dual unpointed exclamation marks in clear snot directly in front of the bug collections. Dad, at the rear, slid his hand down into his purse and extracted a billfold.

"Um."

Johnny McKeon haggled with customers. Price tags, in stores such as *From Attic to Seller*, may just as well been written as fill-in-the-blank forms, as far as most shoppers were concerned.

Johnny knew what to do.

I did not.

"Um," I said again.

"Well?" she asked. She thought I was stupid. I knew the look. "Five dollars."

"I . . . I'm only taking care of the counter for my girlfriend's dad," I said. I suddenly felt virile, capable of breeding, horny. The twins frightened me, though. Their noses pointed upward on the glass, distorting into two peaked snot volcanoes.

My job included keeping the glass cases clean.

"I am not permitted to haggle," I pointed out.

"Pfft!" The mother, obviously used to getting her way, was exasperated. She had to do math.

Nobody likes math.

I took the items and tallied up the prices while the silent husband thumbed through bills.

"Eleven dollars and fifty cents," I said.

I increased the price by one dollar, just because I could, and because I was going to have to clean up a pair of snot streaks left behind by the *Friendship League of Minnesota*.

The man paid what I asked. I bagged my first sale.

Then the man with the purse asked, "Is this Ealing?"

"I know. A lot of people just can't believe they've finally arrived when they get to Ealing," I said. "But this is it."

"This is it . . . heh-heh," the man said. He pulled a small glossy guidebook from his purse and continued, "Ealing, Iowa. Seven unsolved decapitations in 1969."

"Uh."

He proudly held his book up so I could see the cover. It read:

Serial Killer America

"We're on a road trip!" The man with the purse twittered like a gleeful bird.

The twins snarfled and snotted against the glass.

"Cross another one off the list," the mother decided. Then she added, "Please be careful with my corncobs."

I needed a cigarette.

THE BOY IN THE GLASS

I STOOD OUTSIDE in the parking lot and smoked. I watched the traffic of people who came and went and came and went at *The Pancake House*, the launderette, *Tipsy Cricket Liquors*, and, across the street, at *Satan's Pizza*, too.

At 12:45, I phoned Robby.

I lit another cigarette. I was in charge.

Robby was impressed, maybe jealous, that I was alone and

having a cigarette without him. He was still in his bed when I called. I heard him light one up over the phone as we talked. So Robby and I had a cigarette together by cell phone.

It's good to have a cigarette with your best friend.

I told him everything that happened—the history of the morning—even about the snot-faced twin kids from Minneapolis who smeared up the glass case, and how I overcharged them a dollar just because I didn't like them. He asked if I'd gone back into the alley at Grasshopper Jungle. I said no. I wasn't going to go back there.

Everything seemed okay.

It was just another Saturday afternoon in Ealing, Iowa.

But I couldn't shake the feeling that something impossibly huge had happened in the past twenty-four hours. Maybe that's just the omniscience of the recorder who looks back on history as he's painting the walls of his cave. Shit like that.

There is a blissful haze that quietly flies into your head like a swarm of anesthetized butterflies after you smoke a couple fags. Buzzing from nicotine, I went back inside *From Attic to Seller Consignment Store*, wandered my way along the parade route of Johnny McKeon's display maze, and found myself standing once again in front of Johnny's locked office door.

Johnny McKeon obviously didn't really care to hide the things he kept inside his office. Maybe they were an embarrassment. Maybe he just didn't know what to do with the things that once belonged to his dead brother. I thought I might ask Johnny about that if he ever showed me his *experiments*.

I wanted to know *why*.

As my fingers felt along the groove of the molding, I thought about what I would do with Eric's things if he never came home again.

I would probably keep them in my room and not let anyone else look at them.

I understood Johnny McKeon.

The key was still there, where Johnny always hid it.

I went inside his office.

Johnny McKeon did not say anything about the missing globe to the policemen who came out that morning. If he had, he'd have to have shown them the rest of the things inside the office. Johnny would not want to do that.

There were smears on the old library shelf where Tyler's fingers had tracked through the dust at the base of the globe. He didn't even bother to take the stand. It was still there, still announcing the *Contained MI Plague Strain 412E.*

Not so much contained any longer.

That was the first time I'd considered the possibility that maybe those four boys were going to end up getting sick.

But I figured all that shit was from 1969, according to the dates on the labels. Nothing incurable could ever come from 1969.

The Beatles and the Stones came from 1969.

And like Johnny McKeon said, it was only photoluminescent mold, after all.

The two-headed boy, although hardly bigger than a cantaloupe, was older than me. I talked to him.

"You're nearing middle age, my man. You must be tired of being inside that jar."

I put my face close to the glass, resting my chin on the shelf so I could look directly into the little dark sockets of the boy's eyes.

I placed my palm on the cool curve of the glass.

The boy inside twitched.

The movement was so slight. Just a jittering spasm of the fingers. But I saw it.

I snapped my hand away from the glass and took a step back.

I bumped into Johnny McKeon's desk so hard it felt like I ripped a hole in my jeans.

SKATING AND KAYAKING

THE ALLEYWAY BEHIND *Satan's Pizza* wasn't nearly as long or accommodating for skaters as Grasshopper Jungle. The pizza place was a stand-alone business, so all we could really do there was goof around in small circles. Goofing around in small circles was how Robby and I usually skated, anyway.

When I showed up, Robby had on the grimacing lemur mask and the Titus Andronicus T-shirt I loaned him the night before.

After what happened to me in Johnny McKeon's office, everything I saw that day seemed like it oozed out of some twisted nightmare. I kept telling myself that maybe I was only imagining things as a result of too much nicotine and too little oxygen in my brain.

There was no way that little boy could have moved his fingers at me.

"Hey-ho, Lemur Boy," I said.

Robby raised his arms, twisting his fingers into claws above his hairy lemur head. He froze there like that, not saying anything. He stood with one foot on the deck of his skateboard. My board was right beside his.

Grimacing lemurs are a little unnerving.

"Amazingly lifelike," I said.

Robby remained silent and motionless, a taxidermist's display of a lemur-Lutheran-boy-crossbreed experiment.

I shrugged and slid my skateboard away from him. I got on it and pushed off.

"Hey, wait up," Robby said. He followed after me.

When he rolled up alongside me, still wearing the mask, Robby said, "I went through the jungle, Porcupine."

"Did you see anything?" I asked.

"Nah." Robby said, "Somebody pushed the dumpster back. Everything was just like it's always been."

"Are the pubic lice happy and well?" I asked.

"Thriving," Robby said. "I picked up a few hitchhikers who wanted to hang out with you. Let's have a fag."

"Okay. Can you smoke in that thing?"

"I haven't tried yet," Robby answered. "It's probably not flame retardant. Or else it's carcinogenic, or will mess up your sperm and make you have two-headed babies and shit."

"Yeah," I agreed. "You wouldn't want to smoke cigarettes wearing a carcinogenic grimacing lemur mask that's capable of messing up your sperm."

"Nobody wants messed-up sperm."

"Messed-up sperm is the evolutionary slot machine that will destroy mankind."

Robby and I were having a conversation about sperm.

Robby said, "How long are we going to talk about sperm?"

I answered, "I don't know. Talking about sperm is something that people just don't do enough of. It does make me feel a little weird, though."

Robby took off the mask. His face was pink and damp with sweat.

We looked at each other. Robby smiled and nodded. I knew everything between us was okay. He stuck his hand out, and I took it.

It was a real Lutheran-minister-kind-of-awkward-and-sweaty Iowa handshake.

"What is this shit?" I said, "We are shaking hands. We never shake hands."

Robby said, "I know. Well, I just, um, wanted to tell you . . ."

"You don't need to say anything, Rob."

I patted his shoulder.

"I guess not," Robby said. I took out one of the packs of cigarettes Ollie Jungfrau sold me, and Robby added, "I think it is always appropriate to end a conversation about sperm with a sweaty handshake."

"Yeah," I said.

We sat down on our skateboards right next to each other and smoked.

Every Saturday, Robby asked me how many donuts Ollie Jungfrau ate. I could not be certain, but that day I think I counted nine. Robby asked me to swear I would take pictures with my cell phone if Ollie Jungfrau ever exploded.

Then I told Robby about going back inside Johnny McKeon's office, and how scared I was because I believed I saw the two-headed boy inside the jar twitch his fingers at me when I talked to him.

Robby shook his head dismissively. "Last night, after all the shit that happened, we are both probably traumatized. You were seeing things."

"I don't think I'm traumatized, Robby," I said.

"I think the inside of this lemur mask made my face stink," Robby said. He blew out a big gaseous cloud of smoke.

"You're still wearing the T-shirt I loaned you," I said.

"I'll give it back after I wash it."

"Oh. Sure thing, Rob." I asked, "How's the flamingo?"

"Fine. Just fine." Robby rocked sideways on his board. "On

Monday night, my mom's working a double shift. You should come over and get drunk with me."

"Maybe we should do that," I said. "I was thinking. Have you ever popped one of your mom's little blue relaxers?"

"Zannies?" Robby asked.

"Yeah. Ever taken one?" I said, "I was just wondering. They look like little boats, don't they? Kayaks. I just figured they make you all calm and shit. Sailing away. Like you don't have any problems and everything is figured out."

Robby said, "I never tried one. Anyway, *you* don't have any problems, or anything to figure out, either."

"Sure. Sure I don't," I said.

"Like what?" Robby asked.

"Okay," I said.

Okay, at times, can effectively serve as the closing curtain to difficult teenage conversations.

Then I said, "I will come over on Monday and get drunk with you."

"I'll let you wear the lemur mask."

"I don't want my face to stink."

"Yeah. Probably not."

By the time we'd gotten on to our second cigarette, I worked up the nerve to tell Robby about the date I made with Shann. Feeling awkward and guilty about it was stupid, too, but it was just another element of my confusion about things. Robby didn't seem to mind. I was more confused. I thought he'd feel left out, like we were ditching him.

He offered to drive me to Shann's house so I wouldn't have to skate all the way out there. Robby said it would give me B.O., and I probably did not want to have B.O. on a date with Shann.

"You're right," I said. "I don't want to have B.O."

Robby said, "If you have B.O., you might as well have messed-up sperm, too."

"I'll shake to that," I said.

Robby picked up the grimacing lemur mask and sniffed the inside of it.

"This is nasty," he said.

"I thought you'd be disappointed," I said. "Because we're going out on Saturday night without you."

"But it's Shann," Robby said. "She's your girlfriend. You need to go out together. That's what boyfriends and girlfriends do."

"Yeah. Well, I feel bad."

"Why?"

I said, "I don't really know, Robby. What are *you* going to do tonight?"

Robby said, "Me? Laundry, I guess. Shit like that."

"Right."

"Come on," Robby said, "let's head out and pick up the Explorer."

"Maybe tomorrow we could do something," I said. "Just me and you."

"We could fold my laundry," Robby offered.

EDEN FIVE NEEDS YOU

SHANN COLLINS AND I ate burgers and onion rings at *Jackie's Country Kitchen* in Waterloo, Iowa, after the movie.

People in Iowa are real dynamos at naming businesses.

Movies came to Waterloo about a month after they began showing on other parts of the continent. The movie Shann and I sat through was one that all the kids at Curtis Crane Lutheran

Academy had seen on opening day, which happened weeks earlier, just so they could tell everyone who hadn't seen it what it was about and how good it was.

The kids at Curtis Crane Lutheran Academy all agreed the movie was terrific.

It was probably the dumbest movie I'd ever seen in my life.

But since I was with Shann, I didn't actually pay attention to much of it.

It is difficult for any movie to keep my attention. That's something else wrong with me, I think. It's all part of the big confusing history behind Austin Andrzej Szerba. I don't know why I am the way I am. I knew I should talk to my father about things. I just needed to find a way to get that conversation to start.

Shann and I sat in the corner of the back row.

The movie was called *Eden Five Needs You 4*. I had not seen the first three parts, but it didn't matter since everyone at Curtis Crane Lutheran Academy had, and had told everything about what happened. It also didn't matter because apparently the plot of the movie was not an essential element to the experience.

Eden Five Needs You 4 was a very loud, visually assaulting science-fiction movie about a teenager who was abducted by benevolent aliens and taken to a planet called Eden Five.

The first four Edens were probably shitholes.

The benevolent aliens abducted the teen because Earth was dying, due to all the wars and environmental destruction humans had inflicted on their planet and shit like that. So the benevolent aliens chose the teen because they wanted his sperm to start a new population of human beings on this other, nice planet called Eden Five. Well, the teen didn't want his sperm to be the sole genesis of a new race of mankind on Eden Five, because he did not want to be responsible for all the shitty things human beings are genetically driven to do: War, crucifixions, genocide, religion, television.

He paid attention to history enough to know that Adam should have used a condom.

So the teen stole one of the benevolent aliens' spacecrafts and returned to Earth to get his best friend, another teen, so he could go back to Eden Five with him, and both of their sperm could be used to start a new race of mankind. That way, neither one of them would have to take full responsibility for all the shit human beings are naturally driven to do.

You know, friends blaming friends for the other guy's sperm being messed up.

That's what history's all about.

In the meantime, the president of the United States, who had formerly been director of the Central Intelligence Agency, learned of the plan to start a new world on Eden Five. The president was unhappy that it was not going to be *his* sperm that started an entire new race. He ordered the United States Space Agency to send rockets up and destroy the craft with (now) the two teenagers aboard. The United States spaceships were also loaded with frozen embryos that had all been created from the president's sperm.

The United States spacecrafts also looked like gigantic flying pairs of balls.

Hollywood is good at subtlety.

Like I said, it was the dumbest movie I ever saw.

The actor who played the teenager was thirty years old in real life, but nobody in the paying audience seemed to mind because he was very handsome and well groomed.

I don't really know how the movie ended, or if there was a clear conclusion to the story. While we waited in line for our tickets, I did hear some boys ahead of us talking about next summer's release of

Eden Five Needs You 5, so the movie probably had a real cliffhanger of an ending.

The boys in front of us chewed tobacco. They carried paper coffee cups that were halfway filled with sticky brown saliva. They left these on the floor of the theater, for the future. If you were ever going to start a new planet and needed some sperm, these boys would not be on your list.

During the big in-space fight scene between the flying American testicles and the teens whose sperm was going to create a new race of blameless humans, Shann and I had our tongues in each other's mouths.

It's not that the movie made us particularly horny. If we actually paid attention to it, we might likely have been anesthetized. I read a popular myth somewhere about how schools in Iowa used to put a chemical called saltpeter in their cafeteria food. People believed that saltpeter made it so boys would not get erections.

It was all a bunch of shit, of course.

Nothing, except possibly paying attention to *Eden Five Needs You 4*, could ever make boys not get erections.

I slid my hand up inside the loose sweater Shann was wearing and played with her perfect breasts.

The movie was very loud.

I had never touched Shann's naked breasts before. She liked it.

I liked it more, I think.

In fact, Shann dropped her hand between my legs and rubbed me. Shann had never put her hand there before. This caused a very sudden and accidental eruption of Mount Austin Andrzej Szerba inside my jeans.

I gasped and gulped.

It happened exactly at a moment where the dumb movie went absolutely quiet.

I was mortified. I nearly passed out.

Shann knew what happened. It was obvious.

The tobacco-chewing yahoos in front of us could probably tell what happened.

I slumped down in my seat.

I wondered if it was possible to die from embarrassment.

"Oh," Shann said.

"Uh," I said.

And Shann whispered, "*Eden Five needs you.*"

So, while we eyed each other over our burgers and onion rings, I slipped my foot out of my shoe and caressed Shann's leg with my toes under the table at *Jackie's Country Kitchen*. I was somewhere in the middle of telling her the story about Ollie Jungfrau's uncle's German shepherd that can toast a brownie on demand, and how damaged sperm was probably responsible for every great man-made calamity in history, when Shann said to me:

"You know what I really love about you, Austin?"

I did not know what she really loved about me. Probably not my endurance.

I said, "No. Tell me."

Shann said, "I love how you tell stories. I love how, whenever you tell me a story, you go backwards and forwards and tell me *everything* else that could possibly be happening in every direction, like an explosion. Like a flower blooming."

"Really?" I asked. "I . . . Hmm . . . I never noticed that about me before."

I felt myself getting embarrassed again, but not nearly to the degree I had been when we encountered an accidental spill during the painfully quiet post–epic battle scene in *Eden Five Needs You 4*.

Shann said, "I think you're irresistibly cute, Austin Szerba."

"Thank you, Shannon Collins." I said, "I will shake to that."

Here is what happened that night:

Seven people in Ealing, Iowa, stopped eating food. They began bumping into walls and shit. They were very sick.

Ollie Jungfrau was constipated. He'd eaten too many donuts that day and had a dinner whose principal ingredient was cheese.

There were only six houses on the street where I lived. Two of them had been repossessed by the bank. Their windows and doors were posted with notices printed in very small type. At exactly the same moment *Eden Five Needs You 4* got embarrassingly silent and I erupted, a third home on my street went empty as the owners were ordered out by grim-faced officers of the court who waved official papers.

And in that house, tucked away inside the drawer of an abandoned nightstand were four unopened condoms and a Book of Mormon that had been taken from a room at a Marriott Hotel in San Diego, California.

The family had been to Sea World.

Pastor Roland Duff ate a personal-sized *Stanpreme* pizza at *Satan's Pizza*. While he sat alone, Roland Duff read the Waterloo paper and looked up movie listings. He thought he might enjoy seeing *Eden Five Needs You 4*. Pastor Roland Duff had never seen the Pacific Ocean.

Shann's stepfather, Johnny McKeon, who was also my employer, drove out to Waterloo to pick us up at *Jackie's Country Kitchen* at 10:30.

On the drive back to Ealing, Shann sat next to me with her head resting on my shoulder.

It was a quiet ride.

Most of the way home, I was trying to decide if what happened to me could technically be considered *having sex*; if that was the first time I actually *had sex* with someone else. I decided it was close enough. Close enough to repopulate *Eden Five*. Close enough to be a forbidden subject in the library at Curtis Crane Lutheran Academy.

Thinking about what happened in the movie theater made me hope Shann would touch me like that again.

I also desperately wanted to change out of my soggy Iowa plaid boxers.

"So, how was the movie?" Johnny asked.

"Huh?" I said.

Sweaty, damp, and oddly energized, I got home at 11:15. My predictable parents were already asleep at that time. The house was dark. Ingrid waggled and quivered excitedly. She stuck her bowling-pin nose into my crotch when I opened the door.

"Go toast some brownies, Ingrid," I said.

I stood on our front step and waited for Ingrid to shit. Then we both went upstairs into my room, where, at last, I could peel myself out of my ruined clothes.

At 12:04 I slipped between the coolness of my sheets just as my phone rang.

I thought it was Robby, but it was Shann.

She told me the typing-ticking sound had come back and she was scared.

"Tomorrow, after church, me and Robby are coming over," I said. "We're going to find out what's inside the wall."

"Okay," Shann said. "I love you, Austin."

"Eden Five needs me," I said.

I was very horny again.

AN AWFUL LOT OF MATH

WENDY MCKEON LOOKED so much like her daughter, Shann, that people sometimes assumed they might be sisters.

Robby and I went directly to Shann's house after church. Johnny and Wendy didn't take Shann to services that week. They made the excuse that they were settling in to their new old house. When you didn't go to church in Ealing, sometimes it was almost necessary to stick a sign in your yard asking forgiveness from your neighbors.

God cuts slack to people who need to settle in, but your neighbors might not.

Students from Curtis Crane Lutheran Academy were required to wear our ties and sweaters at church, even though most people in Ealing did not dress up on Sundays.

"Don't you two look handsome?" Wendy McKeon said when she greeted us at her door.

Robby and I hadn't changed into our non-Lutheran-boy clothes yet.

"Like candy canes," I said.

"Kind of makes you want to beat us up, doesn't it?" Robby asked.

"Oh, you," Wendy said and put her hand flat on Robby's chest.

Robby was so much funnier and better looking than I was. I believed Wendy sometimes wondered why Shann wasn't *his* girlfriend, instead of the Polish kid's. Robby wasn't *out* to anyone but me and Shann. Wendy McKeon didn't know anything about teenage boys unless she learned it from one of those daytime television talk programs.

Wendy McKeon would have thought it was not normal for Robby and me to experiment.

There was an exterminator service van parked in front of the McKeon House. Shann had told her mother about the noises coming from the wall, and Johnny and Wendy decided it was most likely rats.

"Old houses like this *do* often have rats inside them," I said to Shann when Robby and I were in her room. I couldn't help but play with the idea of asking Shann for an *Eden Five Needs You 4* threesome with me and Robby. The amount of math in that thought made my head ache.

"Rats with typewriters," Robby added.

"These rats type every six hours," Shann said, continuing the numerical assault on my head. "At exactly six and twelve. I've been keeping track."

"So they're obsessive-compulsive rats with typewriters," Robby said.

"Just wait a moment," Shann said. She looked at her wristwatch. It was 11:50.

I was horny and mathematically confused.

The exterminator men crawled all around the floor, looking for holes rats could use to get inside the walls. When they didn't find any, they crawled up into the attic and around the perimeter of the home's foundation, setting traps and putting out attractive dishes of poison that looked like candy corn.

They did not find any rats because there weren't any.

At exactly noon, the noise inside Shann's wall came again. This time, all three of us were there, and all three of us heard it. The sound went silent in less than a minute, but we triangulated with our ears the precise spot in the wall where it originated.

"Do you kids want some lunch?" Wendy called from deep in the house somewhere.

I nodded at Shann and she yelled back at her mother. The house was so big it wouldn't have been too outrageous to actually use cell phones. In houses, teenagers tend to communicate with their parents by screaming across distances.

"It's some kind of a machine," I said.

The wall there was made from top-to-bottom tongue-and-groove wood plank. Some of the slats were loose and could wiggle. I felt certain we'd be able to pry a board or two up without inflicting any permanent damage to Shann's bedroom wall. I asked Shann to bring us some butter knives or flathead screwdrivers—anything Robby and I could use to get at the boards.

And just when Wendy McKeon hollered up to us that lunch was served, Robby and I peeled back a six-inch-wide slat and found the source of Shann's four-times-per-day haunting.

The ghost in Shann's wall was a machine.

The thing was set back between the wall of Shann's room and a bathroom on the other side. It sat on a low, dust-covered pine shelf. Thick rubberized wires ran from its back, following the roadways of wall studs and joists up and down, out of sight.

The machine was also covered in dust, made of Bakelite and blue rounded metal that had the same aesthetic style of a toaster or an automobile designed fifty years ago. At the front was a keyboard, like a typewriter's, but the thing was much bigger than a simple typewriter.

This was what was called a teletype machine.

From the back of the platen cylinder, a yellowed scroll of perforated paper had been spitting out the same repeated message, typed out in black-ink capital letters that formed ladder-like rungs over several feet:

THE FLAMINGO ALERTS ON ENVIRONMENTAL
PRESENCE OF 412-E. SILO GENERATORS NOW
ACTIVATED. REPORT TO THE SILO WITH
PROPER HASTE.

THE FLAMINGO ALERTS ON ENVIRONMENTAL
PRESENCE OF 412-E. SILO GENERATORS NOW
ACTIVATED. REPORT TO THE SILO WITH
PROPER HASTE.

THE FLAMINGO ALERTS ON ENVIRONMENTAL
PRESENCE OF 412-E. SILO GENERATORS NOW
ACTIVATED. REPORT TO THE SILO WITH
PROPER HASTE.

I looked at Robby.
He looked at me.
Both of us, at the same time, said, "Oh."
And Robby said, "Nobody says '*with proper haste.*'"
"Who would ever say something like that?" I added.
Shann said, "What's going on, Austin?"
I said, "Uh."

TALLY-HO!

"**I DON'T THINK** I'll need to eat again before Guy Fawkes Day," I said.
"*Tallyho* to that," Robby said.
"Chip chip and all that," I said.
That night, Robby drove his car east along the flat straight highway that linked Ealing to Waterloo. We were hanging out together, like I'd promised.
Robby said we would be traveling through time, and it might be ugly.
I did not know why Robby wanted to go to Waterloo, or why

he wanted to travel through time. I only hoped he did not want to sit through *Eden Five Needs You 4*.

Wendy McKeon was raised in southern Indiana. Regionalists sometimes referred to that area as Northern Kentucky. Lunch, for a person raised in that part of the continent, consisted of the following: fried chicken, potato salad, mashed potatoes, creamed corn, deviled eggs, canned fruit cocktail, sweet pickles, American cheese slices, white bread, softened margarine, milk, cake, and peanut butter.

After the orgy of Wendy McKeon's lunch, we unplugged the teletype machine before we left. Robby and I took the printout of the repeating message with us, and we replaced the wobbly board to the wall in Shann's bedroom.

Having a teletype machine built into your wall was not so strange, I offered, considering Shann's room also included a door that went nowhere and a staircase descending to a dungeon for horny Lutheran boys.

Shann agreed. It was just a weird house.

"But it is on the *Ealing Registry of Historical Homes*," Robby reminded us.

"An abundance of distressed bricks," I commented.

"Who knows what other crazy stuff the McKeons did in this house?" Shann said.

"Yes," I said. "Who knows?"

There was some figuring out that had to be done.

Figuring out meant a sort of confession to Shann would be involved if Robby and I were not careful. I did not want to tell Shann about the things that happened in Johnny McKeon's office, and I did not want to say to her what Robby and I did when we were up on the roof of the Ealing Mall.

But I do not lie. If Shann ever asked about it, I would tell her.

So Robby and I opted for a waiting period of quiet consideration before exploring the possibilities of what the teletype message actually could mean.

Robby and I went back to my house and changed out of our Lutheran Boy superhero costumes. I loaned him another Austin Szerba outfit from my closet. Soon, I thought, all my clothes as well as Robby's would be scattered, unwashed, over the backseat of his Ford Explorer.

"There is no silo at the McKeon House," I said. "I looked."

I pulled on a pair of jeans and slipped my feet into some loose skate shoes.

"So did I," Robby said. I gave him some Levis and my Pink Floyd T-shirt to wear. Mine said LCD Soundsystem.

"You're not planning on taking me to see *Eden Five Needs You 4*, are you?"

"No," Robby answered. "I'm going to see something I always wondered about, but was too chicken to go by myself."

"Sounds like what I'd say about Eden Five," I said.

Eventually, I was relieved. I was grateful that Robby truly was not interested in the film I'd seen with Shann the night before.

Robby didn't even slow the car when we drove past the Waterloo *Cinezaar*.

Another brilliant job of name branding by an Iowa entrepreneur.

Finally, Robby pulled the Explorer into the parking lot of a squat and dim strip mall. The place was dismal, but not nearly as run-down and left in abandon as the Ealing Mall at Grasshopper Jungle. The signs above each of the businesses were lit up, despite the fact that the majority of places were closed on Sunday nights.

There was a launderette, and it appeared to be clean and condom-free. Naturally, there was a liquor store, another business called *Cheap Smokes* that had a decal of a marijuana leaf in the corner of its front window, a barbershop, and an indoor shooting range and gun shop called *Fire at Will's*.

Waterloo was definitely the place.

And at the end of the mall, in an area where four or five cars had parked beneath a lonely overhead light facing the unit's front door, was a bar called the *Tally-Ho!*

The *Tally-Ho!* was widely known in the area as being a secret place for homosexual men to hang out and meet.

The secret was not well kept.

People in Ealing just didn't talk about the *Tally-Ho!*, or if they did, it was in a very low register, so other ears would not perk up at mention of the name.

The *Tally-Ho!* was Waterloo, Iowa's one and only gay bar.

"Uh," I said.

"What?" said Robby.

"Why did you come to the *Tally-Ho!*, Robby?"

"I wanted to see what it looked like," Robby explained.

"We can't go inside," I argued. "People might think we're . . . Um. Prostitutes, or something."

"Did you actually just say *prostitute*?" Robby asked.

"I can't be certain," I said. "I think I did."

"We can't go *inside* because we're only *sixteen*," Robby said.

"Do you *want* to go inside?" I asked.

"Are you asking me on a date, Austin?" Robby said.

"No."

I was so confused.

Robby went on, "I wanted to come here just so I could see what the future is like. What if I end up *here*, with nowhere else to go? What will I look like?"

"You could wear the grimacing lemur mask," I offered.

"I always wondered who came to this place," Robby said.

"I guess everyone kind of wonders that, but they're just too afraid to admit it," I said.

Robby shook out some cigarettes, held the pack so I could take one. I pressed the lighter into the dash. I thought I knew why Robby came here. It was sad.

We smoked.

"Do you want to go look?" Robby said.

"What? Like, *inside*?"

"No. Maybe we could just poke our faces in the door and say something like we're lost and need to know how to get back to Ealing."

"Nobody would believe it," I said. "Nobody *ever* wants to get back to Ealing."

"You may be right," Robby said. "Still, what would they do to us?"

"What if they think we're gay or something?"

"What are you trying to say, Austin?"

"Um. Sorry, Rob." I took a drag off my cigarette. "I guess I better just shut up."

Robby got out of the car.

Robby wasn't angry or upset at what I'd said. Real friends know what they mean when one of them says clumsy or stupid things. History shows that.

History also shows there aren't an awful lot of *real* friends on the record.

So I got out of the car, too.

THE INNER TOMB

IT WAS FRIGHTENING and thrilling, following Robby to the door of the *Tally-Ho!*

It seemed as though hidden eyes were out there in the dark of the parking lot, and they were watching us and constructing stories—histories—about what these two boys from Curtis Crane Lutheran Academy might be up to.

The *Tally-Ho!*, as it turned out, was not a vibrant, happening scene at all.

It was exactly what Robby expected.

He stood with his hand on the door's pull bar. A sign hung from metal S-hooks beneath clear plastic suction cups on the inside of the glass. It said:

NO PERSONS UNDER 21 ALLOWED

I expected to hear happy music seeping out from the door, the sound of laughter and boisterous barroom conversations, but the *Tally-Ho!* let no such atmosphere leak out from its small, encapsulated world.

The place was as quiet as a cemetery in a morning snowfall.

Robby took a deep breath, pulled open the door, and stepped inside.

And, like a sedated Chihuahua on a jeweled leash, I followed him.

I was so nervous I thought my knees would buckle. My head swam in agitated seas of conflict and confusion: What if people thought we were gay? Why did I care what people thought? What if I really *was* gay? I kissed Robby, after all. What would Shann say about us being here? What if someone started hitting on me or

Robby? What if we got in trouble for walking into the place? What if we got beat up again by some assholes like Grant Wallace and his friends?

Robby Brees was much braver than I could ever be.

We stood there, dumb and quiet in the dark alcove just inside the front door of the *Tally-Ho!*

The place was as tired and mournful as the library at Curtis Crane Lutheran Academy after the masturbation scandal. Nobody so much as turned to glance at the two nervous kids who stood at the door.

I hid behind Robby.

The bartender washed glasses. He wore a T-shirt that was too tight. It accentuated the roll of his belly. He was balding and showed a blurring tattoo of Bettie Page, blanketed beneath the swirling shrubbery of black hair on his forearm. Two other men sat at the bar. They both appeared to be tired, in their forties. They stared straight ahead as though watching something other than their own reflections in the mirror behind the bartender.

They were separated by three barstools.

The closer of the two had dirty hands. He bit his fingernails, too.

At the back of the room sat an undersized pool table with worn felt. It was tucked too near a corner to actually be playable. A man with a Royals ball cap shot pool by himself. He scratched the cue ball while we watched him. After he took another shot, he glanced up at me and Robby. He smiled.

I whispered, "Aren't you going to ask them? You know . . . say we're lost or shit?"

Robby shook his head and backed himself into me.

He said, "No. Let's get out of here, Austin."

Robby leaned on me, pushing me back.

We quietly slid out the door.

Nobody even watched us leave.

AND HERE'S NUMBER FIVE

ROBBY AND I sat against the tailgate of the Explorer. We smoked cigarettes and watched cars on the highway. Robby said he wished we'd have brought our skateboards with us.

"Skating would be good," I said.

The alley behind *Tally-Ho!* looked like a real clean place to skate.

"I never knew there were four gay guys in Waterloo," I said.

That number involved making an assumption about the bartender.

"It's Sunday," Robby said. "I bet when this place gets really busy, there might be five or six."

"You're not going to be like that, Rob," I said. "I mean, all lonely and shit."

"Is that what you think?" Robby asked.

"I'm pretty sure that *is* what I think," I said.

Out on the highway, a car slowed and then pulled into the parking lot at the opposite end, near *Fire at Will's Indoor Shooting Range*. It was a newer Honda Accord. The car drove along the front aisle of parking stalls and then turned left into a slot beside the other vehicles lined up near the *Tally-Ho!*

Robby and I watched from our hidden spot behind his old Ford.

"And here's number five," I said.

The Honda's door opened. Freshly pressed slacks and shiny black loafers with dangly tassels that flapped from their insteps like beagle ears lowered mechanically from the bottom of the driver's door. Then Pastor Roland Duff got out, straightened and brushed off his trousers, shut the door, and entered the *Tally-Ho!*

"Uh," I said.

"Uh," Robby answered.

"I wonder what Pastor Roland Duff is doing here," I said.

"Do you *really* wonder?" Robby asked.

"I guess not," I said.

"He must be lonely," Robby said.

"I'll buy that, Robby," I said. "But if Pastor Roland Duff *is* lonely, it isn't because he's gay. It's because he's a shitspoon."

Robby nodded thoughtfully and smoked.

Then he said, "I'll buy that, too, Austin."

"I would like another cigarette, Robby," I said.

Robby pulled the crumpled pack from his back pocket and handed it to me.

He said, "Where did you get that word from? I admire it."

"What?" I said, "*Shitspoon?*"

"Uh-huh," Robby said.

"It was the name of the alien's spacecraft in *Eden Five Needs You 4*," I said.

"You're making that up," Robby said.

"I know. I didn't pay attention to that shitspoon flick at all, Rob."

TAKING DRAGS

"**WERE YOU SCARED** in there?" I asked.

"I wasn't scared," Robby said.

"I was," I said.

"I could feel your heartbeat through the floorboards. I thought it was because you found the bartender to be attractive."

"Uh. *Was* he attractive?" I asked.

"Kind of," Robby said.

I smoked.

"Do you think I'm queer, Rob?" I asked.

"I don't *care* if you're queer," Robby said. "*Queer* is just a word. Like orange. I know *who* you are. There's no one word for that."

I believed him.

"I know I'm not orange," I said.

"Kind of oatmealy," Robby said.

I always let Robby read the books. He was the only one allowed inside Austin Andrzej Szerba's history department.

"Sometimes I'm confused," I said. "Actually, pretty much all the time I am. I wonder if I'm normal. I think I might ask my dad about it. You know, if he ever felt this way. Or if maybe he still does sometimes. Because I feel . . . Uh . . . I wonder if I am queer or shit."

"You should ask your dad, Porcupine," Robby said.

"Would you ask *your* dad?"

"My dad doesn't give a shit about me," Robby said.

"Uh."

I took another drag. "It made me feel weird. The other night. But I keep thinking about you, and I think doing that means there is something wrong about me."

"I'm sorry. I won't do what I did ever again. You know. Sorry, Austin."

"Nuh." I said, "It's not something to be sorry about. I just don't know what to do, Rob."

"You worry too much," Robby said.

"I know."

And then Robby said, "I do love you, though."

"Yeah, Rob. I know." I blew out a cloud of smoke. I tried to make it all perfect and cool like Robby could, but it didn't work.

So I said, "I love you, Robby."

I did not say *too*.

Robby said, "I know that, Austin. It *is* nice to hear you say it, though."

"I wish we brought our skateboards."

"Uh-huh."

I didn't know what to do.

A VISITOR COMES AND GOES

SO WE STOOD there and smoked our cigarettes down.

In the paralytic coma that is a Sunday night in a strip mall parking lot paved atop the scraps of a cornfield somewhere imprecisely located on the outskirts of Waterloo, Iowa, the whooshing excitement of passing cars came once or twice, every five minutes or so.

And that was our day. You know what I mean.

The *Tally-Ho!* turned out to be not so much a disappointment for Robby as the sad realization of everything he expected to see.

That is, except for Pastor Roland Duff showing up.

But history does consistently prove that whenever guys go out to visit someplace they've never been before, they're going to see shit they did not expect to see.

The Age of Discovery had come to Ealing, Iowa.

Experiments and shit like that.

Krzys Szczerba never expected to see the frosted cupcake

breasts on Eva Nightingale's pillowed mounds of peach ice cream body. He never thought he would see his father, who was also named Andrzej, slipping down into the cold, green-black Atlantic with nothing more than a silver chain for Saint Casimir jingling upon the Quaker Oats whiteness of his still and empty chest.

And as strange and discomforting as it was to watch the headmaster from Curtis Crane Lutheran Academy pull up in freshly pressed attire and then casually step inside the *Tally-Ho!* with the carriage of a man entering the most familiar place on his planet, what we saw next was even stranger.

Out from the darkness in back of us, loaded down with plastic bags, bundles of clothing, suitcases, and a cardboard box lashed by three bungee cords to a broken saddlebag frame that vibrated over a half-flat back tire, a squeaking and tottering rusted old bicycle wobbled and creaked its way into the lamplight.

Hungry Jack had come to pay a visit.

Hungry Jack got around for an old guy on a crooked bicycle.

"He's a real dynamo on the two-wheeler," I observed.

"I don't think he's a *Tally-Ho!* kind of guy," Robby said.

"You never know," I offered.

Robby took another puff and shook his head. "You never do, Porcupine."

It was Robby who'd spoken to Hungry Jack in the past.

I was afraid of the toothless old war criminal.

Robby was much braver than I was, except when it came to shit like breaking into *From Attic to Seller Consignment Store* in the middle of the night.

Robby had given Hungry Jack cigarettes in the past, and, on occasion, the two of them smoked together in Grasshopper Jungle while I worked inside Johnny McKeon's store. That was how Robby found out all the history about Hungry Jack and the things he'd done in Vietnam.

"You want to know what happens?" Hungry Jack had said to Robby.

"What happens?" Robby said.

Hungry Jack said, "You could do whatever you wanted to do over there."

"What I would want to do is get on a boat and come home," Robby told him.

"No boats!" Hungry Jack jumped up and down and repeated himself, "No boats! No fucking boats home! What are you, a crybaby?"

"I suppose I am a crybaby," Robby said to him.

"You could do whatever you want," Hungry Jack said. "Any kind of drug you like. Heroin. Pot. Heroin. Heroin. You could fuck anything you wanted. All the time. Drugs and fucks. I bet you'd like to fuck anything, wouldn't you? Wouldn't you?"

"Uh," Robby told him, "I don't think I would like to fuck *anything*."

"Yes you would fuck anything," Hungry Jack told him.

"No I wouldn't," Robby affirmed.

"You would, too," Hungry Jack argued.

Robby told me this back-and-forth rally of counter-shot verbal tennis balls continued for several rounds.

"Well, that's what *we* did," Hungry Jack said. "Fucked everything. Fucked everyone who'd hold still long enough. We fucked the planet if we wanted to. And no boats! But you know what happened?"

"I suppose you cooked your brain on dope and a little while later your penis scabbed up and fell off from all the dirty shit you fucked," Robby ventured.

"As soon as one boy shoots, everyone starts shooting," Hungry Jack told Robby.

And then Hungry Jack said, "Then, it's time to come home."

Then Hungry Jack told Robby about all the people who died in the village.

Robby told me.

But I never talked to Hungry Jack before or since that day Robby told me the old man's stories.

So that night, Robby Brees and I stood there in the parking lot of the *Tally-Ho!*, which was Waterloo, Iowa's one and only gay bar.

I thought about fucking things.

And while I thought about fucking things, and Robby and I smoked cigarettes, we witnessed firsthand what happens to a person who swallowed a mouthful of *Stanpreme* pizza that had been contaminated by *Contained MI Plague Strain 412E*.

Here is what happened:

Hungry Jack tottered toward us. The front tire of his bicycle jerked this way and that, but somehow the man kept rolling. Hungry Jack's eyes were fixed directly on Robby and me.

When he stopped his bicycle, Hungry Jack was ten feet away from us. He stood at the edge of the dark near a low easement that separated the blacktop of the parking lot from the blacktop of the highway.

At first, the old man was motionless, straddling the top tube of the bike frame with his feet planted on either side. Hungry Jack's chin was slick with drool, but that wasn't uncommon for him.

Hungry Jack had no front teeth.

He stared at Robby. Hungry Jack knew Robby. For all I could tell, I was invisible to the man.

Robby took a big drag from his cigarette.

Robby said, "Hey, Jack. You want a cigarette?"

Jack stared and drooled.

"He's freaking out on you, Rob," I whispered. "Let's just leave."

"Maybe he's exhausted from the long ride," Robby said. Then he asked again, "Want to smoke, Jack?"

Hungry Jack wobbled. He raised his right knee and got off the bicycle.

Hungry Jack released his grasp on the handlebars and his bicycle crashed in a noisy heap. A thermos bottle with a small amount of gasoline in it rolled away toward the curb.

Robby smoked.

Hungry Jack looked at Robby. He took two steps toward us and stopped. The whole time I never saw the man blink once.

He also never said anything to Robby.

Then Hungry Jack turned around and stepped over the low hedge that bordered the parking lot. He lumbered like a sleepwalker, out onto the highway.

Hungry Jack walked directly into the path of a Dodge pickup that was speeding in the direction headed away from Ealing.

The truck never slowed, even after the concussive thud the old man's body made when Hungry Jack went spinning and cartwheeling down the road.

Things like that happened in Iowa all the time, but Robby and I never saw it right in front of our faces.

"Holy shit, Rob," I said.

Robby said, "Holy shit."

THE THING IN THE CORNFIELD

SOMETHING ELSE HAPPENED, too.

We did not talk about it at school.

Shann wondered why Robby and I were both so sullen that

next day. We told her we were tired. I asked if the noise in her wall had come back, but our unplugging the teletype machine had put an end to the typing rats problem in the McKeon House.

"What are we going to say, Rob?" I had asked him. "Are we going to tell Shann we were hanging out in the parking lot of a gay bar smoking cigarettes and we saw Pastor Roland Duff out cruising just before some homeless guy stepped in front of a Dodge truck? Are we going to tell her what happened after that?"

And Robby said, "What *did* happen after that, Austin? I still don't believe we saw that shit."

Because what happened was this:

We ran out onto the highway to see if we could help Hungry Jack.

It was terrible.

It took us several minutes to find him.

The truck had thrown the old man's body more than a hundred feet through the air. We found Hungry Jack lying in a field of waist-high corn on the opposite side of the highway from the *Tally-Ho!*

He had been knocked completely out of his shoes, and his dirty pants had been pulled down, turned entirely inside out, and twisted around his broken legs.

Hungry Jack wasn't just dead. He was destroyed.

I had never seen anyone dead before. Neither had Robby. I thought about Krzys Szczerba saying good-bye to his father on the boat in the middle of ocean, how scared and alone he must have felt. I thought about Saint Casimir, and Pastor Roland Duff across the street from us.

"Holy shit, Rob," I said again.

I stepped closer to the mangled wreckage of the old man.

Robby said, "Don't touch him."

"He just walked right out in front of that shit," I said.

"We need to call someone," Robby said.

I took my phone out of my pocket and turned it on.

Then Hungry Jack moved his arms. His chest heaved and collapsed, and he wriggled around in the dirt between the young cornstalks that had been mowed down when he tumbled and tumbled through the field.

"Stay still!" I tried to tell him.

Robby and I stood back, afraid to get too close. From the light on my cell phone's screen I could see how there was blood all over the place. Pieces of Hungry Jack were sticking out from his belly and from the top of his head.

But the old man wheezed and writhed around in the dirt.

It looked like he was breaking apart.

He was coming apart like a soft-boiled egg oozing thick, yolky blood.

"Let's get somebody," Robby said.

My hand shook so bad I could not even punch three emergency digits on my phone. I also could not look away from the thrashing heap in the cornfield.

Hungry Jack split entirely in half, the same way you'd cleave the husk of a roasted peanut, all the way from his skull to the fork of his crotch. Then he began turning inside out.

That is exactly what happened.

It wasn't that Hungry Jack was actually *turning*, but something was coming *out* of the peanut shell of the old man's body. The thing flopped and crawled stiffly, like a newborn calf, all slick and covered with blood and slippery goo.

"Holy shit," we both said, over and over.

Robby grabbed my shoulder.

I grabbed him back.

We stood there, shaking and holding each other, and we watched as a six-legged bug the size of a small man crawled like some kind of windup mechanized toy out of the hollowed remains of Hungry Jack.

It wiped itself clean with four of its appendages, bringing its spiny hands up to its mandibles, licking itself clean and dry with crackling, smacking bug-mouth sounds.

The thing's head was triangular. It looked like a praying mantis, only it was as tall as we were.

It was identical to those things—pieces of giant bugs—Robby and I had seen floating inside sealed aquarium displays in Johnny McKeon's office two nights before.

Those things were not alive.

This one was.

And it came out of Hungry Jack's body.

The thing hissed and moved toward us. Its head pivoted and turned in a near-complete circle. It froze the point of its chin directly at Robby, looking, looking, and then it backed away.

I pulled Robby's shirt so hard, it nearly came off over the top of his head.

We took off running.

We did not look back.

PART 3:
THE SILO

SAINT CASIMIR'S REAL name was Kazimierz.

He died very young, in his twenties.

Kazimierz refused to be married, even though his father had arranged for a princess as the boy's bride. Because of that, Kazimierz is revered for his chastity and purity. He is considered the patron saint of Poland, and also patron saint of the young.

Maybe Saint Kazimierz was considered the patron for the young because he refused to do what his father told him to do.

History shows that all teenage boys can empathize with that.

But maybe Kazimierz did not get married to the princess because he was confused about what he wanted and what was expected of him, just like me.

Among the wonders credited to Kazimierz is an account of how the young prince somehow miraculously contributed to a victory of the Polish Army over the Russians.

Apparently, the Russians masturbated excessively.

———

A TOUGH DAY AT CURTIS CRANE LUTHERAN ACADEMY

HISTORY LESSON FOR the day: The more time you wait before telling somebody the truth about a secret you've been keeping, the longer your path out of the woods gets.

"What am I going to do, Ingrid?" I said.

I came straight home from school that day. I threw my Lutheran Boy patriotic candy cane outfit on the floor of my bedroom and sat down at my desk. I tried to figure things out as I drew pictures and wrote my stories, but everything only became more muddled and confused.

It had been a tough day at school.

I did not know what to say to Robby. I tried all day to come up with some coherent story to tell Shann. The story would have been an abbreviation, naturally, but I would have to go back to the moment Robby and I left her alone in the backseat of his Ford Explorer on Friday night in Grasshopper Jungle.

I would not tell her about *experiments* or what was, and was not, normal for teenage boys to do, according to the popular psychologist who, although a middle-aged female with cosmetic lip surgery, was a foremost authority on teenage boys. I thought about how I would describe the things Robby and I saw inside her stepfather's office, and I could only hope Shann would not ask me why I'd taken Robby down there in the first place.

Because I was not sure why Robby and I did go down there. All I knew was that I liked doing things with Robby that we were not *supposed* to do, normal or not.

I curled my bare toes in Ingrid's fur.

She let out a big, contented breath, like she was exhaling a billowing puff of soothing cigarette smoke.

"What am I going to say to Shann, Ingrid?"

Robby phoned after that. He asked if I was mad at him, and I told him of course not. That was a dumb thing for him to ask.

Then he said, "Okay, Porcupine. I was just scared about it since you wouldn't talk to me at school. Can you skate down to Grasshopper Jungle? I need to show you something."

I needed a cigarette, too.

So I said, "Okay, Rob. Give me fifteen minutes."

I kicked around through my scattered wardrobe.

I was running out of non-Lutheran-boy clothes.

I slipped on my basketball shorts. I closed my eyes and imagined a prayer to Saint Kazimierz to protect me against getting hit in the balls or having an erection in front of anyone. I pulled on a black Shins T-shirt, found some socks under my bed, got my skate shoes and board, and went out into the hallway.

I said to Ingrid, "Don't toast any brownies till Dad lets you out."

Ingrid made a dog sigh and put her chin down between her paws.

BUGS DO TWO THINGS

AND ON THAT Monday night, Robby Brees and I were going to get drunk together for the first time in our lives.

We had already planned it out. I had obtained permission from my mother and father to spend the night at the Del Vista Arms Luxury Apartments and go to school with Robby in the morning.

It was not like I could back out now.

I had spent the night at the Del Vista Arms before. My father trusted Robby. Robby was never late to class at Curtis Crane Lutheran

Academy. Robby never caused school-wide controversies by doing such things as reading books about Catholic boys who masturbate. Also, there was no reason for anybody to ever *not* trust Robby Brees.

I trusted Robby enough to stay at the Del Vista Arms.

Two of the people who lived on Robby's floor smoked meth.

The night before, on Sunday, Robby and I stood in a young cornfield and watched Hungry Jack's body split apart. We saw a bug the size of a small bear climb out of him.

The other six victims of *Contained MI Plague Strain 412E* had not hatched yet.

Bugs do two things.

They eat and they fuck.

Bugs are soldiers, machines, just like Hungry Jack was.

Bug One—the bug that hatched from Hungry Jack—wanted to eat and fuck. It ate most of what was left of Hungry Jack. It wanted to find Eileen Pope, Travis Pope's wife. It wanted to make more bugs with her.

Ealing, Iowa, was just like Eden Five for a new planet of horny soldiers.

Robby was already in the alley when I got to Grasshopper Jungle. He waited for me behind *Tipsy Cricket Liquors*. When I skated up to him, he held an unlit cigarette in his mouth.

Robby always waited for me. It made smoking better.

Louis, the cook from *The Pancake House* whose real name was Ah Wong Sing, had just thrown a cardboard box full of potato peelings, empty milk cartons, and eggshells into the dumpster. He spilled some peelings onto the sleeper sofa. He brushed them away with his hands.

"I wonder if he knows what pubic lice are," Robby said.

"I have seen Louis take a nap on that couch before," I said.

Louis smiled and nodded at us as he walked across the alleyway.

Louis did not speak English very well, so when Robby asked me if I wanted a fag, Louis got embarrassed. He made it obvious that he was trying not to listen to us, which made it obvious that he *was* listening to us.

"Hello, Louis," I said.

Robby struck a match for me and I got my cigarette going.

Louis said, "Hello, Dynamo."

Ah Wong Sing believed that *Dynamo* was my real name.

Louis hung out with Ollie Jungfrau. They played online alien hunter games and looked at porn together. I thought maybe if I did more shit like that with Robby it might make me feel normal and not so confused.

Louis kept smiling nervously and disappeared through the back door to *The Pancake House*'s kitchen.

We smoked.

"You're still coming over to get drunk with me, right?" Robby said.

"I don't know about getting drunk, Rob. It's been a weird couple days. Maybe I'll just watch *you* do it. You know, like keep you safe and shit." I said, "Like in the sixties, guys used to do that for their buddies when they dropped acid."

"I'm not dropping acid, and I'm not going to get drunk if you don't," Robby said.

I felt guilty about my attempt to back down.

We skated through the alley without saying anything.

When we were down by the dumpster, I stopped and asked Robby what it was he wanted to show me. He carried the rolled-up front section of the *Waterloo News and Gazette* in his back pocket. When he unrolled it, I already had a premonition that there would be something about the accident outside Waterloo, about what had happened to Hungry Jack.

"Look at this," Robby said.

There was a photograph of Hungry Jack's dirty and laceless shoes lying beside the highway. In the grainy background, I saw the *Tally-Ho!* and *Fire at Will's Indoor Shooting Range and Gun Shop.* The photograph was like staring through a portal in time.

The short article said that a transient had been struck and killed by a motorist and there were no witnesses.

Transient is a nice way of saying *homeless. Homeless* makes people think of despair. It makes you think that the United States of America doesn't care about people.

Transient sounds like you have a case of *wanderlust.*

Wanderlust is part of the American Spirit.

The *transient* in the article had been carrying a military I.D. card that gave his name as Charles R. Hoofard.

Hungry Jack's real name was Charles R. Hoofard.

He was born in Indianapolis in 1950.

In 1950, Harry S. Truman was president of the United States.

Harry Truman, as far as I can tell, also never took a shit in his life.

In 1950, the same year that a boy named Charles R. Hoofard was born in Indianapolis, President Harry S. Truman sent military assistance to the French. They were trying to maintain their French Catholic colony in Vietnam. That military aid would grow and blossom to the point that a boy with *wanderlust* from Indiana named Charles R. Hoofard ultimately took time out from fucking whatever he wanted to fuck to participate in the killing of an entire village of women, elderly people, and children.

History is full of shit like that.

All roads intersect on pages on my desk.

All roads spring up along trails worn down by boys on bikes.

All roads lead past shooting ranges, liquor stores, and gay bars.

Wanderlust is part of the American Spirit.

The article went on to say that Charles R. Hoofard's body had been brutalized by coyotes before being discovered by a farmer Monday morning.

It asked for anyone with information to phone the Iowa State Patrol.

"Uh," I said.

I rolled the newspaper up and handed it back to Robby.

We never called anyone about what happened to Hungry Jack.

We had been uncharacteristically silent back inside Robby's Explorer in the lot outside the *Tally-Ho!*

Robby sped all the way home to Ealing.

We smoked and smoked.

I think Robby was crying, too.

Robby and I were in shock.

That is a poor excuse for someone who feels obligated to record history, but that's what happened.

It was our day, and you *do* know what I mean.

"We *did* see the same thing, Rob. People would think we *were* dropping acid," I said.

"Shit like that isn't supposed to happen," Robby said.

"But it did," I said. "Maybe we *should* get drunk."

Then Robby said, "That bug. It was the same thing we saw inside Johnny's office."

"Like I said. We saw the same thing, Robby."

It was getting on to evening. We decided to take Robby's car and pick up my school clothes and sleeping bag.

I always slept on the floor at Robby's apartment. If I put my ear to the floor, I sometimes could hear the meth smokers down the hall fighting with each other.

But as we were skating back through the alley, just when we came to the spot where Grant Wallace and the Hoover Boys had beaten us up three days earlier, Robby and I noticed something on the piss-covered blacktop of the alley:

GRANT WA

It was the message Robby started spelling out in the blood that dripped from his nose.

The letters gave off a pale blue glow in the dimming light of evening.

"Um," Robby said.

I said, "Yes. I see that, too, Robby."

A GIFT FROM JOHNNY MCKEON

JOHNNY MCKEON WAS just locking up the front door of *From Attic to Seller Consignment Store* when Robby and I skated past.

He frowned at me, shook his head, and made a two-fingered gesture to his lips as a kind of sign language reproach about Robby and me skating around in front of his place of business with cigarettes in our mouths.

I was embarrassed.

"Sorry, Johnny," I said. I dropped my cigarette onto the blacktop.

Robby did, too.

Johnny said it was a great coincidence that I happened by, because he'd gotten something that afternoon that he meant to bring home for me. I felt guilty and scared because Johnny McKeon had never given me anything more than a paycheck and a couple free packs of cigarettes in the past. I'd never asked for anything more from Johnny McKeon, either.

"Wait up," Johnny said, and he went back inside his store.

Robby and I waited.

"I found this today in a jewelry box," Johnny said when he came back. He locked the door to the secondhand store and held out his hand to me. His hand was cupped closed, the way a kid might hold on to a bug or something.

"I thought you might get a kick out of this, Austin," Johnny said.

Robby was curious. He leaned in closer to see what Johnny McKeon was offering me. When Johnny unfolded his tentacle fingers, I saw a coiled silver chain with an oval medallion strung on its links. In the center of the pendant was the image of a man with a halo, his chin turned downward in an attitude of something that looked like modesty. The bauble was worn, but the man held what looked like a tree branch in his hand. Around the rim of the outside, in raised letters, was the inscription: **SAINT KAZIMIERZ**

And Johnny McKeon said, "Isn't that a kick? You were just telling me about that guy, and I never heard of him before. Ever. Isn't that a kick?"

"That's a kick, Johnny," I said.

"Anyway," Johnny said, "it's for you, Austin. What would I want with something like that, anyway?"

"I don't know," I said. "Thank you, Johnny."

Robby watched me slip the chain around my neck.

"This is the nicest thing in the world," I said.

I meant it, too.

"You're welcome," Johnny said.

It felt cool and powerful against my skin. The thought of wearing the medal under my Lutheran Boy clothes, against my naked body at Curtis Crane Lutheran Academy made me feel wicked and daring. It also made me very horny to think about breaking such a long list of theoretically unbreakable and ancient Lutheran Boy rules.

I decided I would never take it off.

"Thank you so much, Johnny," I said again. "What a kick."

"That's what I was thinking," Johnny said. "It's a real kick, ain't it?"

Johnny McKeon was in a generous mood. He offered to drive Robby and me to my house so I could pick up the clothes and things I needed to spend the night at the Del Vista Arms.

He and Robby even waited in Johnny's car while I let Ingrid out to take a shit.

I kept playing with the medallion inside my T-shirt. I pressed it against my bare chest. I took it out at least a dozen times to look at Saint Kazimierz.

It made me feel magic.

SHANN CALLS

I IMAGINED A SILVER chain washing up on the cold shoreline in Massachusetts or Maine. Somehow the thing had slipped away from Andrzej Szczerba's body, and had been carried slowly for a century until being discovered in a tangled mass of seaweed and fishing line.

It *had* to come to Ealing.

It *had* to end up around Austin Andrzej Szerba's neck.

I sat in the front seat and Johnny McKeon drove us to the Del Vista Arms from my house. Shann called when we were about halfway there.

"I found something out," Shann said.

"What?" I wondered.

There were an awful lot of things I thought Shann might be talking about, but none of them was correct.

"I found the silo," she said.

"Uh," I said.

There were also an awful lot of silos in Iowa. I did not know what Shann was talking about.

"You know," she went on, "the message from the machine in the wall? Well, today after school I went down to City Hall and looked up the *Ealing Registry of Historical Homes*."

"You did? They actually *have* that?" I asked.

Now there was a book that could have absolutely *everything* about its subject fully contained within its bindings.

"I saw photos of my house. Old ones. There *used* to be a silo on the property. I *found* the silo," she said.

But there was no silo on the property now.

I pointed that out to Shann.

Shann said, "We have to go look, Austin."

"But it's dark and shit," I said. "Do you think someone is hiding the McKeon silo?"

You can't hide a silo in Iowa.

The best you could do is maybe disguise it to look like someone *else's* silo, or maybe something like a penis.

People in Iowa were generally too reserved for such antics.

"No," Shann chided. "I don't think someone's hiding our silo. But there *was* one here at one time."

"Uh," I said.

"Tomorrow. After school. You, Robby, and me. We'll go see if there's anything left of it. I have a copy of the picture."

"Uh," I said again. I glanced back at Robby.

Shann knew we were going to get drunk. We told her. She didn't approve of it. What can you do?

Somewhere, there was a middle-aged, nice-looking woman psychologist with voluptuous, artificially induced lips who, as a foremost expert on teenage boys, could serenely explain to Shann that boys sometimes need to be boys and do dumb things that can get boys in lots and lots of trouble and shit like that.

But Shann did not watch much television.

"Okay, Shann," I said. "I think we can do that. Maybe there is something there, after all."

"I just know we're going to find some other weird stuff that Grady McKeon was doing here," Shann said.

I agreed, and said, "There's probably more than anyone will ever know."

Then Shann said, "I love you, Austin."

I looked at Robby in the backseat, then at Johnny behind the wheel, and I said, "Um. Me too, Shann."

In my defense, and with plenty of history to back me up, it was a perfectly acceptable response considering the environmental realities I had to contend with.

Shann certainly understood the translation: *I am sitting next to your stepfather and my best friend.*

You know what I mean.

MY MOM'S LITTLE BLUE KAYAKS

I HAD TWO of my mother's little blue kayaks.

They were hidden inside a matching pair of clean gray Curtis Crane Lutheran Academy regular boys' socks I brought with me to Robby's apartment for school the next day.

Robby did not know I had them.

I unrolled my sleeping bag on the floor in Robby's room and left my stack of Lutheran Boy clothes on top of his dresser. Robby brought in a bottle of wine he'd hidden in the back of his refrigerator.

His mother never knew anything about it.

The bottle was so cold the glass fogged and dripped.

Then I showed Robby the Xanax pills I'd stolen. He was not happy about what I did.

Robby said, "I'd *never* take one of those, Porcupine."

"Uh," I said. "Why not? Everyone else does."

History lesson for the early evening: When a teenage boy says *everyone else does*, he's usually not being mathematically precise. Robby knew that. We spoke the same language.

Robby said, "I just don't want to ever do shit like that."

I came to my own defense, rationalizing, "I always thought they'd make me feel better."

"Better than *what*?" Robby asked.

"I don't know," I said. "Better than shitty and scared all the time."

"Don't be dumb, Austin," Robby said.

Robby unscrewed the cap on the wine. I watched him swallow. He liked it.

"Well, I'm taking one anyway," I said.

"Go ahead," Robby said.

Robby would not take one. He looked unhappy when I put the tiny blue pill on my tongue. But it was something I always wondered about. I hoped my mother's little kayak would help me figure things out.

Get things to fall right into place.

I washed it down with some wine.

The wine tasted sweet, and it burned at the same time.

Robby kept the grimacing lemur mask and the plastic yard flamingo in his bedroom. I tried the lemur mask on. It did make my face stink, and the lenses in the eyes made everything look strange. There was some kind of refractive prism on the lenses of the mask that made Robby look blue. I took it off.

"Yes," I confirmed, "now my face really *does* stink."

"I told you," Robby said. "Did that Xanax do anything to you?"

"Uh. I don't think so," I said. "But it's only been a minute."

I picked up the flamingo. I shook it.

"What are you doing?" Robby said.

"Shaking the plastic lawn flamingo," I explained.

"Why?" Robby asked.

"I want to see if candy will come out of its ass," I answered.

Maybe I *was* starting to feel different.

We shared more wine. We drank straight from the bottle. I was kind of messy. The wine ran down my neck. It baptized Saint Kazimierz. But it also made my face not stink so bad.

"Maybe the message was about *this* flamingo," I said.

I was somewhat impressed by my brilliance.

"Uh," Robby said.

Robby wasn't really paying attention. He opened up his record player and was flipping through a bookcase of vinyl LPs that used to belong to his dad.

"Yeah," I went on, "maybe it's like a smoke detector for that shit in the globe Tyler dropped. McKeon Industries *did* used to make Pulse-O-Matic® brand smoke detectors."

"I think you're high, Porcupine," Robby said.

He shook his head and carefully grooved the stylus onto the edge of the spinning record.

I don't know exactly what the Xanax did to me. All I can remember is how relaxed and not-uptight I felt. I did not care about anything.

Everything was nice, very nice.

As I sat there on the corner of Robby's bed, I was aware that nothing at all mattered anymore, and I wasn't confused about feeling happy.

I was floating away.

We finally could forget about everything.

Robby played a crackling vinyl recording of *Exile on Main Street*, and we got drunk on screw-top wine and smoked cigarettes and took off our T-shirts.

I opened my notebook and drew sketches of Robby as he reclined, bare chested, on the floor in the slate-colored streetlight that came through the apartment's open window.

It was warm, and outside the sound of insects in the night was electric.

The music sounded better than anything I'd ever heard.

I had never been so happy in my life.

I played with the little silver medal against my bare chest.

I wrote poetry while we sat there like that in the dark and talked about our favorite poems and books and laughed and smoked.

And Mick Jagger sang to us.

The song was called Sweet Virginia.

PAGES FROM HISTORY

IN THE MORNING, Robby's alarm clock buzzed like an air-raid warning.

We had to get up to go to school.

When I opened my eyes, I was lying next to Robby on his bed.

My arm stretched across the space between us, and my open hand lay flat in the middle of Robby's chest. I had my legs pressed up against his leg. One of my feet was completely underneath Robby's calf.

The covers of Robby's bed had been thrown down on the floor around his footboard, and we were sprawled out on top of the bottom sheet.

At that moment, all I had on were some boxers, my left sock, and the silver chain Johnny McKeon gave me with Saint Kazimierz on it around my neck.

I sat up, still drunk and woozy from the pill.

I felt drained and rushed, like my brain had just flushed itself down the toilet of my throat.

I was vaguely aware that Robby sat up in the bed. He turned off his alarm and watched me while I rolled my legs over the edge of his bed. It was all I could do to will myself not to vomit until I staggered and tripped in my drooping boxers out of Robby's bedroom.

I needed to find the toilet.

Robby's favorite poem is Dulce Et Decorum Est by Wilfred Owen. It is a poem about war and lies, youth and thievery.

It begins:

Bent double, like old beggars under sacks,
Knock-kneed, coughing like hags, we cursed through sludge.

Robby has very good taste for words.

My favorite poem is The Emperor of Ice-Cream by Wallace Stevens. It is a poem about everything else: sex, lust, pleasure, loneliness, and death.

It tells the story of a party at a dead woman's house, where a bare-chested man whips ice cream in the empty kitchen, while young boys and girls posture and tease one another suggestively.

Robby recited his poem from memory that night, and I fumbled over some of the last lines in my poem, but finally got it right.

They were both so beautiful, and their sound, as we said them to each other above the music, made our chests fill up with something electric and buzzing, like love and magic.

When I finished throwing up, I flushed the toilet and turned on Robby's shower.

I dropped my orphaned sock and Iowa plaid boxers onto the floor below the sink. I climbed into the tub and got under the water.

It was cold, and there was a grimy ring of brown that had accumulated around the bottom of Robby's bathtub. The apartment had only the one bathroom. It was right in the middle of a T-shaped hallway that separated Robby's bedroom from his mother's.

Connie Brees was not home from work yet.

I put my face under the water. I felt terrible. My eyes blurred and I fingered the medal of Saint Kazimierz and looked at his modest eyes and little upside-down halo. I put the thing in my mouth.

I heard the bathroom door open.

Robby said, "Austin? Are you okay, Austin?"

"I'm okay," I said. There was an edge in my voice.

And I said, "Can you just let me have *five minutes*, Robby? Okay?"

Robby said, "Sure. I brought your school clothes in for you."

Robby was sad because I was being an asshole.

I did not want to go to school.

I never wanted to get out of that dirty shower.

I did not want to look at Robby Brees.

I said, "Okay. Thank you."

But I said it in such a tone that it meant: *Get out of here and leave me alone.*

At exactly that moment, Shann was eating a toasted bagel and looking at a black-and-white photograph of the McKeon House.

And while I was standing under the shower in Robby's

apartment, Travis Pope passed out behind the wheel of his Nissan truck and crashed into a shallow drainage ditch on the practice fields at Herbert Hoover High School. His wife, Eileen, was sitting beside him. She was not wearing her seat belt. They were hatching.

Someone down the hall from Robby's apartment at the Del Vista Arms was holding a torch lighter below a glass pipe and cooking methamphetamine smoke into his face.

Ollie Jungfrau was finally taking a shit. He was going to be late for work.

Johnny McKeon was driving to the Ealing Mall. He was in a good mood. Johnny was always in a good mood.

Ah Wong Sing was looking at video from a porn site in the Netherlands. He was going to be late for work.

I was combing Robby's conditioner with my fingers through my hair. It smelled like bubble gum.

My brother, Eric Christopher Szerba, was on his way to a hospital in Germany. He had lost both of his testicles and his right leg from the knee down. Two other boys died in the same explosion. We would not learn this until the following day.

Robby Brees was in his underwear, sitting on his bed. He put his face into his palms and cried.

SCHOOL PRAYERS

EVERYTHING FELL INTO place, all right.

But things dropped so hard the entire world broke.

I learned this:

My mother's little blue kayaks were perfectly seaworthy. Her Xanax did make me feel not stressed out. They took away my confusion and worry. They made me believe that I only had one head on my shoulders, and that head had everything all figured out. Everything is nicely, sweetly normal when you are floating on the kayak.

But I would need to take them forever if I wanted things to stay that way.

There was one Xanax left.

It was inside the matching, clean gray Curtis Crane Lutheran Academy regular boys' socks Robby carried into the bathroom for me while I was under the shower.

I flushed it down the toilet with the last of my vomit.

While Robby showered, I quietly left his apartment at the Del Vista Arms. I counted three yellow Pay or Quit notices taped to doors on Robby's floor. I walked to Curtis Crane Lutheran Academy alone.

I was not late to class.

I did not say anything to Robby.

Every morning began with a prayer. Robby came in to class. He was almost tardy for the first time in his life. He was flustered and his cheeks were red. Robby's tie was crooked and his shirttail hung down in back of his sweater like he'd been running. He'd obviously been looking for me. Robby would have to fix his appearance or Pastor Roland Duff would call him in for counseling about proper grooming for Lutheran boys.

I prayed with the other students in the classroom, but I only thought about Robby Brees and the chain around my neck.

I did not talk to Robby for days after that.

I needed to talk to my father.

I did not have any idea what I would say.

I told Shann I was sick.

She thought it was from drinking wine with Robby the night

before. That may have been true. I had no way of figuring out if anything was true or not true on that Tuesday after I spent the night with Robby.

So I told her we would have to go searching for her invisible silo after school on Wednesday. I needed to go home and let Ingrid out and then go to bed and shit like that, I told her. Shann understood.

It was already getting too late to do anything about the entire world falling off the cliff that opened at our feet in Grasshopper Jungle. All I could think about was how the pull of gravity was screwing with one particular Polish kid from Ealing, Iowa.

Shann said, "I think you're *both* hung over. Robby looks sicker than you."

"Uh," I said.

"I hope this teaches you something," Shann scolded.

"So do I," I said.

"Tell Robby to come over tomorrow," Shann said.

"Uh. Robby can do whatever he wants."

Shann and I walked out of Curtis Crane Lutheran Academy at the end of the day. Robby had already gone home without saying anything to either one of us.

"What's the matter with you?" she asked.

"I'm not sure," I said.

It was the truth.

Shann repeated her history lesson for the day: "I hope you learned your lesson, is all I can say."

"I'm sorry, Shann," I said. Then I added, "I love you, Shann."

Shann looked around to see if anyone was paying attention to us. We were alone.

She pressed up against me. It was a very daring move for a pair of Lutheran kids in eyeshot of the front doors of Curtis Crane.

For some reason, the medallion of Saint Kazimierz seemed to get heavy and burn against my bare chest. And I thought about Robby again.

Shann whispered, "I love you, Austin."

I rubbed my hips into her. I had to say it: "Shann, do you think... Um. Maybe... if I got some condoms..."

She cut me off. "No! Go home, Austin Szerba. You're sick. You're not even thinking like a normal boy."

I thought that was what normal boys *did* think about.

I tried to prove something, but my experiment failed.

"Sorry, Shann. Um. Are you sure?"

She said, "Can you for one moment stop being silly, Austin?"

She said *moment* again. I was horny, and scared, and so confused about everything.

"I will," I said. "I need to go lie down. I'm sorry."

I was not thinking like a normal boy.

What was I going to do?

THE VICE PRESIDENT'S BALLS

SOME NIGHTS MY mother stayed at work at the Hy-Vee until late, so my dad and I would have to prepare dinner for ourselves.

There was once a time when it was against the law in Iowa for women to allow boys and dads to cook dinner for themselves.

Now, kids like Robby Brees and me often had to survive on our wits and by eating shit like Cup-O-Noodles and Doritos.

Most of all, I wanted to go to bed and mope, but that evening I cooked fish sticks and frozen french fries for my dad. I waited for him to come home from school, so we could talk.

The fish in the sticks claimed to come from Alaska.

The fries were not from France. The package said they were grown in Oregon and Idaho.

If there's one thing America can do well, it's freeze shit.

I waited.

I was nearly asleep with my head on the table when my father came in.

"You stayed up too late with Robby last night, didn't you?" my father, whose name was Eric, said.

"Uh," I answered. I picked my head up and rubbed my eyes.

I was still wearing my Lutheran Boy tie and sweater.

For the first time I realized I'd left my sleeping bag, underwear, socks, toothbrush, sneakers, and cell phone in Robby's bedroom. At least I had the foresight to stuff my history notebooks into my Lutheran Boy school backpack.

"Yes," I said. "I think I'm not feeling well, Dad."

My father sat at the table and began eating. I got up and went to the refrigerator and took out a bottle of ketchup. My dad was a ketchup man. Not me.

The ketchup was made in Nebraska.

So they do something there, after all.

I watched him.

He ate.

I was getting ready to say something. I just needed to know what words to start with.

My dad said, "Is something wrong, Austin?"

"Uh," I said. I was determined to do it. So I said, "Dad, when you were about my age . . . Did you ever . . . Um . . . experience a . . . I mean, did you ever get a . . . have guy friends who you . . . Um . . . did you ever *experiment* with another . . . Um . . ."

It was a mess.

That is exactly how it came out.

My father stopped chewing. Fish sticks are not things that require any degree of jaw strength.

I wished my brother, Eric, was still at home.

He had been gone so long that it was as though I were an only child. Having a brother there would help. Eric was someone I could have talked to about things like erections and sex and making mistakes and accidental spills and being confused and all that kind of shit.

At exactly that moment, Eric Christopher Szerba was in a morphine-induced coma.

As I sat there nervously watching my father, there was a small earthquake in Guatemala. Robert Brees Sr. was sleeping naked in a queen-sized bed with his new Guatemalan wife. Her name was Greta. Robert Brees Sr.'s two-year-old son, whose name was Hector, was lying on Robert's chest. In the sky above them, hot ash from a volcano named Huacamochtli began billowing soundlessly into the atmosphere.

And at that precise moment, there were three bugs in Ealing, Iowa: Hungry Jack, Travis Pope, and Travis's wife, Eileen. They all wanted to do only two things.

The four Hoover Boys had not yet hatched. They were sick. Young people don't break down as fast.

Robby Brees was lying in his bed at the Del Vista Arms Luxury Apartments. He was wearing my T-shirt and the boxers that I'd taken off and dropped on his bathroom floor. Robby was listening to the Rolling Stones.

Shann Collins was writing in a diary she kept locked in the nightstand beside her bed. She theorized how she might get away with her wish to have sex with her boyfriend, who sensitively promised her he would use a condom.

When my father and mother did learn about what happened

to Eric, they left Iowa and flew to the military hospital in Germany where my brother was undergoing treatment. At first, they tried to arrange for me to stay at the Del Vista Arms with Robby and his mother. I begged them to leave me home alone because I was old enough, and somebody needed to let Ingrid out to shit, after all.

It was really only that I was afraid to face Robby Brees. I knew I would have to face him eventually, but I did not want to do it yet.

My parents would not take me with them.

They said I should stay in school, and they would call me twice per day.

When Eric Christopher Szerba was recovering from his wounds, the vice president of the United States of America came to the hospital and visited him.

The vice president was from Delaware.

I never knew anyone who'd even *been* to Delaware.

The vice president of the United States of America took a shit that day in the men's toilet of the cafeteria at the military hospital before visiting my brother's room. The vice president of the United States of America had two testicles that he liked very much, and neither one of his legs had been blown off.

When the vice president of the United States of America was a teenager, he also *experimented*.

My father stopped chewing and stared at me. I could see in his eyes that he knew exactly what I was trying to talk about. There is a certain dark and faraway look that fathers get in their eyes when their sons uncomfortably venture toward asking them questions about their penises and shit like that.

I could see that look right away.

"Um," he said. "You mean, like in *chemistry class*?"

"Uh," I said.

For the last few days in chemistry class at Curtis Crane

Lutheran Academy, we had been making a slippery, gooey, milky white polymer from borax and some other shit.

A polymer is something that is heavy and thick, made up of lots of small molecules. The word *polymer* came from Greece.

The Greeks were good at making up words for shit.

Robby Brees was my partner in the lab.

Robby said the polymer we made in chemistry class looked and felt exactly like sperm. Everyone else in the class also thought it was exactly like sperm.

Actually, not *everyone*. Only the physically and spiritually weak boys who masturbated thought our polymer looked and felt exactly like sperm. That was every boy in the class, considering we were all in tenth grade and fifteen or sixteen years old, which made all us boys physically and spiritually weak masturbators who could never be relied on to effectively defend the United States against foreign invasions. Only a couple of the girls thought our borax polymer looked and felt exactly like sperm.

Shann did. But she sat beside me during the awkward eruption at *Eden Five Needs You 4*.

Mr. Duane Coventry, our chemistry teacher, got mad and embarrassed by the behavior of the boys in the class. He obviously thought the stuff was exactly like sperm, too. So Mr. Duane Coventry brought in small vials of blue food coloring and made us tint our borax-polymer sperm experiments, so they wouldn't look so much like sperm.

"Yeah, Dad. In chemistry," I said.

"I once made a battery with a lemon," my father said.

"Uh. I did that, too, Dad," I said. "Everyone does that shit when they're kids."

My father swabbed his Alaska fish stick through his puddle of Nebraska ketchup.

"Yes, Austin," he said. "I *did* do experiments when I was your age."

He said it with finality and relief.

That was the end of the history lesson about my dad and what he did when he was a teenager.

"Uh. Thanks, Dad. Well, good night."

"Good night, son," my father said.

I went to bed.

I realized that was the last time in my life I would ever attempt to speak to my father about sperm, or about my sexual curiosity and confused feelings. I'd be just as well served watching daytime television programs for women, or speaking to Ollie Jungfrau about those kinds of things. Or to any complete stranger sitting on a bus bench, for that matter.

In the morning chaos before school, my parents were up and speaking with two liaison officers in the kitchen when I came downstairs. That was the day they left Ealing to go to Germany and see my brother, Eric, who no longer had any balls. My mother and father both agreed it would be all right if I stayed in bed that day.

So I did not go to school.

MODERN-DAY NIGHTINGALES

KRZYS SZCZERBA STARTED a factory in Minnesota.

He manufactured urinals.

There is something grandly American in the story.

Krzys Szczerba came to America and earned a living by making things for guys to piss on. The urinals he made were big. They were shoulder height, spanning entire walls with thick porcelain backs and drainage gutters all along the floor where you would carefully distance the toes of your shoes.

Americans like big things to piss on.

In those days, guys didn't feel the need for seclusion or personal space when they pissed. American men and boys lined up shoulder to shoulder and unashamedly pissed like a choreographed army on everything in front of them.

That was our day.

Krzys Szczerba's urinals were big enough so a dozen or more guys could all piss on the same wall together, all at the same time.

We had a similarly designed group urinal at Curtis Crane Lutheran Academy. It was the one with images of disembodied praying hands hanging above it at eye level to remind us boys not to get any *experimental* ideas with our hands while they were holding our penises.

But the urinal at Curtis Crane Lutheran Academy was stainless steel and shaped like a knee-high watering trough for livestock. The urinal chimed a musical song whenever boys would piss down onto its flat metal bottom. And only four boys at a time could use it. More than that, and there would be some uneasy trespassing into your neighbor's personal space.

We kept our eyes on the praying hands.

Besides freezing shit and making it food, pissing on things was something American boys have always been real dynamos at.

Krzys Szczerba called his urinals Nightingales, after his wife, Eva Nightingale, who, like the urinals Krzys made, was big, accommodating, and perfectly white.

There were birds with ribbons streaming from their happy beaks etched along the top rail of Krzys Szczerba's Nightingale urinals.

It was a good name for a urinal, I thought.

Krzys Szczerba's urinal factory went out of business during the Great Depression.

During the Great Depression, I think American boys pretty much pissed wherever they wanted to.

There was also a stainless steel trough urinal at *Satan's Pizza*, but it was only wide enough for two guys to use at once. It was extremely awkward, being paired up with a complete stranger like that at a pizza place.

It was like being on a blind date.

Worse yet would be if I was standing there peeing, and then one other guy would come into the men's room and stand beside me, unzip, and when I glanced over, it would be Louis, the cook from *The Pancake House*, or maybe Ollie Jungfrau or Pastor Roland Duff.

I always tried to hold my pee whenever I ate at *Satan's Pizza*.

Sometimes, a guy just can't, though.

There were old color photographs of Italy that hung behind glass-faced frames above the urinal at *Satan's Pizza*. One of them showed the Coliseum in Rome, and the other showed Michelangelo's statue of David.

You know what I mean.

What guy doesn't like to think about Italy and civilization and shit like that when he is holding his penis and pissing into a steel trough?

I am the great-great-grandson of Krzys Szczerba, a man who made things for other guys to piss on.

My brother, Eric Christopher Szerba, got pissed on, too.

In a way, Krzys Szczerba made me and my brother. When you think about it, Krzys Szczerba's factory was still in full operation, and we were his modern-day Nightingales.

Everyone at Curtis Crane Lutheran Academy heard about what

happened to Mr. Szerba's son, Eric Szerba, who was in Afghanistan.

Robby did not go to school that day, either.

There was something wrong with both of us, but it was not something like what was happening to those Hoover Boys, although there was equally little Robby Brees or I could do about it.

SHANN, THE HORNY POLISH KID, AND SATAN

JOHNNY MCKEON CAME over to my house that afternoon. He said he wanted to check on me and see if I needed anything. There were lots of things I needed, but Johnny couldn't give any of them to me.

I certainly couldn't talk to Johnny McKeon about my confusion, or about what was happening between me and Robby; and between me and Shann.

"I came to see if you needed anything," Johnny said when I opened the front door. He added, "You know, if I could do anything for you, Austin."

I was still in my boxers. I had not gotten out of bed all day. Ingrid squeezed between my legs and wriggled past Johnny out into the yard. The poor dog was about to explode.

I combed my fingers through my messed-up hair. I said, "Thanks, Johnny. I think I'm okay. I could use a cigarette, I think."

"I brought some for you." Johnny said, "They're in my car. Hang on."

"Watch out for dog shit, Johnny," I said. "And, thank you."

"If your mom or dad says anything about this, I'm telling them you stole them."

Johnny always said that.

So Johnny McKeon stayed there with me on my front porch while I smoked a cigarette and talked to him. I'd forgotten all about my plan to look for the missing invisible McKeon silo with Shann. Everything had been such a nightmarish blur since Robby Brees and I had gotten beaten up for being queers by those four assholes in the alley at Grasshopper Jungle.

It was like swimming through a big bowl of alphabet soup, where all the letters are alive and flash little dancing horror shows for you: grimacing lemurs, two-headed baby boys, accidental eruptions at the Waterloo *Cinezaar*, little blue kayaks, enormous green praying mantises, praying hands, the *Tally-Ho!*, my pissed-on brother, Eric Christopher Szerba, and my best friend, Robert Brees Jr., whom I loved very much and felt a terrible sadness for at the same time.

"You're a good dog, Ingrid," I said.

Ingrid lay beneath my bare feet and I sat on a wicker chair in my boxers and smoked a cigarette with Johnny McKeon in front of my house.

At that moment, my parents were on an airplane flying over Scotland.

"Why don't you put some clothes on and I'll take you and Shann out and get you pizza or something?" Johnny McKeon asked.

"You mean you don't want to just take me to dinner in my underwear, Johnny?" I said.

Johnny shook his head gravely. For someone who was always in a good mood, Johnny McKeon never really knew when people were joking around with him.

"No, kid," he said. "Put some trousers and a shirt on or I ain't taking you anywhere."

I waggled my Saint Kazimierz medal at Johnny and told him thanks, but I hoped he wasn't planning on sitting in the middle, considering he was going to be chauffeuring his stepdaughter and me out on another date.

He didn't get *that*, either.

Johnny said, "I'll drop you two off, and come pick you up. But in Ealing, not Waterloo. Now go put some britches on, Austin."

I found some 501s that weren't too dirty. They were lying on my bedroom floor. I slipped into Robby's Spam T-shirt. He'd left it there at my house the day we went up on the roof of the Ealing Mall. It still had a few faded bloodstains and it smelled like Robby, which kind of made me a little sad. I didn't bother putting on any socks. I got the Adidas I'd loaned to Robby a few days earlier and slipped them on.

It made me feel lonely to wear Robby's shirt.

I went to pee in the men's room at *Satan's Pizza* before our *Stanpreme* arrived at the table. It was taking a chance because the pizza place was unusually busy for a Wednesday evening.

Nobody came in to share the trough with me and the photos of Rome and naked David.

I sat beside Shann and we looked out the window, across Kimber Drive to Grasshopper Jungle, the Ealing Mall.

We talked.

At first it was almost as uncomfortable as standing next to Ollie Jungfrau at the little trough urinal in the back of *Satan's Pizza*. I kept thinking about Robby. I felt so guilty about the things we did.

I do not lie, but I did not want to tell Shann about Robby, and I did not want to tell Robby about Shann, either.

So I sat there and thought about how I was ripping my own heart in half, ghettoizing it like Warsaw during the Second World War—*this area for Shann; the other area for queer kids only*—and wondering how it was possible to be sexually attracted and in love with my best friend, a boy, *and* my other best friend, a girl—two completely different people, at the same time.

I was so confused.

There had to be something wrong with me. I envied Shann and Robby both so much for being confident in who they were and what they felt, and for knowing what part of my ghettoized heart they lived in.

Eventually, Shann worked up the courage to talk to me about Eric.

We were eating our pizza by that time, and I had pushed all those thoughts about my brother into a dark place in my head. The pissed-on Polish boys' ghetto. Now a light shined on them.

So I told her this:

Eric Christopher Szerba and I got pissed on. I could not remember any image of my brother where we were not boys together. Eric Christopher Szerba was still a boy. Eric Christopher Szerba was my big brother. Now he was ruined, destroyed. He would be somebody else the next time we talked. It would be awkward, like peeing next to a stranger. We got pissed on, Eric and me. Everyone did. Nobody was better off anywhere. Nobody learned a lesson. Nobody got saved.

I could not eat any more pizza after that.

I think I might have been crying.

I have to be honest. This is history. I *was* crying while I sat there at *Satan's Pizza*, looking out the window at Grasshopper Jungle. I was crying, and it wasn't only for Eric Christopher Szerba. It was for Robby Brees, my mother, my father, Robby's mother, Krzys Szczerba, and for Saint Kazimierz, too.

Shann was crying. She put her face against my neck.

Shann said, "I've always been in love with you for how you say things, Austin. Ever since that day in eighth grade when we sat together and had Cokes and talked about *The Chocolate War*.

Do you remember that?"

"Yes," I said. "It's that book about the peacock who shits gumballs and Sugar Babies out of its ass, right?"

Shann laughed a little and we kissed.

And I told her: "Shann, sometimes I do really dumb things and I don't think about the people I might be hurting. I want you to know that I love you, no matter how dumb I am. No matter what I do."

I was trying to tell her the truth—my abbreviated truth—about me and Robby. Shann thought I was talking about the day before, at school, when I attempted to start a conversation involving the use of condoms.

Shann said, "You are not dumb, Austin. I love you very much. I was thinking about what you said, about . . . Um. You know. If you used a condom."

I nearly fell off the bench at *Satan's Pizza* when she said that.

I said, "You mean you *would*?"

I tried to devise a means of getting Shann Collins over to my empty house *that night*.

"Maybe we could try to do that sometime. When the time is right," Shann said.

I thought the time was right.

Hearing her say the words *do that* made me very horny.

Shann tried changing the subject. She placed her purse on the table beside the remains of our *Stanpreme*. When she opened the purse, I hoped she was going to show me how she'd brought along a pack of condoms or shit like that. Not that I needed any. I had dozens of condoms from cleaning out the furniture for Johnny McKeon at *From Attic to Seller Consignment Store*.

I fought with myself.

There was rioting in the ghetto.

That is the truth.

I was being such an asshole to my two best friends.

I decided to shut up. Like Shann told me, she'd let me know when the time was right to *try to do that*, and that was much closer to a *yes* than a *no*.

Eden Five needed me.

Maybe I could prove something to myself, eventually, and watch how everything might fall perfectly into place for me.

Shann pulled a small black-and-white photograph out from her purse. It was the picture she'd gotten from the *Ealing Registry of Historic Homes*.

And, yes, I was disappointed, and very horny, too.

FOUR PHOTOGRAPHS

Here, our history looks at four photographs:

1. THIS IS THE MCKEON SILO.

In grainy black and white it looks like a galvanized steel penis with Saturn booster rockets, sitting on a launch pad a quarter mile behind Shann's historic home, preparing to blast off for Eden Five.

"I found it," Shann said.

2. THIS IS A PHOTOGRAPH OF ME AND MY BROTHER, ERIC Christopher

Szerba. The picture was taken when Eric was twelve years old. That would make me about five or six. In the picture, we are standing on the shore of Lake Minnewonka, in Canada. The sun is setting into our eyes. Our mother, Connie Szerba, was morbidly obsessed with having the sun shine in our white Polish faces whenever we posed for pictures.

In the photograph, my hair is messy, sticking up unevenly. It is also much lighter in color than my hair is now. I am wearing Velcro-laced *Teenage Mutant Ninja Turtles* sneakers. They had lights along their soles and flashed when I walked. I loved those shoes.

Eric is tall and skinny. He wears a red plaid shirt, untucked, an Iowa boy after all. Eric also has on brand-new cuffed Levis. I can almost feel their stiffness in the photograph. His legs are like matchsticks in them. The jeans have not been washed yet. Eric Christopher Szerba has his arm around my shoulder, but the way he is standing is not the uncomfortable posture of a boy about to turn teenager who is coerced into hugging his little brother to falsely freeze a peaceful moment for a family snapshot while on vacation.

Both of us have those Polish Boy bags under our eyes.

Eric is very handsome. His hair is the color of maple syrup and he has a spray of freckles on his cheeks. The way he smiles, you can see his two big front teeth. His lips are wet. The shadow of my father stretches all the way past our ankles. You can see, in silhouette on the ground, how my father's elbows point out like wings on a nightingale where he holds the camera up to his eyes.

3. NEITHER OF THE OTHER BOYS killed in the same explosion that removed both of Eric Christopher Szerba's balls and one of his legs were younger than my brother. But they were boys, too. Julio Arguelles was thirty-four years old. There is a snapshot of him that was taken when he was six years old. He grew up in Brooklyn, and in the photograph he is standing in the driveway beside his family's home. There is a low redbrick wall at the end of the driveway. On the other side of the wall, you can see the white T of a wood-framed laundry post sticking up. There are some white T-shirts and underwear hanging from the clotheslines. It appears there is no wind blowing. Julio is wearing a Superman T-shirt with a red-rimmed collar, the triangular S, and there are fierce abdominal muscles drawn onto the fabric that loosely drapes over Julio's six-year-old chest. At the very bottom of the T-shirt is a band of yellow— Superman's belt—and the red swath that marks the upper waist of his briefs. It is a funny shirt. I would have worn it when I was a kid. Julio Arguelles's dark chocolate hair sweeps down over his forehead, and Julio is holding up a hand in a permanent Number One gesture. I can't guess what question Julio was answering when that photograph was taken. Julio Arguelles has a faint orange Kool-Aid mustache. He is wearing blue sweat pants, but the legs are pulled up to his knees. He has black sneakers and no socks. Julio Arguelles had three daughters. The oldest of his girls was nine.

4. PAAVI SEPPANEN'S FAMILY came from Finland. Paavi means small. Paavi also died in the explosion that took my brother's right leg below his knee and obliterated both of Eric Christopher Szerba's testicles. Paavi Seppanen was twenty-six years old when he died in Afghanistan. There is a photograph of Paavi that was taken at Easter when Paavi Seppanen was ten years old. Paavi has airy, thin red-blond hair the color of clover honey. He is wearing a collared, white long-sleeve shirt that is tucked into belted black slacks. He has a black clip-on necktie and is standing between his younger brother and sister. He looks like their protector. You can see they believe that about Paavi. Paavi has his arms around his brother and sister and they are all smiling. The younger boy and girl are holding empty woven baskets in their hands. The egg hunt has not started yet. The girl is maybe three in the photograph, and Paavi's younger brother is wearing gray pants, a necktie, and suspenders. Paavi was homosexual. Nobody knew anything about it.

THE PRESIDENT'S SPERM

"**I FOUND IT,**" Shann said.

"It's difficult to miss, I suppose," I agreed. "Maybe it's painted like the sky, instead of a penis, and so we just don't notice it nowadays."

Shann bumped me with her shoulder.

Johnny McKeon could not tell when people were messing around with him, but his stepdaughter could.

"I mean, I *really* found it," Shann insisted. "I hiked out along the old service roads. There are some broken-down henhouses there and old troughs for the milk cows."

"Maybe those are urinals," I offered.

"Be serious," Shann said.

"Uh. Okay." I decided to be serious.

Shann said, "I found the old foundation to the silo. It's concrete, and there's a circular hatch in the middle of it. It looks like something you'd climb through to get into a diving bell or something."

"Uh," I said. "Nobody uses diving bells in Iowa. It's not natural. Besides, there's nothing to see beneath the surface of Iowa."

"I couldn't open it," Shann said.

"You tried?" I was impressed.

"Well . . . no. I was actually afraid to do it alone," Shann admitted.

"That was probably wise of you, Shann. There could be lost Russian sailors down there," I offered. "They would be very horny if they'd been down there ever since Iowa was last covered by a vast sea. Or maybe it's full of the president's sperm."

That made Shann laugh.

I was horny.

I felt like I scored points toward getting her to come over to my lonely house with me. I desperately wanted her to, but I was not going to ask her to please do that. Johnny would probably say *no*, anyway, in spite of the condoms.

But Johnny McKeon waited in his car and pretended not to watch us when Shann walked me to my front door and we kissed good night.

THE VIRGIN SAINT AND HIS WARD

I WROTE.

At the bottom of the first page, I penciled in a picture of a big galvanized steel silo that towered in the distance behind the McKeon House, which was Ealing, Iowa's solitary listing on the *Registry of Historic Homes*.

Ingrid squirmed beneath my bare feet. She perked her ears up. If she hadn't been stricken by cancer when she was a puppy, she may have barked. She looked like she wanted to bark. So I thought maybe she wanted to bark at me because she needed to shit, which was the most predictable quality Ingrid possessed.

She was a quiet fountain of shit and reliability.

Outside, in the distance, a police siren wailed like a plaintive coyote.

We never heard sirens in Ealing. It's not that bad things never happened here, it's just that nobody ever bothered to complain about it when they did.

A few miles away from my house, Ollie Jungfrau was locking up *Tipsy Cricket Liquors*. He had called the Iowa State Patrol, reporting that some kind of wild animal had attacked Wayne DeLong in the parking lot after Wayne left *Tipsy Cricket Liquors*. Wayne was carrying a paper sack with a bottle of El Capitan Vodka and a twelve-pack of Dura-Flex Extra-Sensitive Condoms.

The wild animal that attacked Wayne DeLong was Hungry Jack.

Wayne's friends called him *Wayne-O*. Wayne-O was a pilot. He didn't drink too much on nights before he flew, he said. He was supposed to fly a commuter plane from Cedar Rapids to Omaha in six hours.

Wayne-O wasn't going to make that flight.

Ollie Jungfrau told the Iowa State Patrol officers the animal he'd seen attacking Wayne DeLong looked like a six-foot-tall grasshopper. The troopers requested that Ollie Jungfrau breathe into a machine.

Wayne DeLong was eaten right in front of the *Ealing Coin Wash Launderette*. The only thing left of Wayne-O was his belt buckle, eyeglasses, and the *Tipsy Cricket* paper sack containing the twelve-pack of condoms Wayne-O would never get to use, and the bottle of El Capitan Vodka that Wayne-O would also never drink.

"Okay, Ingrid," I said. "Come on."

I stood up from my seat at the desk. Ingrid raced ahead of me and ran downstairs to the front door, wagging her tail and panting.

"Uh. Wait, girl," I said. I turned back. I'd forgotten the cigarettes Johnny McKeon brought for me in my bedroom.

It was a nice night.

I sat on the front porch in nothing but my boxers and Robby Brees's Spam T-shirt. I put my bare feet up on the railing while Ingrid sniffed around in the yard. I lit a cigarette and considered staying home from school for a second consecutive day.

I thought Robby was right. I would surprise my dad by cleaning up all the dog shit and mowing the lawn before my parents came back home from Germany.

"There goes my Nobel Prize and my trip to Sweden with Robby Brees," I said.

I was talking to Saint Kazimierz.

I smoked.

Saint Kazimierz chose to maintain his virginity until his death.

I could not comfortably wrap my head around that thought.

Saint Kazimierz must have been a real dynamo at saying *no* to his penis.

After he died a virgin boy in his twenties, Saint Kazimierz's body was wrapped in silk. Saint Kazimierz's corpse reportedly cured all kinds of people who were afflicted with untreatable illnesses. He even brought a dead girl back to life.

This is all true.

The maintenance of his virginity was more remarkable than any of that shit, as far as I was concerned.

I couldn't see how a Polish boy could do that.

I wondered if, in the 1400s in Poland, being a virgin boy meant you were still technically permitted to *experiment*, or at least allowed to produce a little polymer from time to time. Otherwise, it had to be some kind of hoax or, perhaps, a genuine miracle.

Saints, like Kazimierz, I decided, truly *were* superhuman.

When his original tomb crumbled, the clergy decided to transport the boy's body to a new crypt. When the priests opened his tomb, Saint Kazimierz's body was miraculously preserved, and smelled like flowers.

Maybe shit like that will happen to any Polish boy who can actually fight off the urge to lose his virginity.

It was hopeless for me.

I was destined to be a stinky Polish corpse that would never cure diseases or shit like that.

A gray fog of headlights came sweeping like a sandstorm down the middle of our street.

Nobody ever drove out this way in the middle of the night.

Then Robby Brees's old Ford Explorer pulled up and parked along the curb in front of my house.

I was scared, but also very happy to see Robby.

I had been a ridiculous asshole to Robby Brees over the past two days. And now, here I was: caught red-handed smoking on my porch, alone, in my underwear and Robby's Spam shirt that he'd been wearing when we got called queers and beaten up by the Hoover Boys.

Seeing Robby Brees get out of the car made me feel guilty and nervous. It was the same way I'd felt the day Pastor Roland Duff called me in to the headmaster's office at Curtis Crane Lutheran Academy to counsel me on the history and consequences of masturbation.

Robby did not expect to see me sitting there on the front porch, smoking in my boxers. In fact, he did not see me at all, which is why he let out a little startled squeal when I said, "Hi, Robby. It's really good to see you."

Nobody ever expects to be cheerfully greeted at midnight by a kid smoking in his underwear on a deserted street in Ealing, Iowa.

I may just as well have been a six-foot-tall praying mantis, or shit like that.

Robby regained his composure.

He said, "Hey, Porcupine."

"Want a cigarette?" I asked.

Robby said, "Uh."

He looked around, like he was trying to see if there was some kind of joke being played on him. Ingrid came up and sniffed his hand and then transformed herself into a doggy rug beneath my chair.

I took my bare feet down from the porch rail and curled my toes in her fur.

She sighed contentedly.

I said, "You're a good dog, Ingrid."

The sirens in the distance went silent.

Robby said, "I didn't mean to bother you, Austin. I just came to drop off some things on your porch. I didn't think you'd be out here."

He went back to get what he'd brought from his car.

"Watch out for dog shit," I warned.

"I *am* watching out," he confirmed.

It must have been the end of the world or some shit like that. Robby Brees, who never did his laundry, had been washing laundry all day, which is why he did not go to school. It was *part* of the reason why Robby did not go to school. Most of the reason was that his Polish-kid best friend had been acting like a complete asshole.

He carried a neatly folded stack of half my entire non-Lutheran-Boy wardrobe in his arms.

On top of it were two pairs of sneakers, my toothbrush, and cell phone.

"Sorry it took so long to get all this stuff back," Robby said. "Your sleeping bag's in the Explorer, too."

I took the bundle from Robby. Our hands touched.

Everything smelled really good.

"This stuff smells good," I said.

Robby said, "Thanks. I tried."

Robby shrugged.

"You actually did *all* your laundry today?" I asked.

"Yeah," Robby said. "It's not too bad. I couldn't find one of your socks, though."

Socks and underwear have a way of disappearing with me.

"Maybe it's under your bed," I said.

I immediately felt the flush of embarrassment. I silently prayed to Saint Kazimierz to make me not say anything else that was as stupid as the shit I just said to Robby.

"Your dad's been calling," Robby said.

"Uh."

"I talked to him. He said everything is going to be okay. I hope you don't mind that I answered your phone." Robby said, "Austin, I'm really sorry about Eric."

Robby was such a good person.

"You are such a good friend, Rob," I said.

I gave Robby a cigarette. Then we went to his car to get my sleeping bag. I could hardly believe my eyes: Robby Brees's backseat was completely cleaned out. All the dirty clothes were gone. It was like there was a new Robby.

"The new Robby," I said.

"Yeah," Robby agreed.

"Uh." I said, "Now I feel guilty about wearing your Spam shirt. I think I might have B.O. I've been lying in bed all day."

"Austin, you *do* have B.O.," Robby confirmed. "I can smell it from here. You smell like leftover pizza in a locker room."

Robby, who swore that Doritos smelled like a six-year-old boy's feet, had an acute sense for smells.

"Uh. I will do laundry tomorrow, too," I said. "We'll be, like, laundry buddies, or shit like that, and we can chat about how we manage to get our things to smell so fresh."

We sat on the porch, next to the stack of all my clean-smelling laundry that was missing at least one sock, and Ingrid, my golden retriever, who was missing her vocal cords, and smoked together.

I tried making small talk.

I said, "I ate a *Stanpreme* tonight with Shann."

"Oh," Robby said.

"It always tastes better when you're there. I think Satan dislikes you," I said.

"He hates everyone who asks for ice water. What do you expect? He's *Satan*," Robby theorized.

"Oh yeah," I said. Robby was very smart about theology, too.

"Look, I wanted to say something, Porcupine," Robby began.

"Don't say anything, Rob. I don't want you to."

I waved my hand in the air between us like I was erasing words from an invisible blackboard.

"Okay," Robby said.

THE DIVING BELL

THE THREE OF US marched through waist-high weeds and brambles, across fields that at one time were forests of corn, out to Shann's launch pad.

Shann Collins found the invisible McKeon silo.

The silo was just as Shann had described it to me: A circular pad of concrete thirty feet in diameter. Around the circumference, corroded anchor bolts that used to support the structure's cylindrical outer wall poked up like a mummy's rusted fingers. In the exact center was a steel hatch, tightened shut by a spoked metal wheel that looked entirely like something you'd find on top of an old diving bell.

I was nervous.

"We should have brought flashlights," I said.

And then I added, "Let's go back and get some flashlights."

Robby, who was never scared of anything unless we were breaking in to Johnny McKeon's museum of horrors in the middle of the night, said, "Let's have a cigarette and then open this shit up, Porcupine."

"You boys smoke too much," Shann said.

So Robby and I lit cigarettes, and before he'd taken the second drag on his, Robby squatted down above the hatch wheel and began forcing it counterclockwise.

As soon as the wheel rotated a quarter turn, we heard a low buzzing sound coming up from beneath the hatch.

"Um," I said. "Robby? That thing's full of bugs or shit."

"It's not full of bugs," Robby argued.

"If it's full of bugs, I'm going to be mad," Shann offered.

"If it's the kind of bugs I'm thinking of, you won't be mad for too long," I said.

"He is thinking of butterflies that shit raspberry cupcakes on your head," Robby said.

That made me hungry for cupcakes.

"No," I said. "No, I am not thinking of butterflies that shit raspberry cupcakes, Rob."

Robby knew what kind of bugs I was thinking about, but Robby was not afraid.

Finally, the wheel would turn no more. The hatch came loose, and Robby stood up and lifted it open.

åI took a drag, exhaled, and said, "Roof access, Rob."

THE POPULAR GIRL

AT EXACTLY THE same moment Robby Brees opened the hatch to the McKeon silo, my mother and father stood at the bedside of Eric Christopher Szerba. It was nearly midnight in Germany. My parents were trying to talk Eric into speaking with his younger brother on their cell phone. My father held his phone above Eric's bed like it was a fragile baby bird. Eric did not want to talk to his younger brother. Eric Christopher Szerba told my father to get out of his goddamned room and leave him alone.

At that moment, my cell phone was sitting on the coffee table in our living room beside an empty container of chicken-flavored Cup-O-Noodles.

I often forgot to carry my phone with me.

At that moment, Grant Wallace fell down in his bathroom while taking a piss. Grant hit his head on the rim of his toilet. It was not a Nightingale. Grant Wallace's head broke open. It didn't matter. Grant was hatching. The bug that came out of Grant was young and powerful. He was hungry and also very horny. He needed to eat, and he needed to find Eileen Pope. He could smell and hear Eileen Pope, even though she was four miles away from the Wallace home.

Grant Wallace made a terrible mess in his bathroom. There was nothing that was not covered by spatters of blood after he finished eating. But Grant was still hungry, and he also wanted to fuck and make more bugs with Eileen Pope.

When he came out of the bathroom, Grant Wallace ate his two younger brothers, his mother, and the family's Yorkshire terrier, which was named Butterfly.

Grant Wallace's father, Will Wallace, was not home from his job in Waterloo yet.

Will Wallace owned *Fire at Will's Indoor Shooting Range and Gun Shop.*

At that moment, Will Wallace was selling a 9mm Ruger over the counter to a drunk man who claimed he was going to use it to shoot his ex-wife's cat.

Will Wallace had a sign behind his counter. The sign displayed Will Wallace's two favorite mottos. It looked like this:

A GUN IS NOT A TOY
ALL SALES FINAL

The three Hoover Boys Grant Wallace enjoyed hanging out with hatched within minutes of one another. Like Grant, Travis Pope, and Hungry Jack, they wanted to do only two things.

Now there were seven bugs in Ealing, Iowa: Eileen Pope and her six suitors—Hungry Jack, Travis Pope, Grant Wallace, Tyler Jacobson, Devin Stoddard, and Roger Baird. Eileen Pope was going to be very popular.

Eileen's dance card was full.

At that moment, the vice president of the United States of America was performing his monthly testicular self-exam. His balls felt perfectly fine. The vice president of the United States of America named his balls Theodore and Franklin. Theodore was a little bigger than Franklin.

And Johnny McKeon was inside his office. He watched the little two-headed baby boy inside the jar. Johnny had seen the boy move before. The two-headed boy was moving his hands now: open and closed, open and closed, open and closed.

Johnny said, "Ain't that a kick?"

Johnny thought the thing inside the jar was some sort of deranged toy.

Two-Headed Boys Are Not Toys.

Ollie Jungfrau was lying in his bed. He lived in a bachelor apartment at the Del Vista Arms. He needed to take the day off after the stressful ordeal with Wayne DeLong in the parking lot at Grasshopper Jungle the night before. Ollie Jungfrau thought masturbating would make him feel more cheerful. He also phoned out for pizza delivery from *Satan's Pizza*.

Customers for *Tipsy Cricket Liquors* had to bother Johnny McKeon at the secondhand store if they needed booze, cigarettes, or condoms. Johnny didn't mind. Johnny McKeon never minded much of anything.

Louis, the Chinese cook at *The Pancake House*, whose real name was Ah Wong Sing, met Connie Brees in the alley at Grasshopper Jungle.

They went back to the Del Vista Arms together.

At exactly the same moment the hatch on the McKeon silo came up into the Iowa sky for the first time in forty years, Connie Brees was making certain her son, Robert Brees Jr., was not at home. She went through Robby's room, looking for a box of condoms she found on the floor of Robby's bedroom on Tuesday afternoon when Robby was at school. Ah Wong Sing sat naked, waiting for Connie Brees in her bedroom, which was just on the other side of the little bathroom where I'd vomited and taken a shower on Tuesday morning.

And, at exactly the moment Robby lifted open the old hatch and the subterranean chamber below our feet lit up in pale fluorescent-green light, I was thinking about having an underground threesome with Shann and Robby, and feeling myself turn red and hot with my sweating, embarrassed horniness.

I also wanted cupcakes.

WELCOME TO EDEN

IF DRIVING OUT to the *Tally-Ho!* with Robby Brees was like traveling forward in time, then climbing down into the belly of the McKeon silo with him was like going backwards.

First: Robby climbed down the rounded steel ladder, and Shann and I followed. As soon as Robby was halfway down to the floor, which was fifteen feet below the hatch opening, a welcoming sound chimed us into the silo.

It was a recording of a very sterile, anesthetized-sounding woman's voice that said:

Welcome to Eden. Please secure the hatch upon entry.

Welcome to Eden. Please secure the hatch upon entry.

Welcome to Eden. Please secure the hatch upon entry.

"Uh," I said. The message kept repeating without any indication that it would stop. I added, "Shann, if this place ends up being full of sperm, I'm leaving."

The place did have sperm in it. We found it later.

You will see.

"It's just like our mothers or something," Shann said. "I bet she won't shut up till one of us closes the front door."

Shann pointed up to the hatch and the disc of blue Iowa sky above our heads.

Shann was very smart.

I thought it was like our mothers because the voice sounded like the two Connies—Connie Brees and Connie Szerba—when they were floating along on little blue kayaks.

Welcome to Eden. Please secure the hatch upon entry.

Welcome to Eden. Please secure the hatch upon entry.

"Okay," I said. "I can't take it anymore."

But before I could do anything, Robby was back up the ladder, sealing shut the hatch above us.

The welcome announcement stopped.

Robby looked down at us from the top of the ladder.

"Uh," I said. "What if we can't get out, Rob, and this chamber suddenly begins filling up with sperm or shit like that?"

Robby said, "Eden Five needs us, Porcupine."

"Uh," I repeated.

"You worry too much," Robby said.

That was very true.

Everyone knew I worried too much.

Absentmindedly, I fiddled with the silver Saint Kazimierz bauble dangling from the chain around my neck.

SOME KIND OF SIGN

THE DIVING BELL turned out to be much more than a diving bell. It was a bunker fortress, a preserved glimpse, like Paleolithic cave art, at the paranoia that gripped Cold War Ealing, Iowa, and the United States of America.

It was everything in the entire world down there.

You will see.

The first room below the hatch was something like a mudroom. There were benches all along its circular wall, with coat and hat hooks positioned at even distances above them. The wall was painted an industrial shade of gray with bold yellow block letters that said:

MCKEON INDUSTRIES INFESTATION COMPLEX
EDEN PROJECT • EALING, IOWA

There was a pair of scuffed wingtip shoes left beneath one of the benches, as well as a powder-blue windbreaker hanging from a hook. There was also a matching set of three of the same plastic pink lawn flamingos with the wire stakes coming out of their asses. The wire stakes were fed through perfectly drilled holes in the benches. The flamingos were turned with their beaks toward the center of the mudroom, like they were watching us.

"This must be some kind of nuke shelter," Robby said.

"Nuh," I said. "It has something to do with that shit Tyler dropped."

Shann said, "What are you talking about?"

"Let's see what's down here," I said.

A single metal door led out of the entry room. The fact that this door also had a sealing airlock mechanism convinced me that the silo had been created for some anticipated disaster. A reasonable observer might conclude that Dr. Grady McKeon had prepared the structure, as many Americans did during the 1960s, as a type of bomb shelter for his family. But I knew after what I'd seen inside Johnny McKeon's office at *From Attic to Seller Consignment Store* that there was something much more to this silo and to Grady McKeon's creations.

I was certain Robby believed it, too.

None of us had any way of knowing it at the time, but Robby Brees and the bloody message he left on the pavement at Grasshopper Jungle had just as much to do with the end of the world as old, dead Dr. Grady McKeon ever did.

We went through the first door.

Robby said, "I don't mind telling you this, Shann, but I think you should keep this place secret from your parents, so we can have a raging party down here."

"*Like an orgy,*" I whispered.

"Uh," Shann said.

"We could rule the world from this place," Robby offered.

I wasn't really listening to them. I was nervous about being there, and I was silently communicating to Saint Kazimierz, asking him if he could make me stop thinking about having an orgy.

In the early 1970s, among the last times anyone had ever been down inside the McKeon silo, which was technically called the Eden Project, scientists and workers from McKeon Industries actually did come down here to have sex parties.

We would find this out later, much to Shann's embarrassment.

The doorway led us into a vast tiled hallway of lockers, which in turn opened on either side to a wide shower room on our right, sinks and mirrors to our left, with gleaming stainless fixtures and hospital-clean floors and walls. I went inside the shower room. The showerheads were arranged like sunflowers blooming outward from the tops of central posts that looked like columnar periscopes in old submarines. Twenty people could shower in there at the same time. The place was obviously designed with the idea of not segregating shower-takers and clothes-changers by gender.

I opened one of the spigots.

The water came out hot.

The place was suitable for an army, and it was also ready to be used.

"Too bad I already took a bath today," I said.

"Yeah. Too bad," Shann said.

She was joking.

In the shower chamber, at the end of the room where there were polished redwood benches and cubbies for towels and clothes, there were three doored stalls to toilets, and an enormous twenty-foot-long porcelain communal wall urinal. I examined the top of the urinal. There were birds on it with ribbons coiled around their happy beaks. The urinal was an antique Nightingale.

I knew I would have to pee in that thing.

My destiny was calling.

Once again, every highway that had ever been laid was

intersecting right at my feet. I rubbed the Saint Kazimierz medal against my chest and thanked the virgin boy.

Robby had opened some of the lockers. They all contained identical sets of supplies: clean towels and shower kits with soap and razors, fresh white-and-blue nylon jumpsuits that zipped up the front, sealed packages of white socks, and cloth caps, all of which had been embroidered in blue and gold thread with the McKeon Industries Scientific Labs Department logo.

All the jumpsuits were numbered and said *Eden* on their chests.

"I wonder if we should change our clothes or shit," Robby said.

"If there's one in there that says *Eden 5*, I am putting it on," I decided.

Robby waved a hanger like a banner in front of me. On the left chest, the jumpsuit said this:

EDEN

5

"This is like some kind of sign or shit," I said.

GIMME SHELTER

THE UNIFORM MADE me look like someone who worked at a place that sold hot dogs and ice cream cones.

I stripped down to my boxers and slipped myself hurriedly inside the jumpsuit. Shann and Robby gave in to their desire to conform. All teenagers really want to be exactly alike, so why wouldn't they?

Shann and Robby put on uniform jumpsuits as well.

Watching Shann and Robby take off their clothes made me realize that nylon jumpsuits were also not very good at hiding erections. Saint Kazimierz kept me strong.

I wanted a cigarette.

Shann Collins was Eden 49.

Robby Brees became Eden 133.

We put on our white caps and socks. We were an army now.

There were a lot of lockers down there, enough to find suits that fit us perfectly. Enough to last forever.

"Do you think this place would explode or shit if we smoked down here?" I asked.

Robby said, "I was wondering the same thing, Porcupine."

The place did not explode.

I noticed there were ashtrays built into the walls of the locker room. Everyone smoked in the 1970s, especially in Iowa. Who wouldn't smoke if you were sealed underground and the world above was going down a cosmic shithole?

Walking silently over the cool, slick floor in our brand-new McKeon Industries Scientific Labs Department white socks, we left the locker room through the only hatched doorway at the opposite end from the entry.

We came out into a massive auditorium with rows of cushioned seats that all faced a podium and rolling blackboards at the front of the room.

It was like a lecture hall.

The stage area was lit up in track lights that pointed down at the lectern, so the audience's attention would be focused on whoever might be up there telling them all the important shit they needed to know.

On one of the chalkboards behind the speaker's podium, a diagram had been drawn.

It looked like this:

412E→HUMAN BLOOD HOST→
LARVAL STAGE→METAMORPHOSIS→
SEXUAL REPRODUCTION→INFESTATION

It was just like biology class with pollywogs.

I hated biology, and as far as I know, pollywogs cannot destroy the world. Then again, I never paid attention in biology class unless the teacher was talking about sexual reproduction with humans.

Our ninth-grade biology teacher at Curtis Crane Lutheran Academy was named Mrs. Edna Fitzmaurice. She had a mustache and would not tolerate nervous giggling when she said a word like *penis* or *vagina*. Edna Fitzmaurice's main function at Curtis Crane Lutheran Academy was to make teenagers morbidly terrified of sex.

History lesson: Over the course of centuries in the history of education, although fought valiantly by endless armies of pedagogues, the attempt to frighten teenagers away from sex has proven to be a losing battle.

The lecture hall had multiple sets of doorways leading out from each of its three curved walls. There was so much for us to explore. The place was easily five times larger than the McKeon House where Shann lived, maybe bigger than that.

The first door we opened took us into a type of lounge. It looked like a television set from a 1960s-era family comedy, with low, straight-backed sofas perched on narrowly tapered birchwood peg legs, shag carpeting, and coffee tables shaped like kidney beans. On one of the tables was an assortment of magazines. They were perfectly unwrinkled, dustless, hardly touched. The most recent date on any of the magazines was 1971.

There were framed photographs on the walls: an image of the flag of the United States of America planted on the surface of the moon, the faces of presidents carved into Mount Rushmore, a herd of longhorn cattle, what apparently were Iowa cornfields, Willie Stargell swinging at home plate in the 1971 World Series, and a black-and-white picture of President Richard Nixon and his family, taken in the White House in front of a fireplace, and a painting of President George Washington. It was everything that made America worth living in an underground cave for, while the rest of the world went entirely to shit.

That was our day. You know what I mean.

And there was a cigarette machine in the lounge.

Discovering it had an almost religious impact on Robby and me.

"Thank you, Saint Kazimierz," I said.

I pulled my medal out from my jumpsuit and kissed the saint.

"You're going to go to hell for turning Catholic," Robby said.

Robby pulled one of the levers on the machine. Out popped a red pack of Pall Mall cigarettes and a book of matches that advertised how you could get into art school by drawing a cute little fawn named Winky.

You did not need to put money into the machine to get cigarettes out of it.

It was a miracle.

Robby said, "Thank you, Saint Kazimierz."

We sat on one of the couches and smoked.

The Pall Mall cigarettes were a little stale, but they were free.

I had read somewhere that cigarette manufacturers during the 1970s also put saltpeter in their tobacco. I wondered if Americans had fewer erections during the 1970s than during other decades. Apparently, the saltpeter in my Pall Mall was not having much of an effect on my penis. I sat beside Shann and rubbed her leg with mine. The jumpsuits felt very nice. I put my hand on her neck. We kissed, and I slipped my tongue into Shann's mouth.

I believed Robby was a better kisser than me. I tried to kiss Shann like Robby would.

Robby watched us. He was not bothered at all by what I was doing with Shann.

He got up from the couch and went over to the wall, where a built-in shelf surrounded an old reel-to-reel tape recorder. There was a big spool of tape that had been left threaded across the machine's playheads.

Robby pressed the power button and the two level-meter windows on the bottom of the machine flickered with yellow light. There were red needles that looked as fine as strands of horsehair, and they pricked up inside each window. Robby flipped a switch. It made a soft click, and the reels jerked and spun.

Music came from everywhere around us.

It was a recording of the Rolling Stones's album, *Let It Bleed*.

Robby said, "Oh, hell yes."

Robby danced and smoked.

He was such a great dancer. It was just like when he taught me how to dance in his room at the Del Vista Arms so I could win Shann's attention when we were in seventh grade. I wanted to dance with Robby, too.

Robby said, "I never want to leave Shann's silo."

Mick Jagger sang Gimme Shelter.

History will show that Gimme Shelter is one of the greatest songs ever recorded. It sounded so beautiful down inside Shann's silo. Robby danced in his jumpsuit, which he had unzipped all the way past his belly button, so you could see his brightly colored, non-plaid, non-Iowa boxers. They had pictures of ice cream cones with rounded scoops of colorful ice cream melting down the diamond-patterned waffle cones in suggestive drips.

Robby always had the coolest boxers.

He waved his hands around and tilted his cigarette daringly from his lips.

I got up and danced with Robby there in my jumpsuit and socks on the thick shag carpeting in the lounge room. It all felt very good. Shann joined us. The three of us danced together. It made me very horny.

I said, "I never want to leave Shann's silo."

Shann smiled and danced between Robby and me.

We were in Eden.

Eden needed us.

All roads crossed on our dance floor.

THE DRAGON PARADE

WE DANCED AND DANCED.

The tape played. We were sweaty and hypnotized, and we lost ourselves as the music fell all around, washing over us.

I said, "I love you, Shann. I love you, Robby."

What was I going to do?

Shann and Robby smiled at me.

Shann combed her fingers through my wet hair. Robby touched my hand with his.

We danced and danced.

And while I danced with Robby and Shann below the ground, things happened in the world above.

Ingrid, my golden retriever that could not bark, was exhausted from being outside and watching me mow the lawn and scoop up dog shit all day. She was curled up beneath my desk, asleep and content, waiting for me to come home.

Ah Wong Sing and Connie Brees were lying naked together in bed. They had had sex three times in one hour.

Ah Wong Sing was a real dynamo for such a quiet guy.

The Pancake House cook and Connie Brees smoked a marijuana cigarette that Ah Wong Sing had rolled before coming over to the Del Vista Arms. They also used up the last of the condoms Connie Brees had found on the floor of Robby's bedroom.

The family from Minnesota who had come through Ealing the previous Saturday on their serial-killer road trip were heading back home to Minneapolis. They bought a *Stanpreme* pizza to go and had a picnic on the benches at Amelia Jenks Bloomer Park.

It was not a good idea.

Nobody in Ealing, Iowa, ever went to Amelia Jenks Bloomer Park.

Some parks are unexplainably like that: Unused, as though there is some unspoken recognition there might be a sort of toxic pall hanging over them. In fact, Amelia Jenks Bloomer Park was built on the site of an old chemical milling and etching plant. The tanks there had corrupted, and poisonous metals from them seeped into the ground. Swallowing water from the drinking fountains at Amelia Jenks Bloomer Park was just a little safer than sucking on a nozzle of unleaded premium at the Arco on Kimber Drive. Nobody knew anything about that. The twin boys drank and drank from the fountains at Amelia Jenks Bloomer Park in Ealing, Iowa. They filled squirt guns again and again with Amelia Jenks Bloomer Park's drinking water.

It did not matter.

The family sat and looked over their memories in their guidebook. Before Amelia Jenks Bloomer Park was an abandoned park, *United Chem-Etch Incorporated*'s parking lot occupied the exact spot where the picnic tables were located. In 1969, the decapitated head of an adult white male had been discovered in that parking lot. It was a perfect place to have a family picnic. The father remarked how fresh the sausage meat was on the *Stanpreme* pizza they had bought.

The Hoover Boys—at least the bugs that hatched from the Hoover Boys—Tyler, Devin, and Roger, scampered with clicking, mechanical jerkiness across the Little League field adjacent to the picnic area.

They audibly buzzed with horniness and hunger.

One of the twin boys saw them. He said, "Look! A dragon parade!"

It was not a dragon parade.

Mantises are very quick. It's not that the bugs that hatched from the Hoover Boys and the other victims of *Contained MI Plague Strain 412E* were precisely mantises, but they were close enough in physiology, with their triangular heads and viciously barbed tri-segmented striking arms. And they also stood six feet tall.

In battle, a six-foot-tall praying mantis could easily destroy a six-foot-tall grizzly bear. They were like grizzly bears with steel plating and lightning-fast arms studded with row upon row of shark's teeth.

The bugs that hatched out from the victims of *Contained MI Plague Strain 412E* liked to snatch their prey up by the head, and then commence eating their thrashing victims straight down to their shoes.

The dragon parade made a bloody mess at Amelia Jenks Bloomer Park.

They were very quick.

They even ate what was left of the tourist family's *Stanpreme* pizza before scurrying off to look for more food and also for Eileen Pope, who they could hear and smell and wanted to fuck.

And while we danced and danced, my mother swallowed another of her little blue kayaks. She had gone back to the hotel with my father. My father was leaving a voicemail message on my cell phone at exactly the same moment that Shann and Robby danced with me.

The message was this:

> *Hey, Austin. We've been sitting with Eric, and he looks good. Real good. He is going to be fine, son, so there's no need to worry about your big brother. He is a hero. Call me and let me know how things are going at school. I hope you're eating okay, and not just Cup-O-Noodles and shit like that. And don't forget to let Ingrid out. I love you, son.*

Happy hour was beginning at the *Tally-Ho!*

Thursdays were good days there for men to meet new men who were daring enough to finally try their luck at the *Tally-Ho!* Will Wallace was drinking a beer at the bar while Shann ran her fingers through my hair and Robby brushed my sweaty hand softly with his.

Will Wallace was not homosexual. The *Tally-Ho!* sold beer for seventy cents per glass during Thursday happy hours. Will Wallace also enjoyed the attention he got from men who showed up at Waterloo, Iowa's one and only gay bar for the first time.

Will Wallace had no idea he was spending his last evening on earth in a bar for homosexual men.

At the same time Will Wallace was finishing his second glass of beer at the *Tally-Ho!*, Mr. Duane Coventry, our chemistry teacher at Curtis Crane Lutheran Academy, was tapping on the front door at *Tipsy Cricket Liquors*. He needed a bottle of whiskey. Duane was single, and he drank a lot. Nobody opened the door for him, so he got back into his car and drove to the Hy-Vee, where Connie Szerba worked as a bookkeeper.

At the Hy-Vee, Duane Coventry purchased two boxes of antihistamine tablets for his allergies. He did not have allergies. The chemistry teacher from Curtis Crane Lutheran Academy was a real dynamo when it came to cooking methamphetamine in his kitchen. Duane Coventry was very lonely. He should have tried hanging out at the *Tally-Ho!*

Hungry Jack, whose real name was Charles R. Hoofard, but was now a massive green bug that looked like a praying mantis, and Travis Pope, who was also a massive green bug that looked like a praying mantis, were back in the alley at Grasshopper Jungle. They were fighting over mating privileges with Travis's wife, Eileen Pope, who was also a massive green bug that looked like a praying mantis.

It didn't matter. Travis had already inseminated her a dozen times that day, and now he was more hungry than horny. There was plenty of Eileen Pope to go around.

Eileen Pope was about to become queen of a new world.

Once her six suitors got to her, they would collectively fertilize millions of eggs inside Eileen Pope's burgeoning abdomen. It would take her several days to produce and hide her egg mass, but then in a matter of hours there would be more hatchlings from those first seven victims of the *Contained MI Plague Strain 412E* than there were people in the entire state of Iowa.

The world would have just about seven days before the bugs started taking over.

And bugs only want two things.

So Travis Pope submitted to Hungry Jack and scuttled away down the alley behind the Ealing Mall.

Travis Pope hunted for someone to eat.

Hungry Jack joined himself to Eileen Pope as she clamped four of her arms onto the dirty convertible sofa in Grasshopper Jungle and buzzed with contented, fizzling coos like a short-circuiting wall socket.

We danced until the entire tape played through and flapped its disconnected end over and over around the receiving spool in an unending counterclockwise loop.

Shann and Robby and I were soaked with sweat. The three of us collapsed onto the thick shag carpeting, panting and staring up at the high ceiling overhead.

Shann said, "Let's try to find something besides shower water to drink."

I said, "I want to go piss in my great-great-grandfather's urinal."

"So do I," said Robby.

History often loops around into complete circles.

The spool of tape spun and spun.

SOUP FROM PAINT CANS

ANDRZEJ SZCZERBA'S AMERICAN name, the one with swapped-out consonants and shit, was Andrew Szerba. Andrzej Szczerba was my great-grandfather. His mother was Eva Nightingale, and his father was Krzys Szczerba, who Americans renamed Christopher Szerba, manufacturer of palatial urinals.

Robby and I peed all over the gleaming receiving wall of Krzys Szczerba's beautiful urinal.

"This is the greatest urinal ever made," I said.

Robby stared at the spot on the wall where the disembodied praying hands would be hanging if this were Curtis Crane Lutheran Academy.

"Very accommodating *and* unoppressive," Robby offered.

"If the act of urination had self-esteem, it could not help but feel better about itself after occurring in such a splendid location," I said.

Robby said, "Without a doubt, this is the nicest thing I have ever urinated on, with the possible exception of Sheila's husband's new Harley-Davidson."

Sheila was Robby's sister, who lived in Cedar Falls.

"You peed on your brother-in-law's Harley-Davidson?" I asked.

"He wasn't my brother-in-law at the time, but, yes, Porcupine, I peed all over the seat," Robby explained.

"Why?" I asked.

"I'm not really sure," Robby said. "Something inside me just told me that motorcycle needed a good peeing-on."

"Well, I have never peed on anything that was particularly nice. Except for maybe the grass on the football field at Curtis Crane Lutheran Academy," I said.

"You *peed* on our school?" Robby asked.

"Yes," I said. And then I asked, "Robby? Are we done talking about peeing yet?"

"I'm pretty sure we've said everything that needed to be said, Austin," Robby answered.

"We probably should shake hands," I said.

"Meet me at the hand soap dispenser," Robby answered.

Andrzej was seventeen years old when he left home, the same age his father was when Krzys Szczerba found himself entirely alone in the middle of the Atlantic Ocean. The Great Depression had arrived in the United States of America, and urinals—even beautiful ones with names that sang—were no longer in high demand.

Growing up, Andrew—Andrzej—always felt there was something quiet and troubling that made him different from other boys.

You know what I mean.

Krzys Szczerba's boy was often afraid and confused, just like another Andrzej who was going to be his great-grandson. Since he was born, his father, Krzys, only spoke to his son in Polish.

Andrzej Szczerba rescued an injured bird when he was thirteen. That would have been about the same year he was in seventh grade in Minnesota, where his father ran the *Nightingale Convenience Works*.

History shows that lots of shit happens to Polish boys when they are in seventh grade.

I do not know why, but that is not my job. My job is saying *what*. The shit that happens to us Polish boys is causally related to the bags under our eyes.

The bird Andrzej found was a European starling. Andrzej kept it and raised the bird as a pet. He named the bird *Baby*.

By the time Andrzej was seventeen and left home, Baby could talk. Baby spoke English as well as Polish, which displeased Eva Nightingale, who believed that Krzys and his son frequently conspired against her will, and plotted in their anarchists' tongue. She thought the bird was in on the Polish conspiracy, too.

Whether or not Baby actually understood the things he said was always a matter to be decided by the person listening to Baby speak.

Andrzej loved Baby. He never kept the bird in a cage, either. In fact, Andrzej tried to encourage the bird to fly away and find a suitable mate or a more natural place to live, but Baby would not leave Andrzej. Baby preferred to stay inside Andrzej's coat, or perched near his collar at all times.

People in southern Minnesota, where Andrzej was a boy, thought Andrzej was crazy. You must be crazy, after all, if a bird loves you.

In 1933, when Andrzej was seventeen years old, he and Baby found themselves at the very center of a vast continent. They were somewhere in the state of Iowa, in a place called Boatman's Bluff. Andrzej, like a lot of young men during the Great Depression, was more or less a hobo.

I also do not know why people say *more or less*. Everything is *more or less* of anything you can think of. Iowa is *more or less* the French Riviera. The French Riviera has the largest per-capita consumption of Spam in the world, *more or less*.

That is more or less the truth.

Andrzej was a hobo.

On a frozen morning in April, Andrzej arrived at a farm foreclosure auction. Sometimes, he went to these auctions just to stand in the midst of the people, where he could stay warm. Often, when auction-goers saw how young Andrzej was, and what a beautiful face the boy had, they would invite Andrzej home and feed him and allow him to take a warm bath or sleep for a while in their outbuildings.

It was natural for kindhearted people to feel a sense of sadness or obligation when they looked at young Andrzej, all alone and helpless. He looked like an angel, or like an injured bird.

Perhaps it was that people were also attracted to the strange talking bird that stayed inside Andrzej's collar and nuzzled against the boy's neck, which was the color of hominy grits.

That kindness people sometimes showed him was what Andrzej was looking for on the morning in April at the farm foreclosure auction. Andrzej was very hungry, and the ground of the dead farm was frozen in such deep black ruts that it hurt his feet when he walked through the crowd.

Andrzej ran into another drifter among the people at the auction: a nineteen-year-old boy named Herman Weinbach, who had come from Michigan. Herman Weinbach's straight hair, which was the color of pot roast gravy, hung down across one eye. His skin was the color of soda-and-flour biscuits.

Herman Weinbach had been a member of the American Communist Party, but he quit all political activities due to hunger, he explained. People were leaving the American Communist Party in the early 1930s, and Herman simply didn't believe anything was ever going to change, whether it was destined to, as Karl Marx said, or not.

Herman Weinbach was also homosexual, but nobody knew anything about it.

When Herman Weinbach saw Andrzej Szczerba at the auction, he asked Andrzej if he was a Jew. Andrzej told him no, that he was Catholic, and Herman said that would have been his next guess, after Quaker.

Herman Weinbach was a Jew, but nobody knew anything about that, either. He told Andrzej he was an atheist.

Andrzej Szczerba had never met an atheist before. At least, he had never met anyone daring enough to say they were atheists. Just the thought of denying God frightened Andrzej, who, like me, frequently touched a silver medallion of Saint Kazimierz he constantly wore on a chain around his neck.

Before Herman Weinbach died, he told Andrzej Szczerba that being a Communist homosexual Jew in Iowa in 1933 was like being a European starling that spoke two languages.

Andrzej did not know what Herman meant when he said that, but I believe he meant it was something beautiful and wonderful.

The boys found a man in the crowd who was smoking. He gave Herman and Andrzej some tobacco, and he let them roll cigarettes. Cigarettes were a good way to not feel so hungry.

That day Andrzej and Herman became great friends and

traveling companions. They shared their hunger, and Andrzej showed Herman the tricks he could do with Baby.

The boys had to go to a soup kitchen in Ames to get a meal that day. They had to wait for other boys to finish eating, so they could borrow something to hold soup for themselves. Herman and Andrzej had nothing except a talking bird named Baby.

They ate out of borrowed paint cans.

The boys who loaned them their paint cans waited for Herman Weinbach and Andrzej Szczerba to finish their meal.

You just don't give away empty paint cans when there's soup that needs to be ladled out.

This is the truth. It was America, and America had very little to spare for boys like Herman Weinbach and Andrzej Szczerba.

Herman was going to California, he said. He told Andrzej about his uncle, a man named Bruno Wojner, who had trained an amazing dog act for a circus.

The name of the circus act was *Bruno's Amazing and Incredible Dogs*. Herman said his uncle, Bruno Wojner, would be very excited about Andrzej's talking bird, and maybe they could go to work at Bruno's circus in California.

Andrzej thought California would be much better than Iowa, even if it was only a different place to starve and be cold, so the boys decided to try to go to California together, and find Uncle Bruno and his amazing dogs.

They made a pact to stay together—Herman, Andrzej, and Baby.

Of course, Andrzej never managed to leave Iowa, but the idea was good and romantic. That's what all Polish boys like when they are seventeen years old: Romantic ideas and somewhere to go.

Andrzej and Herman ate their soup from paint cans and saved half of their bread for later, and also to feed to Baby.

Things like this were what made America great: romance, talking birds, eating dinner from paint cans, and setting off with your friend to see the world.

There was an entire world inside Shann's silo, which was actually called *Eden*.

The world was frozen in time from around 1971.

That world included telephones wired into the walls. The phones were made from heavy plastic. Their mouthpieces were connected to the machinery of the telephone with tightly corkscrewed rubber cables. The phones had rotary dials on them and illuminated square buttons along their bottoms that were labeled with the names of other extensions within the silo called Eden.

Not one of us had ever used a phone like the ones we found in the silo.

I could hear a dial tone in them, and I'm certain I could have figured out how to place a call, but we decided there was no one any of us wanted to talk to, anyway.

We found out that Shann's and Robby's cell phones did not work inside the silo.

We discovered Eden's cafeteria, a museum piece in stainless steel and formica.

There were soda taps behind the buffet lines, with machines that must have been producing ice cubes for several days. The only soda brand I recognized was Coca-Cola. There was also something called Nesbitt's, which was orange, and another, piss-colored beverage named Vernors. The taps worked. The sodas came out cold and carbonated.

It was another miracle.

Free sodas.

And there was a warehouse filled with food. The food was all boxed in cardboard and contained green cans of just about every imaginable concoction you could eat. There were green foil pouches of peanut butter, and every one of the boxes contained small packs of cigarettes. This was the same kind of stuff the United States of America sent to its troops fighting in Vietnam, cigarettes and all.

"Thank you, Saint Kazimierz," I said.

"Thank you, Saint Kazimierz," Robby repeated.

Shann would not compromise her unsteady Lutheranism, most likely because she did not smoke.

"Robby and I *both* went to church on Sunday," I pointed out.

"I was moving in," Shann explained. "No one expects you to go to church when you're unpacking boxes."

There were enough boxes in Eden for us to unpack that we'd never have to go to church again.

GIDEON'S BREEDING RIGHTS

SHANN'S BEDROOM HAD a door that led into a brick wall and another that dead-ended at the foot of a stairwell. It was what I called a dungeon for horny Polish boys.

In truth, the silo called Eden went all the way into the foundation of the McKeon House, and the doorways in Shann's room had been bricked off when the Eden Project work crews finished construction on Dr. Grady McKeon's subterranean shelter.

Just as those McKeon Industries scientists back in the 1960s had been playing with self-sustaining universes they trapped inside globes of glass, the bigger enclosed bubble project they'd been working on lay beneath the ground under Shann's bedroom and stretched beyond the derelict cornfields on Dr. Grady McKeon's own property.

Here is what we found: Eden had a gymnasium, a fitness center with polished wood floors and weightlifting equipment, a sauna, and another shower room. There was a small facility for laundry that put the *Ealing Coin Wash Launderette* to shame in terms of its cleanliness and lack of discarded condoms and cigarette butts on the floor.

There was even a salon with those old-fashioned hair dryers that looked like brainwashing torture machines from science fiction movies, barber chairs, and haircutting tools.

Shann looked at her hair in the mirror. As always, it was beautiful, the color of mature wheat in late August. Her skin was perfect and unblemished.

I said, "Would you like us to do something with your hair?"

Shann said, "Do either of you guys know anything about hairstyles?"

And Robby continued our string of unanswered questions with, "Why are you both looking at me? Do you think it's just natural that I'd be, like, into doing hair and shit?"

Later, we found Eden's dormitories. Naturally, I was incapable of wandering through the bedrooms with Shann and Robby without feeling horny and guilty. I wondered if there had ever been threesomes inside Shann's silo.

Each room had two double beds. They looked, in style, like hotel rooms, except they lacked bathrooms and toilets, which were all located at the center of a hub of hallways that connected the fitness center and the lecture hall and entry room where we had changed out of our Iowa surface-dweller clothing.

There wasn't much room for argument in the discussion we had as we explored the bedrooms: Eden was built to house survivors for the end of the world. We could say the idea was to protect a few human specimens in the event of a nuclear war, but Robby and I knew Eden was probably built for something else entirely.

The idea that Robby and Shann and I were inside some kind of breeding compound for the genesis of an entire new species of humans was particularly thrilling and attractive.

"If we never came out of Eden, the three of us would be able to start an entire new race of underground Iowans," I said.

"Uh." Robby was unenthusiastic.

"Well. If we had to," I offered. "Between you, me, and Shann, we would have enough genetic diversity to not breed two-headed boys and shit like that."

I was somehow working into a long-range threesome strategy.

"Uh," Robby repeated.

Shann said, "I bet that's what Grady McKeon had in mind with the whole idea of *Eden*: starting everything over."

"Everyone who eventually came out would just end up doing the same stupid shit that always happened up there," I said, and pointed my thumb at the world above us.

"We should leave a copy of *Porcupine's History of the World* down here, just to save mankind the trouble," Robby said.

"That would be a good strategy," I said. "When do you two suppose we might start working on the new species?"

Shann rolled her eyes and pushed my chest.

I liked that.

She also changed the subject: "There must be books or stuff like that down here," Shann said.

Robby jumped on one of the beds like it was a trampoline. He said we should all do that, so Shann and I joined him. It was fun. We made a mess of that room. It was ours, anyway. Nobody could stop us.

I pulled out my little medal of Saint Kazimierz and looked at him and thought about how difficult the boy-saint's life must have been.

I hopped down onto the floor. I pulled open the drawers on the nightstands at the head of the double bed Shann and Robby were jumping on. There was a Gideon's Bible inside, but, naturally, there would be no condoms in Eden.

Every room had a Gideon's Bible in it.

Grady McKeon must have worked some kind of deal with those Gideon people. Maybe he promised to let them leave some sperm down here, besides just a bunch of Bibles, I thought.

We had no idea of the time when we were down in Eden.

We also had no idea about what was beginning to happen up above us in Ealing.

Nobody did.

———

THE QUEEN OF THE UNIVERSE

WE FOUND EDEN'S library at exactly the same time the Hoover Boys and Grant Wallace found Eileen Pope and Hungry Jack in the alley at Grasshopper Jungle.

Now Eileen was very busy. She was getting filled up with the seeds of a new apex species for Planet Earth. She was happy. Eileen was the queen of the new universe. But she was hungry, too.

While Devin Stoddard, the same Hoover Boy who had kneed me in the balls the Friday before and was now a lumbering six-foot-tall mantis beast, pumped future generations of little Devin bugs into Eileen Pope's swelling abdomen, she pivoted her thoracic midsection around clockwise and clamped Devin's head in the toothy mace of her grasping arms. Devin Stoddard did not resist. He pumped and pumped and pumped. Devin Stoddard continued pumping semen into Eileen Pope even after she had eaten his entire head.

Eileen Pope was doing the two things bugs like to do.

The other bugs watched and waited. They wanted more turns on Eileen Pope, even if she was still hungry after eating Devin Stoddard. When Eileen Pope finished eating, the only thing left of Devin Stoddard was a gooey smear across the floral sofa in Grasshopper Jungle.

And, at the exact moment we found Eden's library and Eileen Pope was crunching her way through Devin Stoddard's exoskeleton to get to the slick and nourishing goodness inside her mate, Johnny McKeon was locking up *From Attic to Seller Consignment Store* for the night.

Johnny decided to take a box of garbage out to the dumpster in the alley of Grasshopper Jungle.

It was not a good idea.

———

THE LIBRARY AND THE NEW TALLY-HO!

HISTORY SHOWS THAT an examination of the personal collection of titles in any man's library will provide something of a glimpse into his soul.

Such was the case with Dr. Grady McKeon's library beneath the ground.

Here was Dr. Grady McKeon's collection of books: There was a wall of novels. And every one of the novels in Dr. Grady McKeon's library was an American work. Also, every novel had been written by a man.

Before going down into Eden, I never knew that American

men had written so many books and shit. The men who wrote the books in Dr. Grady McKeon's library weren't just *guys*, they were monuments, and had names like Melville, Hawthorne, Twain, Fitzgerald, Faulkner, Dreiser, and on and on. The most recent novel, if you could call it that, was *The Old Man and the Sea*, by Ernest Hemingway.

There was not a copy of *The Chocolate War*, however, but that stood to reason.

Another wall in Dr. Grady McKeon's library was filled with books on all kinds of scientific subjects: botany, evolution, taxonomy, genetics, and reproduction. The books on reproduction caught my eye. They were very old and conservatively worded, however.

But the most wonderful feature of Dr. Grady McKeon's library were the rows of desks, each of which had been furnished with supplies for writing and drawing.

It was meant to be that Eden would have its historian.

"This is meant to be," I said.

I sat down at one of the desks and looked through the assortment of pens and empty leather-bound logbooks. I felt around with my feet in the carpeting beneath where I sat. It was difficult for me to adequately concentrate on writing without Ingrid sighing under my toes.

So I said, "What am I going to do, Shann?"

Shann said, "I don't know, Austin."

Shann was smart. She knew I was troubled about things. She always let me have room. In some ways, Shann was like Ingrid.

"This is where I will write the history of the end of the world," I said.

Shann said, "Uh."

Then I picked up some thick permanent markers and opened their caps. Naturally, I smelled them. I do not know why, because that is not my job, but history shows that every time a teenage boy opens a permanent marker, he will first sniff it before deciding how to go about defacing the planet.

That is what I did.

On the empty wall above the desk where I sat, I drew a big hairy thing—a bison—in as close a likeness as I could manage to the figure that had been drawn so many centuries before on the wall of a cave at a place called Altamira. Maybe it was my great-times-one-thousand-grandfather who'd drawn the Altamira bison. It would have been back when the world was like this: messed-up and poisonous, and a few scared and confused specimens found their way inside a cave called Altamira that may just as well have been a silo called Eden.

They would have gone down in that cave to start things over again. Perhaps my great-times-one-thousand-grandfather also smoked cigarettes and wore a medallion of a virgin Polish saint around his neck. He would have *experimented*, too. Maybe he was also confused about the people he was in love with, and whether or not there was something wrong with him for frequently finding himself sexually attracted to the guy he grew up with.

You know what I mean.

Thinking about being inside a cave with Robby and Shann made me feel very horny.

Robby said, "Nice cow, Austin."

"It is a bison," I pointed out.

"Oh," Robby said. And he added, "Nice buff, Porcupine."

Robby and Shann were great friends, true friends. They both allowed me the space that I needed. While I wrote the history of our day inside Eden, Shann and Robby sat and waited quietly. But there was still much of the silo we had to explore, so I rushed and abbreviated, and when I was satisfied that I had gotten down the important details of our discovery, I tucked the logbook under my arm and led the way out of the library and deeper into the mysteries of Dr. Grady McKeon's sealed-in universe.

Just across the hallway from Eden's library was a bar.

An actual bar, inside a compound designed to resurrect mankind.

Robby said, "I christen this bar *New Tally-Ho!*"

"Eden Five needs a gay bar," Shann said.

"Everywhere needs gay bars, Shann," I pointed out.

This was true.

We went inside the *New Tally-Ho!*

In the same way the *Eden No Coins Required Launderette* put to shame the dirty laundry joint at Grasshopper Jungle, the *New Tally-Ho!* was immeasurably more luxurious than Waterloo, Iowa's one and only gay bar.

There were built-in wine coolers and every kind of liquor I had ever heard of in my life, and some others that I had not.

There was a bottle of something called *Krupnik*, which came from Poland.

Once again, all roads crossed where I stood.

The *New Tally-Ho!* was impressively furnished, with a wide mahogany serving bar and a floor-to-ceiling mirror behind racks of immaculately arranged bottles and crystal ware. There was a pool table with a perfect felt surface. It sat in the middle of the floor with plenty of space around for proper play. A dart board hung on one wall. The chalkboard beside it still recorded a match from four decades back, between someone named *Doc* and another player named *Virgil*. Doc, apparently, was not such a good dart player.

We killed this big hairy thing. We played darts. And that was our day.

None of us was in the mood to try drinking alcohol. Drinking was reckless, and made us unconcerned about doing stupid shit.

"Um," I said. "Let's not get drunk, Robby."

We agreed to save that experiment for some other time.

Robby knew what I meant.

After our trip through the bar, we found a medical clinic that looked like it was equipped to do surgery.

"Lots of drugs in here," Shann said.

"An entire navy of kayaks," I added.

Eden was built like a starfish. Its arms radiated outward from the room we called the lecture hall, which was just beyond the mudroom and lockers and showers, where Dr. Grady McKeon had somehow managed to install a salvaged antique Nightingale urinal.

At the end of the arm that housed the medical clinic, there was a full-sized bowling alley with two complete lanes and a rack of balls and shoes, all of which had been personalized with the names of their owners.

Seeing those relics, as well as the scoreboard that had been kept for darts in the bar, made me suddenly aware that all the first people who had ever been down inside Eden were most likely dead.

"This is kind of creepy," Shann said. She stared at a swirling pink bowling ball with dainty finger holes and a gold-etched name on it that said *Wanda Mae*.

Wanda Mae was the first Queen of Eden.

She was fertile, left-handed, and enjoyed having sex with multiple partners in Eden. Wanda Mae also liked to bowl.

People in Iowa liked to bowl.

Robby said, "Bowling creeps me out, too, Shann. Except for the fact that it is the only sport that encourages its participants to smoke cigarettes."

I wanted a cigarette.

I tapped Robby's shoulder. I did not have to say anything to him. Robby Brees always knew what I was thinking, even when I was thinking about something other than smoking.

We lit cigarettes and backtracked to the final unexplored arm of the place called Eden.

And there we found the most important treasure the silo had yet to offer up: Eden's Movie Theater.

I will tell you.

VENTILATOR BLUES

BACK IN THE lounge, Robby uncovered a cache of reel-to-reel tapes in the cupboard below the tape machine.

"I would be happy to stay down here forever," Robby said.

"The future of mankind is . . . Um. Inside our jumpsuits," I said.

"I wonder what time it is," Shann said.

"It is time to begin the rebuilding of the universe with hybrid Austin-Shann-Robby offspring," I answered. I did not want Shann to think about leaving the silo.

Robby held up a box with a glossy black-and-white photo printed on its cover. It held a reel copy of *Exile on Main Street*.

"It's a miracle. This is like heaven," Robby said.

"Eden," I corrected.

Exile on Main Street, according to Robert Brees Jr., was the most brilliant rock album ever created.

"In Eden, it is permanently the nineteen-seventies," Robby affirmed.

"I never want to go home again," I said.

Robby wanted us to spend the night in Shann's silo.

He said, "Let's sleep here tonight."

"I'll cook dinner," I offered.

The opportunity was daring and thrilling to me. My heart raced with the thought of an Eden slumber party.

Shann said, "I can't spend the night with two *boys*. What would my mom say?"

I said, "She will probably say for you to use condoms."

"Shut up!" Shann answered.

"You are right, Shann. Eden needs us to not use condoms. It is our duty to repopulate Planet Earth with our handsome Iowan children," I said.

Robby threaded the new tape onto the machine.

Robby and I smoked. The three of us were having a beautiful time in Eden. We laughed, and I drew pictures of Shann and Robby in their jumpsuits, dancing together.

I asked Robby to recite Dulce Et Decorum Est, and he did. It was beautiful. I wanted to watch Robby kiss Shann. I wanted Robby to kiss her the real way, like I would, but there was no way Robby would just do something like that.

The song that played was called Ventilator Blues.

———

SOMETHING ALWAYS HAPPENS WHILE SOMEONE ELSE DANCES

HERE IS WHAT happened while Shann and Robby danced together, and I fantasized about watching Robby put his tongue in Shann's mouth:

Johnny McKeon stepped out into the alley at Grasshopper Jungle. Johnny carried a cardboard banana box someone had left behind in the garage of a foreclosed home in Ealing.

Johnny McKeon intended to toss the garbage into the same dumpster that Hungry Jack ate from at least once per week.

Hungry Jack's real name was Charles R. Hoofard. Charles R. Hoofard was born in Indiana and had served in the United States Army in Vietnam, where he participated in the extermination of an entire village of women, children, and elderly people. Hungry Jack was now a claw-armed six-foot-tall praying mantis thing, and he was waiting in line to fuck Eileen Pope.

Eileen Pope had been breeding all day and she was near exhaustion. Eileen Pope was also a claw-armed six-foot-tall praying mantis that had just eaten her most recent sexual partner, the Hoover Boy named Devin Stoddard. Devin Stoddard kneed me in the balls on the previous Friday when he and his friends beat me and Robby Brees up for being queers.

I was pretty sure I was not exactly queer.

But I was not certain.

Devin Stoddard was born in Crete, Nebraska. He once got fired from a part-time job bagging groceries at the Hy-Vee for smoking marijuana in a parked car when he was supposed to be gathering shopping carts.

At that moment, Eileen Pope's husband, Travis Pope, was inside *The Pancake House*, which looked as though it had been fire-hosed with blood and ground meat.

Travis Pope ate nine people inside *The Pancake House*.

It was a terrible mess.

Travis Pope had been very hungry after fucking Eileen all day long, ever since they had hatched out in the wreckage of Travis's Nissan truck. Travis Pope also enjoyed the sugary taste of spilled imitation-maple-flavored syrup on raw human beings.

Travis Pope had never been a blueberry syrup man.

The imitation-maple-flavored syrup served by *The Pancake*

House was made in New Jersey.

At the same time, Johnny McKeon opened the back door to *From Attic to Seller Consignment Store*, Eileen Pope clamped her four bristly upper arms into the woven fabric on the sofa in Grasshopper Jungle while Grant Wallace impregnated her over and over and over.

Hungry Jack and the two remaining Hoover Boys, who were also now claw-armed six-foot-tall praying mantises, postured and hissed with their toothy arms erect, sparring over who would get to deposit his semen inside Eileen Pope next.

Eileen Pope was nearly finished getting pregnant. She was as fertilized as a genetically modified cornfield in Kansas, and was getting ready to lay millions of squirming eggs. Eileen Pope was still hungry, too.

Eileen Pope decided she would eat Grant Wallace soon, and then she could go find a dark, protected place to build her foaming mass of eggs.

Johnny McKeon did not notice the breeding swarm of bugs as he walked out into Grasshopper Jungle carrying his box of refuse.

The box Johnny carried was full of VHS porno movies.

The movies were made in a place called the San Fernando Valley, which is near Los Angeles, California.

Johnny McKeon did not enjoy watching pornography anymore. He had grown out of that preoccupation. Johnny would have given the tapes to Ollie Jungfrau, but Ollie stayed home from work at *Tipsy Cricket Liquors* that day.

Ollie was lucky.

Ollie Jungfrau would have wanted those movies. Ollie was a connoisseur of porn, and he especially enjoyed sex films from the 1980s, which was when these particular ones had been made.

It was just past 8:00 on Thursday evening.

Ingrid was still sleeping beneath the desk in my bedroom.

Will Wallace was driving home from the *Tally-Ho!* in Waterloo. Will Wallace was drunk. He glanced at himself repeatedly in his rearview mirror, and he thought about the young man from Vinton, Iowa, who had been hitting on him during happy hour at the *Tally-Ho!*

The man who'd been hitting on Will Wallace was a paramedic. He was handsome and lonely. Will Wallace wondered what it would be like if he tried being queer. He had never *experimented* when he was a teenager, but he tried to imagine himself doing something sexual with the handsome young paramedic from Vinton. Will Wallace was drunk and excited by the thought. He was very horny by the time he got to Ealing. Will knew what he would do to his wife as soon as he got the chance.

Will Wallace had a vasectomy.

He thought about buying some condoms at *Tipsy Cricket Liquors*, just in case he ever got especially drunk and daring with anyone in Waterloo.

Will Wallace tried calling home on his cell phone, but there was no answer. Sometimes his wife got angry at him for coming home drunk after hanging out at Waterloo, Iowa's one and only gay bar. Will assumed his wife was not answering her phone because she was mad at him. The actual reason she was not picking up her phone was that she had been eaten by Grant Wallace, who was at one time Will's son.

Will Wallace decided to make amends for flirting with a gay man. He stopped off at *Satan's Pizza* and ordered a surprise *Stanpreme* for his wife and children. For dessert, he thought his wife, whose name was Dorothy, would like something sweet and alcoholic. So Will Wallace drove across the street to *Tipsy Cricket Liquors*, where he planned to buy some condoms for himself, and coffee liqueur and vanilla ice cream for Dorothy Wallace.

It was not such a good idea.

Here is what happened at Grasshopper Jungle while I watched and dreamed about Shann and Robby dancing together:

Johnny McKeon dropped his box of VHS pornos at his feet. He said something like *What the hey?* or *Ain't that strange?* when he saw the six-foot-tall bugs that buzzed and vibrated around the abandoned sofa in the alley.

Johnny McKeon never cussed.

Eileen Pope was crunching her way down through Grant Wallace's triangular head. Grant was still pumping his semen into her oviduct and his pinchers clamped rigidly into Eileen's thorax. One of Grant Wallace's arms broke off and it flexed, opened and closed, opened and closed, wriggling in the stew of piss and insect semen on the asphalt of Grasshopper Jungle.

Tyler Jacobson, one of the other Hoover Boys who was now a six-foot-tall, tooth-armed monster, picked up Grant Wallace's twitching arm and began eating it like a massive stalk of celery. Roger Baird, the remaining Hoover Boy bug, attempted to mount Eileen Pope and impregnate her as she ate Grant Wallace, who was also still joined with Eileen in the final act of making future clusters of little Grant Wallace larvae inside her.

Hungry Jack rotated his head toward the sound of the crashing box of porno tapes. His arms spiked high and his useless wings flared out from the carapace coverings along his backside. It was an impressive and threatening pose for a large male mantis. Then Hungry Jack came scuttling straight across the alley at Johnny McKeon.

Johnny probably said *What the hey?* again and fell back through the open door to *From Attic to Seller Consignment Store*.

Will Wallace was just pulling up to the front of *Tipsy Cricket Liquors*. He was horny and drunk, and the inside of his Volvo smelled like a *Stanpreme*. He did not even notice Travis Pope standing in front of *The Pancake House*. Will Wallace just took Travis Pope for someone having a cigarette break, as opposed to someone who had been transformed by *Contained MI Plague Strain 412E* into a gigantic carnivorous bug that was more powerful than a wild tiger.

By the time Will Wallace's eye caught hold of the unnatural form of Travis Pope, he was already within striking range of Travis's lightning-fast barbed arms. Travis Pope wasn't exactly hungry, but prey excited him as much as Eileen Pope's oviduct did.

Travis fired his clawed arms at Will Wallace and crushed Will's rib cage between them. Will Wallace did not even have time to gasp.

Travis carried Will Wallace, who thrashed and kicked uselessly, into *The Pancake House*. Travis Pope smeared Will Wallace's hair through a puddle of imitation-maple-flavored syrup. Then Travis ate him like a piece of French toast.

Johnny McKeon managed to slam shut the thick, solid-core door that opened from his secondhand store onto the back alley at Grasshopper Jungle. Johnny had stumbled upon the scene of cannibalistic bugs as big as grizzly bears that fucked and ate at the same time, which were the two things that bugs like to do.

Hungry Jack was a mere half second too slow to catch Johnny McKeon. As Johnny bolted shut the door, Hungry Jack punched his spiked arms into the wood. The barbs on Hungry Jack's arms bored two-thirds of the way through the door.

Bugs are not smart.

Hungry Jack could have easily hammered the door into toothpicks.

As soon as the door was shut, Hungry Jack forgot all about Johnny McKeon. Although he knew he was still hungry, Hungry Jack went back to wait on another turn with Eileen Pope.

Eileen Pope and the two surviving Hoover Boys were gone.

Hungry Jack sniffed and sniffed at the air, trying to smell her, but Eileen Pope was no longer emitting the powerful hormones that had attracted him and the other males in the first place.

Johnny McKeon was smart.

Since the break-in at *Tipsy Cricket Liquors* the previous Friday, Johnny had installed an alarm system that connected his businesses to the Iowa State Patrol.

Johnny McKeon activated his alarm.

The Iowa State Patrol, which operated from a substation in Waterloo, was alerted to an emergency at the Ealing Mall. A patrol car with a state trooper from Waterloo was on its way.

It was not a good idea.

At that moment, it was early morning in Germany. My brother, Eric Szerba, was lying on his back in a hospital bed. An intravenous needle pumped drugs and fluids into his arm, and other things had been taped to his body to tell whether or not Eric Szerba was still alive.

A thin plastic tube had been inserted into the opening of Eric Szerba's penis so he could urinate.

The tube was manufactured in Ohio.

It was called a catheter, as opposed to a Nightingale.

Eric pushed numbers on the display of a cell phone. Eric Szerba was calling me, but I left my phone inside my house. Eric Szerba would not have known that cell phones do not work in Eden.

Eric Szerba was also crying.

Ingrid rolled herself out from her place at my desk. She went across the room and pulled a pair of my discarded blue Iowa plaid boxers out from under the bed. She sniffed the boxers and rested her damp nose in them. This is what Ingrid did sometimes when she was lonely, or when she needed to take her mind off shitting.

It was Ingrid's silent way of kissing me.

Ah Wong Sing, who most people called *Louis*, kissed Connie Brees one last time before leaving the Del Vista Arms. Connie was in the shower. She was standing naked in the same grimy tub where I took a shower Tuesday before school. I had also vomited in that same bathroom.

Louis pulled the yellowed curtain back and looked at Connie Brees. He wanted to have sex again, but Connie told him no because her son would probably be home any minute now.

Connie Brees had to get ready for work.

She took two Xanax as soon as Ah Wong Sing left the apartment.

When the song finished playing, Shann kissed Robby and told him thank you for dancing.

It was not the kind of kiss I hoped to see. Shann kissed the side of Robby's cheek. I stared at Robby's perfect neck and jaw. Shann's breasts looked especially full and heavy beneath the shimmer of her jumpsuit. Robby was a little embarrassed. He knew what I was thinking.

Robby always knew what I was thinking.

Robby Brees turned red when Shann kissed him.

I lit a cigarette.

———

LUCKY, IN POLISH BOY NAMES

GOOD BOOKS ARE about everything.

This is my history.

Andrzej Szczerba and Herman Weinbach became great friends.

Andrzej Szczerba was also my great-grandfather.

After they left the soup kitchen in Ames, Andrzej Szczerba and

Herman Weinbach walked through the night. They tried to find a place where they could sleep and stay warm. They fed bread crumbs to Baby, who almost immediately began to impersonate Herman Weinbach.

Herman habitually used expressions like *Ach!* And *Nu?*

Baby began saying *Ach* and *Nu*, too. Andrzej thought it was funny.

The boys believed they were headed toward California, but the following day they took a ride from a family whose pickup truck had been loaded with all their household belongings, and Herman Weinbach and Andrzej Szczerba ended up at an abandoned farm outside of a place called Midvale, which was also in Iowa.

Nobody even knew the boys had moved themselves into the place.

They lived there together, with Baby, a talking European starling, for nearly a year. On their third night in the abandoned farmhouse, Andrzej Szczerba and Herman Weinbach slept together. Herman Weinbach was homosexual.

At first, Andrzej found the situation to be awkward and frustrating.

What Herman Weinbach and Andrzej Szczerba did together evolved into something substantially more than an *experiment*. So Andrzej was confused, very much like his great-grandson, who would also be named Andrzej. But Andrzej Szczerba also enjoyed the closeness of sleeping with Herman Weinbach.

Andrzej had never kissed any person other than his mother, Eva Nightingale, and his father, Krzys Szczerba, in his entire life. Young Andrzej enjoyed kissing Herman Weinbach very much. Herman Weinbach was experienced, and Andrzej felt tremendous pleasure and satisfaction in sharing the sex the two of them enjoyed together.

Nobody knew anything about Andrzej and Herman.

They fell as deeply in love with each other as anyone in the entire history of mankind.

That is the truth.

Andrzej loved Herman, but he told him he would never become a Communist.

Herman Weinbach laughed about that.

Baby imitated everything the boys said to each other.

Baby said, *Ach! Being a Communist homosexual Jew in Iowa is like being a bird that speaks Polish.* And Baby also said, *I believe I am in love with you, Herman Weinbach* and *I love you with all of my heart, Andrzej Szczerba.*

The boys hunted and scrounged, sometimes begging for food to stay alive. They were very happy together in Midvale. Nobody bothered them at all. Baby flew around the house with them, and every night Andrzej and Herman slept together in their lovers' bed. They had found the bed in the home's attic on the morning after their initial *experiment.* They had pulled the bed down to the home's living room so they could sleep beside the fireplace, where they burned furniture and sometimes even the doors from kitchen cupboards to stay warm.

They loved each other.

In January of 1934, Herman Weinbach became ill with pneumonia. He died while Andrzej held him in bed.

Andrzej Szczerba was completely lost without Herman.

Andrzej asked the bird, *What am I going to do, Baby?*

Andrzej cried for days and days without leaving the house. Finally, Andrzej Szczerba wrapped Herman Weinbach's gray body in their bedclothes and he carried his friend out into the frozen winter.

Baby flitted around Andrzej Szczerba and lit on his collar or atop his head as the boy toiled at digging Herman Weinbach's grave.

All the while the bird sang out about how much Herman loved Andrzej, and vice versa. Baby said things that were sexual and suggestive, too—things the boys sometimes said to each other openly in the solitude of their squatter's home.

Andrzej Szczerba was like me in many ways. He was confused and troubled by things, and he loved his friend as much as it was possible to love anyone. But there were those things that set Andrzej Szerba apart from me, too.

This is what happened:

Andrzej knew he had to leave Midvale after he buried Herman Weinbach on the old farm. Maybe it was that he was crazy with grief. I believe that is the truth. Andrzej knew he could not keep Baby with him any longer. Baby said too many things that could make problems for a young man in Iowa in 1934. Andrzej Szczerba was eighteen years old in 1934.

Andrzej Szczerba killed his bird and left the farmhouse in Midvale, Iowa, on the same evening he buried Herman Weinbach's body in a ruined cornfield.

That spring, Andrzej Szczerba found himself in Iowa City. He was still greatly tormented over the things he had done with Herman Weinbach, and about losing everything he had ever loved.

Andrzej Szczerba needed to prove something to himself.

In this way, he was very much like me.

He found a job cleaning up at a butcher's shop. There, Andrzej met a young woman named Phoebe Hildebrandt. Phoebe Hildebrandt was plain and uninteresting at seventeen years of age. Her father was the butcher who had hired Andrzej to clean.

They knew my great-grandfather as Andrew Szerba.

Phoebe Hildebrandt and her father, whose name was Edmund, both took pity on Andrew because of his age, the softness of his features, and how quiet and sad the boy was. They never knew anything about Andrew's love for a boy named Herman Weinbach.

Andrew Szerba, whose Polish name was my name, Andrzej, also had bags under his eyes.

Andrzej means man in Polish boy names.

One night in June, Andrzej Szczerba and Phoebe Hildebrandt went for a walk. Andrzej forced himself sexually onto Phoebe. Phoebe Hildebrandt did not resist his advances.

Phoebe cried. Sexual intercourse was painful. She lay on her back in the dirt, wondering how long it would take for him to finish. But she also allowed Andrzej Szczerba to insert his erect penis into her vagina. The act hurt Phoebe Hildebrandt, who was a virgin.

Andrzej Szczerba wanted to find something out about himself, which he did. He found out he thought only about Herman Weinbach while he engaged in sexual intercourse with Phoebe Hildebrandt.

Afterward, Andrzej Szczerba was disgusted in himself, and he was disgusted by Phoebe and her uninteresting personality, too.

But Andrzej Szczerba's semen found its way deep into Phoebe Hildebrandt's body from that unloving sexual act in June of 1934 outside a place called Iowa City, Iowa.

Phoebe Hildebrandt was my great-grandmother.

In 1935, a boy named Felek Szczerba was born. This happened only two months after Andrzej and Phoebe were married.

Andrzej Szczerba never put his penis inside Phoebe Hildebrandt again after that first time beside a dirt road in Iowa City.

And that was our day. You know what I mean.

Andrzej loved Felek, his son, as much as he had ever loved anything, but Andrzej Szczerba was very unhappy.

Felek means lucky in Polish boy names.

Felek Szczerba's American name was Felix Szerba.

Felix Szerba was my grandfather.

MOVIE NIGHT IN EDEN

THE THEATER IN Eden had half as many seats as the *Cinezaar* in Waterloo.

It was comfortable and clean. Like everything in Eden, the theater sat unused, brand-new, and at the same time it had been preserved like some kind of fossil.

This was where we learned the most about the history of McKeon Industries, and about the things that started happening up above us in Ealing after the unfortunate coincidence of Tyler Jacobson dropping the globe of *Contained MI Plague Strain 412E* directly onto Robby Brees's blood.

The screen of the *Edenzaar* was a bit smaller than the screen in Waterloo. The projector sat on a stand, atop a raised platform behind the rows of crushed velvet seats. But all things considered, it was one of the nicer movie venues in this part of Iowa.

Growing up, Robby Brees had always been *projector monitor* in our classes at Curtis Crane Lutheran Academy. He knew everything about how to operate a 16 mm film projector. It took no effort to get him to volunteer to see what had been left behind in Eden for our viewing pleasure.

As he searched through the cabinets behind us, Shann and I took seats in the back row. I slid my hand into the warm spot between Shann's thighs.

I said, "Eden Five needs you."

Shann said, "Eden Five has to wait until Eden Five grows up."

Robby held up a big steel canister of film and told us the movie inside was called *Five Easy Pieces*.

I thought it was a funny name, especially since I was *Eden 5*. I was waiting, too. I thought I *was* grown up. I wished Shann would ask me to go back to one of the dorm rooms with her while Robby *experimented* with the projector.

"Never heard of it," I said.

"It's from 1970. And it's probably the greatest movie ever made," Robby answered.

Robby missed being born at the right time by four decades.

My father, Eric Andrew Szerba, was ten years old in 1970.

Eric Andrew Szerba's Polish name would be *Arek Andrzej Szczerba*.

His father, Felek, who everyone called *Felix*, was thirty-five when *Five Easy Pieces* was made.

"You should have been alive in the seventies, Rob," I said.

"Hell yes," Robby affirmed.

We did not watch *Five Easy Pieces* that night. Robby found another stack of canisters that were labeled *Eden Orientation Series*. It felt like we were being indoctrinated into an army or some shit like that. And I hoped it was an army for repopulating the planet, so it made me very horny to think about my mission down here in Eden with Shann and Robby.

"Duty calls," I said.

Shann said, "Huh?"

I told Robby it was our duty to get oriented.

"We owe it to the world, and to history, to watch *Eden Orientation Series*, Robby," I pointed out.

There were three film reels in all. Robby and I noticed they were numbered One of Five, Two of Five, and Three of Five.

Two canisters of the five films were missing.

Robby also found reels of a film called *A Clockwork Orange*, but Reels Four and Five of *Eden Orientation Series* were nowhere in the theater.

That was because those particular reels were up on the roof at Grasshopper Jungle. They were there when we found a plastic flamingo with a steel spike coming out of its ass, a grimacing lemur mask that makes your face stink, and two bottles of wine, one of which Robby and I drank on Monday night in his bedroom at the Del Vista Arms.

It took me and Robby a while to figure that part out.

Not too long, though. We were probably a little more intelligent than most cave people.

You know what I mean.

Robby Brees fed the leader of Reel One into the projector, and a grainy numbered countdown squiggled and danced on the screen in front of us.

Robby hopped over the seats and sat beside me.

I was in the middle of Shann and Robby. I was always in the middle of them. It made me feel horny and awkward, too.

Most boys would have sat next to Shann.

Boys from Curtis Crane Lutheran Academy would never sit without an empty seat between them at a movie theater. That's what Lutheran boys do. They project their fear of being thought of as homosexual, so they do uncomfortable things like sit with empty seats between them, and then end up wondering if they or their friend on the other side of their sexual buffer zone might be curious about being gay. The uptight straight-kid Lutheran Boy Code of Conduct mandates the maintenance of THE EMPTY SEAT between boys in a movie theater, so you don't get any funny ideas about your friend, and nobody looking at you will think you're queer, either.

Lutheran Boys in Iowa know those rules and follow them like lemmings on a springtime jog.

But not Robby Brees. He sat so close to me, our knees rubbed against each other.

Shann knew Robby was in love with me.

How could she *not* know it?

She probably knew I loved Robby, too. I said it when we danced, after all. And I meant it. Shann definitely knew I was in love with her, too.

What was I going to do?

I felt nervous and guilty when Shann held my hand and Robby's knee pressed so comfortably against mine.

"I wonder if they have any popcorn in the cafeteria," Shann said.

"Or ice cream," Robby added. He touched my hand with his fingers. It electrified me.

"Call the roller of big cigars," I said.

That was the first line from my favorite poem, The Emperor of Ice-Cream.

The line sounded so sexually suggestive. It was like something Herman Weinbach might have said to his lover, Andrzej Szczerba. I felt myself turning a brilliant, heated red.

The film's sound came on just then.

And there was the face of Dr. Grady McKeon.

THE GOOD DOCTOR ACCOUNTS FOR HISTORY

DR. GRADY MCKEON looked like an old movie star.

Well, he looked like an old movie star with a slight twitch in his right eye, which was magnified through the thick lenses of his black-framed glasses. Dr. Grady McKeon looked like an old movie star with a psychopath's twitch in his eye. He looked calm and reassuring, how you might imagine a serial killer to look at you while he was sharpening his knives and discussing which parts of your body produce the best-tasting sausage meat.

Dr. Grady McKeon also had a very small L-shaped scar between his eyebrows. When he was twelve years old, Grady McKeon was struck in the head by an unoccupied wooden swing. The swing was unoccupied because he had just pushed his younger sister, whose name was Arlene, onto her face.

Grady McKeon did not want his sister to be on the swing.

Arlene was not very talented when it came to sitting on things like bench seats on swings. In 1974, she fell from a ski lift in Jackson Hole and died.

Jackson Hole is in Wyoming.

Arlene was a real dynamo on snow skis. Not so much on ski lifts.

Dr. Grady McKeon was comfortable narrating the filmed history of his life's accomplishments. Grady McKeon's hair was perfect. He carried a strong resemblance to Shann's stepfather, Johnny McKeon, who was Grady McKeon's decades-younger and immensely less talented brother. Also, Grady McKeon had never physically abused Johnny the way he had inflicted harm on their sister, Arlene.

Arlene McKeon was also Miss Iowa in 1969.

Iowans love shapely young women with names that have lots of long rhyming vowels, even if their brothers are psychopaths.

The film was in black and white, but I feel safe making the claim that Dr. Grady McKeon's hair was the color of Smith Brothers licorice cough drops, and his skin was the same color as French vanilla non-dairy creamer.

Dr. Grady McKeon wore a blue-and-white Eden jumpsuit, too.

His jumpsuit was monogrammed, the same way a doctor's smock at a hospital would be. The monogram said:

DR. GRADY
EDEN
1

Reel One opened with Dr. Grady McKeon's personal message to the audience. It was a frighteningly sober introduction, despite the fact that Dr. Grady McKeon maintained a comforting butcher's smile while he spoke.

Dr. Grady McKeon looked like he was floating on a fistful of little blue kayaks. He could have easily been sitting across from us at a desk, selling us his top-of-the-line casket for our departed loved ones. Whoever that might be.

After his introduction, the film went through a history of McKeon Industries from its founding in 1957 through 1971, which was the year the *Eden Orientation Series* films were produced.

In 1971, a film called *The French Connection* won the Academy Award for Best Picture. Voting members of the Academy probably did not get a chance to see *Eden Orientation Series*.

This is exactly what Dr. Grady McKeon said at the beginning of his film:

> *Welcome to the Eden Project, my friends.*
> *Welcome, welcome.*
> *If there are any McKeon family members in the*
> *audience, would you please stand and make your presence*
> *known?*

This is where Dr. Grady McKeon smiled and nodded and panned his head from one side of the screen to the other, as though he could somehow look out at us from his black-and-white celluloid universe.

"Stand up, Shann," I said.

"Stand up," Robby urged.

"This is so dumb," Shann said.

Shann stood up. Robby and I clapped for her.

Shann said, "Shut up."

Then Dr. Grady McKeon nodded and continued:

> *Thank you.*
> *Each of you is fortunate to be part of the Eden*
> *Project. You are fortunate to have survived, but you also*
> *bear a tremendous responsibility to mankind.*
> *You must breed, my friends. You must breed.*

"You heard the man," I blurted out.

Shann said, "Shhh—"

Dr. Grady McKeon seemed to pause, anticipating the instructions he delivered might cause nervous comments among his audience.

Robby said, "Uh."

And Grady McKeon continued:

> *The event that brought you here today was one of*
> *two things.*
> *First, if there has been nuclear fallout detected in*
> *the atmosphere, you would have been directed into the*
> *showers upon arrival. The world above is no longer*
> *habitable. You will be alerted as to when it will be*
> *appropriate to return to the surface. Until that time,*
> *this is the New World, my friends, and you all are the*
> *New Men and Women. The men and women of*
> *the future.*
> *You have a responsibility to breed.*
> *Do not despair.*

I was not despairing.

Here, Dr. Grady McKeon looked very serious and clinical. The camera zoomed in so Dr. Grady McKeon's face occupied the entire screen. Grady McKeon's twitching right eyeball was as big as an Ozark watermelon. Dr. Grady McKeon stared directly out from the screen with the same expression a doctor performing a physical gets just as he grabs your balls and tells you to cough.

When a doctor grabs your balls, how can you think about coughing?

Coughing when someone is grabbing your balls requires as much concentration as riding a unicycle while carrying an Ozark watermelon.

History shows that when your balls are being grabbed, you can only think about your balls and nothing else.

"See? I told you that's why we're here," I said. "Eden Five needs us."

Shann pointed out that there was no nuclear war taking place at the moment.

"Nobody's dropped any bombs," Shann said.

It was something of a disappointment to me.

"Oh," I said.

Robby said, "Um."

Then Dr. Grady McKeon went on:

> Second, in the event of a 412E alert, the world aboveground will unfortunately become an interspecies battlefield, tremendously dangerous for human beings. You must pay close attention to all the training films we have prepared. Your survival—and the future of humanity—depend on this.
>
> Pay attention and breed, my friends.
>
> Breed.

> *If the flamingo at the entry chamber did not activate a warning signal upon your arrival, then you are all safe and free from 412E contamination.*
>
> *Make note: If the 412E event is more than twenty-four hours into its cycle, you must not return to the surface unless you have prepared the appropriate tools.*
>
> *You will be instructed, my friends.*
>
> *This is your new world, and you are the new race.*
>
> *You are Unstoppable.*
>
> *Please, do not despair my friends. I think you will enjoy living in this most remarkable world.*
>
> *Live in love. Live in love.*
>
> *Eden is love, my friends.*
>
> *In Eden, a new human race will begin. It is your duty to do this. You will find the Eden Project Compound to have sufficient resources for years, perhaps decades. You must prepare to recapture the world from the mantid armies above. If you have arrived within the window of infestation, then you may be able to halt what will invariably be the end of the world.*
>
> *But you must act.*
>
> *Pay careful attention, my friends.*
>
> *Pay careful attention and breed.*

Then Dr. Grady McKeon smiled a very creepy smile, like he was imagining pornos from Eden. I happened to be imagining pornos from Eden, too, and they involved the three of us: me, Shann, and Robby.

The introduction shot lap-dissolved into old newsreel clips

that took us through the history of Ealing, Iowa, and its most notorious scientist, Dr. Grady McKeon, founder of McKeon Industries.

Robby said, "What a fucking psycho."

Robby and I never dropped f-bombs.

Obviously, he was as impacted by Dr. Grady McKeon as I was, even if I did appreciate the frequent directive to have sex down there in our new world.

Shann squirmed in her seat. She said, "Uh. Am I wrong about something, or do you two boys actually *know* something more than I do about what he's talking about?"

I said, "Uh."

Robby said, "Uh."

UNSTOPPABLE CORN! UNSTOPPABLE CORN!

ALL ROADS INTERSECTED at our feet.

We watched the first three reels of *Eden Orientation Series*.

This is what we learned:

Dr. Grady McKeon's original business venture, which he founded in Ealing, Iowa, in 1957, which was the same year that his little baby brother, Johnny, came into the world, initially developed fertilizers aimed at increasing corn yields. At that time, McKeon Industries had a workforce of three scientists, one secretary, and a man who drove packages in his pickup truck and swept the floors of the old service station Grady McKeon had taken out on lease. The fertilizer produced was a tremendous hit throughout the Corn Belt, and McKeon Industries expanded rapidly.

In 1961, which was the year after my father, Eric Andrew Szerba, was born, McKeon Industries moved into its main plant, the one that recently shut down in Ealing. At the new facility, Dr. Grady McKeon unveiled the redesigned company symbol.

The Great Seal of McKeon Industries looked like something you might find in an Ayn Rand novel.

Ayn Rand was an author who had no books at all on the shelves of Dr. Grady McKeon's library in Eden.

The new symbol for McKeon Industries depicted a gigantic woman, sitting calmly with her legs folded beneath her, apparently gazing out from her two-hundred-foot-high face upon the beautiful and fruitful fields of Iowa. She had an expression like she had just swallowed some blue kayaks.

They would have naturally been full-sized kayaks, since the woman was as tall as an oil derrick.

Arranged before her bare knees (she was wearing a modestly styled dress that adequately covered her perfect thighs), like a child's toys at Christmas, were hand-sized factories with smokestacks, a gleaming and modern steel locomotive, and, for whatever reason, a trio of bare-chested men in overalls working behind what looked like yoked teams of oxen.

Ahead of the unnaturally enormous woman, perfect rows of sequoia-sized cornstalks grew, stretching off forever into the Iowa horizon. And inscribed around the curving edge at the bottom of the McKeon Seal were the words:

INFINITA FRUMENTA! INFINITA FRUMENTA!

Infinita frumenta! is Latin for Unstoppable Corn! or some shit like that.

You could pretty much put anything you wanted to in Latin at the bottom of a picture and people in Iowa would either beat you up, or think you were a messenger from God.

Dr. Grady McKeon believed he was God.

He preached the gospel of *infinita frumenta*.

History provides evidence that *infinita frumenta* made Dr. Grady McKeon one of the Cold War's largest profiteers. His success entirely resulted from an accident of nature.

In Reel Two of *Eden Orientation Series*, Dr. Grady McKeon narrated from off-camera as we saw clips of hardworking scientists in perfectly clean white lab coats, while they peered into microscopes and tilted their cigarettes with smirking intelligence and engaged in academic discussions with one another.

Scientists loved a good smoke back in the 1960s.

There were also ashtrays built in to the armrests of the Eden theater. When Robby and I saw those smart, hardworking scientists lighting up their *fags*, we couldn't resist the urge to join them.

It was our duty to smoke along with the *Eden Orientation Series*.

"Ahhh . . . ," I said, after I took a drag.

"Ahhh . . . ," Robby said.

In the 1960s, *infinita frumenta* meant that McKeon Industries was working toward the development of corn plants that could not be eaten by insects.

Unstoppable Corn.

Like smoking cigarettes on the job, they probably thought Unstoppable Corn was a good idea at the time.

Scientists working for Dr. Grady McKeon experimented with corn.

I know that's an oddly funny thing to say, and I may have to strike that line from my history book, but that's what they did.

They *experimented* with corn.

Scientists at McKeon Industries, like Robby Brees and I, had no idea what the results of their experiment would be, but they did it anyway.

Dr. Grady McKeon and his colleagues attempted to blend genetic material from the semen of grasshoppers into the pollen from corn plants.

Pollen is plant sperm.

It was not a good idea.

The corn they produced from their plant-sperm-and-grasshopper-semen experiment was lively and strong. It was also true that, as hoped, bugs would not eat it. It was unstoppable. Dr. Grady McKeon was very happy. His company's stock was worth an incalculable fortune.

Fortune is also an odd word.

Unfortunately, the corn that was produced by the plant-sperm-and-grasshopper-semen experiment at McKeon Industries also caused an undesirable side effect in teenage boys: Their balls dissolved.

Testicular dissolution among developing adolescent males, is how Dr. Grady McKeon described it.

That sounded nicer.

If a doctor told me, "You are merely experiencing testicular dissolution," it would not frighten me nearly as much as if he said, "Your balls are going to dissolve, Austin."

Actually, the scientists from McKeon Industries at first concluded that their Unstoppable Corn only caused boys undergoing puberty to have their balls dissolve. That was because the slightest amount of Unstoppable Corn affected adolescent boys that way. Ultimately it was discovered that Unstoppable Corn would pretty much dissolve anyone's balls if you ate enough of it, and if you also had balls.

Enough of it turned out to be about an ear and a half.

The corn that was harvested in all the McKeon farms across Iowa that year was shipped as a goodwill gesture from the United States of America to the people of Canada.

That was the end of Reel Two.

Robby and I both squirmed at the thought of eating some of the McKeon plant-sperm-and-grasshopper-semen corn. We also felt sorry for Canada.

"I am *never* eating anything with corn in it again," Robby said.

"Do they even *make* food that doesn't have corn in it in Iowa?" Shann asked.

"Uh," Robby said.

I wondered, "Did Dr. Grady McKeon ever get married?"

"It seems like he probably practiced breeding a lot," Robby said.

"He never was married," Shann answered.

"Maybe he ate some of his own corn," I suggested.

"I need a cigarette," Robby said.

We found out later that Dr. Grady McKeon, indeed, did not eat his own corn and experience testicular dissolution. You will see.

INFINITA FRUMENTA! INFINITA FRUMENTA!

THREE OF FIVE

REEL THREE, WHICH was the final part of the film we saw that night, ended on a cliffhanger.

Dr. Grady McKeon's *Eden Orientation Series Part Three* was a true corker.

At the end of it, all I could say at first was, "Holy shit."

Robby said, "Holy shit."

Here is what happened in Reel Three:

Fortunately for Dr. Grady McKeon and his company, it turned out that during the 1960s anything that could look like corn *and* make your balls dissolve was of tremendous interest to the Department of Defense. McKeon Industries received its first of many lucrative contracts to develop Unstoppable Weapons and, later, Unstoppable Soldiers.

That was how the six-foot-tall, tooth-armed mantises that were more powerful than grizzly bears came about. But that was through an accident of nature, too.

By 1965, McKeon Industries employed 2,700 people in Ealing, Iowa.

In 1965, Ealing, Iowa, was a Cold War boomtown.

That year, my father, Eric Andrew Szerba, who had been baptized in the Catholic Church, enrolled in kindergarten.

After the mishap with the grasshopper-semen-and-plant-sperm experiment, McKeon Industries went to work on a variety of theoretical methods aimed at stopping the global spread of Communism. There were multiple units within the scientific department at McKeon Industries, each of which was developing its own creative anti-Communist ideas.

One of the units worked with the Unstoppable Corn material. In that particular lab, scientists attempted to invent some type of delivery system that would result in the testicular dissolution of enemy armies.

Nobody would ever take an army of Communists without balls seriously.

Another of the units worked on a human replication project. It was a first attempt to actually clone soldiers. That was where the human head, penis, and the praying hands in the jars came from. Robby and I found those when we broke into Johnny McKeon's office the night we climbed up on the roof at Grasshopper Jungle. The Human Replication Unit was also where the little two-headed boy was created.

We found this out later.

Reel Three of *Eden Orientation Series* involved Robby and me in ways we never anticipated.

This was how it happened:

The film showed how the Unstoppable Corn lab team had been extracting cellular material from crop yields that had been stored in a silo on one of the remaining McKeon Industries Unstoppable Corn farms.

Their goal was to dissolve Russian balls around the world.

Later, I did find out by researching archived records in Eden that President Richard Nixon also brought some of Dr. Grady McKeon's Unstoppable Corn to China as a gift. In what was called Eden's *Brain Room*, I discovered a black-and-white photograph that showed the prime minister of China, a man whose name was Chou En-lai, eating some of Dr. Grady McKeon's Unstoppable Corn while the president of the United States of America looked on and smiled warmly.

Prime Minister Chou En-lai's balls dissolved.

When the Unstoppable Corn team began off-loading silos of Unstoppable Corn in Iowa, they discovered the corn, when decaying, produced a new variety of mold that they had never seen before. They had never seen it before because the mold was an accident of nature. The mold gave off a blue photoluminescent glow.

This second accident of nature became known as *Plague Strain 412E.*

There was no significance to the *412E* part of the name. The marketing division of McKeon Industries believed the name sounded good for a sales pitch to the Defense Department, as though it came about after hundreds of trials and tests. In reality, *412E* was just an accident of nature that occurred when scientists attempted to splice together the genetic material from grasshopper semen with plant sperm and fertilize corn with it.

Scientists at McKeon Industries took the mold into their labs, where they grew great heaps of the stuff inside long glass boxes that looked like massive aquariums. They didn't know what to do with the mold, but they were fascinated by the sponge-like form of the mold, and how it moved and pulsated, and gave off light.

Despite seeing it in the black-and-white film, Robby and I recognized the familiar glow of the *412E* mold when the camera captured its luminescence after the scientists in the film turned off the laboratory's lights.

Dr. Grady McKeon, the film's narrator, said this:

Behold the wondrous glow of a new being!

I said, "Uh."

Shann said, "He's a little overly impressed by something that looks like rotten cauliflower."

"That's the same shit Johnny had in his office," Robby said.

"*What* is?" Shann asked.

"*That* shit," I said.

Robby added, "Um. Yeah."

Robby Brees and I had some explaining to do.

"Your stepfather," I said. "He had some of that stuff inside his office at *From Attic to Seller Consignment Store*. Robby and I saw it."

"When were *you* inside Johnny's office?" Shann asked.

"Shh—" Robby said, playing the part of the irritated moviegoer who is distracted by talkers in the theater. "Be quiet and listen to the film."

Here was where *Eden Orientation Series* turned into a horror show.

It turned into a horror show for two reasons.

First, the scientists who were working on the Unstoppable Corn/Unstoppable Soldier project decided to try mixing the genetic material from the mold with a fresh sample of human blood.

They decided to use Dr. Grady McKeon's own blood.

Dr. Grady McKeon thought of himself as a kind of God. So he drew his own blood to mix with the genetic material from the photoluminescent mold.

It was not a good idea.

The idea to mix human blood material with the *412E* mold was even less reasonable than laboratory scientists deciding it was a good idea to smoke on the job and screw around with grasshopper semen by grafting it into plant sperm and injecting it into corn seeds.

Dr. Grady McKeon's blood made the *412E* mold very happy.

Here was the beginning of the end of the world, and it took place in the 1960s.

"This is the shit that was drawn on the blackboard in the lecture hall," I said.

"Huh?" Shann said.

Robby said, "Uh-oh."

It was all starting to come together.

The roads were intersecting.

But it got worse, too.

I said, "Robby, hop back there and freeze the film on that part."

Robby, who was our *projector monitor*, said, "What?"

I said, "Back up to that part where the scientist is adding blood to the petri dish and stop it on *that* frame."

Robby did what I asked him to do.

And here was the second reason *Eden Orientation Series* truly turned into a horror show right before my eyes: The scientist who was feeding the human blood host to *412E*, who also happened to be starting an initial infestation event, looked exactly like my father, Eric Andrew Szerba.

Of course, the scientist in the film could not be my father because Eric Andrew Szerba would have been a kindergartner at exactly the same time that portion of the film was shot.

"Hey, Porcupine," Robby said, "that guy looks exactly like your dad."

I said, "Uh."

Shann agreed, "He *does* look exactly like your dad, Austin."

The film was grainy, but we all could see how the scientist's lab coat had been monogrammed with a name: Felix Szerba

It was my grandfather, Felek Szczerba, whose father, like me, had been born with the name Andrzej.

Felek Szczerba, whose American name was Felix Szerba, was the first victim of *McKeon Industries Plague Strain 412E.*

Nobody knew anything about it.

They sure found out fast, though.

As we let the film play through, Dr. Grady McKeon's voice spoke over a series of frozen pictures. The pictures showed the faces of the scientists and secretaries who worked with Felix Szerba at McKeon Industries. Dr. Grady McKeon explained how these brave patriots lost their lives while developing an Unstoppable Soldier to fight against Communism.

Unfortunately, the Unstoppable Soldiers McKeon Industries created were nothing more than accidents of nature resembling six-foot-tall praying mantises with lightning-fast arms that were studded with rows and rows of needle-sharp, barbed teeth.

Unstoppable Soldiers liked doing only two things: fucking and eating.

They were also nearly impossible to stop.

Dr. Grady McKeon said that, through research, scientists at McKeon Industries did find one way to stop his Unstoppable Soldiers.

And that was exactly when Reel Three of Five ended.

"We need to go back," I said.

Robby said, "Uh."

Shann said, "Back *where*?"

"We need to go back to Grasshopper Jungle. Robby and I need to go back up on the roof. We left something there," I said.

"What did you two leave up there?" Shann said.

I could have said a lot of things about what Robby Brees and I left behind up on the roof of Grasshopper Jungle.

I said, "The rest of this film is up there. Shann, we *need* to see the rest of this film."

Shann said, "Oh."

And Robby said, "And I think we need to hurry."

THE ORPHAN FELEK

FELEK SZCZERBA WAS nine years old when his father was killed.

It happened at a place called Cisterna.

Cisterna is in Italy.

Andrzej Szerba had joined the United States Army in 1942. He enlisted in the Army because he wanted to fight against Hitler, and because he was so unhappy living in Iowa with Phoebe Hildebrandt.

Andrzej Szczerba was homosexual, but nobody knew anything about that.

The only person who ever knew about Andrzej Szczerba's homosexuality was Herman Weinbach.

Herman Weinbach died from pneumonia in Midvale, Iowa, in 1934.

Andrzej Szczerba never got to meet Herman Weinbach's uncle, a man named Bruno Wojner, who performed with *Bruno's Amazing and Incredible Dogs* with a circus in California.

In the summer of 1944, Andrzej Szczerba was shot through the back of his head while he was crouching down to take a shit in a little place called Cisterna, Italy. He received a medal for getting killed while shitting.

Andrzej Szczerba's great-grandson, Eric Christopher Szerba, also received a medal for having his balls torn off by an unstoppable homemade bomb.

Dulce Et Decorum Est.

Felix Szerba was very intelligent. He graduated from high school in Iowa City at the age of fourteen. His mother, Phoebe Hildebrandt, remarried when Felek was ten years old.

Phoebe Hildebrandt began having sexual intercourse after the long lonely spell that followed the time Andrzej Szczerba stole her virginity and gave her his son, Felek.

Phoebe Hildebrandt hated Felek's name.

Against Felek's will, Phoebe Hildebrandt had her new husband, whose name was Daniel Barton, adopt the boy and change his name to Felix Barton. It is a little-known fact of history that I was nearly named Austin Barton, a name that has the kind of ringing sound Iowans appreciate.

Daniel Barton owned a radio station in Iowa City. He was fifty-two years old when he married Phoebe Hildebrandt in 1945.

Daniel Barton also had defective semen. He had a low sperm count, but Daniel Barton never knew anything about it. He never knew because his wife, Phoebe, became pregnant three times from three different men before Felix graduated from high school.

Daniel Barton was convinced he had very powerful sperm.

Phoebe Barton was a real dynamo at having sexual intercourse with numerous men in Iowa City.

Phoebe Barton was unstoppable. She liked doing exactly the same two things that bugs like to do.

Phoebe Barton never knew how much she would enjoy sexual intercourse until Andrzej Szczerba was shot in the head while taking a shit. Before that, Phoebe only believed that sexual intercourse was painful, interminably long, and sad—and that it would make you bleed. Phoebe Barton's three new children— a boy named Eldon Wayne and two girls, Chastity and Linda— were presumed by everyone to be full-blooded Bartons. Daniel Barton believed it, too.

Phoebe Barton's youngest daughter, whose name was Linda, was a product of semen that was produced in the testicles of Felix's high school physics teacher.

After Felix Barton, whose real name was Felek Szczerba but was called Felix Szerba by American people, graduated high school at the very young age of fourteen, Daniel Barton and his wife, Phoebe, enrolled the boy into Stanford University.

Stanford University is in a place called Palo Alto, California.

Palo Alto means tall stick in Spanish.

There are big trees near Stanford University.

Spanish missionaries were real good at naming shit.

Felix Barton was very lonely and unhappy in California. At Stanford, Felix tried to kill himself once by mixing chemicals that created a poisonous cloud of gas.

It was not a good idea.

Felix Barton only ended up burning the lining of his airways.

As a result, Felix Barton, who had been born Felek Szczerba, had a chronic cough for the rest of his life.

After he graduated the university, Felix had his name legally changed back to Felek Andrzej Szczerba. He sometimes went by Felix Szerba, because Americans get so uptight about all those bunched-up consonants and shit like that.

Felek married a Catholic Polish girl he met in California. His wife was named Ksenia. She was very beautiful. Ksenia Szczerba was my grandmother.

Unlike his adoptive father, Daniel Barton, Felek Szczerba did not have any problems at all with his sperm.

In 1960, when Felek was twenty-five years old, his first son, Arek Andrzej Szczerba, was born. Arek Andrzej Szczerba was my father, Eric Szerba.

Felek and Ksenia Szczerba had four more strong Polish sons together. Their names were Krzys, Mieszko, Gabrysz, and Jacek.

In 1965, Felek Szczerba and his family moved back to Iowa, to Ealing, where Felek accepted a position in the research laboratories at McKeon Industries.

In 1968, Felek Szczerba was killed in a motorcycle accident. The history recorded in the Waterloo paper described how Felek Szczerba apparently lost control of his motorcycle and ran himself beneath the wheels of a freight car that was carrying liquid fertilizer.

The fertilizer was made in Ealing, Iowa.

What actually happened to Felek Andrzej Szczerba that day was this: Felek Andrzej Szczerba hatched out.

Felek means lucky.

Felek Szczerba was the first Unstoppable Soldier.

PART 4:
THE END OF THE WORLD

SAINT KAZIMIERZ WAS not an Unstoppable Soldier.

When he was a teenager, his father ordered Kazimierz to lead the army of Poland to conquer Hungary. Some Catholic scholars claim Kazimierz refused to do it. They say Kazimierz did not refuse because he was afraid. Kazimierz refused because he thought it was unjust to go to war against Hungary. Some historians claim Kazimierz, who was only thirteen at the time, went to war, but was defeated.

Hungarians may have masturbated less often than Polish boys. This is probably true.

Kazimierz's father punished him for not going to war. It is difficult to imagine how you could punish a boy for *not* going to war. It is kind of like punishing a boy for skipping dinner by giving him cake.

In order to resist sexual temptation, Kazimierz wore a hair shirt, which was something coarse and irritating that was made from goats' hair. Devout people like Kazimierz would wear this garment as underwear so it would rub against their skin. The only purpose of a hair shirt is to cause injury and pain. Some historians claim that Saint Kazimierz may have worn his hair shirt in direct contact with his penis.

Hair shirts work like dynamos.

Nobody makes hair shirts nowadays.

———

WE, THE NEW HUMANS

I TOLD SHANN Collins everything that night.

I told her about what happened at Grasshopper Jungle. I said Grant Wallace and the Hoover Boys had broken into the place looking for alcohol, and that Robby Brees and I should not have been there, but we were. I told Shann Collins what we found inside Johnny McKeon's office, and how Tyler Jacobson dropped the glass universe and splattered what we knew was *412E* all over the alley behind *From Attic to Seller Consignment Store.*

This is what I said to Shann Collins: Robby Brees drove me out to Waterloo, so we could look into the future. We went to the *Tally-Ho!*, where a homeless man we called Hungry Jack stepped in front of the path of a speeding Dodge truck, and then this horrible creature hatched out of his body and ate him.

Shann had to go home. It was late.

Shann changed out of her Eden Project jumpsuit. She could not go home dressed in a strange uniform. Wendy McKeon, Shann Collins's mother, was one of those types of mothers who paid attention to things like what their children were wearing when they left the house. Wendy McKeon would ask questions, and we did not want anyone to know about Shann's silo.

Nobody knew anything at all about Eden.

Robby Brees and I kept our Eden Project jumpsuits on. We left all our clothes, except for our shoes, down inside the silo. Wearing the jumpsuits made us feel like we were an Army or something. It made us feel like we belonged together.

Anyway, Robby Brees and I had some shit to do.

Nobody would ever know if Robby and I didn't go home that night.

It was 8:30. Shann had missed dinner with her family. Her cell phone hadn't worked when we were down inside Eden. She was going to be in trouble. Good Lutheran kids in Iowa do not forget to come home for dinner with their families.

Coming up out of Eden under a big, black, star-filled Iowa sky made us feel like we were climbing from a spaceship and onto the surface of some alien world. Everything was different.

We were the New Humans.

That was exactly what Dr. Grady McKeon told us we were.

Robby waited for me in his old Ford Explorer, so I could walk Shann to the front door of the McKeon House. I asked her if she wanted me to say something to her mom or to Johnny McKeon, but Shann said no, that she was going to be in trouble and I couldn't possibly make things better.

So I hugged Shann. It felt really good squeezing my body against hers in my jumpsuit, like I wasn't wearing anything but my boxers. I kissed her for a long time and ran my hands up and down from her butt to her shoulders. I was trying to get her to accept Dr. Grady McKeon's advice about our mission. I had forgotten all about Robby waiting in his car and about big monstrous bugs. I pressed my hips into Shann's.

That was exactly when Shann whispered, "I think Robby is in love with you, Austin."

I felt a lump in my throat, and I asked Saint Kazimierz to make things okay.

"Uh," I said.

"I can tell he is," Shann said.

I said, "Is there something wrong with that?"

Shann backed away from me a half step. Her eyes tracked up and down, up and down, all over my body. Jumpsuits are no good for hiding erections. I tried to adjust myself.

Shann said, "Is there *something wrong* with that? Don't you think there's *something wrong* with that, Austin?"

"Uh," I said.

I honestly did not think there was anything wrong with Robby Brees being in love with me.

I was probably wrong about that.

Shann said, "Have you guys ever *done* anything?"

I felt all the blood draining out from every part of my body. It felt cold and wiggly.

"What do you mean? Like skate? We do lots of things," I said.

I do not lie. It is my job not to ever lie.

I wanted a cigarette.

"Have you ever kissed Robby?" Shann said.

I had to tell her. I loved Shann, and I do not lie.

"Um. Yes," I said.

"Oh," Shann said. "Like, I mean, a *real* kiss?"

"Yes, I did," I said.

I looked away. I was suddenly aware that Robby was waiting. I could hear the *clunk-clunk-clunk* of the old Ford's engine.

Shann backed up against the front door.

Then Shann said, "Have you and Robby ever had sex with each other?"

"Uh. Um," I said, "no."

I did not lie to her.

"Come on, Shann. Please." I said, "You know I am totally in love with you."

Shann looked as though I'd just kicked her in the stomach. She did not say another word. She went inside and closed the door behind her. I heard the sound of the deadbolt turning within the door's locking mechanism.

And that was my day. You know what I mean.

What was I going to do?

The end of the world was nearly one week old.

The end of the world was nearly one week old and only three people in Ealing knew about it: Me, Robby Brees, and Shann Collins.

LAST LEGS

ROBBY SLID A PACK of cigarettes across the top of the dashboard toward me when I climbed into his car.

He did not say anything.

I did not say anything.

Robby could tell something else had gone wrong. Another something else. Robby always knew everything about me.

I lit a cigarette.

The engine clunked and clunked.

"This car's on its last legs," I said.

DAVY CROCKETT AND DANIEL BOONE NEVER WORE COONSKIN CAPS

ROBBY TOOK ME home. I needed to get my history books, and Ingrid, too.

I wanted to take Ingrid with us to Eden.

Maybe I was crazy with grief. Maybe all the shit—thinking about my brother, Eric, my grandfather, Felek, and his lost and sad father, Andrzej, poor Herman Weinbach who loved him, Saint Kazimierz, Shann Collins, and the talking European starling named Baby—playing all of those thoughts through the reel-to-reel between my ears made me feel like I was all alone and standing on the edge of a razor blade.

Robby played one of his father's old cassette tapes in the Explorer. We listened to *Exile on Main Street*.

And the car shuddered past Curtis Crane Lutheran Academy, which was located in Ealing, Iowa, on *Main Street*.

"So. You want to tell me about it, Porcupine?" Robby said.

I knew what Robby was talking about. I played dumb, anyway.

I said, "Tell you about *what*, Rob?"

"What happened between you and Shann back there. That's what," Robby said.

"Oh." I said, "Nothing."

History does show that *nothing* means a hell of a lot more than *nothing* when teenagers talk. In this case, Robby knew it meant that I did not want to talk about it, so he left me alone.

Robby Brees was such a good friend.

It was awkwardly quiet inside my empty house with Robby Brees that night. It was one of those exceedingly dumb moments where I did not know whether I was supposed to actually say something to him. I felt myself wanting to act like an asshole to Robby again, so I closed my eyes and asked Saint Kazimierz to help me shut the hell up.

Ingrid came bounding for the door as soon as we were inside. She ran out into the nicely mowed front yard.

I left the door standing open, a kind of message to anyone passing by that Robby Brees and I were *not* conducting experiments inside my house while my parents were gone.

Robby knew what I was doing.

Leaving the door open like that was the kind of thing an uptight asshole would do.

I grabbed my cell phone from the coffee table where it had been sitting all day. I saw that I'd missed a phone call from Eric, my brother. Eric left a message. I sat on the sofa and listened to my brother's voice. Robby stood by the door and watched me. He knew what was happening. We were soldiers in this together, wearing our Grasshopper Jungle uniforms.

Robby Brees and I could be unstoppable, too, if we told ourselves to be.

This is the message Eric left for me on my phone:

> *Hey, Booney. I miss you and I hope you're out having*
> *fun and smoking cigarettes and shit like that. I wish*
> *you were here instead of Dad and Mom. I'm sorry if I*
> *scared you or anything. I'm going to be okay, Booney. I*
> *promise. You be okay, too. I'll see you soon.*

When I was nine years old and Eric was fifteen, my family took a trip to Nashville, Tennessee. I still do not understand why we went to Nashville, but I do remember that my mother and father enjoyed the trip quite a bit.

Because Eric was a teenager, my father and mother would go out at night and listen to music. They felt comfortable leaving my brother and me alone at our hotel.

Eric was mature and sensible enough at fifteen to take care of me.

These days, mothers and fathers end up in jail for doing shit like that. At least, you frequently hear terrible stories about what happens to kids left alone in hotel rooms, even if the kids happen to be sensible and mature.

While we were in Tennessee, my father bought me a fake coonskin cap, which I wore for so many continuous days and nights

I began to develop a bald spot on the back of my scalp. My bald spot was right below the place on the cap where a plastic button had been stitched to the inside, in order to secure the fake raccoon tail.

The coonskin cap was a souvenir from a place called Crockett-Land.

The coonskin cap was made in China.

Richard M. Nixon, president of the United States of America, brought some Unstoppable Corn to China in 1972. He used the Unstoppable Corn to dissolve Prime Minister Chou En-lai's balls.

To my knowledge, my fake coonskin cap did not adversely affect my balls.

CrockettLand sold souvenirs that cashed in on a man named Davy Crockett, who was a frontiersman from Tennessee.

Eric started calling me *Booney* that summer when I was nine and he was fifteen because he said I looked like Daniel Boone, who was also a frontiersman from Pennsylvania.

History shows that neither Davy Crockett nor Daniel Boone ever wore coonskin caps, but movies made people believe they did. Meriwether Lewis wore coonskin caps, however.

I was happy my brother did not start calling me *Meriwether*.

I do not know if movies ever showed Meriwether Lewis wearing a coonskin cap. When you think of exciting movies about frontiersmen, you tend to think about Daniel Boone and Davy Crockett, as opposed to some guy named Meriwether.

Movies made people believe a lot of shit about history.

Robby Brees and I believed what we saw in *Eden Orientation Series*. It was the truth.

There were two prostitutes who lived in the same hotel in Nashville where we stayed.

One night, Eric and I were playing catch with a foam rubber football out on the balcony that connected all the rooms on the third floor, which was the floor our room was on. We said hello to the prostitutes.

The prostitutes were named Tiffany and Rhonda.

I do not know their last names.

History shows that a lot of prostitutes do not necessarily need last names.

Tiffany had hair the color of whipped sweet potatoes and skin like creamy hot cocoa. Rhonda had lemon meringue hair and always wore lipstick the color of cotton candy.

Eric knew what Tiffany and Rhonda were doing. I thought it was curious how my brother would watch Tiffany and Rhonda come and go, and come and go, and how Eric always acted so nice and proper toward them. The girls winked at us both, and sometimes Tiffany, who was quite fat, would comb her hands through Eric's hair and flirt with him suggestively, and rub the back of my neck with her thick warm fingers.

Tiffany and Rhonda were very nice.

On the third night, Eric went into Tiffany and Rhonda's room with them.

Eric left me alone on the balcony for nearly an hour. It may have been more or less than an hour. When you are nine years old, five minutes can seem like a week, *more or less*.

When he came out of Tiffany and Rhonda's room, Eric looked pale, like he was sick or something. Eric's hair was sweaty around his ears and along the back of his neck, and somehow his T-shirt had been turned backwards and inside out. Eric's eyes were funny, too, like he was sleepy and startled at the same time.

I asked him why he left me alone, and Eric told me that Tiffany and Rhonda gave him a blow job.

To me, hearing that those girls gave my brother Eric a *blow job* sounded very nice.

257 | GRASSHOPPER JUNGLE

History shows that all boys consider *blow job* to be a nice-sounding set of words.

I thought a *blow job* was putting your face in front of an air conditioner, which is something all nine-year-old boys love to do, even though Eric did not look like he had been cooled off very much.

I asked Eric if Tiffany and Rhonda would give me a blow job, too.

Eric laughed and laughed.

Then he told me what a blow job was.

Eric lifted up his shirt and showed me how there were perfect kisses of cotton candy lipstick all down below his freckled, cream of wheat belly and over both of his nipples.

At that time, being nine years old and dressed in a coonskin cap in Nashville, Tennessee, as I was, I could not understand at all why anyone would ever let someone give them a blow job.

I listened to my brother's message a second time. I realized I'd almost forgotten how Eric liked to call me *Booney*.

Sometimes, when I teased Eric afterward, during that summer when he was fifteen, I would call him *Cotton Candy* and Eric would get embarrassed in front of my mother and father, and tell me to shut up, too.

While I listened to my brother's voice, a text message came in from Shann Collins. It said this:

You are disgusting.

I did not even know that I was sitting there on my sofa in my living room crying.

I don't cry.

I suppose I was tired, and disappointed, too, for what I had done to Shann and Robby, and especially because I missed my brother and I wanted him to get better, even if I knew nothing would ever be better than it was for Eric and me on those summer nights when we played catch and shit like that, all alone in that hotel in Nashville.

Robby put his hand on my shoulder and shook me.

He said, "Hey. Hey. Don't do that, Austin."

I wiped my face and told Robby I was sorry for crying.

Then I went back into my room and grabbed my history books. It was a heavy stack.

GARLIC, DR PEPPER, AND CRYSTAL METH

WE WERE NOT heading toward Grasshopper Jungle.

I said, "Robby, where are you going?"

Robby said, "I need to go to my house. I need to grab some shit, too."

Ingrid curled up on the backseat. I reached between Robby and me and stroked her fur.

"You're a good dog, Ingrid," I said.

There was something unnaturally still and menacing about the night. Maybe I was only working myself up, getting too emotional.

Ealing would always be a ghost town. It just felt like *more* of a ghost town that night, after Robby parked the Explorer along the curb in front of the Del Vista Arms.

Robby said, "You want to come in with me, Austin?"

I said, "I better wait here with Ingrid. You wouldn't want her to shit in your car, or shit like that."

Robby shrugged.

We both knew what we were thinking about.

Robby said, "I'll be right back."

I turned around and patted Ingrid again. I tried not to be nervous about things, but my head was swimming, drowning actually, in uncertainty. I unzipped the top of my jumpsuit and played with the Saint Kazimierz medal that hung from my neck.

And then I whispered, "What am I going to do, Ingrid?"

Robby ran around the front of the car and disappeared inside the Del Vista Arms.

I thought about Shann Collins, and how she told me I was disgusting.

At exactly that moment, Ollie Jungfrau was killing aliens in an online space-shooter game. He was sitting up in his bed, in his underwear, with his laptop resting on his thighs. Ollie had eaten a large pizza and drank five cans from a six-pack of Dr Pepper. Tiny speckles of pizza sauce dotted Ollie's swollen breasts. Ollie Jungfrau needed to piss, but he did not want to get up from bed. He tried to calculate whether he could get away with peeing in his empty Dr Pepper cans. Ollie Jungfrau decided trying to do that might cut his penis, which he could not actually see due to the roll of his belly, or it might cause him to piss in his own bed. Ollie had pissed in his bed before, when he was too tired to get up and walk to the toilet. Ollie Jungfrau got up. He walked past his window and looked down at the street.

Ollie Jungfrau saw Robby Brees running around the front of a Ford Explorer parked in front of their apartment building. Ollie hated Robby Brees because Robby was gay, and Ollie knew it, and also because Robby was so young and good-looking. Ollie wished Robby Brees would fall down, trip on the curb or shit like that, but Robby was also coordinated and balanced.

Ollie Jungfrau hated young, good-looking, coordinated kids.

Especially ones like Robby Brees, who were gay.

Ollie Jungfrau's eye caught the movement of something farther down the street in the dark. Ollie Jungfrau's eyes were good at noticing quick movements. That was how he killed so many aliens in the game he played every day. The motion Ollie detected was not caused by an alien, however.

Ollie Jungfrau saw the dark form of an Unstoppable Soldier crossing the street ahead of Robby Brees's Ford Explorer. He saw the creature just as Robby disappeared into the foyer at the Del Vista Arms.

The Unstoppable Soldier, a six-foot-tall mantis thing with spike-studded arms, was Hungry Jack.

Hungry Jack was hungry again.

I sat inside Robby Brees's Ford Explorer. I was turned toward the backseat, stroking Ingrid's fur and flipping the silver Saint Kazimierz medallion with my left hand. Ollie Jungfrau did not know the Polish kid he sold cigarettes to and called *Dynamo* was down there in the gay kid's car on the street.

Ollie Jungfrau stood at his window, frozen in fright. He was in his boxers and socks, and he was standing in a puddle of his own steaming piss.

Ollie's piss had the slight smell of garlic and Dr Pepper.

And at the same time that Ollie Jungfrau was urinating down his bread dough thighs, watching in horror as Hungry Jack scampered like a metal windup puppet through the dark toward me and Ingrid while we sat in Robby's car, Duane Coventry, the chemistry teacher from Curtis Crane Lutheran Academy, put down his glass meth pipe after smoking three peanut-sized rocks of crystal.

Duane Coventry sat completely naked at his computer. The chemistry teacher from Curtis Crane Lutheran Academy could look at pornography for endless hours when he smoked meth. The only thing that sometimes interfered with viewing pornography, which frequently lasted until daybreak, was if Duane Coventry turned the computer's camera on himself. Then Duane Coventry used his monitor as a mirror, so he could study his face, scratch at it, pick spots out of his skin that were not there, until he made them real with his own yellowed fingernails.

That was what Duane Coventry was doing at the exact moment Ollie Jungfrau was pissing himself, and Hungry Jack was click-stepping toward the smell of Robby Brees and the food-meat things that sat inside Robby's car. Duane Coventry was picking his face, naked, seated at his computer, picking and picking and picking.

Duane Coventry thought he left his doors and windows open. Duane Coventry always had to check his doors and windows whenever he smoked his meth. He stood up, took a step toward the front door of his small Iowa house. Then Duane Coventry turned around and grabbed his pipe. He burned the amber residue inside the little glass globe and inhaled deeply.

Duane Coventry forgot why he'd been standing up. He sat down again and began picking his face.

Every night Duane Coventry smoked methamphetamine was exactly like this.

Nobody knew anything about Duane Coventry.

Duane Coventry wanted to look at pornography and masturbate, but he needed to check his doors and windows. Duane believed people were always outside, always watching him.

Duane Coventry went into his kitchen, where he'd been cooking methamphetamine for over a year without anyone knowing about it.

Duane Coventry loved methamphetamine more than he could ever love anything else.

He checked the door that opened onto the kitchen porch.

It was locked.

Duane Coventry walked through the small living room and checked the windows behind his sofa. The windows were latched secure. Then he checked his front door. The front door had not been closed all the way.

Scrawled into the plasterboard wall, all down along both sides of Duane Coventry's front door were letters and numbers. They were license plate tags from cars Duane Coventry saw outside his house whenever he smoked meth.

There were exactly 464 different license plate numbers etched into Duane Coventry's living room wall. Duane Coventry knew there was always someone out there watching him, waiting for him.

When Duane Coventry opened the front door, he stepped outside. As soon as Duane Coventry went outside his little Iowa house, he strained to think about why he was going out into the night. He had forgotten what he needed to do, but Duane Coventry, our chemistry teacher from Curtis Crane Lutheran Academy, did realize he was completely naked.

He thought that maybe he was supposed to check to be certain his car doors had been locked.

Duane Coventry's car was parked in the driveway beside a hedge of rosebushes.

Duane walked across the yard toward his car.

It was not a good idea.

Tyler Jacobson and Roger Baird had caught up to the exhausted Eileen Pope, who was trying to find something as big as an empty house or a garage in which to lay her millions of fertilized eggs. Roger Baird had Eileen Pope pinned down. He was fucking her on the lawn just beyond Duane Coventry's rose hedge. Roger Baird was doing one of the only two things Unstoppable Soldiers ever want to do. Eileen Pope was too tired to eat Roger Baird. Tyler Jacobson was tired and hungry. Tyler Jacobson smelled Duane Coventry's sweat as soon as the meth smoker opened his front door.

Duane Coventry looked over the hedge and saw the three monstrous things in the grass of his lawn.

Duane Coventry said, "Big fucking bugs."

That is exactly what they were.

Tyler Jacobson, Roger Baird, and Eileen Pope were the materialization of a meth smoker's most horrible delusion: gigantic bugs with jagged bear-trap mandibles and folded claw-arms prickled with mountain ranges of knife-blade, triangular teeth.

In the last second of his life, Duane Coventry felt a sort of jubilant vindication: He had been right after all this time. There really *were* horrible things waiting to get him outside his house.

Duane Coventry was right.

Tyler Jacobson left little more than a few dime-sized bloodstains from the meal he made of the chemistry teacher from Curtis Crane Lutheran Academy.

Tyler Jacobson was unstoppable.

And at exactly that moment, Ingrid's ears perked up.

If Ingrid were a normal dog that hadn't lost her throat's barking mechanism to cancer, Ingrid would have barked and barked.

Ingrid heard and smelled the monster named Hungry Jack as he got right up next to Robby's old Ford.

I scratched Ingrid's ears.

I said, "What's wrong, Ingrid?"

I turned away from her and I saw the triangular, glistening head of the giant bug that stared at me, fascinated, watching me through the windshield of my best friend's car.

"Holy shit," I said.

I am not certain that is *exactly* what I said, but I did say something.

Sometimes historians need to fill in the blanks on their own. It is part of our job.

You trust us because we are historians.

Historians are reliable blank-fillers.

It is my job.

Hungry Jack's mandibles yawned open. A gooey string of bug saliva hammocked between his jagged side-hinged jaws. The mandibles opened and closed, opened and closed. Hungry Jack wanted to eat me and Ingrid. Hungry Jack pressed his head into the windshield of Robby's Explorer. He tried to bite me through the glass, but he could not figure out what was keeping him from getting me into his mouth.

He bit and bit at the windshield, each time leaving streaks of milky bug spit on the glass.

Ingrid squeezed her way up between the front seats, into my lap, and also tried to bite Hungry Jack through the unyielding windshield.

Bugs are not very smart, but Hungry Jack was persistent.

I reached over to the steering column, but Robby had taken the car keys with him. Of course Robby would have taken the keys. He would have no way to enter the Del Vista Arms without his keys.

I pressed down into the car's horn.

Robby's Ford Explorer was exactly like Ingrid: barkless. The horn did not work.

I pushed Ingrid back and scooted my way deeper into the rear cargo compartment of the car. Hungry Jack whipped his arms up and struck them into the windshield. He was figuring out the puzzle. Cracks starred outward from the impact, fracturing the windshield in every direction, all the way to the rubber gasket frame.

At exactly that moment, Robby Brees stepped out from the foyer at the Del Vista Arms. When I saw Robby, he was standing on the sidewalk with some objects under one arm, only a few feet away from Hungry Jack.

It was not a good idea.

"Robby!" I screamed, but it was too late.

CLICKETY CLICKETY

THE COMPOUND EYES on an Unstoppable Soldier take up approximately three-fourths of his head.

Hungry Jack could see the entire world around him at all times, even when he was focused on getting to me and Ingrid, who were hiding inside Robby Brees's Ford Explorer.

The poor old car took a beating from Hungry Jack's tooth-spiked arms.

Hungry Jack's head swiveled entirely around when he detected the movement of Robby Brees outside the doorway to the Del Vista Arms.

Robby Brees was going to be easy prey.

Robby stood, frozen. I screamed for him to run, but Robby was not paying attention to me.

I realized I was going to sit there and watch my best friend get killed if I did not do something about it. I crawled up from the rear compartment and grabbed the latch on the rear passenger door. I was not even thinking at that moment about how Robby and I were going to die together.

All I knew is I had to do something for the person I loved.

I opened the door and screamed at Robby again.

Hungry Jack sprang down from the hood of the Explorer and landed squarely on his four rear feet. Hungry Jack was so close to

Robby that his folded and spiked arms were practically touching Robby's shoulders.

Then Hungry Jack backed away from Robby. The monster butted up into the fender of Robby's Explorer without ever looking toward me or Ingrid again.

Hungry Jack ran, *clickety clickety*, down the street and disappeared into the night.

Unstoppable Soldiers could run at speeds exceeding forty miles per hour.

Hungry Jack was afraid of Robby Brees.

I had seen it before. The first night—when Hungry Jack hatched out in that cornfield across from the *Tally-Ho!*—he did the same thing. He ran away from Robby Brees.

It was because Robby Brees was God to the Unstoppable Soldiers.

We found this out later.

"Holy shit," I said.

"Uh," Robby said.

Robby Brees had still not moved from the spot I thought he was going to die in.

"Holy shit, Rob."

I grabbed Robby and hugged him. We stood there on the street holding each other. Ingrid curled her body around our legs, wagging her tail.

Above us, Ollie Jungfrau looked down from his window. He had regained his composure, but was still standing, soaked, in a puddle of his own piss.

Ollie Jungfrau said, "I might have known little Dynamo was a queer, too. Dumb stupid lucky queer kids."

Robby and I had to get out of there.

Robby Brees and I had shit to do, and monsters to kill.

ON THE ROOF AGAIN

ROBBY SPED ALL the way to Grasshopper Jungle.

It turned out the things Robby wanted to get from his apartment at the Del Vista Arms were these: some clean underwear and socks, his toothpaste, the plastic lawn flamingo with the steel spike coming out of its ass, and the grimacing lemur mask.

"I should have gotten some underwear, too," I said. "What if we end up having to *stay* down there?"

"I don't know, Austin," Robby said.

"Neither do I," I agreed.

Nobody knew anything about what we should do.

It was why we needed to get those last two reels of film from the roof of Grasshopper Jungle.

Dr. Grady McKeon *told* us to get those films.

We had to get the films and go back to Eden. Robby and I both knew that it was not too late, that the infestation was still in its first stage. We still had time, and Dr. Grady McKeon said there would be instructions for what to do on the last reels of the *Eden Orientation Series*.

Maybe Robby and I could stop the Unstoppable Soldiers.

Maybe Shann Collins would forgive me.

Maybe that plastic flamingo would start shitting candy bars and vanilla ice cream out of its ass, too.

When Robby rounded the turn onto Kimber Drive, his phone chimed.

It was a text message from Shann Collins.

Shann's text message to Robby Brees said this:

I hate you.

Robby glanced at the message on the screen of his phone. I watched him. He did not show any reaction at all. Robby knew it was not a joke message, though. Then he handed his phone over to me so I could see what Shann had written, too.

"I had a feeling you told her about me and you," Robby said.

I said, "I never lie, Rob. Shann asked me about it. I don't know what I am going to do."

Robby sighed.

I answered Shann's text message using Robby's phone:

Shann, it is me, Austin. Please do not make this about Robby. I love you both too much. Can we talk?

Shann's answer came to my phone:

You are disgusting. I hate you both.

Robby pulled the Explorer into the alley at Grasshopper Jungle. If we had gone around to the front of the mall, we might have seen the mess Travis Pope had made at *The Pancake House*.

Robby and I had no idea what had been going on at Grasshopper Jungle.

He eased the Explorer along the back of the mall and parked beneath the metal ladder that came down from the roof behind *From Attic to Seller Consignment Store*.

Robby and I left Ingrid inside the car and climbed up onto the roof racks of the Explorer. From there, it was an easy reach to the bottom of the ladder.

"Um," Robby said, "that creature-thing really messed the shit out of my car."

"Sorry, Rob," I said. "We might as well call them what they are: Unstoppable Soldiers, created from the sicko brains at McKeon Industries who thought it was a good idea to mix bug sperm and blood with anything that happened to show up in their petri dish."

"Who would think it *wasn't* a good idea to mix bug sperm and blood with shit?" Robby said.

I said, "Uh."

Robby said, "I wonder what a can of bug spray would do to them."

"Uh," I said. "I think Eden One Thirty-Three and Eden Five better get their butts onto the roof and find the rest of that movie."

"I *do* hate stopping a film right in the middle," Eden 133 said. "Just when it was getting good."

Actually, we stopped the film just when my grandfather, Felek Andrzej Szczerba, became McKeon Industries's first Unstoppable Soldier.

We climbed up onto the roof of the Ealing Mall.

Johnny McKeon was hiding inside, just waiting for somebody to respond to his emergency alarm. Johnny McKeon was also going through the stock of handguns he had on display in the glass case at *From Attic to Seller Consignment Store.*

Johnny McKeon had a lot of guns for sale.

Robby and I had no way of knowing Johnny McKeon was directly below our feet.

"Smoke?" I said.

"Fags," Robby agreed.

"I guess so," I said.

We lit up.

The steel film canisters were right where we had left them. I bent down and picked up both canisters. What we hadn't noticed the first time we were up on the roof became strikingly obvious

270 | ANDREW SMITH

now. The film cans were wrapped with tape and marked with a thick black pen: Four of Five, and Five of Five.

Robby said, "Can I ask you something, Austin?"

I said, "Sure."

"Was it hard for you to tell Shann the truth?" Robby asked.

I shook my head.

"No," I said.

It was the truth.

"Oh." Robby said, "And you really don't know what you're going to do?"

I took a drag and exhaled.

"No," I said. "I think I should just leave you both alone before I ruin everyone's life."

"You wouldn't ruin my life," Robby said.

"I don't want to hurt you or Shann, Rob," I said.

I *was* ruining Robby's and Shann's lives, even if Robby told me I wasn't.

I was disgusted with myself.

We threw our cigarette butts down and stamped them out on the grit of the roof.

A police siren wailed. We could see the pulse of red lights coming closer through the night toward Kimber Drive.

"Do you think someone saw us come up the ladder?" Robby said.

"I don't know," I answered. "We should get out of here before we get arrested, or shit like that."

DENNY DRAYTON HAS A GUN, MOTHERFUCKER

JOHNNY MCKEON TURNED off all the lights.

He was inside *From Attic to Seller Consignment Store*, waiting for the coyote cry of the Iowa State Patrol car that had been dispatched from Waterloo.

The State Patrol was responding to an emergency alarm Johnny McKeon rang when he saw Hungry Jack and the other Unstoppable Soldiers in the alley at Grasshopper Jungle.

There was only one bored trooper in the patrol car. He sat behind the wheel. He was bored because he was coming to Ealing. Nothing ever happened in Ealing, and he figured it was going to be another pile of Ealing nothing crap from a false alarm at an abandoned business in a loser town.

Ealing, Iowa, was the elephants' graveyard for American entrepreneurism.

The trooper was named Denny Drayton.

It was a good Iowa name.

Denny Drayton's skin was nearly translucent white, the sickly color of the coconut center in a Mounds bar. He had absolutely no hair.

Denny Drayton needed to take a shit. He hoped wherever he was heading to had a shitter that worked, and toilet paper, too. Denny Drayton carried a pack of baby wipes in his patrol car for emergencies, like when he'd pull off to the side of the road and shit in someone's yard.

The baby wipes in Denny Drayton's patrol car were made in a place called Eden Prairie, Minnesota.

That is the truth.

Denny Drayton chewed tobacco while he was on patrol. He

held a plastic liter Diet Coke bottle between his thighs as he drove. The Diet Coke bottle was three-fourths full of hot tobacco spit. Iowa State Troopers were not supposed to chew tobacco on the job, but Denny Drayton had a motto for just about every situation he encountered.

His motto was this: *Fuck that shit. I have a gun, motherfucker.*

Denny Drayton's motto was tattooed in an arc of Old English lettering that made a semicircle like a rising sun over his white and hairless belly button.

Fuck that shit. I have a gun, motherfucker.

Denny Drayton shaved his entire body every morning. He shaved all his hair off, even his eyebrows and pubic hair.

Trooper Drayton also had a tattoo of the flag for the Confederate States of America. The stars and bars flag was tattooed directly on the front of Denny Drayton's hairless scrotum.

Denny Drayton was most likely insane.

Denny liked to show off his hairless body and the tattoos of his motto and the Confederate flag in the shower room at the police station in Waterloo. Denny Drayton told his police officer friends that he got the tattoo of his motto for reading material, just in case he ever hooked up with a bitch who was smart enough to read *and* give blow jobs at the same time.

Denny Drayton had one joke, and that was it.

It wasn't a particularly good joke, and everyone knew it. But Denny Drayton had a gun, motherfucker.

The six-foot-tall praying mantis beast that used to be named Travis Pope lumbered out of *The Pancake House* on his four clicking lower legs. He was a little groggy. Will Wallace had been exceedingly drunk, and Unstoppable Soldiers are sensitive to eating drunk people and people who smoke meth and shit like that.

Travis Pope only wanted to find the swarm and go dormant with them overnight.

Denny Drayton was just pulling into the parking lot.

Johnny McKeon noticed the flashing red lights through the glass front of his secondhand store. Johnny McKeon had a gun—a Smith & Wesson .500 magnum.

The gun weighed six pounds.

A Smith & Wesson .500 magnum could blow a man's head off.

Pastor Roland Duff saw the lights on Trooper Denny Drayton's patrol car, too. Roland Duff had come back from Waterloo, where he had met a nice Christian man at the *Tally-Ho!*

Roland Duff sat alone inside *Satan's Pizza*. He was eating a small *Stanpreme*. Roland Duff was exchanging text messages with his new friend. Roland Duff was very excited. He had an erection. Pastor Roland Duff and his new friend were flirting suggestively, and arranging a date for Saturday evening.

Roland Duff's new friend was named Shaun Doherty.

Shaun Doherty owned a septic pumping business. He lived in a town called West Bazine, which was in Iowa. East Bazine did not exist at all.

Shaun Doherty and Pastor Roland Duff planned on meeting at the Waterloo *Cinezaar* on Saturday evening.

They were going to see *Eden Five Needs You 4*.

That was the plan, at least.

Denny Drayton turned his spotlight onto the dark front of *The Pancake House*. His keen sense of Iowan normalcy alerted Denny Drayton that something was not right. Windows were shattered, the front door had been torn from its hinges, and it looked like there were some bloody shoes and a belt lying on the sidewalk in front of the mall.

"Something's not right here," Denny Drayton said.

Denny Drayton spit into his Coke bottle and pinched another wad of black, moist tobacco from a can of Copenhagen he kept pinned behind the patrol car's sun visor.

He farted. Denny Drayton admired the smell of his own farts.

"I really need to take a shit," Denny Drayton said.

Then the Iowa trooper saw Travis Pope, an Unstoppable Soldier, moving with mechanical jerkiness through the debris field of blood, glass, clothing, and imitation-maple-flavored pancake syrup.

Denny Drayton opened the door on his patrol car. He spit onto the asphalt of the Ealing Mall's parking lot and then stood up, angling his spotlight so it would fully illuminate the strange creature in front of *The Pancake House*.

It was not a good idea.

Denny Drayton thought it must have been some kind of prank. Maybe somebody was making a movie or something. Denny Drayton wished he could be in a movie.

"What the heck is that shit?" Denny Drayton said.

Denny Drayton drew his pistol. His gun was a 9mm Sig Sauer model P250.

Denny Drayton's pistol was made in New Hampshire.

Compared to Johnny McKeon's Smith & Wesson .500 magnum, Denny Drayton's weapon was a rubber band gun.

Travis Pope's attention was riveted to all the lights blazing from the patrol car. He was not hungry, but he decided to kill the man making all the noise and light, anyway. Unstoppable Soldiers do that kind of shit.

Johnny McKeon came outside just then. Johnny pointed his powerful pistol in the direction of Travis Pope. Johnny McKeon was not a good shot. He knew he would miss hitting the creature unless he got very, very close.

Pastor Roland Duff had never had sex with another person

in his entire life. He believed he was ready to have sex with his new friend, Shaun Doherty. Roland Duff imagined the thrill of *experimenting* with another man after all his lonely years. He was very excited about it. Roland Duff adjusted his uncomfortable erection and sat watching the police lights from across the street. He was curious. Pastor Roland Duff could not tell what was going on.

Sometimes, Pastor Roland Duff counseled himself over his own doubts and weaknesses. He could not decide whether he was a virgin or not. Pastor Roland Duff did believe that masturbation was immoral and compromising. Roland Duff was frequently wracked by guilt. He was uncertain if he could still be a virgin *and* masturbate as often as he did. Pastor Roland Duff thought he would masturbate when he got back home that night.

Pastor Roland Duff did not really get the chance.

At exactly that moment, ash flakes fell like snow in Guatemala on the home of Robert Brees Sr. For some strange reason, Robert Brees Sr. thought about the son he'd left behind in Iowa. Robby would be sixteen now, he thought. Robert Brees Sr. watched the ashes falling and falling. He had not thought about his son in years.

Eric Christopher Szerba was lying awake in a hospital bed. Eric was looking at the tubes and medications near the head of his bed, and wondering if anything there could be useful to him in committing suicide.

Robby Brees and I were driving out from Ealing toward the McKeon House. We were going back to Eden to watch the last reels from *Eden Orientation Series*. Robby played *Let It Bleed* in the tape deck.

And Robby sang along with Love In Vain.

Robby Brees reached across the center console and put his hand on top of mine.

The wife of the vice president of the United States of America was performing oral sex on the vice president. It was the vice president's birthday, and the vice president of the United States of America was getting a blow job. Franklin and Theodore were very happy.

I had not named my balls.

Robby Brees had not named his balls, either. I asked him about it.

And Robby said to me, "Who would ever name his balls?"

I said, "I would like to, but once you give your balls names, there is no going back."

"Well, if you do think up names for your balls, let me know what they are. I would hate for us to have balls with the same names in such a small town as Ealing," Robby decided.

Robby was always so smart about small town social blunders and shit like that.

"Having balls with the same name as your best friend's is a serious social blunder," I said.

That is the truth.

"Get down on the ground!" Trooper Denny Drayton said to Travis Pope.

Johnny McKeon was very scared. He crept across the parking lot. The Smith & Wesson .500 magnum was so heavy, it hurt Johnny McKeon's wrist just to hold it.

Travis Pope got closer and closer to Denny Drayton.

The last thing Denny Drayton said was his motto. He said, "Fuck this shit. I have a gun, motherfucker."

Then Denny Drayton began shooting at Travis Pope.

Johnny McKeon ducked.

Across the street, Pastor Roland Duff ducked.

Denny Drayton fired and fired and fired.

Unstoppable Soldiers do not like being shot at. They also have exoskeletons that are as bulletproof as the hull of an aircraft carrier.

They are unstoppable.

Denny Drayton emptied his gun. He was in the process of reloading when Travis Pope unhinged his barbed arms and picked Denny Drayton up by his head. Travis Pope bit most of the trooper's head off and let Denny Drayton's hairless and tattooed body fall down onto the blacktop.

Johnny McKeon whispered, "Well, I'll be danged."

Johnny was smart. He did not fire his pistol at the monster. Johnny McKeon quietly went around to the driver's side of his truck, got behind the wheel, and drove off.

Stan, the owner of *Satan's Pizza*, and Pastor Roland Duff, the headmaster from Curtis Crane Lutheran Academy, were not so smart.

But they were curious. Pastor Roland Duff was curious about a lot of things. He was still fantasizing about Shaun Doherty.

Nothing exciting ever happened in Ealing. Pastor Roland Duff and Stan, the owner of *Satan's Pizza*, who had come from behind the counter when he heard what sounded like gunfire, stepped out onto the street to see what was causing all the commotion across Kimber Drive at Grasshopper Jungle.

It was not a good idea.

EXILE IN EDEN

ROBBY DROVE THE Ford Explorer through the fields of weeds and brambles behind Shann's house.

He parked beside the dilapidated chicken coops where the

hatch into Eden sat nearly unnoticeable in the center of an old concrete pad.

Ingrid was excited. She had found a new place to shit.

Robby opened the hatch. The welcome recording began again and the room below us lit up.

I took my phone out of the pocket of my Eden 5 jumpsuit. I did not need to explain to Robby that I was calling Shann Collins. Robby knew what I was doing. I wanted to try to get Shann to listen to me.

We all needed to be safe now, and the Unstoppable Soldiers had come out in Ealing.

Shann would not answer my call. I knew she was not asleep. It was 11:00. No teenager in the world goes to sleep before 11:00. I left a voice message as Robby stood near and listened. There was no need to hide anything from Robby Brees.

I had no secrets with him.

I had no secrets with Shann Collins, either.

This is what I said:

"Shann, I am sorry. I told you I do stupid shit without thinking about who I might hurt. But the truth is, I think you need to come to Eden. Me and Robby are going back inside now, so my phone won't work, just in case you want to tell me I am disgusting again. We have the rest of the film. I think something terrible is happening in Ealing, and maybe we are the only ones who can stop it. Well. Uh. I love you, Shann. I really do love you. You have to know that, Shann. Please come to Eden with me and Robby. Hurry."

I put the phone back inside my jumpsuit. I rubbed the silver medallion of Saint Kazimierz between my thumb and finger.

I said, "Saint Kazimierz, I am Polish. I am a kid. I'm not sure if I'm technically a virgin or not. But a solid two out of three gives me hope you might look out for me and Robby and Ingrid."

Robby stood, watching me.

And I said, "I really do love you, Robby. How can I be in love with two people at the same time?"

Robby said, "I don't know how you can do that, Austin."

It was very difficult carrying Ingrid down the ladder.

Not only did I fail to think about bringing clean underwear and shit like that, I never even thought about how I would get a sixty-pound golden retriever down a very tall ladder.

Robby had to help. We sandwiched Ingrid between us and climbed down. We must have looked like a reject hybridization of two boys and a barkless dog. That was probably some kind of shit they pulled at McKeon Industries back in the sixties, too.

By the time we finally got down into the mudroom, we were both damp with sweat, we smelled like dog fur, and the repeated welcoming tape was driving us crazy.

"I have B.O.," I said.

"I know," Robby agreed.

Robby and I went back up one final time to get my history books and the things Robby had brought from the Del Vista Arms. Then we sealed the three of us—me, Ingrid, and Robby— inside the Eden Project.

Robby and I put on clean pairs of white Eden scientist socks in the locker room. I thought about changing into a clean jumpsuit, but I did not want to give up the number 5. I wanted to take a shower, but we had too much shit to do.

Robby Brees left his bundle of things on the bench we'd been sitting on. I carried the two final reels of film, and Robby followed me into the theater room.

A CHANCE MEETING UNDER A PORTRAIT OF A PRESBYTERIAN, OR, CALVIN COOLIDGE'S CANOE

MY FATHER'S NAME is Eric Andrew Szerba.

His Polish name was Arek Andrzej Szczerba.

His father, Felek, was a scientist at McKeon Industries.

Felek Andrzej Szczerba was the world's first Unstoppable Soldier.

All roads cross here on my desk. As a historian, I realize, too, that we are all on the same road, all the time.

Sometimes we drive in circles or the wrong way, because we are stupid like that.

And that was my day. You know what I mean.

Eric Szerba, my father, was only a little boy when Felek was killed.

Raising five fatherless Polish boys in Ealing, Iowa, was a tremendous challenge for my grandmother, Ksenia Szczerba. Dr. Grady McKeon saw to it that the family was provided for, so Ksenia never had to go to work, and McKeon Industries subsidized the five brothers' education.

All the Szczerbas moved far away from Iowa after my grandmother died. Ksenia Szczerba died of exhaustion in 1992, several years before I was born. Only my father, Eric, stayed in Ealing, where he became a teacher after graduating college.

Eric Szerba's first teaching assignment was at Herbert Hoover High School, Ealing's public school. He began teaching when he was twenty-two years old.

In his first year of teaching World History, Eric Szerba met a fifteen-year-old boy named Kelly Kenney.

Kelly Kenney is a true Iowa kind of name for a boy. It is a name that almost tastes like buttermilk biscuits and honey.

Kelly Kenney was not such a good student. But Kelly Kenney was persistent. At least once per week, Kelly Kenney would say this to Eric Szerba:

"Hey, Mister Szerba. You should meet my sister, Connie. She is twenty years old and a real dynamo. You are single, right, Mister Szerba? You should go out with Connie. Here is our phone number. Connie likes going to the movies, and you would make a nice couple. Connie is not a slut, either. Ha-ha. You should call on her, Mister Szerba. That would be neat!"

Eric Szerba was not the kind of young man who would ever call a girl based on urgent pleading from a fifteen-year-old boy. Eric and Connie would never have met solely as a result of Kelly Kenney's persistent prodding.

It was Connie Kenney who came in to Eric Szerba's classroom on behalf of her parents, at Herbert Hoover High School's Open House in the fall semester of 1982.

In 1982, every classroom at Herbert Hoover High School had a portrait of Ronald Reagan hanging above the blackboard. Ronald Reagan was president of the United States of America in 1982. I can find no historical records anywhere that detail whether Ronald Reagan ever took a shit, or if he named his balls.

I believe Ronald Reagan most likely did name his balls.

I believe that Ronald Reagan, the president of the United States of America, named both of his balls the same thing: *Calvin Coolidge*. Ronald Reagan would have named both of his balls *Calvin Coolidge* just to avoid any confusion on his part.

It may have been a social blunder, but it made remembering your balls much easier. No one wants to be caught in the embarrassing situation of forgetting the name of only one of your balls.

Connie Kenney, who was Lutheran, met my father, Arek Andrzej Szczerba, a Catholic who smoked cigarettes, beneath a portrait of Ronald Reagan.

Ronald Reagan was Presbyterian.

Kelly Kenney claims to have been responsible for Eric and Connie's eventual marriage, but history shows that it was the result of a meeting of the two in a classroom at a public school, beneath a portrait of a Presbyterian who never took a shit and named his balls Calvin Coolidge.

I once saw a photograph of Calvin Coolidge in an exhibit at the Library of Congress. Calvin Coolidge was riding in a canoe.

The canoe was named *Beaver Dick*.

I could not make that up if I tried.

That is the truth.

Eric Andrew Szerba changed his life for Connie Kenney. He quit smoking cigarettes and he converted to Lutheranism. In exchange for Eric Szerba's devotion to her, Connie Kenney allowed Eric Andrew Szerba to put his penis inside her vagina. This happened several times before the two were actually married, although it was an act that good Lutherans in Iowa look askance at.

After they were married, Eric Andrew Szerba, a non-smoking Lutheran teacher of history, took a position at Ealing's private school, Curtis Crane Lutheran Academy. Eric Andrew Szerba's non-smoking Lutheran Polish semen created a son named Eric Christopher, who was born in 1989, and a second son named Austin Andrzej, who was born in 1995.

This is my history.

A MOST SOOTHING SHOWERHEAD

"**YOU ARE A GOOD** dog, Ingrid," I said.

Ingrid curled up beneath my feet. I sat in the back row of Eden's theater.

Behind us, Robby Brees fed the leader strip for Reel Four of *Eden Orientation Series* into the toothy cogs of the theater's projector. Then Robby jumped over the seat back and sat down right next to me, like he always did when we went to the movies together.

Robby Brees put his hand on the armrest, so he was touching me.

The final two reels of film in *Eden Orientation Series* contained some of the most horrible things either one of us had ever seen.

We lit cigarettes and watched.

This is what we found out:

McKeon Industries worked frantically toward the development of Unstoppable Weapons and Unstoppable Soldiers during the second half of the 1960s.

McKeon Industries wanted to make Unstoppable Anything. They would have made Unstoppable Cup-O-Noodles if they could. The scientists who worked for Dr. Grady McKeon didn't seem to be overly concerned about consequences, like how to stop shit once they made it *unstoppable*, and shit like that.

Reel Four of *Eden Orientation Series* opened with a headshot of the insane Dr. Grady McKeon himself. Dr. Grady McKeon sat behind his mahogany desk in what was called Eden's Brain Room, wearing a thin white, V-neck T-shirt.

"I'll bet you anything he wasn't wearing any pants when they filmed that," Robby said.

I had been thinking exactly the same thing.

Dr. Grady McKeon rambled on about his projects, and bragged

about corn and the dissolved balls of Maoist thugs, while he smoked a cigarette and his eye twitched like a strand of Christmas tree tinsel during a springtime Iowa thunderstorm.

Robby Brees and I found the Brain Room later that night.

Dr. Grady McKeon licked his lips and began:

> *Ah. My friends. Tell me, are you breeding?*
> *Are you? Hmmm?*
> *Breed, my friends. Breed and love. You are the New Humans.*
> *It's a lovely place, our Eden, don't you agree?*

Robby said, "Thinking about that guy kind of has a damping effect on the drive to conjugate."

I said, "Uh."

McKeon Industries experimented with several methods for creating an Unstoppable Soldier.

Dr. Grady McKeon's Human Replication Unit actually grew human body parts that floated in polymer suspensions. The polymer suspensions created their own electrical charges, like jellied batteries. This was where the praying hands, the penis, and the little two-headed boy came from. They were all created from Dr. Grady McKeon's own tissue samples.

So each jar actually *was* Dr. Grady McKeon, *more or less*.

Apparently, all of the things inside the jars filled with electrical polymers were *more or less alive*, too, according to Dr. Grady McKeon.

More or less.

Johnny McKeon didn't know anything about the somewhat-living penis, hands, and baby boy he'd been keeping inside his office at *From Attic to Seller Consignment Store*.

Dr. Grady McKeon had been a sick monster.

"Well, he did develop a most soothing showerhead," Robby pointed out.

"I will give him that. There is nothing quite like showering beneath a Pulse-O-Matic® showerhead," I agreed.

I could not help but feel sad about the poor little boy with two heads. I really *did* see his hand move that day when I was alone inside Johnny McKeon's office. The two-headed boy had been imprisoned within that glass container, *more or less alive*, for over forty years.

But the man's head in the jar came from something else entirely.

We found out about that in Reel Five.

The Human Replication Unit at McKeon Industries also collected and experimented with sperm. Dr. Grady McKeon had no apparent difficulty obtaining sperm samples from very powerful and important American men. Dr. Grady McKeon's power sperm had been frozen and stored in a cryogenic vault inside Eden's Brain Room.

It was exactly like *Eden Five*.

On the door of the freezer vault were framed photographs of men, including President Richard Nixon, Vice President Spiro Agnew, the Director of the Central Intelligence Agency, whose real name was Richard Helms, and, of course, Dr. Grady McKeon.

Each of them had donated multiple samples of their Unstoppable Sperm.

The Unstoppable Sperm was intended as the beginning of a New Universe.

Robby said, "Um."

I said, "This place really *is* full of sperm, Robby."

Dr. Grady McKeon explained that the vault full of Unstoppable Sperm was a precaution. What if, he postulated, only women managed to escape to the Eden Project, or if there was a depletion of desirability among male breeders? Dr. Grady McKeon confidently answered his hypothetical question: Unstoppable Sperm would become the genetic seed bank for the New Universe.

It was most likely something that Dr. Grady McKeon had intended all along.

Much later, in conducting further analysis inside the Brain Room, and through reading Dr. Grady McKeon's barely legible and ranting diaries, I did discover that in 1975, McKeon thawed out the sperm from CIA Director Richard Helms, President Richard Nixon, and Vice President Spiro Agnew.

Dr. Grady McKeon discarded that sperm unceremoniously into his prized *Nightingale Urinal*.

Dr. Grady McKeon replaced the Unstoppable Sperm with his own.

The Brain Room was pretty much full of Dr. Grady McKeon's sperm.

From the Unstoppable Sperm experiments, Reel Four jumped across the McKeon Industries Complex to the Unstoppable Corn Unit, where a series of catastrophic accidents of nature sprang up like milkweed in well-watered fields of Iowa corn.

INFINITA MILITES! INFINITA MILITES!

HERE WAS REEL FIVE:

Felek Szczerba was the first Unstoppable Soldier.

The end of the world began in Ealing, Iowa, in 1968. Nobody knew anything about it. The scientists at McKeon Industries were crazy and drunk on money. Dr. Grady McKeon would have done anything to be the man responsible for creating an unstoppable force in the universe.

He nearly got away with it, too.

Initially, there were five people infected by Dr. Grady McKeon's *412E*: three scientists and two secretaries. The five victims made a mess of McKeon Industries in 1968.

They were Unstoppable Soldiers. All they wanted to do was fuck and eat.

Because McKeon Industries maintained such extreme levels of security during the Cold War, the Unstoppable Soldiers that had been accidentally created there never got a chance to step outside into the Iowa daylight. If they had ever gotten outside, the world would have certainly come to an end, and there would have been a new apex species in charge of Planet Earth—one that wanted only to fuck and eat.

Besides fucking and eating, a few of us human beings are driven to paint on the walls of caves. Other than that, and the fact that we die relatively easily when you shoot at us, I think human beings are very much like Dr. Grady McKeon's Unstoppable Soldiers.

INFINITA MILITES! INFINITA MILITES!

Despite images of all the dead people inside the lab building, the destruction of an entire research wing of the facility, and shit like that, Dr. Grady McKeon's voice had a gleeful chime to it as he narrated over grainy black-and-white surveillance footage of the beasts, while cameras caught them unreservedly engaged in the two things that Unstoppable Soldiers like to do.

There were several unfortunate clips of the Unstoppable Soldiers eating a few of their co-workers, but what can you do?

It was all in the name of science and anti-Communism.

A commercial had been spliced directly into the middle of Reel Five. The commercial was a sales pitch to the Defense Department for McKeon Industries's Unstoppable Soldiers. It suggested exposing prison inmates, the unemployed, welfare recipients, and hippies to *412E*, and then dropping them off in sunny Havana, or possibly deep inside Red China.

> *Bulletproof, tireless machines of conquest. McKeon*
> *Industries presents to the world our Unstoppable*
> *Soldiers!*

The commercial footage kept replaying the image of Felek Szczerba in the process of hatching out.

As soon as an Unstoppable Soldier hatches out, he is a bit puffy and wilted, kind of like a butterfly when it sheds the husk of its chrysalis. But as soon as the Unstoppable Soldier ate what remained of Felek Szczerba's corpse, it also ate two attending nurses and a physician.

All of this was captured on camera.

> *Bulletproof, tireless machines of conquest. McKeon*
> *Industries presents to the world our Unstoppable*
> *Soldiers!*

The Unstoppable Soldier that hatched out of Felek Szczerba ate the cameraman, too.

Apparently, the scientists at McKeon Industries did not have any ideas for what to do about the Unstoppable Soldiers that had taken over their Unstoppable Corn Research Unit. They only knew that they wanted to sell the Unstoppable Soldiers, and that they were unsuccessful at shooting them. So the leaders of McKeon

Industries did the worst possible thing you could do with an Unstoppable Soldier infestation: They waited to see if the Unstoppable Soldiers would simply die, or go away on their own.

Unstoppable Soldiers do not just go away.

Unstoppable Soldiers can live a very long time between meals.

McKeon Industries eventually learned these two details. Unfortunately for an entire crew of McKeon Industries scientists, they also learned that Unstoppable Soldiers were bulletproof.

Dr. Grady McKeon narrated:

> *In the spring of 1968, tireless scientists at McKeon*
> *Labs kept round-the-clock vigil on our formidable*
> *troops, observing carefully while the burgeoning females*
> *deposited egg masses as large as a high school basketball*
> *court!*
> *Imagine the reproductive and growth potential of*
> *such an army, my friends!*

Robby said, "Uh. Those egg things look exactly like the shit inside the globes."

He was right.

The third stage in the infestation of Unstoppable Soldiers—the breeding and egg-laying phase—reverted back in appearance to the original black-pulsing and cauliflowered mass of the *412E* mold; but on a much grander scale.

Like the contained mold specimen Robby and I first saw inside Johnny McKeon's office the night we climbed down the Roof Access ladder and into *From Attic to Seller Consignment Store*, the egg masses laid by the two female Unstoppable Soldiers quivered and writhed, radiating an obviously powerful light.

The egg masses swelled with small volcanic bulges that would rise up and spit globules of snot-like eruptions, only to be reabsorbed into the pulsating blob. And the female Unstoppable Soldiers never moved from their guardian positions over their rookeries. They stayed with their spiked arms spring-loaded, just waiting for anything to get near enough to become a next meal.

Dr. Grady McKeon appeared once again in the role of on-screen narrator before the end of Reel Five.

Dr. Grady McKeon had aged considerably between the filming of the first reels and the reel that showed the siege of the Unstoppable Soldiers. His hair was thinner, and behind the thick distortion of Dr. Grady McKeon's eyeglasses, his eye twitch fired and fired like an inexhaustible machine pistol.

Dr. Grady McKeon said:

> *It was merely by blind chance, my friends, that we at McKeon Industries ultimately discovered the secret to de-mobilizing our Unstoppable Soldiers. Pay attention, my friends, for you may be able to affect a similar salvation if the conditions are favorable in your situation.*
>
> *If not, then take heart. Enjoy your lives here in Eden. And, by all means breed, my friends. Breed and live in love. The New Universe depends on your success.*
>
> *I love you. I do love you all.*

Then Grady McKeon began to weep on camera.

Robby said, "He is fucking insane."

"Uh," I said. "Let's have another cigarette."

Scientists at the lab dared to enter the sealed-off Unstoppable Corn Unit where the eggs had been laid. The McKeon Industries scientists formed an armed phalanx in their Eden jumpsuits. Dr. Grady McKeon himself led the entry of the scientist army into the secure laboratory.

Dr. Grady McKeon and his scientists were armed with flame-throwers.

History provides a compelling argument that every scientist who tinkers around with unstoppable shit needs a reliable flame-thrower.

When Dr. Grady McKeon entered the lab, however, the Unstoppable Soldiers reacted to him in exactly the same manner I had seen Hungry Jack respond to Robby: The Unstoppable Soldiers were afraid of Dr. Grady McKeon.

They tried to get away from him.

Dr. Grady McKeon was clearly the God of Unstoppable Soldiers.

So McKeon Industries reasoned that since Dr. Grady McKeon had brought the Unstoppable Soldiers into being, it was he that could erase their existence as well.

So they *experimented*.

The notable characteristics of McKeon Industries experimentation entailed two prominent features: First, scientists working alongside Dr. Grady McKeon seemed to have no logical expectation for any particular outcome. They simply randomly selected any convenient biological agents and threw them into the paint cans of their soup kettle.

Second, for whatever reasons, the McKeon labs seemed a bit overly obsessed with blood or sperm as their default catalysts.

ROBBY THE THEOLOGIAN

UNSTOPPABLE SOLDIERS WERE ridiculously easy to kill.

It cost McKeon Industries a few more scientist-meals to figure that simple fact out, but eventually the problem of the first infestation had been clearly put to rest.

They started, naturally, with sperm.

Scientists at McKeon Industries's Unstoppable Soldier Unit used Dr. Grady McKeon's sperm. They loaded plastic capsules filled with sperm into ink-marker guns and shot the capsules at the Unstoppable Soldiers.

Unstoppable Soldiers do not appreciate being shot with somebody's sperm.

One Unstoppable Soldier snatched the unfortunate scientist with the plastic-capsule-sperm-pistol, and picked him up by his head, while the other two males played wishbone with his legs.

It was a gruesome spectacle.

"You can't really blame them for doing that," Robby said.

"No," I agreed. "Can't blame them at all. Who *wouldn't* get ticked off if you shot them with plastic capsules filled with Dr. Grady McKeon's sperm?"

"Even Saint Kazimierz would get mad at a guy over shit like that," Robby said.

Robby Brees was such a gifted theologian.

The two female Unstoppable Soldiers remained, poised motionless in their guarding positions over their pulsating mountains of eggs.

The scientist who lost his life in the failed sperm attack was named Heinrich Fuchs. It was an unfortunate surname, by Iowa standards.

Heinrich Fuchs was born in a place called Splugen, which is in Switzerland.

I researched Heinrich Fuchs. There were a lot of Fuchs in Splugen. Splugen was full of dumb Fuchs.

The Swiss are famous for maintaining neutrality, except, apparently, when it comes to shooting at monstrous bugs with someone else's sperm.

Dulce Et Decorum Est.

If McKeon Industries ever reworked its motto following *infinita frumenta!*, which basically means Unstoppable Corn, and its successor, *infinita milites!*, which means something like Unstoppable Soldiers, or shit like that, they might have considered a slogan along the lines of *post sperma sanguine conantur!*

I believe, from Latin, the phrase might be translatable to something like this: *After sperm, try blood!*

It rings nicely, but it is not nearly as melodious as a good old rhyming Iowa name.

"I'm glad it didn't work," Robby decided. "I would hate to have to fill up little bullets with my sperm just so we could go out and kill Hungry Jack."

"Uh," I said.

We realized that in the same way the 1968 Unstoppable Soldiers cowered away from Dr. Grady McKeon because it was *his* blood that created them, the Unstoppable Soldiers in Ealing today would only be stopped by Robby Brees.

That was what the insane Dr. Grady McKeon meant when he told us, "Pay attention, my friends, for you may be able to affect a similar salvation if the conditions are favorable in your situation."

It was the blood that did the trick, and Robby Brees was God to Ealing's newest crop of Unstoppable Soldiers.

The scientists at McKeon Industries, none of whom had ever received a Nobel Prize and its accompanying million dollars and trip to Sweden for a threesome with Robby Brees and Shann Collins, nearly drained Dr. Grady McKeon dry collecting blood from the twitching man. Once they did, their initial method of delivery was

294 | ANDREW SMITH

less sophisticated than the plastic capsules filled with sperm: One of the scientists went into the lab where the Unstoppable Soldiers had taken over, and he squirted them with Dr. Grady McKeon's blood from a large plastic hypodermic.

That particular scientist lost his right arm from the elbow down.

"That is a really dumb way to lose an arm," I pointed out.

"Those guys actually went to college and shit," Robby said.

"I think a lot of colleges in the sixties offered degrees in taking LSD, Rob," I said.

"It is fortunate you were not born with two heads," Robby concluded.

But a remarkable thing happened once the targeted Unstoppable Soldier had come into contact with the blood of his God. The Unstoppable Soldier stopped, and fell to pieces.

The six-foot-tall praying mantis with tooth-spiked arms simply broke apart, segment by segment.

That was the first Unstoppable Soldier. It was the one that hatched out of Felek Szczerba.

At that exact moment, as Robby and I sat watching Reel Five of *Eden Orientation Series*, the disconnected pieces of Felek Szczerba's Unstoppable Soldier body were floating in a brine of preservatives, sealed within large glass cases resembling aquariums, inside Johnny McKeon's private office.

So McKeon Industries was able to clean up the first infestation of Unstoppable Soldiers in Ealing, Iowa, during 1968. They let the eggs begin to hatch, unfortunate as it was. Film images captured the black creatures as they began bursting out from the gooey egg masses. The miniaturized Unstoppables were about as large as third-graders as soon as they hatched, and the first ones immediately began feasting on their brothers and sisters.

They were, after all, Unstoppable Soldiers. Actually, until they'd eaten and molted several times, the hatchlings were more like Unstoppable Cub Scouts.

Unstoppable Cub Scouts only want to do one thing, at least until they enter Unstoppable Puberty, which happens in about four hours.

Within days, the sealed-off McKeon Industries lab facility was completely packed—from attic to cellar—with full-grown, hungry Unstoppable Soldiers, all of which engaged in a round-the-clock unstoppable orgy of sex and cannibalism.

The experiment had to be halted.

More blood was drawn. Dr. Grady McKeon became frail and anemic. But finally, all the Unstoppable Soldiers had been erased.

It was not the end of the film, however.

The worst was yet to come.

Robby Brees and I did not know anything about it.

SATAN AND THE PASTOR

"UM, ROBBY," I said, "I just thought of something."

"I don't like the idea of draining my blood, Porcupine," Robby said.

"Not that. I was thinking, what if Ingrid needs to shit?" I said.

Neither one of us considered the fact that getting Ingrid *up* the ladder to the entry hatch was likely going to be far more difficult than getting her *down*.

Robby said, "You might just have to put her inside the Nightingale."

I shook my head.

"I could never do that to a genuine Nightingale," I said.

The movie played on.

And, at that exact moment as Robby and I sat next to each other inside Eden's theater, Pastor Roland Duff and Stan, the Mexican man who owned and operated *Satan's Pizza*, cautiously made their way across Kimber Drive toward the red and blue flashing lights of the Iowa State Patrol car.

It was not a good idea.

Stan, whose real name was *Sevastián Hernandez*, walked one step in front of Pastor Roland Duff. The two men saw Johnny McKeon driving away from the Ealing Mall.

Grasshopper Jungle was eerily quiet. The shops were all dark. This was normal for the most part because so much of the mall had shut down. But even the *Ealing Coin Wash Launderette* was lightless; and that was unusual.

Pastor Roland Duff assumed the power on the south side of Kimber Drive must have gone out. The lights were still on at *Satan's Pizza*.

Roland Duff glanced nervously at Stan Hernandez illuminated by the silent flickering lights from the patrol car. The alternating washes of blue and red made it seem like the men were standing on the dance floor at a discotheque. Pastor Roland Duff realized he had never actually *looked* at Stan Hernandez before.

Stan Hernandez was very handsome.

Too bad Stan Hernandez was Catholic, thought Roland Duff.

Roland Duff, who had never had sex with anyone, was very aroused.

Unfortunately for Pastor Roland Duff and Stan Hernandez, so was Travis Pope.

Stan Hernandez and Pastor Roland Duff got right up alongside Denny Drayton's abandoned patrol vehicle. The driver-side door had been left fully open, and the vehicle's motor was idling. The two men saw the sideways Diet Coke bottle that leaked its viscous contents of tobacco spit all over the cushioned upholstery of the driver's seat.

Denny Drayton's emptied Sig Sauer was on the ground next to the rear tire.

Trooper Drayton's mostly headless and entirely hairless corpse lay in the parking lot in front of the car.

The Unstoppable Soldier that had been Travis Pope flitted up to the roof of Denny Drayton's patrol car. He perched like an obscene living gargoyle atop the rack of flashing colorful lights.

Stan Hernandez looked up and said, "Holy shit."

Those were the last words Pastor Roland Duff, who was mostly a virgin, ever heard in his life.

Holy shit.

Excrementum Sanctum.

Travis Pope killed Stan Hernandez and Pastor Roland Duff. Travis Pope also ate Pastor Roland Duff's entire aroused body. The headmaster from Curtis Crane Lutheran Academy was very tender and moist. Travis Pope made bug shit all over the Iowa State Patrol car, then he scampered away, sniffing the air, trying to find where Eileen and the other bugs had gone.

And at exactly that moment, Ollie Jungfrau opened the door to his Dodge Caravan minivan. He put his laptop and a plastic Walmart bag, into which he'd stuffed some clean clothes, onto the passenger seat.

Ollie Jungfrau was going to get the hell out of Ealing if it was the last thing he'd ever do.

It was.

As Ollie Jungfrau made his way toward the east-west highway that connected Ealing to Waterloo and Dubuque, he noticed a

298 | ANDREW SMITH

figure running along the side of the road.

Ollie Jungfrau imagined he was stuck inside a video game.

He imagined he was in charge of driving a Dodge Caravan minivan, and the object of the game was to run down big fucking bugs.

"Suck on the front end of a Dodge fucking Caravan, you big fucking alien bugs," Ollie Jungfrau said.

Ollie Jungfrau's penis was hard.

Ollie Jungfrau got erections whenever he killed aliens in video games.

The thing Ollie Jungfrau saw running along the roadside was not a big fucking alien bug, however. The thing Ollie Jungfrau saw was Louis, the cook from *The Pancake House*, whose real name was Ah Wong Sing.

Louis was five foot four inches tall.

Louis had fucked Connie Brees three times that day, using condoms that Connie Brees found on the floor of Robby's bedroom.

Ollie Jungfrau nearly ran his friend over before he realized it was not a big fucking alien bug.

And running next to Louis was another person Ollie Jungfrau recognized: It was the eighth-grade English teacher from Curtis Crane Lutheran Academy. Her name was Mrs. Edith Mitchell.

Mrs. Edith Mitchell sometimes shopped at *Tipsy Cricket Liquors*. However, Mrs. Edith Mitchell did not purchase condoms there. Mrs. Edith Mitchell smoked Marlboro menthol cigarettes and drank white wine from cardboard boxes.

Ollie Jungfrau pulled his Dodge Caravan over to the side of the road.

"Hey, you two," Ollie Jungfrau said, "I think Ealing's being invaded by aliens or something. I'm not joking, you better get in."

Ah Wong Sing and Mrs. Edith Mitchell were frantic.

They had seen the bugs, too.

Ah Wong Sing slid open the rear side door on Ollie Jungfrau's Dodge Caravan.

"Thank God," Ah Wong Sing said.

"Thank God," Mrs. Edith Mitchell echoed.

They got inside Ollie Jungfrau's minivan. Ollie accelerated as fast as a Dodge Caravan carrying three Iowans could go. He headed toward the bridge that led out of town, just on the other side of Amelia Jenks Bloomer Park.

It was not a good idea.

SERIAL KILLER USA

I KNEW HOW to kill the Unstoppable Soldiers.

"We could use my paintball gun," I said.

Paintball is a game teenage boys like to play. We dress up in old clothes and shoot one another with mushy plastic balls filled with paint. The balls are about the size of a nickel. They burst open and leave a splatter mark upon impact, like blood.

"Uh," Robby said.

"We could take some of your blood and inject it with a hypodermic into paintballs." I said, "That's how we can kill the Unstoppable Soldiers. I am certain they have the needles and shit to do it in the clinic."

"You are insane, Austin," Robby said.

Robby crossed his arms tightly in front of his chest. He did not want me to take any of his blood.

"Do you want to stay down here forever?" I asked.

"Yes," Robby said. "I *do* want to stay down here forever. As long as the Rolling Stones are here, it's fine with me."

The film continued:

From mid-1968 until early 1970, there were a series of unsolved beheadings in Ealing, Iowa.

Robby Brees and I solved them that night, as we watched Reel Five of *Eden Orientation Series*.

Newspapers, and even the few books that had been written about the Monster of Ealing serial killings put the number of victims at seven. There were actually a lot more than that.

A head belonging to one of the victims was floating inside a large glass jar that sat on a shelf in Johnny McKeon's office in *From Attic to Seller Consignment Store* at the exact moment Robby Brees and I sat and watched our film play out.

Dr. Grady McKeon got his contract for Unstoppable Soldiers.

What engineer of warfare could possibly pass up a chance to set free a breeding, self-regenerating horde of horny and hungry Unstoppable Soldiers inside enemy territory? The Defense Department of the United States of America wanted Unstoppable Soldiers very much.

McKeon Industries tested their *412E* strain on prison inmates. The prison inmates had all volunteered for the program. They had been told it would be an opportunity to leave the country and kill Communists.

Offering the possibility of such an experience to an incarcerated prisoner in the Iowa Men's Reformatory, which is now called Anamosa State Penitentiary, is kind of like offering a lazy white kid one million dollars, a trip to Sweden, and a threesome with Shann Collins and Robby Brees.

Sign me up.

So the scientists at McKeon Industries exposed the inmate volunteers to their *412E* plague mold, strapped them down naked to hospital beds, pumped them full of liquid sedatives, and filmed the *volunteers* while McKeon Industries teams waited for the hatching to begin.

Monsters were making monsters.

At first, Dr. Grady McKeon's staff assumed the Unstoppable Soldiers that hatched would be placid and sedated from all the drugs, too.

It was not a good idea.

History shows that, as a group, scientists tend to not be very aggressive when it comes to physical attacks. The scientists who worked for Dr. Grady McKeon were like good-morning breakfasts for the first hatchling Unstoppable Soldiers.

It also became apparent to the McKeon Industries scientists that the Unstoppable Soldiers are always very horny. The Unstoppable Soldiers needed females, but, unfortunately, there were no female volunteers for the *Unstoppable Soldiers Project, Phase 2.* This made the Unstoppable Soldiers very edgy.

Six-foot-tall praying mantises with jagged rows of serrated teeth on their arms are not very good at masturbating. This made them even angrier.

Dr. Grady McKeon decided to halt the experiment a second time.

Again, the Unstoppable Soldiers proved difficult to stop. Ultimately it was discovered that the only way to prevent hatching-out among the exposed inmate volunteers was by removing their heads.

This is what the scientists at McKeon Industries did.

And they cleaned up their failures as sloppily as they did everything else, which accounts for the discovery of headless corpses in fields around Ealing, Iowa, in 1969.

Robby posed a question: "Austin, is it just me, or do you feel *dumber*, too, after spending the last couple hours watching those

McKeon scientists experiment with shit?"

"No doubt, Rob, we have lost some brain cells," I answered.

And Robby said, "What are we going to do, Austin?"

Ingrid sighed beneath my feet.

That was usually Ingrid's question.

The film ended with footage of the McKeon Industries Family Picnic Day: happy scientist families eating corn on the cob and playing softball or running three-legged races. It was all very creepy, made more so by Dr. Grady McKeon's voiced-over exhortations:

Breed, my friends, breed. Breed and be the New Human Race.

"I wonder if that corn they're feeding the kids is Unstoppable," Robby said.

I said, "Uh."

Fuck corn.

I never wanted to eat corn again.

Just as the film ran its last strip of leader through the projector, Robby and I heard another sound coming through Eden's speaker system:

Welcome to Eden. Please secure the hatch upon entry.
Welcome to Eden. Please secure the hatch upon entry.

Someone had opened the hatch from outside.

Someone was coming down the entry ladder.

Welcome to Eden. Please secure the hatch upon entry.

LOOKING FOR WIGGLES

THE MOVIE MADE quite an impression on Robby Brees and me.

We were terrified.

Robby and I stared at each other, both of us uncertain as to which course of action to take: Run and hide, prepare to fight, or go out to the mudroom and see who might be calling on us so late at night.

It was past midnight, Friday morning.

The end of the world was one week old and it was getting out of hand.

"What are we going to do, Ingrid?" I said.

I pinched the silver medallion of Saint Kazimierz between my finger and thumb, raised it to my lips, and kissed it.

At exactly that moment, Eric Andrew Szerba, my father, and Connie May Kenney Szerba, my mother, were drinking cups of strong German coffee. They sat at my brother's bedside in a military hospital, where he was not recovering very well from losing the lower half of his right leg and both of his testicles to a shrapnel bomb in Afghanistan.

On the other side of Ealing, on Onondaga Street, the Unstoppable Soldier that hatched out of Eileen Pope entered Duane Coventry's house through the open front door. Eileen Pope began filling the rooms of the small house with jellied clusters of translucent gray eggs. In a few hours, the house would be entirely filled with Eileen Pope's egg mass, which would turn black and boil with mountainous eruptions of oily unstoppable goo.

The males would have to leave Eileen Pope alone now. Tyler Jacobson and Roger Baird perched alongside each other, up on the roof of the house. Unstoppable Soldiers do not sleep; they rest.

Unstoppable Soldiers cannot close their massive compound eyes.

The Unstoppable Soldier that hatched out of Tyler Jacobson would not have slept even if he could shut his massive, lidless eyes. Tyler Jacobson was hopped up on all the crystal meth that had been coursing through Duane Coventry's body. The crystal meth made Tyler Jacobson very edgy and extremely horny. Tyler Jacobson scrambled on top of Roger Baird, who was also an Unstoppable Soldier, and attempted to copulate with him.

Roger Baird had been in a resting state.

Roger Baird was not very happy after being disturbed from his rest by another male Unstoppable Soldier that was in the act of copulating with him. Tyler Jacobson was confused. The two six-foot-tall praying mantis monsters fought.

Roger Baird was pinned. Tyler Jacobson bit Roger's head completely off. Roger Baird's head rolled down the slope of Duane Coventry's roof like a noisy pinecone felled by a gust of wind.

Clop clop! Clop clop! Thud! went Roger's triangular head as it tumbled unevenly down the shingled pitch of the roof, dropped, and landed below the front porch.

Undeterred, Tyler Jacobson continued doing the two things that Unstoppable Soldiers on crystal meth like to do.

Tyler Jacobson was very confused.

Connie Brees was very tired. She worked on the night staff at the FedEx facility outside Waterloo. She sorted and scanned flats and packages. While she worked, Connie Brees's brain floated along on little blue kayaks.

She floated and floated.

Connie Brees thought about Ah Wong Sing, the man she'd had sex with all afternoon long. Connie Brees wanted to have sex with Ah Wong Sing again. She thought about the ocean, volcanoes in Guatemala, and her son, Robert Brees Jr.

Connie Brees had never actually seen the ocean in her entire life.

Connie Brees wondered if her son, Robert, and the Polish kid he constantly hung around with were gay. Connie Brees glanced at the clock to see if it was time to go outside and have a cigarette. She decided that her son, Robert Brees Jr., and the Polish kid he always hung around with were most likely homosexual for each other. It did not matter, Connie thought. She wanted Robert Brees Jr. to be happy.

The Polish kid seemed nice.

Connie Brees would rather Robert be happy than grow up and float around on little blue kayaks going nowhere.

Connie Brees looked up at the clock again.

Travis Pope made his way through the pitch dark at Amelia Jenks Bloomer Park. Unstoppable Soldiers can see very well at night. Travis Pope sniffed and sniffed at the air. He could smell Eileen Pope, and he was making his way out of the park toward an older neighborhood of small homes along Onondaga Street.

Travis Pope scurried out onto the highway behind Amelia Jenks Bloomer Park. A two-lane, steel Warren truss bridge crossed Kelsey Creek there.

Kelsey Creek is a tributary of the Cedar River, which runs through Waterloo.

Travis Pope stood in the center of the highway at the threshold of the Kelsey Creek Bridge.

The headlights from Ollie Jungfrau's Dodge Caravan minivan washed over Travis Pope, making him glow like a pale green ghost. Everyone inside Ollie Jungfrau's Dodge Caravan minivan could see the six-foot-tall, spike-armed Unstoppable Soldier that stood in the middle of the bridge.

Ollie Jungfrau laughed.

"Ha-ha," Ollie said.

Ollie Jungfrau was in a video game, and he had two passengers who were watching him play from the backseat of his Dodge Caravan.

"Suck on my fat Dodge Caravan cock, you sonofabitch fucking alien bug," Ollie Jungfrau said. Then he added, "Welcome to Earth, motherfucker. Next stop: Hell."

Ollie Jungfrau was a tool.

Ollie Jungfrau jammed the accelerator all the way down to the floor.

Ollie Jungfrau had an erection.

Louis, whose real name was Ah Wong Sing, knew that Ollie Jungfrau regularly used obscene language when he became caught up inside his video games. Mrs. Edith Mitchell, on the other hand, was disgusted by what she heard and saw.

It did not matter. Mrs. Edith Mitchell was in shock, anyway.

Earlier that evening, Mrs. Edith Mitchell had been outside in her neighborhood, which was just west of the Del Vista Arms. She had been looking for her blue Maine coon cat. The cat had not been home in two days.

Edith Mitchell's blue Maine coon cat was named Wiggles.

Wiggles had no balls, but this was neither a result of having eaten Unstoppable Corn, nor because Wiggles had ever been in the blast pattern of a roadside bomb in Afghanistan.

Wiggles's balls had never been named, as far as I can tell.

Mrs. Edith Mitchell did not find Wiggles.

When she returned to her home, the Unstoppable Soldier that had hatched out from Hungry Jack in the middle of a cornfield across from a Waterloo gay bar was inside her living room eating her husband.

Tally-Ho!

It was a mess.

Edith Mitchell's husband was named Leslie Mitchell. Leslie Mitchell was a retired veterinarian. Leslie Mitchell cut Wiggles's balls off.

Wiggles's balls ended up in a trash can, which is what animal doctors tend to do with all the testicles they cut off things. Wiggles's balls ended up in the same trash can that contained a thumb-sized tumor that had been cut from the throat of Ingrid, my golden retriever.

Ingrid never barked after that.

When Mrs. Edith Mitchell came home and saw an enormous bug devouring her husband inside her living room, she ran off screaming down the street.

The television was on. Leslie Mitchell had been watching a program about how to cook lamb when Hungry Jack came in and started eating him.

Now Mrs. Edith Mitchell was staring through the windshield of a Dodge Caravan minivan, while Ollie Jungfrau zeroed in on one of the monsters poised motionless in the road directly ahead.

"Suck this dick, bitch," Ollie Jungfrau said.

Ollie Jungfrau dripped sweat that smelled of garlic and urine. His arms locked straight on the steering wheel.

The Dodge Caravan minivan impacted squarely with the Unstoppable Soldier that had been standing in the roadway at the Kelsey Creek Bridge.

Dodge Caravan minivans do not hold up so well against Unstoppable Soldiers with exoskeletons as tough as the exterior hull of an aircraft carrier.

It was like an Ozark watermelon throwing itself onto the cutting edge of a samurai sword.

The front end of Ollie Jungfrau's Dodge Caravan minivan shattered. The impact of the collision with Travis Pope drove the Dodge's motor all the way back to the front seat. Ollie Jungfrau's right foot was severed in the crash. Travis Pope's enormous head slapped through the Dodge Caravan's windshield and crushed Ollie

Jungfrau's rib cage.

The crumpled Dodge Caravan grinded and scraped its way to the center of the Kelsey Creek Bridge before coming to rest against the steel trusses. Before the van stopped moving, Travis Pope had climbed in through the broken windshield.

Travis Pope, who was not very hungry, began picking disinterestedly at Ollie Jungfrau's fleshy corpse.

In the backseat, Ah Wong Sing and Mrs. Edith Mitchell had been dusted with gems of safety glass and flecked by Ollie Jungfrau's blood, but they were still very much alive. They were also trapped inside a crumpled Dodge Caravan minivan.

Ah Wong Sing attempted to open the side door, but it would not move. The frame of Ollie Jungfrau's Dodge Caravan minivan had twisted inward on itself, so nothing would open.

Mrs. Edith Mitchell covered her face with her hands.

The Unstoppable Soldier that hatched out from Travis Pope sat up front, watching the two frightened humans in back while he chewed and chewed at Ollie Jungfrau.

Kelsey Creek Bridge is a good spot for walleye fishing.

The vice president of the United States of America once caught an eleven-pound walleye in the Allegheny Reservoir in Pennsylvania.

One female walleye can lay 500,000 eggs during a spawn.

Travis Pope made shit all over the front seats. Then Travis Pope climbed out through the van's shattered windshield and scampered off into the Iowa night, sniffing the air, looking for Eileen Pope.

The vice president of the United States of America was asleep. He dozed off after receiving a blow job. Blow jobs always made the vice president drowsy. The vice president of the United States of America was scheduled to fly to Germany early the following morning, to visit in the afternoon with American soldiers who had been wounded in Afghanistan.

The vice president's wife, who has no formal title, was having a glass of Scotch whisky.

And at that exact moment, Wiggles, Mrs. Edith Mitchell's wayward blue Maine coon cat, came back home looking for food.

CONCERNING THE BISON, AND FREE WILL

LATER, AFTER ROBBY and I left Eden, I came to a sudden realization about history.

Here is what I concluded:

All this time, I have been devoting too much thought to the guys who painted the bison on the wall of the cave, and too little attention to the bison itself.

I mean, the bison is the important member of the team, isn't he?

But once the historians put the thing on the wall, it was almost as though every bison for all eternity became doomed to face the hunter's interminable slaughter.

We killed this big hairy thing and this big hairy thing. And that was our day. You know what I mean.

I began to consider the fact that maybe history is actually the great destroyer of free will. After all, if what we blindly believe about history is true—the old cliché admonishing us to learn how *not* to repeat the same shit over and over again—then why do the same shitty things keep happening and happening and happening?

I felt guilty for ever having written anything at all about me, about Robby or Shann, Johnny McKeon, Pastor Roland Duff,

Unstoppable Corn, Saint Kazimierz, Krzys Szczerba, *Contained MI Plague Strain 412E*, Andrzej Szczerba, Herman Weinbach, a talking European starling named Baby, Felek Szczerba, Phoebe Hildebrandt, Eva Nightingale, my brother, Eric, and two prostitutes named Tiffany and Rhonda, whom we met on the third-floor balcony at a hotel in Nashville, Tennessee.

Each of us became a bison on the wall of my own cave.

Paavi Seppanen.

Julio Arguelles.

Everyone on every road that crossed beneath the point of my pen was always going to do the same things over and over and over.

I was confused.

How could I be in love with a girl *and* a boy, at the same time?

I was trapped forever.

You know what I mean.

POPULATION EXPLOSION

WELCOME TO EDEN. *Please secure the hatch upon entry.*

The repeating message finally stopped.

Whoever had joined Robby and me in Eden closed the hatch after they came inside.

But it was no six-foot-tall praying mantis army of spike-armed killers, nor was it some crazed hermit McKeon Industries Unstoppable Scientist. Our new arrivals in Eden were Shann Collins, her stepfather, Johnny McKeon, and her mother, Wendy McKeon.

Johnny McKeon was carrying the biggest handgun I had ever seen.

Johnny McKeon's Smith & Wesson .500 magnum was made in

Massachusetts. A bullet fired from the pistol travels at nearly two thousand feet per second.

"*I wonder if Johnny kills queers,*" Robby whispered.

"Uh," I said.

Johnny McKeon did not come down into Eden to kill Robby Brees and me.

Shann and her family had come down to Eden because they knew the Unstoppable Soldiers were running wild in Ealing, Iowa.

Robby and I stood in the doorway to the locker room. Ingrid, never one to get too worked up about such things as late-night visitors, sat on the floor between us and yawned.

To Johnny McKeon and his wife, Robby Brees and I must have looked like players in a science fiction movie, dressed as we were in our matching and numbered Eden Project jumpsuits.

Shann Collins, who now officially hated me and Robby Brees, avoided my eyes when I tried to look at her.

"Welcome to Eden, Johnny," I said. "I think you are safe down here."

"Uh," Johnny McKeon said.

Johnny McKeon was pale and shaken. He looked at the gun in his hand, then back at me with an apologetic expression like Johnny McKeon wasn't aware that a gun the size of a small bazooka had somehow attached itself to the palm of his right hand.

"You can't shoot them, anyway," I said.

"Uh. I know that, Austin," Johnny McKeon said.

And then Johnny asked, "Are you okay?"

I caught Shann's eye.

Shann Collins had been looking at my face. She turned pale and immediately lowered her gaze. Shann Collins was confused. She was in love with the Polish kid who was also confused.

I said, "Yes. We are okay, Johnny."

Johnny McKeon walked across the floor of the mudroom and placed his Smith & Wesson .500 magnum on the bench just below the scientist's old windbreaker that had been hanging from a hook on the wall for nearly half a century.

I said, "I suppose it's time for me and Robby to show you what has been going on."

Shann coughed nervously.

You know what I mean.

EVERYTHING A GUY COULD NEED, AND THE TWO BEST ROCK ALBUMS EVER MADE

WE WERE THE New Humans.

Johnny McKeon, Shann Collins, and her mother, Wendy Collins McKeon, changed into Eden Project jumpsuits and white scientist socks. Robby and I did not stay in the locker room and watch them change their clothes. Things were weird enough without doing shit like that.

When the newest New Humans joined us in the lecture hall, I pointed out the chalkboard diagram of the development from *412E*, the Unstoppable Corn mold, to the creatures Johnny McKeon had seen fucking and eating earlier that evening in the alley at Grasshopper Jungle.

Although we suspected it, Robby and I did not know for certain that there were several more Unstoppable Soldiers up above us in Ealing until we heard it from Johnny McKeon.

Up until that moment, Robby and I had only seen one Unstoppable Soldier, the one that came out of Hungry Jack.

Despite that, we did believe the Hoover Boys and Grant Wallace had to have hatched out as well.

Johnny McKeon also confirmed the Unstoppable Soldiers were spawning.

Robby Brees and I had watched all five reels of *Eden Orientation Series*. We knew the world had less than twenty-four hours before every human being on the planet dropped to a lower level on the food chain.

It was not a good level to be on.

"Uh, Rob," I said. "You still against the paintball idea?"

Robby said, "Uh."

Johnny McKeon drank Scotch, and Wendy made herself a vodka gimlet at Eden's *Tally-Ho!*, which was the nicest bar in a thirty-mile radius for this part of Iowa.

Things would be better for Johnny and Wendy McKeon if they were drunk.

Robby Brees reached across the bar and nonchalantly grabbed the bottle of Scotch whisky and poured some out into two glasses.

Nobody said anything about it.

Robby said, "*Tally-Ho!*"

Robby Brees and I drank the Scotch whisky. It tasted like hot cinnamon and dried fruit.

Johnny McKeon said, "This Scotch must be sixty years old."

Johnny McKeon appreciated good Scotch whisky.

"It is like drinking history," I said.

Johnny said, "Cheers."

Robby Brees and I got drunk with Johnny McKeon and Shann Collins's mom in Eden. It only took two small glasses of Scotch whisky to make me feel like everything was funny, and I wanted to dance with Robby Brees again.

We lit cigarettes.

Wendy McKeon might have known Robby and I smoked cigarettes, but we had never done it in front of her. She was distant and unaffected by what was going on. Johnny and Shann must have scared the shit out of her with the stories about what they knew was happening in Ealing.

And Johnny and Shann didn't know half of it.

Wendy McKeon was very pretty. Her breasts were tight and sharp beneath the shimmering fabric of her jumpsuit. I wanted to touch them.

Wendy McKeon was Eden 93.

Johnny McKeon was Eden 7.

Wendy McKeon's hair was the color of ground coriander.

I fantasized that somebody would suggest we all have an orgy when we got to the parts of the film where Dr. Grady McKeon commanded us to breed. The Scotch whisky made me feel very horny and confused. I would be the first one to volunteer to strip naked out of my clothes, but Johnny McKeon kind of made me feel nervous.

I could not imagine Johnny McKeon ever having sexual intercourse with Wendy Collins McKeon.

Johnny McKeon was the only person in Eden I did not want to take a shower with at that exact moment.

I realized I was getting a Scotch whisky–fueled erection. I did not believe anyone would approve of my erection at that moment. So I sat at the bar and asked Robby for another cigarette.

Robby knew what I was thinking. He always did.

"*Tally-Ho!* Porcupine," Robby said.

Robby Brees was drunk. He lit a cigarette for me and passed it to me.

The filter end was just a little bit wet with Robby's spit.

"I'll be danged if they don't have everything you'd ever need down in this place," Johnny McKeon said.

Johnny McKeon got up from the barstool. He threw a dart at the board that hung on the other side of the pool table.

"I'll be double-danged," Johnny said, daringly.

"A proper Eden will always have everything a guy could ever need or want, Johnny," I said.

"That, and the two best rock albums ever made in the history of humankind," Robby added.

THE BLOOD OF GOD

WE TOOK JOHNNY McKeon and his family on a tour of the silo.

We did not show them the entire *Eden Orientation Series*. Johnny McKeon only wanted to see a portion of the final film. He wanted his wife to know what the creatures he saw at Grasshopper Jungle looked like.

It did not matter. You could not watch five minutes of *Eden Orientation Series* and not witness some experiment with sperm, or shit like that, or hear Dr. Grady McKeon telling us that it was our duty to start having sex.

"My big brother was a nut case," Johnny McKeon concluded.

"Isn't there television down here?" Wendy McKeon asked. "Maybe there would be something on the news about what's going on."

It was a good question.

The lack of televisions did not register with me until Wendy McKeon asked about it. We hadn't seen one television set in Eden. I imagined Dr. Grady McKeon concluded that when the Eden Project became a necessary sanctuary for humanity, there would be nothing at all worth watching on any broadcast stations.

New Humans would be without commercial television.

Maybe there was hope, after all.

Dr. Grady McKeon was probably correct about post-apocalyptic television broadcasts, although we eventually did find a bank of five side-by-side televisions that night in Eden's Brain Room.

Here is what happened:

We were all very tired after watching the final few moments of corn eating and three-legged-race running in Reel Five. Shann would neither speak to me nor sit near me inside Eden's theater. I thought Johnny McKeon or Wendy might have seen Shann's behavior as cold or unexpected, but if they did, I could not tell.

I began to think guilty thoughts that maybe Shann had said something to her parents about me. I was confused and frustrated, and I desperately wanted to have an opportunity to speak to Shann.

Robby Brees and I were also drunk. The Scotch whisky made us brave and reckless.

I admitted to Johnny McKeon that we had come up with a plan to kill the Unstoppable Soldiers—a plan involving Robby Brees's blood and the paintball guns that had been stored inside my garage ever since my brother, Eric, went away to join the Marines and have his testicles blown off.

Robby announced that if he could have one more drink of Scotch whisky he would let me take blood from him.

It was all a very ghastly proposition.

I did not think I could actually do something like stick a needle into Robby Brees's arm. The thought of inflicting pain on Robby nearly made me cry. With everything that had been going on in my life that past week, and now with Shann treating me like an enemy, I was an emotional disaster.

Shann's mother, Wendy McKeon, had been a registered nurse before marrying Johnny McKeon and moving to Ealing. She said if she could have one more vodka gimlet, she would draw a few vials of blood from Robby Brees.

I went pale.

Robby went pale.

It was all very ghastly.

The clinic filled with the steaming smell of alcohol breath. There is something about the sterility of clinics that repels everything, as though they are vacuums unto themselves, like the glass globes into which the McKeon scientists trapped all kinds of shit. As soon as the five of us entered the Eden Project clinic, the place absorbed the odors of booze, sweat, cigarettes, and golden retriever.

"I have B.O.," I said.

Ingrid sighed and curled up on the floor beneath the flat, padded examination table.

"Saint Kazimierz brought a dead girl back to life, and he also made a blind boy see," I said. I unzipped the top of my jumpsuit and slipped the silver chain over my head. I told Robby he should wear the Saint Kazimierz medal while Wendy McKeon drew blood from him. I put my chain on Robby. He looked scared.

Wendy McKeon told Robby to lie down on the table and strip to his waist. Wendy began opening cupboards and drawers in the clinic, gathering the things she would use to collect blood from Robby Brees.

Robby undid the top of his jumpsuit and slid it down around his hips. He lay there, half naked on the operating table.

"I wonder if those McKeon sickos ever operated on teenagers here," I said.

Robby said, "Uh."

I touched the Saint Kazimierz medal and pressed it against Robby's heart.

Wendy put two wadded balls of gauze into Robby's palm and

told him to squeeze them.

"I bet that's the first time you ever squeezed someone else's balls in a doctor's office," I joked.

Robby said, "Shut up, Austin."

"Okay," I agreed.

Shann was exasperated. She said, "I can't watch this."

Shann *thud-thudded* in her padded scientist socks out into the hallway.

I wanted to follow her, but I was stuck. I could not just leave Robby alone in the clinic. I looked back and forth, from the door to Robby's pale chest as Wendy McKeon tightened a rubber tube around my best friend's bicep.

Robby gripped the wads of gauze in his hand. He was scared. I didn't want to see Robby Brees scared and hurt.

Robby's skin was the color of the insides of sweet Babcock peaches.

He knew what I was thinking.

Robby Brees whispered, "You should go talk to her, Porcupine."

Robby Brees always knew what was going on.

I wanted to ask Ingrid what was I going to do, but I did not want Johnny McKeon and Shann's mom to think I was an insane kid who talked to his non-barking dog and shit like that.

"Uh . . . Um . . . ," I said.

Wendy McKeon stabbed a thick needle right into the bend of Robby's arm.

"Gee whiz, babe," Johnny McKeon said.

Thick maroon blood began filling up the cylinder on the syringe.

Blub-blub! went Robby's blood.

Robby winced.

I felt my knees buckle. "Uh. I better step outside," I said.

WANDA MAE'S PINK BOWLING BALL

SHANN COLLINS HAD gone down to the end of the hallway. She stood outside the doorway to Eden's bowling alley. Shann faced away from me, but I could tell she was crying.

I felt like shit.

"Please don't cry, Shann," I said.

I put my hand on her shoulder and slid it up beneath the soft warm fluffs of her perfect hair. She did not pull away from me. That was progress, I thought.

History is all about progress.

"And please don't hate Robby. Uh. Or me. I would never lie to you, Shann. I love you too much." I said, "And, uh, be honest: How many boys do you know who actually have the ability to save the entire world? Robby Brees is like a superhero."

Shann laughed and cried at the same time.

History does show that Shann Collins was a complex person, capable of doing such things simultaneously.

All my best friends were very complex.

"Why didn't you ever tell me, Austin?" Shann said.

I nearly gave Shann Collins the automated teenage boy response, which would have been *I don't know*. I stopped myself.

"Do you really want to hear about Robby? Because I will tell you everything I know about him, Shann," I said.

Shann said, "No."

I said, "I love you, Shann Collins."

She wiped at her face. It was my fault Shann was crying.

"Tell me the truth. Are you gay, Austin?" Shann Collins said.

"I really don't think so. Uh. I don't know, Shann." I said, "Maybe there is something wrong with me."

"But I love you, Austin," Shann said.

"I know that. I'm sorry for hurting you, Shann." I said, "I can't even begin to tell you how much I love you."

Then Shann turned around and put her arms around me. We kissed, more deeply and passionately than we had ever kissed in our lives. I pressed my hips into hers. She did not back away from me at all.

Shann Collins clearly approved of my erection.

She said, "I'm scared, Austin."

I whispered, "I guess I am, too."

"Okay."

"I'm sorry."

We moved like tangled dancers through the doorway and into the bowling alley.

That was a lot of progress.

The world was turning, and mankind was marching onward, doing the same stupid shit over and over and over.

I unzipped Shann Collins's jumpsuit and did the same to mine, so I could press my bare chest against her full breasts. My throat tightened. My heart felt like it was squirming up inside my neck, just like a fat walleye forcing its way through a shallow creek during the spring spawn.

Eden 5 needed to spawn.

We went deeper into the bowling alley.

I imagined being inside a cave, fifteen thousand years in the past.

Shann Collins and I threw off all our clothing. Naked, we went down onto the floor together.

"Do you think this is the end of the world, Austin?"

"We'll be okay. We'll be okay."

Shann kissed me. She put her mouth everywhere on my body.

It was electric.

But I could not stop myself from thinking about my brother, Eric, and the two prostitutes named Tiffany and Rhonda. I thought about Saint Kazimierz and his hair shirt, about Krzys Szczerba, and all the Szczerba men after him. I thought about Robby in the clinic.

I thought about naming my balls.

Shann Collins helped me put my penis inside her vagina, and we had sexual intercourse right there on the floor of Eden's bowling alley, below a pair of shoes and a pink ball that had *Wanda Mae* embossed in gold on it.

Our sex was noisy and urgent and wet. I rubbed my kneecaps raw, scraping them on the rough carpeting at the shoe-changing station. I pushed Shann along on her butt until her head and mine bumped against the rattling rack of bowling shoes.

I did not care about anything at that exact moment.

No one knew anything about it.

Dr. Grady McKeon would be proud of Shann Collins and me. We were unstoppable.

At exactly that moment, Louis, the cook from *The Pancake House*, whose real name was Ah Wong Sing, climbed over the bloody, shitty mess in the front seat of Ollie Jungfrau's Dodge Caravan minivan. He got out of the van through the shattered window, the same way the Unstoppable Soldier that once had been Travis Pope did.

Ah Wong Sing wanted to help Mrs. Edith Mitchell get out, too.

"Climb over the seat," he said to her.

Mrs. Edith Mitchell shook her head and said no.

Ah Wong Sing tried all the doors on the Dodge Caravan. He could not open any of them.

"Climb over the front seat," Ah Wong Sing repeated.

But Mrs. Edith Mitchell would not move.

Ah Wong Sing said he would get somebody to help. He ran

off, across the Kelsey Creek Bridge toward Amelia Jenks Bloomer Park, which was the opposite direction from where he had seen the Unstoppable Soldier going.

Ah Wong Sing was smart.

Mrs. Edith Mitchell waited in the crumpled Dodge Caravan minivan.

It was not a good idea.

At exactly that moment, Robby Brees was lying back, dizzy. Robby stared up at the soft fluorescent lights inside the clinic while Wendy McKeon smoothed a plastic bandage across the small dark hole she had left in Robby's arm.

"Just lie there for a few minutes," Wendy McKeon told him.

Then Wendy McKeon put the three large syringes she had filled with Robby Brees's blood inside a small steel clinical refrigerator.

Johnny McKeon was asleep on a wheeled doctor's chair with the back of his head propped against the wall.

In the bowling alley, Shann Collins and I hurried to put our clothes on. We were both sticky and smeared all over with semen and saliva. I wanted to take a shower.

Neither of us said a word.

I was more confused than ever.

I felt terrible for all the things I had selfishly done to Shann and Robby. I shut my eyes and asked Saint Kazimierz to help me.

Outside, I heard Wendy McKeon calling for us in the hallway.

I stuttered guiltily, offering something shitty about bowling a few frames when I saw Robby Brees, Ingrid, and Shann's parents looking for us in the hallway.

I do not lie, and now I was a liar, too.

Shann and I were mortified with embarrassment.

Robby's mouth tightened in a disappointed frown. He looked drained and tired.

Robby knew what we did. He could tell.

Robby Brees always knew everything about me.

Robby Brees slipped my silver chain over his head and handed the medallion with Saint Kazimierz back to me.

Robby said, "Thanks for this, Austin. You probably need it more than me now."

A cigarette was what I needed, but I did not have the guts to say anything to Robby Brees.

I looked at Ingrid and said, "What am I going to do, Ingrid?"

Ingrid yawned, which is what Ingrid always does when she is confused.

I was confused, too.

Johnny McKeon said, "Dang. A dog who understands English. Ain't that a kick?"

RULES ARE RULES, BUT THE BRAIN ROOM IS NOT PARTICULARLY BRAINY

JOHNNY MCKEON DID not have to try very hard to convince me and Robby that we should wait until daylight before going back to my house for the paintball guns.

Robby Brees and I were going to use my paintball guns and Robby's blood to kill the Unstoppable Soldiers and save the world.

Nobody wants to go out in the dark with Unstoppable Soldiers on the loose, even if you happen to be hanging around with their God, who is armed with a paintball gun, or shit like that.

I hoped the God of Unstoppable Soldiers was not too upset with me for sneaking away while his blood was being drained so I could have sexual intercourse with Shann Collins on the floor of a bowling alley.

Unlike my great-grandfather, Andrzej Szczerba, I was not testing myself or trying to prove anything.

That was what I told myself, at least.

I was probably wrong.

I mumbled something about wanting to take a shower. I stunk.

Wendy McKeon said that if we had to stay in Eden for a while, we would have to make some kind of rules about when boys could shower and when girls could shower.

It was a ridiculous thing to make a rule about. Wendy McKeon may just as well have made a rule about the rotational speed of the earth.

History shows that as long as there have been human beings on this planet, once you put two of them together, rulemaking will start up before you know it.

"I sometimes take showers with Ingrid," I confessed.

Ingrid yawned.

We made this stupid rule and this stupid rule.

Boys are not allowed to love each other.

Then we painted a bison on the wall.

I wanted to take a shower. I was sticky and scratchy between my legs. I felt like the abrasive acrylic carpet fibers from the bowling alley were boring into my balls. I had B.O., and I needed to pee really bad.

Everyone else wanted to go to sleep. It was very awkward and nerve-wracking for me, talking about going to bed. I wanted Shann and Robby to sleep in the same room with me. I wanted to hold them both and tell them how sorry I was.

I knew that would not happen. You know, rules, and shit like that.

It was on our way through the hallway of Eden's dorms that we discovered the Brain Room.

Here is how we discovered it: The door had a brass plaque with etched banker-font letters that said this:

BRAIN ROOM

Robby, Shann, and I did not notice it before when we were running crazy through the sleeping compartments, jumping on beds and not making rules, and shit like that.

"What the heck?" Johnny McKeon said.

"Maybe it's some kind of command post," Wendy, Johnny's wife, offered.

"Uh," I said. "After watching and listening to Dr. Grady McKeon for about three and a half hours tonight, I would not be surprised if the room on the other side of this door was filled with actual brains."

"Or sperm," Robby added.

"Uh," I said.

I turned red.

Shann was absolutely silent.

Nobody wanted to hear about sperm at that exact moment.

But Robby was actually closer to winning the guess-what-is-inside-the-Brain-Room game.

It turned out there was quite a bit of sperm inside the Brain Room.

Robby Brees, the God of all Unstoppable Soldiers, pushed his way between Johnny McKeon and me. Robby turned the knob on the door.

We went inside Dr. Grady McKeon's Brain Room.

To be more precise, we went into the *receptionist's office* of the Brain Room.

Dr. Grady McKeon kept a secretary. History will verify that his secretary was highly involved in Dr. Grady McKeon's mission to breed. Dr. Grady McKeon attempted to breed with his secretary on top of her desk, on the floor of the reception area, on the pool table in Eden's *Tally-Ho!*, and even on the stainless steel tray caddy in the cafeteria.

Dr. Grady McKeon's sperm was not very lively. Dr. Grady McKeon's sperm was not unstoppable. In fact, Dr. Grady McKeon's sperm never got started.

Dr. Grady McKeon's secretary's name was Wanda Mae Rutkowski.

She had a nameplate on her desk that said so.

Moments earlier, Shann Collins and I had sexual intercourse below Wanda Mae Rutkowski's pink bowling ball and tricolor bowling shoes. Wanda Mae Rutkowski had feet like Godzilla. While my penis was inside Shann Collin's vagina, I noticed that Wanda Mae Rutkowski's shoes were women's size 11.

It is my job to notice accurate details, no matter what is going on.

Wanda Mae Rutkowski's desk was frozen in time.

"Hey! Gum!" I said.

Wanda Mae Rutkowski left an opened, pale green rectangular package of Wrigley's Doublemint gum on her desk. There were three sticks left inside the pack. I took one and began chewing it. The texture at first was cardboard-like and somewhat disappointing, but there was still a remarkable double-mintiness locked within the sugary gum.

"Unstoppable Chewing Gum," I said.

Robby said, "Um."

I prayed to Saint Kazimierz that he would see to it my balls would not dissolve.

Wanda Mae Rutkowski also had a pack of cigarettes called *Virginia Slims*. I wanted to smoke one of them. There were two cigarette butts in an ashtray that came from Clement's Motor Inn in Cedar Rapids. Wanda Mae Rutkowski had cotton candy lipstick. It made me horny thinking about Wanda Mae's lips. My penis was a real dynamo. I finally settled on names for my balls.

My balls deserved names.

The *Virginia Slims* cigarettes were menthol, and very thin. They looked like candy.

Wanda Mae Rutkowski obviously enjoyed minty pleasures.

A rotary-dial phone sat on her desk, too. Like the others we had seen in Eden, it had a row of clear plastic buttons across its base.

NEVER LOOK FOR ICE CREAM IN A SPERM FREEZER

"WELL, I'LL BE a monkey's uncle," Johnny McKeon said.

I never knew what that meant, but in Dr. Grady McKeon's case, it would have to mean that someone's sperm got inside a monkey.

Ingrid yawned.

Johnny McKeon picked up the handset for the phone. "I haven't seen one of these beauties in a coon's age."

In the wild, North American raccoons live approximately three years.

Doublemint gum was invented in 1914.

Krzys Szczerba was twenty-six years old in 1914.

I stuck my stale Doublemint chewing gum under Wanda Mae Rutkowski's desk.

Johnny McKeon dialed Ollie Jungfrau's phone number. Ollie

Jungfrau could not answer his phone at the Del Vista Arms because Ollie Jungfrau had been eaten by Travis Pope on the Kelsey Creek Bridge.

It didn't matter because the Brain Room's phone did not connect to phones on the surface of the planet Earth.

"This is only an internal line, I guess," Johnny McKeon said.

Who would you call after the end of the world, anyway?

"*Satan's Pizza* does not deliver in the event of global cataclysm," I said, adding, "It says so right at the bottom of the placemat menus."

"I never noticed that," Johnny McKeon, who had absolutely no sense of humor, said.

Satan's Pizza would no longer be delivering because Stan, the owner, whose real name was Sevastián Hernandez, had his head removed by Travis Pope's crushing mandibles earlier that evening.

On the wall behind Wanda Mae Rutkowski's desk hovered the sun-like golden shield of McKeon Industries's *infinita frumenta!* seal. On either side of the seal hung black-and-white, framed photographs of Dr. Grady McKeon with President Richard M. Nixon, Vice President Spiro T. Agnew, and CIA Director Richard Helms. There were two other photographs hanging on the wall. The first was a photograph of a man named James Arness, who was a television star in a program about the Wild West. The second was a photograph of Dr. Grady McKeon standing with Pope Paul VI. The inscription on James Arness's photograph said:

To Grady—Thanks for the Corn!!!

The pope wrote a message across his picture in blue ink:

Dear Grady, This corn is sublime.

Dr. Grady McKeon dissolved the pope's balls.

Excrementum Sanctum.

Below the Great Seal of McKeon Industries was a small brass plate that read:

SPERM VAULT
IN EDEN, MANKIND IS UNSTOPPABLE!

The seal was actually a door cover to Dr. Grady McKeon's bank of frozen sperm.

Robby opened the seal door. Behind the door was a heavy steel freezer.

"They have the president's sperm in there," Robby said.

"Uh," I said. "They have the pope's sperm in there."

"And James Arness's," Johnny McKeon added.

"Oh my!" Wendy McKeon said.

"James Arness was a handsome man. Handsome. My favorite actor, too," Johnny McKeon offered.

"Maybe there's some ice cream in there," Robby suggested.

"Uh," I repeated. I pushed the Great Seal shut. "Let's not look for ice cream in a sperm freezer, Rob."

To the side of Wanda Mae Rutkowski's desk was a windowless door marked:

PRIVATE

It led to Dr. Grady McKeon's Brain Room.

A REAL CONCRETE IOWA THINKER

TWO HEADS, WITH four gaping eyes, sat on Dr. Grady McKeon's desk, staring directly at us when Robby opened the door marked *Private*.

Shann gasped.

Wendy squeaked.

Johnny McKeon said, "Ain't that a kick?"

There were two identical grimacing lemur masks inside the Brain Room.

They were the first things we noticed, simply because they looked like severed monster heads resting atop Dr. Grady McKeon's desk, poised to defend the room against intruders. They were exact matches to the one Robby and I took from the roof of Grasshopper Jungle, only these were cleaner and appeared to be brand-new.

"Grady McKeon must have owned the world's finest collection of grimacing lemur masks and sperm," Robby theorized.

"Holy shit," I said.

"I wonder if they make your face stink," Robby said.

Shann finally spoke. She was not looking at the grimacing lemur masks. She stared in shocked wonder at the cases along the wall behind her dead stepuncle's desk.

"What *is* this stuff?" Shann said.

Johnny McKeon sighed and leaned against his brother's desk.

Johnny said, "It looks like the same boatload of oddities McKeon Industries had delivered to the store when they packed up and closed down the plant."

Robby and I tried to play dumb. Johnny McKeon never found out that Robby Brees and I had been inside his office at *From Attic to Seller Consignment Store* the night Grant Wallace and the Hoover Boys broke in and robbed *Tipsy Cricket Liquors*. We were not about to tell him, either.

I said, "What is it, Johnny?"

And Robby said, "Uh."

Here is what we found inside the Brain Room:

There were ten perfect globes of pulsating black *Contained MI Plague Strain 412E*—more than one for every continent on Earth—enough to ensure the annihilation of the entire human species. And all along the other shelves sat rows of bottles and bottles of deformed, clay-like body parts that had been cultivated from Dr. Grady McKeon's inadequate sperm in the Human Replication Unit labs. I noticed a foot inside one of the polymer-electric cells. It sprouted long nails that grew all the way to the glass barrier and its toes twitched, which made faint *tick-tick! tick-tick!* sounds against the jar. And there were oblong cases that contained some of the segmented parts of the first Unstoppable Soldiers that'd been dissolved with Dr. Grady McKeon's own blood.

It was a deranged carnival sideshow.

Against one of the Brain Room's walls was a bank of five television sets.

The televisions were absolutely useless, as primitive as kerosene lanterns. Each of them had a numbered dial that went from channel 2 to 13. Johnny McKeon explained to me, Shann, and Robby that at one time, televisions had to be calibrated and tuned by hand. Johnny McKeon told us that people stopped having so many children in Iowa after the invention of the remote control. Johnny said when he was a kid in Iowa, there were only five channels broadcasting, and that none of them was on the air twenty-four hours per day.

"Wow," I said. "Did they have programs instructing you on how to paint bisons on your walls?"

Johnny said, "I don't think they had any art classes on TV in those days, Austin."

Johnny McKeon was a real concrete Iowa thinker.

Johnny turned on one of the televisions. It took the picture tube nearly a minute to light up. There was nothing but monochromatic electric sandpaper on every one of the ratchet-knob channels Johnny McKeon clicked through.

"This is a real beauty," Johnny said.

"Oh," I said.

"It sure is," Robby agreed.

The real prize of the Brain Room was Dr. Grady McKeon's personal logbook.

The logbook looked like it had been written by a seven-year-old with a dull pencil. Dr. Grady McKeon's *scientific record* included undiluted details of every time Dr. Grady McKeon masturbated for one of his *experiments*, or engaged in *coitus* with other Eden Project volunteers.

In the frenetic scrawl of a crazed disciple of unstoppability, Dr. Grady McKeon also confessed to flushing Pope Paul VI's sperm down his Nightingale. The other contributors' samples soon followed.

Dr. Grady McKeon saw himself as the future King of a New Universe.

Too bad his sperm never worked for anything.

But the logbook also provided relevant pieces of information about the upside-down universe of McKeon Industries Labs.

"It says here," I said, flipping through the book, "that the lemur masks are detection devices that cause people to glow bright red if they are contaminated with the 412E."

"That's cracker-jack science, right there," Johnny said.

Scotch whisky made Johnny McKeon talkative and enthusiastic, even at the end of the world.

Robby slipped one of the masks over his face and looked around at each of us.

"Red balls," he said.

"What?" I said. I cupped my hands over my balls.

"On the wall. All the balls look red," Robby said, pointing to the globes of 412E. "But we are all a boring shade of blue."

I remembered how, the night I slipped away on my mother's blue kayaks in Robby Brees's bedroom at the Del Vista Arms, when I put his lemur mask on my face, it made Robby appear to turn blue.

I would not say that it was a *boring* shade, however. Robby Brees could never be a *boring* blue.

"And the best part is," Robby continued, "this one does not make my face stink!"

NIGHTTIME IN EDEN

SHANN COLLINS, HER mother, Wendy McKeon, and stepfather, Johnny, all stayed in one room together.

We said good night in the hallway. I tried to catch Shann's eye, but she was nervous and shy—not like Shann at all.

We should not have had sexual intercourse.

It was an unstoppable mistake.

History will show that teenagers are unstoppable horny dynamos once the jumpsuits come off. I knew that well enough after living through the week when the world ended in Ealing, Iowa.

The Collins-McKeons slipped into their room and shut the door.

Then Robby quietly said good night to me and went inside one of the rooms by himself.

"Hey—" I said.

Robby did not want to talk to me.

"What am I going to do, Ingrid?"

I did not know what to do. Everything was a mess. I was in love with my two best friends, and I was making them both miserable at the same time. And there were big horny bugs up above us that were eating the whole planet.

I walked away from the dormitory rooms, carrying Dr. Grady McKeon's logbook.

Ingrid followed me into the locker room.

Ingrid lay on the tile floor and watched me while I took a shower.

Afterward, I put my boxers on and dropped my jumpsuit into the Eden Launderette. I sat on the washing machine while it ran, and I remembered how Robby Brees had told me the *Ealing Coin Wash Launderette* was like a vacation in Hawaii compared to the Del Vista Arms's laundry room.

I left my Eden 5 jumpsuit there, tumbling and tumbling in the dryer, then found my way into my own, lonely sleeping compartment, which happened to be the messy one—the room where Robby, Shann, and I had jumped on the beds.

I sighed and sat down.

I wrote until I fell asleep with the lights on.

Tucked inside Dr. Grady McKeon's personal logbook, I found a 1971 brochure that featured Cypress Gardens's water ski team and a creased glossy photograph of Wanda Mae Rutkowski.

Wanda Mae Rutkowski was the very image of the two-hundred-foot-tall woman on the great seal of McKeon Industries.

At the bottom of the picture, a message that had nothing to do with corn or sperm had been scrawled in smeared blue ink and curling, candy-sweet script. It said:

Grady, I hope you can someday forgive me. We will
always have Eden, Wanda Mae

In her photograph, Wanda Mae Rutkowski is wearing knee-high lemon yellow vinyl boots. Although people in the 1970s did not recycle plastics, those boots could likely have been converted into at least three complete shower curtains; perhaps a full-size Slip 'N Slide, or one of those inflatable bouncy houses parents rent for their kid's birthday. Her dress, low-cut to showcase the perfect V separating her breasts, has long belled sleeves and a wild floral print in pinks and violets. Wanda Mae is wearing a matching headband that spans her forehead from eyebrows to hairline. The hem on the dress barely covers her panties, which I imagine would be a pale lavender. Her hair falls in loose globular curls over her shoulders. It is the color of tangerine marmalade, and Wanda Mae's flawless skin looks like home-churned Indiana butter.

I can't be certain, but I believe Dr. Grady McKeon did not hire Wanda Mae Rutkowski for her stenographic abilities.

Wanda Mae Rutkowski performed in a barefoot water ski show in Florida throughout the 1970s, after Dr. Grady McKeon sealed up his subterranean sexual pleasure dome in Ealing, Iowa, for the last time.

Dr. Grady McKeon became a recluse in his old historic house when Wanda Mae Rutkowski left him. Wanda Mae married a dog trainer who made a fortune racing greyhounds in Florida. The dog trainer's name was Jan Wojner. Jan Wojner learned everything he knew about dogs from his grandfather Bruno, who survived the Great Depression by performing with circus dogs in California.

Unstoppable dogs!

Wanda Mae Wojner won the Women's National Barefoot Water Ski Championship, which was held in Waco, Texas, in 1978.

In 1978, Pope Paul VI died without ever knowing that Dr. Grady McKeon had unceremoniously discarded his sperm in my great-great-grandfather's urinal.

In 1978, McKeon Industries presented four sealed globes of *Contained MI Plague Strain 412E* to the United States Department of Defense.

Nobody knew anything about it.

In his abandonment, Dr. Grady McKeon, who had gone about as far off the deep end as anyone could go following the gruesome disasters of his Unstoppable Soldier experiments, got crazier and crazier. He forgot all about Unstoppable Soldiers and his Eden Project.

In 1978, Dr. Grady McKeon bought a small palace in Costa Rica and boarded up the old McKeon House in Ealing, Iowa.

I could only find evidence of one recorded trip he made back to Ealing to attend a shareholders' meeting, which happened when Robby Brees and I were in seventh grade.

It was not a good time to fly.

TOO BAD FOR BOYS LIKE ME

IT IS THE strangest machine: pencil and paper, paint and wall; medium, surface, and man. The machine stitches all roads into one, weaves every life together, everything.

All good books are about everything, abbreviated.

And maybe it's the words we leave out that really tell us how to stop doing the same meaningless and terrible things over and over and over.

The abbreviations make sense of the roadmap.

The words we cut are vast universes winking out into darkness.

By the time Krzys Szczerba was a middle-aged man, he had grown tired of struggling and feeling so isolated from his identity in the United States of America.

Krzys Szczerba could never stop being the Polish boy who lost his father on the crossing to America. Every day, Krzys Szczerba could shut his eyes and see the gray, wooden body of his father as it slipped into the cold water of the slate sea.

Krzys Szczerba's son, Andrzej, had gone away to Iowa City. Krzys Szczerba never knew anything about how much his son loved Herman Weinbach. Krzys knew something about his grandson, a boy named Felek, which means lucky. But Krzys Szczerba had never seen the child, nor the mother—a butcher's daughter named Phoebe Hildebrandt.

Eva Nightingale, Krzys's wife and the inspiration for his Nightingale urinal, was killed by a street trolley in Saint Louis in 1936, when Krzys was forty-eight years old. Things like that happened all the time, and nobody knew anything about it.

Without the creamy white pillows of Eva's body to enfold him at night, Krzys Szczerba became cold. Krzys Szczerba froze inside. Krzys Szczerba still had brothers and sisters in Poland whom he had not seen since 1905, when Theodore Roosevelt was president.

In 1937, Krzys left the United States of America to return to Poland.

It was not a good idea.

In September 1939, Krzys Szczerba was killed as he walked in a marching column of refugees along a muddy farm road in western Poland.

In September 1939, Germany was unstoppable, and Russia shared in the spoils of Polish conquest. Nobody needed Polish boys.

Too bad for Poland.

Too bad for boys like me.

This was just one of those things in history that gave us Polish boys sleepy bags under our watchful eyes. We see everything. It is our job to pay attention to details.

Wanda Mae Rutkowski had size 11 feet.

One day, I will go to Poland. I will ask Robby Brees to go to Poland with me. I know I will find the same country road where Krzys Szczerba died, and I will bring flowers in last month's newspaper and place them there.

With my finger I will draw the image of a bison in the dirt, and Robby Brees and I will smoke cigarettes and I will tell him all the stories I know, about everything.

This is the truth.

THE WORST IMAGINABLE SMALL-TOWN SOCIAL BLUNDER

"I DECIDED ON Orville and Wilbur," I said.

Robby said, "Huh?"

"My balls," I said. "I have decided to name my balls Orville and Wilbur."

I named my balls after the Wright brothers.

Orville and Wilbur Wright were from Ohio, although Wilbur was born in Indiana. They invented an airplane.

Orville and Wilbur Wright never married anyone in their entire lives. They must have masturbated a lot, which, according to Pastor Roland Duff, would have made them highly stoppable soldiers.

Maybe they wore hair shirts.

"Which one's which?" Robby said.

"Wilbur Wright did not have a mustache and was bald on top. So Wilbur is on the left," I answered. "The left side is . . . Uh . . . kind of bald."

"Um. That makes sense," Robby decided.

Robby Brees nodded appreciatively and took a long drag from his cigarette.

We drove in Robby's old Ford Explorer, away from the McKeon House, which was the only house on Ealing, Iowa's *Registry of Historic Homes*.

It was morning, and it was time for Robby Brees and me to go kill some monsters.

I wore my fresh-laundered Eden 5 jumpsuit. It smelled like detergent and brand-new underwear. We had Ingrid, three syringes full of Robby Brees's blood, six packs of cigarettes from the free Eden vending machines, and the two grimacing lemur masks with us.

Robby looked like he slept well. He had showered and his hair was wet. Robby looked good.

Robby always looked good.

Robby said, "I am relieved to announce we are safe from committing the worst imaginable social blunder, which is giving your balls the same names as another guy in the same town's balls."

"I am thankful for that," I said.

I took a drag from my cigarette.

Robby said, "My balls are named Mick and Keith."

"Those are probably the best names anyone has ever given their balls in the history of naming your balls," I said.

Robby said, "Thank you, Austin."

He pushed a cassette into the tape player in the Explorer's dashboard.

It was *Exile on Main Street*.

That cassette was so old, all the printing had completely worn off it. Robby knew the difference between *Exile on Main Street* and *Let It Bleed* only because of the smudge patterns on the plastic shell casings.

The first song on *Exile on Main Street* is called Rocks Off. To me, it is suggestive and taunting.

Sometimes I understood Robby Brees better than other times. I knew he was mad at me for leaving him there in the clinic the night before, even if he selflessly encouraged me to do it. That was Robby, and I loved him.

I believed Robby was jealous of Shann Collins.

And, looking at the sky and all the light, I also agreed that the sunshine was boring.

I wished we could go back underground and be alone in the dayless and nightless world of Eden, so we could play music and dance together—just me, Robby, and Shann.

And Ingrid, too.

Ingrid does not dance or bark.

I have tried to dance with Ingrid. It makes her nervous.

We headed off toward the town of Ealing, in the direction of my house. After that, who could possibly know? It wasn't like there were any specific instructions on how to hunt down and kill wild Unstoppable Soldiers. Even the lunatics who ran the labs at McKeon Industries only had to deal with bugs in a jar, so to speak.

The state of Iowa is a pretty big jar.

Johnny McKeon urged us to take his gun. We did not. Despite being Iowa boys, neither Robby nor I had ever fired a real gun in our lives. I was afraid one of us would accidentally kill the other. That would be worse than being eaten by an Unstoppable Soldier.

Paintballs are just paintballs, unless they're filled with the blood of your God and you are an Unstoppable Soldier, but a Smith & Wesson .500 magnum could bring down a helicopter.

So we left Johnny McKeon's Smith & Wesson .500 magnum in Eden.

Johnny McKeon made a sling from two Eden Project jumpsuits, and I carried Ingrid up the ladder with me and Robby when we left the silo. Johnny offered to come with us, but I convinced him the Unstoppable Soldiers would leave Robby—and hopefully me—alone.

Johnny McKeon knew he did not want to leave Shann and Wendy by themselves, anyway. He was just doing the Iowa-right thing by offering us his gun and company.

Iowa right is the same thing as blue plaid on your boxers.

Johnny McKeon was a humorless, but good, man.

That morning, we had eaten breakfast in the Eden cafeteria. Wendy McKeon cooked pancakes and brewed coffee. I did not sleep well. Neither did Shann. Her eyes were red and her hair was uncombed. It was a look I had never seen before. Shann Collins looked nervous. She looked like Ingrid when I danced with her.

Shann and I managed to have a few moments alone that morning while Robby showered and Johnny McKeon visited the toilet.

It was awkward and embarrassing. We held hands, but it somehow was not like the *us* we used to be.

"Are you okay?" I asked.

Shann said, "I suppose so. Are you?"

Nobody from Iowa ever says *I suppose so*.

"My knees are scuffed up," I admitted.

It made me feel horny to think about my knees.

"I never did that with anyone before," Shann said.

"I. Uh." I did not know what to say. What could I say? Was

I supposed to apologize or something?

I said, "I thought it was amazing. The best thing ever. I love you so much, Shann. Did you . . . Uh . . . Did you like it? Shann?"

"It hurt," Shann said. "And you told me you would use a condom."

That was an unfair thing for Shann to say to me. It was cold, too. We never talked about condoms or anything the night before at our little *End of the World Party*; we just did it because it was what we wanted, the one thing we needed to do. But Shann sounded like someone at a butcher shop rejecting a cut of meat for having too much fat, or shit like that.

"Uh. I must have left my condoms in my other jumpsuit, Shann," I said.

Shann was angry. She was sorry for what we did.

I felt like shit.

Ingrid was happy to get out of Eden. She shit for a solid ten minutes.

Edens are made for humans, not for animals.

And Dr. Grady McKeon was no Noah. Noah would not have flushed the pope's sperm down a urinal, not to mention James Arness's.

"What am I going to do, Robby?"

Robby drove with both hands on the wheel, a cigarette angled daringly from his lips. He looked cool, like a tough guy in a movie, or maybe someone who was about to save the world, but had to think things over first.

I mean, what if the world was not worth saving, after all? What if, in some twisted way, Dr. Grady McKeon really had the right idea about starting over in a well-stocked Eden with stacks and stacks of blank books just waiting to be filled up by New Humans writing a New History where we did not do the same shitty things over and over and over?

"Why do you want *me* to tell you what to do, Austin? I have a tough enough time figuring out what *I'm* going to do," Robby said.

"Uh."

Robby was right.

"I am sorry for what I did last night, Rob," I said.

"Why do you have to apologize to me for anything?" Robby said.

"You know," I said. "I had sexual intercourse with Shann Collins in the bowling alley while you were lying in the clinic having your blood taken out, so we ... uh ... you ... could save the world."

"The bowling alley sounds like a romantic spot for you and Shann Collins to have sexual intercourse," Robby said.

"Uh," I said.

"It's not like I would have traded places with you," Robby offered.

"Um."

Naturally, that made me think again about having a three-some with Shann and Robby. Normally, the thought would make me feel very horny. Too bad Shann Collins did not seem to like me anymore. Too bad Robby Brees did not seem to like me very much, either.

I reached back and stroked Ingrid's fur.

I did not like myself, but at least Ingrid did.

Dogs are good for that kind of shit.

We drove along Kelsey Creek.

The largest walleye ever caught in Kelsey Creek weighed six pounds, four ounces.

Looking across to the opposite bank, I noticed the streets of Ealing that surrounded Amelia Jenks Bloomer Park were completely deserted. Ealing had become even more of a ghost town than it usually was. Fat, twisting columns of smoke coiled upward into the morning sky. Homes and buildings were burning.

War had come to Iowa.

Robby and I both saw it. We knew what was going on.

It was unstoppable.

"I feel like shit," I said.

"Was it good? Did you like having sexual intercourse in the bowling alley with Shann Collins?" Robby asked. He glanced at me with an inspector's no-bullshit appraisal. He shook another cigarette out and tossed the pack across the center console, onto my lap. I lit one and passed the lighter over to Robby Brees.

"I guess so," I said. "Uh. I skinned my knees on the carpet."

"I have heard that can happen. You have to be careful with that indoor-outdoor shit they made in the 1970s." Robby said, "It's like sandpaper on naked knees when you are trying to put your penis inside someone."

Robby was really smart about carpet burns and sex, and shit like that.

I took a deep drag from my cigarette. It was a brand called *Benson & Hedges*. The name made me feel rich or something. A name like Benson & Hedges says *I spend a lot of money on my cigarettes*.

"So, I am sorry, Rob," I said.

Robby shrugged. "They have a name for guys like you, you know, Austin?"

"Um. Bisexual?" I guessed. I did not think I was bisexual. I was only guessing.

I was always only guessing.

I was trying to talk to Robby and make him not think about things like me betraying my friends; hurting their feelings. But Robby Brees was too smart for that shit.

"No," Robby said. "The word is *selfish*. You don't really care about me *or* Shann."

I slumped down in my seat and stared at the columns of smoke across the creek.

It was like bombs had been dropped, and the biggest one just landed on my chest.

Robby turned right to cross the Kelsey Creek Bridge.

He stopped the car.

I was not looking.

I was not looking because I felt like I was going to start crying or shit if Robby said one more thing to me.

Robby Brees said, "Holy shit."

THE RIGHT KIND OF CIGARETTES TO SMOKE JUST BEFORE YOU KILL SOMETHING

OLLIE JUNGFRAU'S DODGE Caravan minivan sat crumpled against the steel trusses of the Kelsey Creek Bridge.

The nose of the van was folded in on itself, as though it had run head on into an unbendable pole. The front wheels sat in a stew of antifreeze, transmission fluid, and motor oil. There was blood, too. The windshield had been caved in, and dripping smears of blood streaked everywhere, over the shelf of the van's dashboard, the steering wheel, and both front seats.

I slipped one of the grimacing lemur masks over my head.

"Um," Robby said.

I wanted to see if any red lights would show up. I wanted to hide my face from Robby Brees.

Ingrid did not like the mask.

If she were a normal dog, Ingrid would have barked at me.

"Do not get out of the car, Robby," I said from inside my mask.

Robby said, "That's Ollie Jungfrau's van."

I did not say anything. Of course I knew whose van it was.

Robby inched the Ford Explorer slowly past the wrecked vehicle.

I smoked.

The mouth of the grimacing lemur mask served as a kind of cigarette holder. I could easily wedge the filter end of my Benson & Hedges cigarette tightly between two of the grimacing lemur's lower teeth.

It was very convenient.

"Uh," Robby said. "What if smoking a cigarette in that mask messes up your sperm, Austin?"

I did not care if my sperm got messed up. I wanted my sperm to get messed up.

I did not say anything to Robby. I kept smoking with the mask on.

Robby stopped the Explorer and slipped the second mask over his head.

He smoked, too.

And Robby said, "I'm sorry if I hurt your feelings, Austin."

"It's okay." I said, "You are right, Robby. I deserved it. I deserve to have messed-up sperm."

"Nobody deserves messed-up sperm," Robby said.

He drove around Ollie Jungfrau's ruined Dodge Caravan minivan.

Unfortunately, at exactly that moment, Mrs. Edith Mitchell woke up. Mrs. Edith Mitchell was still hiding in the backseat of Ollie Jungfrau's Dodge Caravan. She had fallen asleep, wedged down between the seats and the floorboard of the van. When she poked her head up to see if she was being rescued, what Mrs. Edith Mitchell saw drove her beyond the brink of her sanity.

What she saw were two monsters with rat-like heads in blue-and-white jumpsuits driving a Ford Explorer while they smoked cigarettes.

Mrs. Edith Mitchell thought Ollie Jungfrau was correct: That aliens from outer space had landed in Iowa, for whatever reason.

Mrs. Edith Mitchell believed the end of the world had come to Ealing, Iowa.

She was probably correct.

Robby Brees and I did not see Mrs. Edith Mitchell looking out at us through the dark rear windows of the crumpled Dodge Caravan. As we passed, Mrs. Edith Mitchell finally mustered enough courage to climb through the bloody muck in the front seat and get out of the van.

Mrs. Edith Mitchell removed her shoes and all of her clothing. She jumped, naked and white, like a fluffy marshmallow schoolmarm, from the side of the Kelsey Creek Bridge into Kelsey Creek.

It was not a good idea.

Mrs. Edith Mitchell did not know how to swim.

Beneath the surface of Kelsey Creek, a cluster of walleyes was engaged in the spring spawn.

On the other side of the bridge, past the parking lot for Amelia Jenks Bloomer Park, as Robby drove into the neighborhood where I lived we saw a television news van that had come all the way from Des Moines. The van was painted with a bold design that said *Eyewitness News*. The van sat on its side in the middle of the street. The radar antenna had been deployed and was stretched out across the road like a big broken arm.

The doors on the *Eyewitness News* van were left open.

348 | ANDREW SMITH

We caught quick, passing glimpses of a bloody mess inside the vehicle. There was one black high-top Converse basketball shoe sitting in the road beside the tipped-over van.

Unstoppable Soldiers do not like to be filmed by television news crews from Des Moines.

The first Converse Chuck Taylor signature basketball shoes were made in Massachusetts in 1932. In 1932, Krzys Szczerba's *Nightingale Convenience Works* manufactured the last Nightingale urinal.

That particular urinal, Krzys Szczerba's final, grand porcelain monolith, ended up beneath the ground in an Iowa sanctuary constructed by a madman. Robby Brees and I urinated into it together, in Eden.

We drove past three houses that were engulfed in flames, and two others that had already burned to the ground. Apparently, the people of Ealing tried to come up with some method for fighting the Unstoppable Soldiers.

Their ideas did not appear to have been effective.

There were dozens of dead Iowans, and mere parts of others, scattered like Halloween decorations across yards, on fence posts and mailboxes, or lying in the streets.

Robby said, "When we get to your house, we have to get the guns loaded quick. Then we need to go back to the Del Vista Arms."

I said, "Why?"

"My mom," Robby said. "I have to try to get my mom."

"Oh."

Despite Connie Brees's obvious shortcomings as a single parent, her son, Robert Brees Jr., was a good boy.

Robby Brees really *was* a superhero.

I did not even think about my mother and father until Robby told me he wanted to rescue his mother. My cell phone was with my clothes inside the locker room in Eden. I hoped my parents, and Eric, my brother who had lost half his right leg and both of his testicles in Afghanistan nearly a week before, were not planning on returning to the continent of North America anytime soon.

"You are a superhero or shit like that, Rob," I said.

"A gay superhero," Robby added.

Robby blew a big cloud of smoke out from the mouth of his grimacing lemur mask. It was just about the coolest thing I had ever seen.

"I just realized that the Unstoppable Soldiers' God is gay," I said. "I told you I was—in seventh grade," Robby corrected.

I smiled and nodded. The grimacing lemur mask on my head only grimaced and smoked.

"I am sorry, Rob," I said. I squeezed Robby's hand.

"There's nothing you can do about me being gay," Robby said.

Readers of history may decide that joking while two guys are driving around through a town that has recently been slaughtered by six-foot-tall praying mantis beasts with shark-tooth-studded arms is in poor taste.

It is.

But that is exactly what real boys have always done when confronted with the brutal aftermath of warfare.

Dulce Et Decorum Est.

I said, "I am going to try to be a better person. Not so selfish and shit. And maybe one day you will tell me if I have done it."

"Uh. Let's have another *fag* before we get out," Robby said. He maneuvered the Explorer as close to my garage as he could get it. Then Robby said, "And then let's go kill some big fucking bugs, Porcupine."

"I think Benson & Hedges are the right kind of cigarettes to smoke just before you kill something," I said.

THERE ARE NO CUP-O-NOODLES IN EDEN

EDEN'S ARMY OF grimacing lemurs landed in Ealing, and it was time for them to go to war.

Robby Brees and I charged up the paintball guns. We injected small amounts of Robby's blood into dozens of grape-sized jellied projectiles.

When we finished, we left three bloodstained hypodermic needles on the white tiled countertop in my kitchen. It looked like a heroin den.

It was disgusting.

The smell of blood made me want to vomit. I had been smelling it all day.

We smoked and smoked to cover up the defeated odor that hung everywhere over Ealing, Iowa.

Before we left my house, I grabbed an armload of clean underwear and T-shirts and the razor and shaving cream from my bathroom. Tomorrow would be Saturday. Saturdays were shaving days. I did not take my bottle of bubble bath with me. I would miss taking baths. There had to be a bathtub somewhere in Eden.

There were no Cup-O-Noodles in Eden, so I also filled a paper sack with as many of the paper and Styrofoam containers of the miracle food I could find in the pantry.

All houses in Iowa have pantries.

Cup-O-Noodles are unstoppable food.

Before we left my house, the telephone in the kitchen began ringing and ringing. It was my father calling. He wanted to know what the hell was happening. He wanted to know why the hell I had not called him. And he asked, how the hell did Ealing, Iowa, end up on news broadcasts in Germany, telling stories of enormous bugs that were devouring every man, woman, and child in the town? What the hell was all this about?

"It is a lot of hell, Dad," I said.

At exactly that moment, all the power cut out everywhere in Ealing, Iowa.

The wireless phone in our kitchen went dead.

Robby and I heard gunfire in the distance.

Ealing, Iowa, had gone to hell.

RAT BOYS FROM MARS, AND AN UNFORTUNATE INCIDENT INVOLVING AN INFLATABLE WHALE

PICTURE THIS IF YOU CAN:

Robby Brees and I, wearing fur-covered, full-head grimacing lemur masks that helped identify Unstoppables, smoking cigarettes and dressed in matching form-fitting blue-and-white Eden Project jumpsuits, as we carried fully automatic paintball rifles slung over our shoulders. And we were accompanied by a sixty-pound golden retriever that could not bark.

If we had thought everything out more clearly, we probably would have anticipated the likelihood of being fired upon by *real* guns and *real* bullets from my next-door neighbors, Earl Elgin and his teenage son, whose name was Earl Elgin Jr.

Earl Elgin Jr. was fifteen years old; a redheaded Lutheran boy who attended Curtis Crane Lutheran Academy, and fortunately for me and Robby, he and his father were both terrible shots. They were especially terrible shots because they were scared out of their minds after enduring a night-long rampage of six-foot-tall praying mantis beasts with spike-armed claws. And now they had come face-to-face with what they believed could only be alien invader rat boys from Mars.

We knew Earl Elgin Jr. as EJ.

EJ Elgin had skin the color of cottage cheese.

He also had a real dynamo of an Iowa name—*EJ Elgin*.

In the same way that Benson & Hedges says *I spend a lot of money on my cigarettes*, EJ Elgin says *Sperm met egg in Iowa*.

EJ Elgin only had one ball.

EJ Elgin lost one of his testicles when he was nine years old. EJ's father, Earl Elgin Sr., hired a giant inflatable whale-shaped bouncer house for EJ's birthday party. One of EJ's balls got stuck inside a plastic-rimmed ventilation hole near what was supposed to be the big inflatable whale's spout. It is painful to recall, but I am only doing my job. I was there. I recorded the history of EJ Elgin's detached ball.

Nothing puts a damper on a boy's ninth birthday party like the loss of one of the guest of honor's *guests of honor*.

EJ had to be taken to the hospital in Waterloo after having one of his balls detached when it became lodged in the plastic vent on a giant inflatable whale. He came home the following day with an excess of unoccupied space inside his scrotum. I do not know if doctors discard detached human balls in the trash can or not.

The boys at Curtis Crane pestered EJ for a while.

After his ninth birthday party and the horrible incident with the enormous inflatable whale, all of us, to a boy, were horrified and curious. All the boys at Curtis Crane Lutheran Academy wanted to see EJ's ball sack, now that one of EJ's balls had been lost to a whale attack.

By the time the boys at Curtis Crane Lutheran Academy entered puberty, which is an epiphany, a kind of religious awakening as to the true magnificence of our balls, and shit like that, we all felt mournfully afraid of EJ Elgin, the boy with only one ball.

EJ Elgin, to my knowledge, never named his solitary ball.

The one he lost might have been appropriately named *Jonah*. Perhaps *Ahab*.

"Stay right there and don't move, you motherfucking rat boys from Mars," Earl Elgin Sr. said.

He nervously pointed his emptied assault rifle directly at my belly.

"Dad, we caught us some alien rat fucks from outer space," EJ added. "Let's shoot them in the balls."

EJ plinked a shot level with Robby's crotch. Robby flinched and whined. EJ only had a BB gun.

The Elgin males were not especially brilliant, but they had been through a lot. I had to give them that.

"Uh," I said.

Robby raised his open hand in the intergalactic gesture of peace, and said, "Please do not shoot us in the balls, EJ Elgin. It is only me, Robby Brees, and my friend, Austin Szerba, who is your next-door neighbor, and we are not rat boys from Mars. We come in peace, and smoking cigarettes."

"Benson and Hedges," I said.

Earl Elgin squinted and tilted his head. The weapon he held was a Colt AR15-A3 Tactical Carbine. It looked exactly like the paintball rifles Robby and I carried, except if Earl Elgin had actually shot us with it, Robby and I would both be dead, gory messes. EJ Elgin had a Daisy .177 pellet rifle. If he had actually shot us with it, Robby and I would have stinging welts on our skin, possibly on our ball sacks.

He missed Robby's ball sack.

A Rat Boy from Mars definitely would not want to get shot in the balls with a Daisy .177.

My next-door neighbors, EJ Elgin and his father, had been packing camping equipment into the bed of a pickup truck. They were planning on taking the rest of their family, which consisted of EJ's mother, who was named Rosemary, and his two younger sisters, Edie and Donna, as far away from Ealing and the monster invasion as they could get. When Robby and I came outside of my house, carrying armloads of underwear, shaving stuff, and Cup-O-Noodles, Earl Elgin Sr. and his son, EJ, saw us and grabbed their weapons.

Earl Elgin Sr. let loose a burst of rifle fire that shattered nearly every window on my house, as well as one on the driver's side of Robby's old Ford Explorer—which had really taken a beating since the attack by Hungry Jack the night before.

"Holy shit!" I said.

Boxers, T-shirts, and Styrofoam containers of dehydrated ramen noodles flew everywhere.

Ingrid, who was not particularly startled by the gunfire, was shitting in the front yard when it happened.

That was exactly when Earl Elgin Sr. told us to put our hands up and surrender, because he and his boy were going to become some kind of national heroes for capturing the invading Rat Boys from Mars.

"Shoot them in the balls, Dad," EJ Elgin urged.

"Uh," Robby said.

Both of us had our hands raised in the intergalactic gesture of *Please do not shoot us in the balls.*

"Earl Elgin, you shot my goddamned house!" I said.

Earl Elgin Sr. looked confused.

Earl Elgin Sr. said, "What the fuck did you creatures do with the Szerba boy?"

Robby Brees and I did not get killed that day by Earl Elgin Sr. and his one-balled son, EJ.

But it took some dramatic pleading from me to stop Earl Elgin Sr. from shooting me and allow me to take my head off so I might show him who was actually inside the clinging and form-fitting Rat Boy from Mars jumpsuit.

"Thank you, Saint Kazimierz," I said.

I felt like the virgin saint was looking out for me and Robby.

There was no other way I could explain *not* being shot in the balls.

We left Earl and EJ to their hurried departure preparations and got into Robby's battered Ford Explorer.

And Robby said, "Holy shit, Austin," as we drove away from my house and headed toward the Del Vista Arms.

What could I do?

THE BATTLE OF THE DEL VISTA ARMS

I ASKED MYSELF THIS:

What could I do?

Just one week earlier, everything was perfect. Everything was Iowa blue plaid. Robby and I skated in Grasshopper Jungle. Shann Collins made me very horny. There were no books mentioning Catholics or masturbation available in the library at Curtis Crane Lutheran Academy. Ollie Jungfrau dreamed of internet porn and Saturday morning donuts with me and Johnny McKeon.

All of that equaled *normal*.

Then Grant Wallace and the Hoover Boys beat the shit out of Robby Brees and me. They threw our shoes up on the roof at Grasshopper Jungle because they said we were queers from Curtis Crane Lutheran Academy, and after that, the whole world went to shit.

So, what could I do?

Robby played *Let It Bleed*.

Although it had been made more than forty years before, it seemed like every song on that Rolling Stones album was precisely about Robby and me, or Unstoppable Soldiers, Ealing, Iowa, and McKeon Industries.

And Robby sang something about feeding on people.

"Uh," I said.

We smoked cigarettes.

Ingrid sighed and yawned in the backseat.

And at the exact moment we pulled up to Robby Brees's apartment, the cook from the destroyed *Pancake House*, Louis, whose real name was Ah Wong Sing, happened to be hiding inside a cinder-block cubicle where dumpsters were stored at the Del Vista Arms.

Louis's clothes were ripped. He was missing one shoe and his shirt hung open. Dried blood stippled his torn cook's trousers. But he was very, very happy to see us.

He also did not glow red when I looked at him through the eyes of my grimacing lemur mask.

But Louis was so psychologically worn from what he had seen and been through that he did not even seem startled by the Rat Boy from Mars with the fully automatic AR15-A3 Tactical Carbine replica paintball gun.

"Good morning, Louis," I said.

I waved my open hand in the intergalactic Rat Boy from Mars gesture of *This is the end of the world, but I am politely greeting you anyway*.

"Um," Robby said.

Robby Brees was not wearing his grimacing lemur mask. "It's just us, Louis. Me, and Austin from the secondhand store. You know? Austin Szerba? The dynamo kid?"

Robby Brees held up a lit cigarette in the intergalactic gesture of *We are the skater kids who smoke in the alley, and shit like that.*

Louis had not slept in two days. He was spent. He'd had sexual intercourse with Robby Brees's mother three times in the previous twenty-four hours. After he ran away from the carnage at the Kelsey Creek Bridge, Louis came back to the Del Vista Arms, thinking he would find safety and Connie Brees.

Instead, Louis found the Unstoppable Soldier called Hungry Jack.

The end of the world was one week old, and people everywhere were finding out about it. And the Battle of Ealing began that morning at the Del Vista Arms Luxury Apartments.

Here is what happened:

Hungry Jack was confused, and Louis was a very motivated runner when being chased by Unstoppable Soldiers. Hungry Jack had been huddling beneath the aluminum roof that covered a row of cars at the Del Vista Arms when Louis ran through the parking lot.

Unstoppable Soldiers are like cats in that they are stimulated by movement. They are also like walleyes in that they only want to do two things. The two things walleyes and Unstoppable Soldiers want to do is fuck and eat.

Unstoppable Soldiers are not as intelligent as either cats or fish.

So when Louis managed to slip inside the dumpster corral, Hungry Jack looked around for a while and then forgot what he had been looking for.

Unfortunately for Robby and me, Hungry Jack became stimulated by the movement of a Rat Boy from Mars in a tight blue-

and-white jumpsuit. The Unstoppable Soldier that had hatched out
from Hungry Jack's body in a cornfield outside of Waterloo while
Robby and I stood in horrified amazement and watched it happen
became very aroused by the motion around Robby Brees's Ford
Explorer.

Hungry Jack flitted down to the lot from the rooftop of the car
park.

I saw him first.

Through the lenses on my grimacing lemur mask, a brilliant
flash of red caused me to momentarily consider that I had indeed
ignited the flammable, carcinogenic, messed-up-sperm-causing
mask with my Benson & Hedges cigarette.

Hungry Jack looked like a ball of flame as he flew down from
the awning above the car park.

"Holy shit," I said. "These things really *do* work."

I was impressed by the technology of the grimacing lemur mask.

Unfortunately, I should have been more impressed by the speed
with which Hungry Jack closed the distance between us.

It was also impressive how Hungry Jack picked me up by my
head. Until that moment, I had never in my life been picked up
by my head. I did find myself marveling for an instant at how well
the grimacing lemur mask protected my skull from the piercing
barbs of the studded spikes all along Hungry Jack's tri-segmented
pincers.

But it was only an instant.

Then I screamed.

And while I was screaming, Hungry Jack unhinged his bear-trap
mandibles in order to crush my Rat Boy skull. I looked over at
Robby, thinking my beautiful friend, a person I loved very much
but had also inflicted a great deal of pain upon, was going to be the
last image burned into the screens of my dying eyes.

Robby Brees stood there, looking more cool and superhero-ish than any Lutheran boy from Iowa ever did, calmly smoking a cigarette while his eyes, which were the color of robin egg Cadbury chocolate Easter treats, focused directly on the monster that was just about to eat my head.

Robby raised his paintball gun and let go a burst of three rounds that splattered into Hungry Jack's mouth and compound eyes.

Pop! Pop! Pop!

The paintballs gushed.

The Unstoppable Soldier received a faceful of the blood of his God.

Fortunately, this caused Hungry Jack to release his vise clamp on my head. I hit the ground, and Hungry Jack reeled away from the concussion of the blast.

"Shit! Shit! Shit! Holy shit!" was all I could say.

Excrementum Sanctum.

And while Unstoppable Soldiers' exoskeletons are as impenetrable as the hull on an aircraft carrier, the blood of their God rusts every rivet in their construction, and sinks them on the spot.

"Glad we didn't have to use my sperm," Robby said.

"Uh," I said, dazed, on my hands and knees in the parking lot at the Del Vista Arms. "Thank you, Saint Kazimierz. And thank you, Robby Brees."

Louis, whose real name was Ah Wong Sing, cowered in the doorway to the dumpster corral.

Hungry Jack hissed and gurgled.

The Unstoppable Soldier looked confused, if such an expression could manifest itself on the face of a six-foot-tall beast that looked like a praying mantis. Hungry Jack's left arm fell off first. The right arm disjointed and plunked down onto the ground seconds later. The tooth-spiked claw arms rattled around on the pavement of the parking lot, spastically opening and closing, opening and closing, as they scraped along the ground with no coherent mission.

Where the claw arms had detached from Hungry Jack's thorax, a gooey stream of slick yellow fluid burbled like twin pots of boiling unstoppable cornmeal mush. Then Hungry Jack's chin lowered and his head rolled away from his body, landing on the ground between the two flailing arms.

What was left of Hungry Jack scampered away on four gangly legs, which soon became three, then two, and the entire Unstoppable Soldier collapsed in puddles of oily mush.

Robby Brees saved my life.

Being a historian naturally has its dangers, but this is my job.

I tell the truth.

THE END OF THE WORLD

AT THE CONCLUSION of the First Battle of Ealing, which took place in a parking lot at the Del Vista Arms Luxury Apartments, the Unstoppable Soldier that had once been growing inside a homeless man named Hungry Jack lay in a soupy yellow mess of jumbled bug parts.

At that moment, there were only three Unstoppable Soldiers remaining on the surface of the planet called Earth. They were Tyler Jacobson, Travis Pope, and Travis Pope's wife, Eileen, who had filled Duane Coventry's house on Onondaga Street with a jellied, pulsating black goo of fertilized eggs.

Robby Brees and I, the two Rat Boys from Mars who were the only people capable of saving the planet called Earth, had no way of calculating how many other Unstoppable Soldiers there were, and no way of knowing where to look for them.

So Robby put on his grimacing lemur mask and the two of us entered the hallway of the Del Vista Arms Luxury Apartments. Ingrid, my silent golden retriever, and Louis, the equally silent cook from the most certainly closed-down *Pancake House*, cautiously followed.

We were there to save Robbie's mom, Connie Brees.

"Aaah!" screamed Eunice Mayhew when Robby Brees and I entered the hallway of the Del Vista Arms.

Eunice Mayhew was the manager of the Del Vista Arms. At the exact moment Robby and I stepped through the entrance that led in from the parking lot, Eunice Mayhew was posting two more Pay or Quit notices on locked doors to silent apartments.

Eunice Mayhew did not glow red.

Eunice Mayhew was fifty-three years old. She had a figure like an upended pickle barrel, and was just about the same height. Her hair was the color of cigarette ash, and her skin had a similar hue to the gritty waterline around Robby Brees's bathtub, where I'd showered after spending the night with Robby earlier that week. I know that you would not eat either one of those things: cigarette ash or the ring inside Robby Brees's bathtub.

I also do not believe an Unstoppable Soldier would eat Eunice Mayhew.

"Aaah!" Eunice Mayhew screamed again. She threw her hands up, in what I suppose was the intergalactic gesture of *I surrender to the conquering Rat Boys from Mars*.

If somewhere there existed entire planets of Eunice Mayhews, Robby Brees and I could rule the cosmos.

Eunice Mayhew is also a very solid Iowa name.

A name like Eunice Mayhew says *Sperm met egg in Iowa, and zygote grew up to become a bingo-playing, quilting square-dancer with a body like an upended pickle barrel.*

At the exact moment Eunice Mayhew screamed and two Rat Boys from Mars occupied the hallway at the Del Vista Arms, Shann Collins was lying down on her bed inside the Eden Project silo.

Shann was scared, and she was crying, too.

Wendy and Johnny McKeon assumed their daughter was crying because Shann was scared about the monsters, and worried about her friends who had gone out hunting the beasts.

It was not exactly why Shann Collins was crying.

Earlier, Shann and Johnny had crawled up to the surface in order to use their cell phones.

There was no more cellular service at all in Ealing, Iowa.

Shann and Johnny saw the forest-like columns of smoke that ringed the horizon.

They had gone back inside Eden, and Shann slipped into her bedroom, where she lay down on her bed and cried.

The night before, Shann Collins and I had sexual intercourse on the floor of the Eden bowling alley while I stared at a pair of shoes that had belonged to Wanda Mae Rutkowski.

The healthy Polish sperm I deposited inside Shann Collins's vagina found its way to a receptive egg.

Shann Collins was already pregnant, and she did not know anything about it.

The New Universe began in Eden one week after the end of the world began in Ealing.

Eden Five needed us, and Shann Collins and I were Adam and Eve to every New Human.

I had Unstoppable Sperm.

Dr. Grady McKeon would have been very pleased.

As Shann Collins, who was pregnant with a strong Polish boy who was going to be named Arek Andrzej Szczerba, cried on her bed, a volcano called Huacamochtli in Guatemala exploded in a massive eruption that blacked out the sun.

Everything in the village of Poqomchi rattled and shook. Rocks and burning ash from the angry sky bombarded the little village. Robby's father, Robert Brees Sr., his wife, Greta, and two-year-old son, Hector, tried to leave their small home. Robert Brees Sr. could not start his car. The car's motor was strangled in the steaming ash that turned everything into a dead gray night. Robert, Greta, and Hector Brees choked in the noxious smoke. They covered their faces with damp cloths and began walking away from their small house.

It was not a good idea.

In a cave in Spain, at a place called Altamira, a painted bison lay folded in death, his nose pressed to the ground, mouth open, one tired and defiant eye staring and staring and staring. He had been staring that way for fifteen thousand years, neither dead nor alive, trapped by history with his nameless balls pressed down into the ground between his curled hind legs.

Altamira means high view.

At exactly that moment, the vice president of the United States of America was being escorted through Eric Christopher Szerba's hospital room in Germany. The vice president of the United States of America patted my brother's shoulder and said to him, "The United States of America thanks you, son."

The vice president of the United States of America did not know anything at all about what was happening in Iowa, but he did know that Eric Christopher Szerba had lost his balls.

It made the vice president of the United States of America uncomfortable to think about a healthy young boy like Eric Christopher Szerba losing his balls to a bomb blast in Afghanistan. The vice president did not know exactly what to say to Eric.

What can you say to a kid who lost his balls?

All the boys at Curtis Crane Lutheran Academy already knew

there was no good answer to that. We all learned that lesson when EJ Elgin's ball was torn off by a whale.

The vice president of the United States of America was very pleased that his own balls, which he had named Theodore and Franklin, were just fine.

At exactly that moment, three massive National Guard helicopters flew at very low altitude directly over the Del Vista Arms Luxury Apartments.

The darkened hallway where we stood rattled and shook.

"Don't be afraid, Mrs. Mayhew," Robby said. "It's just me. Robby Brees."

Eunice Mayhew kept her hands up. She recognized Robby's voice.

Anyone who knew Robby Brees would recognize his voice. Robby's voice was perfect and smooth. Robby Brees's voice sounded the way soft vanilla ice cream feels and tastes inside your mouth on a blistering summer day, and when he sang, Robby Brees could make a lump form in my throat.

Eunice Mayhew cocked her head like a confused, barrel-shaped Orpington hen.

She said, "Something crazy is going on around here, Robby. Was that you and your friend dressed up like giant bugs this morning?"

"No, ma'am," Robby answered. "Uh. My friend . . . uh . . . Austin and me were only dressed up like lemurs."

"Rat Boys from Mars," I corrected.

Robby left the key to his apartment hanging from the ignition switch in his Ford Explorer. He knocked and knocked on the door to his apartment.

"Mom," Robby said to the door, "wake up! I left my keys in the car! Mom! You need to let me in!"

Connie Brees was asleep.

She did not expect her son, Robby, to be dressed as a Rat Boy from Mars. It was Friday morning, and Robby was supposed to be dressed up as a Curtis Crane Lutheran Academy Boy from Iowa. Connie Brees also did not expect her son to be accompanied by a second Lutheran Rat Boy from Mars, a golden retriever that could not bark, and Louis, the cook from *The Pancake House*, with whom she had sexual intercourse using condoms she found on the floor of her sixteen-year-old son's bedroom just the day before.

It was obvious Connie Brees did not expect any of this because she was wearing nothing but low-cut silk panties and a pale violet plunge bra.

Connie Brees had very large tits and fine golden strands of silky fuzz that lay smooth and flat between her navel and the waistband on her panties.

Connie Brees's skin was the color of perfectly prepared, soft and warm buttered toast. Her eyes matched Robby's, and her hair, which fell softly over her bare shoulders, was the color of apple spice cake.

"Uh," I said.

Robby's mother made me very horny. I definitely wanted to invite her to Eden.

I was not so sure about taking Louis, though.

Wendy McKeon's pancakes were just fine.

I wondered if Robby Brees would disapprove if I had sexual intercourse with his mother. I already knew how much it hurt his feelings that I had done it with Shann Collins.

I sighed. I was very confused.

Robby Brees was a good son. He did not have to be a good son. Nobody would expect it of him, unless you really knew Robby, and maybe loved him, too.

Connie Brees did not glow red.

Robby took off his grimacing lemur mask and kissed his mother. They held each other like they knew everything that had ever happened on every road that crossed beneath our feet.

I was happy for Robby and Connie Brees.

PICTURES OF ROBBY AND SHANN

HERE ARE TWO pictures I drew the week the world ended:

Robby Brees is sitting on the floor of his bedroom. He leans back on his elbows and there is a half-empty bottle of sweet white wine standing open beside his hip.

Robby is not wearing a shirt. In the picture, which was drawn on Monday night, Robby Brees is wearing nothing but some tight, white cotton underwear with colorful tigers printed on them.

His chest is square and flat, and his belly relaxed and soft. The perspective of the picture is from where I sit, cross-legged and in my socks, on top of Robby's bed.

I am floating.

We are laughing.

There is a cigarette held between the first two fingers of Robby's right hand, which comfortably rests on his belly.

The paper I draw on in my history book still smells of our cigarettes and wine.

Robby's skin reminds me of the warm insides of a late-summer white peach. Those peaches are named Babcock. Robby's hair is the color of graham cracker piecrust.

I can almost hear the music playing from Robby's stereo.

Robby is smiling, and we are reciting our favorite poems above the jangling vocals on a song called Live With Me.

The picture makes me feel like I am floating again.

Shann Collins sits on the staircase that leads to nowhere from her bedroom in the McKeon House. She is framed in an open doorway above, and narrow walls of distressed brick to either side of her.

The perspective is from below, looking up at Shann Collins from her dungeon for horny Lutheran boys. I draw it so her shorts, as they did, gap open just a bit, and there is a mysterious centering to the warm spot between Shann Collins's legs. I think about her pubic hair and the moistness in that perfect locus.

It is history.

It is the truth.

Shann's blouse opens slightly between the third and fourth button. I can almost smell the ginger and orange blossom lotion she smooths on her skin. Her hair is summer wheat and her skin is the color of a perfect October butternut squash. Shann Collins is smiling and her eyes are scolding.

I imagine I am explaining to her every wrong I have ever committed.

There is nothing I can do.

It is my job to tell the truth.

The picture makes me feel like the luckiest boy at the *Curtis Crane Lutheran Academy End-of-Year Mixed-Gender Mixer*, and it is the first time Shann Collins has ever danced with me. It makes me feel like seventh-grade Austin Szerba, whose best friend, Robby Brees, teaches him in secret how to dance with someone you love.

History will show that eighth-grade boys are never aware of the roads they have built, nor the ones they are standing on.

I love Shann Collins so much I am afraid it is killing me.

I love Robby Brees the same way.

I am an unstoppable train wreck to their lives.

THE INTERGALACTIC BUG COPS

ROBBY'S FORD EXPLORER was running out of gas.

It was a matter of reasonable debate, which would happen first: Would the gas run out, or would the old car simply give up and die?

Bang! Bang! Bang! Bang! Bang! went the thrown rod inside the Ford's crankcase.

We left the Del Vista Arms with two new citizens for Eden: Connie Brees and Louis, whose real name was Ah Wong Sing.

I thought Eden would be too crowded now. I did not want any more boys down there. Eden was only big enough for me and Robby Brees. I could make allowances for Johnny. It was selfish, I know, but it was how I felt.

That is the truth.

While Robby drove away from the Del Vista Arms, I plucked up my Saint Kazimierz medallion and put it into my mouth.

We'd found a chapel in Eden. It was little more than a small broom closet, but it had a church-like appearance. There is a particular kind of angle and aesthetic to all churches. The same quality is exhibited by coffins and urinals—you know what function they serve as soon as you see them.

These are the things that require neither signs nor labels.

Churches, coffins, and urinals all proclaim, *This is what I am*.

No questions asked.

At the exact moment Robby and I drove away with Louis, Connie Brees, and Ingrid, my golden retriever, in the backseat, I decided that I was going to become a Catholic, like I was always supposed to be—like all the Szczerba men always had been.

Saint Kazimierz's blood was in me, even if he did die a virgin.

Saint Kazimierz brought a dead girl to life, and he saved me from having my skull crushed by Hungry Jack.

"Thank you, Saint Kazimierz," I said.

Near Amelia Jenks Bloomer Park, two National Guard soldiers stood in the road beside an armored vehicle. They waved their hands at us, palms forward in the intergalactic gesture of *We have guns, so you better stop, motherfucker.*

We should have known the intergalactic bug cops would show up.

"Um," Robby said.

"Uh," I said.

"I wonder if they are going to give us tickets for underage smoking of cigarettes," Robby offered.

"I wonder if they are going to shoot us for being Truant Rat Boys from Mars," I said.

The truth is, the two National Guardsmen nearly *did* shoot Robby and me for being Rat Boys from Mars who were also ditching school.

We had no way of knowing that school, like everything else in Ealing, Iowa, had ceased to operate, due to the end of the world, and shit like that.

Coincidentally, Robby Brees and I were both wearing our grimacing lemur masks as we sat in the front seat of the dying Ford Explorer.

One of the guardsmen glowed red.

"Holy shit, Rob," I said.

"I see it," Robby concurred.

"What's wrong?" Connie Brees asked from the backseat.

"Nothing," I said, in the intergalactic teenage response to any question ever asked.

Robby corrected me, "That stocky guy on the left is going to turn into one of those bugs."

And, from the backseat of Robby's Ford Explorer, Louis finally spoke.

He said, "Shit."

"How could that *happen*?" I said.

"Those McKeon guys didn't know shit about what they were doing. Their experiment never got outside their lab," Robby said.

"You deserve a Nobel Prize, Rob," I said.

I dreamed of going to Sweden with Robby. I hoped he would let Shann come, too.

Connie Brees reached over the seat back and touched Robby's shoulder.

Connie said, "Do you know what's going on, Robert?"

She liked to call her son *Robert*.

I liked the way it sounded, too.

Robby said, "It would take hours to explain, Mom. Austin and I will tell you everything."

"Uh," I said.

I did not want Robby and me to tell his mother *everything*.

Robby stopped the car in the middle of the road.

Both of the National Guardsmen showed edgy, wide-eyed alertness. They were obviously uncertain as to how to respond to the two monsters in blue-and-white jumpsuits driving a beat-up Ford Explorer through the ruined town of Ealing, Iowa.

History will show that it is exactly times like these that having a grown-up *and* a golden retriever in the backseat of your Ford Explorer when you are also dressed as a Truant Rat Boy from Mars has potentially lifesaving benefits. The guardsmen, who were armed with M-16s, also thought Connie Brees was very sexy, which provided a considerable anesthetizing influence over our detainers.

An M-16 rifle is the military equivalent of a Colt AR-15. The difference is that the guardsmen's M-16s had thirty-round clips and were fully automatic. Also, unlike Earl Elgin, I did not believe the soldiers would miss Robby and me if they decided to shoot.

ENOLA GAY AND BEAU BARTON'S BONER

CONNIE BREES SHOWED the soldiers her breasts and FedEx identification badge.

She explained she was taking her "sons" and "husband" to safety in Waterloo.

Robby's mother did not actually expose herself in front of her teenage *sons*, but she did elevate her chest, the way that some women do, as though she were hoisting a battle flag before a lesser enemy.

It made me happy to think of Robby as my brother, but I was not comfortable with the idea of Ah Wong Sing being my father. It was quite obvious that he would have had to be our stepfather, and no son ever likes his stepfather.

That is a fact of history.

The guards' names were Beau Barton and Florencio Villegas.

Beau Barton had a real dynamo of an Iowa name.

Florencio Villegas did not.

Also, Florencio Villegas had somehow been infected by *Contained MI Plague Strain 412E*.

Nobody had any way of knowing how that came to be.

Later, when Robby Brees and I discussed poetry, science, and history one evening in the library of Eden, we concluded that, somehow, the dead Unstoppable Soldiers may have developed Unstoppable Mold; or perhaps the mold grew on the egg masses that were deposited in Duane Coventry's home on Onondaga Street. Maybe, we conjectured, Florencio Villegas happened to pass through the alley where we skated in Grasshopper Jungle when Robby's blood was fresh on the pavement, after Tyler Jacobson dropped the moldy blue universe from inside Johnny McKeon's office to splatter over everything.

Whatever the origin, it did not matter.

We would never know with absolute certainty.

Histories are actually full of conjectures. Those conjectures become so accepted by descendants and readers that time itself is forced to rearrange its own furniture. This is a new history, and I cannot do such a thing.

The end of the world was fully one week old, and the only human being on the entire planet called Earth with the capacity to stop it was my best friend, a sixteen-year-old homosexual Lutheran boy from Iowa named Robert Brees Jr.

Florencio Villegas was born in Topeka, Kansas.

Florencio Villegas was a diesel mechanic in Cedar Rapids.

He would be dead within thirty minutes.

Beau Barton worked as a bagger at a grocery store in Boone County. He would also be dead within thirty minutes.

Beau Barton was twenty-four years old and smelled like mouthwash and chewing tobacco. Beau Barton was actually related to me in a distant and illegitimate, Iowa-by-marriage way.

Beau Barton, like me, was Phoebe Hildebrandt's great-grandson. Nobody ever knew Beau Barton's actual great-grandfather was the Catholic priest who counseled Phoebe for years following the death of her first husband, Andrzej Szczerba. Everyone in Iowa City assumed the semen that created Beau's grandfather, a man named Eldon Wayne Barton, came from the balls of Daniel Barton, whose balls did not work so well. Daniel Barton was the radio station owner Phoebe Hildebrandt married after her husband, Andrzej Szczerba, was shot in the head while taking a shit during the Battle of Cisterna in Italy during World War 2.

All roads keep crossing and crossing at the point of my pen.

Nobody ever knew anything about Beau Barton and me.

Beau Barton adjusted his penis conspicuously as he leaned his face through my window. He was attempting to assess the threat level of the smoking Rat Boys from Mars and the woman with the large tits in the backseat.

Beau Barton, my cousin, had an obvious erection. He stared and smiled, practically drooling at Connie Brees.

Beau Barton thought he would most likely masturbate in the trees by the creek later that day if nothing was happening. He would not get that opportunity.

Beau Barton was sweating. He showed obvious embarrassment when he became aware that I was looking directly at the camouflaged bulge caused by his swelling erection.

Beau Barton was an idiot.

When Beau Barton was fourteen years old, he unintentionally burned down his family's garage in Boone County, Iowa. It happened when Beau Barton set fire to a plastic model of the *Enola Gay*. Beau Barton, the teenager, loved to build models and then set fire to them. Fires and big tits gave Beau Barton, the twenty-four-year-old National Guardsman, unstoppable hard-ons.

Louis and Ingrid may just as well have been invisible to Beau Barton from Boone County. He probably might have noticed them had they been engulfed in flames.

The *Enola Gay* was a plane named after the mother of Paul Tibbets, who was its pilot.

History will show that Enola Gay Haggard Tibbets is the only mother who ever shared her name with an airplane that killed at least one-tenth of one million human beings.

Paul Tibbets was covered for Mother's Day gifts after naming a plane with such a reputation after his mom.

Paul Tibbets grew up in Cedar Rapids, Iowa, which is also where Florencio Villegas repaired diesel engines.

Orville and Wilbur Wright invented the airplane.

All roads converged at Kelsey Creek Bridge.

At that exact moment, Beau Barton, the very aroused National Guardsman, wanted to do only two things: He wanted to put his penis between Connie Brees's breasts, and he wanted to go back home to Boone County, Iowa.

Boone County, Iowa, is named for Nathan Boone, who was the youngest son of Daniel Boone. As far as I know, neither Nathan Boone nor his father ever wore coonskin caps. They also never killed more than a hundred thousand people. I wore an artificial coonskin cap that had been made in China on the day my fifteen-year-old brother, Eric Christopher Szerba, got his first blow job in a Nashville hotel from two prostitutes named Tiffany and Rhonda. Eric liked his blow job. Eric also started calling me *Booney* ever since that trip we took to Nashville when I was only nine and Eric got a blow job.

When I was nine years old, I could not understand why my fifteen-year-old brother, Eric, would let Tiffany and Rhonda talk him into putting his penis inside their mouths, but when I was nine, I also could have just as easily lost my balls in a whaling accident and never known the difference.

Boys' attitudes about their balls and putting their penises in someone else's mouth change significantly sometime after the age of nine.

The soldiers wore the kind of camouflaged battle dress issues that troops used in Afghanistan, which is where my brother lost the lower portion of his right leg and both of his testicles. With those uniforms, the National Guardsmen did not blend in so well among things like Iowa cornfields and rivers with spawning walleyes, and shit like that.

Robby and I took off our masks so Beau Barton and Florencio Villegas would not kill us, and so they could see we were just normal-looking sixteen-year-old Iowa brothers who happened to be wearing matching blue-and-white jumpsuits, which also did not blend in so well.

Beau Barton was mad at me for staring at his erection.

He said, "Are you boys in some kind of dance club or something?"

"Uh," I said.

Robby answered, "We work at a car wash in Waterloo. These are our car wash uniforms."

Robby truly deserved a Nobel Prize, a million dollars, and a trip to Sweden with me and Shann, if he would let her come along.

Beau Barton said, "Those are some real humdinger outfits they make you boys wear."

People in Boone County, Iowa, used words like *humdinger*.

THE BATTLE OF KELSEY CREEK BRIDGE

EALING, IOWA, WAS being evacuated by the National Guard.

Beau Barton and Florencio Villegas had been posted on the road to Kelsey Creek Bridge. Their job was to ensure traffic moved in one direction only.

That direction was *away* from Ealing.

Beau Barton and Florencio Villegas instructed us to follow them across Kelsey Creek Bridge. They drove ahead of Robbie's Ford Explorer in their armored vehicle. They decided to escort us around the wreck of Ollie Jungfrau's Dodge Caravan minivan. Beau Barton and Florencio Villegas wanted to be certain we made it safely to the highway that connected Ealing to Waterloo.

It was very kind of them to do that, but it was not a good idea.

Someone had already placed a yellow tarp over the smashed front end of Ollie Jungfrau's Dodge Caravan minivan. There was also a dripping black X spray-painted on the tarp. The National Guard were real dynamos at covering dead things with plastic.

We had seen dozens of tarps in Ealing on our drive away from the Del Vista Arms. The tipped-over *Eyewitness News* van was entirely blanketed with them. It looked like an inflatable bouncer house you might rent for a kid's birthday party.

Watch your balls.

Ealing had become the plastic tarp capital of Iowa.

Unstoppable Tarps! Unstoppable Tarps!

No one at all knew what the hell was going on in Ealing, Iowa, except for me and Robby Brees.

Unfortunately for Beau Barton and Florencio Villegas, just as their vehicle crept past the wreckage of Ollie Jungfrau's van, the Unstoppable Soldier that used to be a Hoover High School punk named Tyler Jacobson, still hopped up on meth and confused after his first sexual *experiment*, appeared, standing in the middle of the road at the end of the bridge.

And just behind Tyler Jacobson was the Unstoppable Soldier that had hatched out of Travis Pope.

They only wanted to do one thing at that exact moment.

Tyler Jacobson and Travis Pope had also molted during the night. They were now eight feet tall, with abdomens as thick as telephone poles.

Louis whimpered in the backseat.

Louis knew all about Unstoppable Soldiers and the things they liked to do.

The armored vehicle stopped.

Robby said, "Holy shit."

I said, "They . . . um . . . got bigger."

Robby Brees's sputtering Ford Explorer chose that exact moment to die.

We were stuck on Kelsey Creek Bridge.

"Um," I said.

The doors of the National Guard vehicle opened on either side. Beau Barton and Florencio Villegas popped out of the cab, their M-16s raised and ready. It looked like a scene from an action movie.

Beau Barton and Florencio Villegas had guns, motherfuckers.

It was a very bad idea.

Connie Brees said, "Oh my God."

Ingrid yawned.

Louis threw his arms around Connie Brees. He buried his face in Connie Brees's hair and turned away from the spectacle that unfolded on the bridge ahead of us, through the windshield of Robby's dead Ford Explorer.

In the creek below us, walleyes spawned and spawned. Carried on Kelsey Creek's steady current, Mrs. Edith Mitchell's body had already drifted into the Cedar River.

I found myself thinking about Saint Kazimierz, and contemplating why people said things like *Oh my God* at times like these. If there really was a God, I thought, why would Connie Brees want to lay her claim to a deity that unleashed Unstoppable Soldiers on human beings caught on a bridge above Kelsey Creek in Iowa?

Johnny McKeon had one tattoo on his entire body. On his right forearm, in blurry blue-green ink, which is how all tattoos look on men as old as Johnny McKeon who had also served in the United States Navy, was the image of *Sputnik*. Beneath the satellite was an inscription that read *Oh My God!*

Johnny McKeon told me that his father, who was also Dr. Grady McKeon's father, looked up into the starlit sky above Iowa the night the Soviet Union launched *Sputnik*, and said those three exact words.

Oh my God!

Johnny McKeon's father believed it was the end of the world in 1957.

Johnny McKeon's father had a heart attack as soon as he said those three words.

He died when Johnny was an infant.

Oh my God.

History will probably verify that *Oh my God* was among the first idiomatic exclamations uttered by human beings. The phrase has persisted for at least twenty thousand years.

We killed this big hairy thing, and this big hairy thing, and then we did a little experiment.

Oh my God.

You know what I mean.

If God had satellite TV, he was probably tuned in to the Battle of Kelsey Creek Bridge. Maybe he and Saint Kazimierz were sitting on a cloud couch together, nibbling unstoppable popcorn and watching what happened to us, and to Beau Barton and Florencio Villegas, too.

The National Guardsmen's machine guns spit bursts of metal-jacketed bullets at the Unstoppable Soldiers. The sound was electric and terrifying. The bullets may just as well have been candy sprinkles on unstoppable frosted cupcakes, because they had absolutely no effect at all on the monstrous praying mantis beasts with blade-spiked arms.

Tyler Jacobson and Travis Pope walked through the spray of bullets like they were cats walking through darkness; like beauty pageant queens parading through swirling showers of glitter.

If the Unstoppable Soldiers even noticed the bullets careening off their exoskeletons, they did not show it.

Tyler Jacobson snatched Florencio Villegas between the pointed blades that ridged his crushing arms. Tyler Jacobson began devouring the soldier, boots, helmet, body armor, and all. Some of Florencio Villegas's blood splashed over the metal hood of the armored vehicle he'd been driving just moments earlier.

Tyler Jacobson even tried to eat Florencio Villegas's M-16.

He spit it out.

Travis Pope attempted to fight with Tyler Jacobson over the meal he was making of Florencio Villegas. Beau Barton bravely fired and fired at both of the Unstoppable Soldiers while they ate and sparred over Florencio Villegas's right leg.

That was exactly when Travis Pope noticed the other, as-yet-uneaten National Guardsman.

It was not a good thing for my second- or third-cousin, or whatever sharing a great-grandmother made Beau Barton to me.

I got out of Robby's car first.

For a moment, stunned, Robby Brees and I had sat there, watching what was happening on the bridge ahead of us. Then I realized we were all stuck anyway, and Robby and I still had our paintball guns that were loaded with the blood of a real, cigarette-smoking, homosexual teenage God.

As soon as my feet hit the tarmac of the bridge span, Robby shouted, "Austin! Hey! What the hell are you doing?"

Tyler Jacobson was covered with blood and bug spit. He also had a foot-long length of Florencio Villegas's webbed belt dangling from his left mandible like a strand of bloody spaghetti. Tyler Jacobson was aroused by the motion I made as I ran from Robby's Ford Explorer. He watched me for a moment while he excreted a foamy white meringue of bug shit onto the blacktop between his two hind legs.

Tyler Jacobson was already hungry again.

Beau Barton emptied his M-16 on the Unstoppable Soldiers. He tried to run back toward Ollie Jungfrau's van when his gun stopped firing.

Unstoppable Soldiers are very, very fast.

Travis Pope sprang with a single jump over the armored vehicle the guardsmen had been driving. Travis Pope landed directly on top of Beau Barton. It was like a cat playing with a very small mouse.

Travis Pope pinned Beau Barton with his two middle legs.

Beau Barton wriggled and squirmed.

Travis Pope lowered his triangular face, opened his massive jaws, and bit off everything that had once been Beau Barton from the armpits up. Travis Pope chewed and chewed.

The sound was like a starved barbershop quartet engaged in a buffalo-wing-eating contest.

I raised my paintball gun.

I thought about saying something dramatic.

History, when told truthfully, will show that boys never really do make heroic statements while engaged in battle. Historians craftily pen those things in after the fact.

I had nothing to say.

But I did think about Saint Kazimierz. I thought about my brother, Eric Christopher Szerba. I wished he could watch what was happening here on the Kelsey Creek Bridge on satellite television. I thought about my mother and father, too, and I was convinced I would never see them again. And I thought about my balls—Orville and Wilbur.

I cannot say why I thought about my balls, only that I did.

All of that ran through my mind in the exact span of time it took for me to pull the trigger on my paintball gun.

That is the truth.

Bap! Bap! went the paintballs.

At that exact moment, Tyler Jacobson sprang toward me.

Pop! Pop! Pop! went Robby Brees's paintball gun.

Robby, naturally, chased after me when I ran from the car. Robby Brees truly was a superhero.

If Unstoppable Soldiers are capable of showing expressions with their mechanical faces and massive compound eyes, then both Tyler Jacobson and Travis Pope looked at each other in confusion and stunned defeat, possibly horror.

I shot Travis Pope a third time, a direct hit into his thoracic joint.

The Unstoppable Soldier broke completely in half.

"Fuck yeah!" I said.

I had never killed anything bigger than a freshwater perch in my entire life. There was something exhilarating and pure that rushed through me in that moment. I am almost embarrassed to say that it felt somewhat sexual, and made me kind of horny.

It is the truth.

This is why assholes in charge of shit convince boys to go to war, I believe.

"Fuck yeah!" Robby said.

Robby Brees felt the same thing.

Tyler Jacobson staggered away from the front of the guards' vehicle. As he stumbled backward, he began disassembling—*clop! clop! clop!*—in detached segments that looked like goat-sized green lobsters flailing around in puddles of cheesy, shimmering yellow goo.

"Robby?" I said.

"Yeah?" Robby answered.

"Are you okay?" I said.

Robby Brees said, "Yep."

And I said, "That was probably one of the top-three most bitchin' things I have ever done in my life."

Robby said, "The only way it could have been better, Porcupine, is if we were on our skateboards when it happened."

Robby Brees was the brightest boy on the planet called Earth.

At that exact moment, in a small house across Ealing, on Onondaga Street, the Unstoppable Soldier that had once been Eileen Pope came out into the blue plaid Iowa afternoon.

She was very horny and very hungry.

And her eggs were hatching.

GREAT BIG JAR

WE TRANSFERRED OUR belongings from Robby's dead Ford Explorer into the National Guard armored vehicle.

Robby drove.

The armored vehicle did not have a cassette tape deck.

It would have been a perfect time to listen to *Exile on Main Street*.

"They should put tape decks in this shit," Robby said.

"They don't even have a lighter for our *fags*," I pointed out.

"What could they possibly have been thinking?" Robby offered. "Anyone knows boys are better soldiers when they can smoke cigarettes and listen to the Rolling Stones."

"We are unstoppable," I said.

It was just as well. I had matches, and half a pack remained of my Benson & Hedges cigarettes. I lit one for Robby and then reached across and put it into his mouth. I touched his lips. I was still very confused about everything. I cared so much for Robby Brees. I would do anything for him. But at that exact moment, I was worried about Shann Collins, and I needed to get back to Eden.

What was I going to do?

I caught Connie Brees watching me when I put a lit cigarette into Robby's mouth and my fingers touched his lips. Connie Brees smiled.

"Um," I said.

Robby said, "Thanks, Austin."

I lit a cigarette for myself and passed the pack and matches to Robby's mom. Louis did not smoke.

Ingrid yawned.

Robby and I explained as much as we could. It was really too much to fit inside one car ride, and who could ever expect Connie Brees and Louis Ah Wong Sing to make any sense of what had been happening in Ealing, anyway?

It would take time.

Robby and I smoked.

Robby Brees sang Let It Loose. I had to be quiet when he sang because the sound of it made me want to cry, in a good way.

After he finished, Robby said, "There are other Unstoppable Soldiers out there somewhere."

I nodded.

I said, "Uh. What can we do, Rob?"

Robby said, "It is a big jar we're in, Austin."

"It's a great big jar," I said.

Here is what the end of the world looks like:

It looks like a child running out into the road, eyes focused only on some destination ahead—the future, which is on the other side—and the child fails to notice the speeding truck that is there, on that same road, in the present.

This is what the end of the world looks like.

All roads cross here.

Thu-Thump!

Robby slammed on the brakes.

The armored vehicle completely ran over the small pedestrian, front wheels and back wheels.

"Shit!" Robby said.

"Uh," I said.

We sat there for a moment, not really knowing what to do.

What do you do when it is the end of the world and you run over some dumb kid who jumps out in front of your armored vehicle?

"I will go look," I said.

I climbed down from the cab.

In truth, I was afraid to look at the road behind us and come face-to-face with the bloody mess that would be there. This is history. I was standing in the present, looking back at the past with the empty road ahead of us.

What could I do?

And in the road behind us, stiffly clambering up onto shaky legs was a dark, confused Unstoppable Soldier that stood no taller than shoulder height to me.

And it was hungry.

I ran before the thing realized I was food.

"Holy shit! Holy shit! Holy shit!"

Excrementum Sanctum.

I slammed the door shut just as the hungry beast crumpled its arms against the side of the cab.

"What the—" Robby began. Then he saw the folded, spiked arms of the Unstoppable Soldier as they scraped against the bulletproof window on my door.

"Gun it, Rob," I said.

This is what the end of the world looks like.

Leaping and skittering over the strands of barbwire that lined the highway out toward the old McKeon House came dozens and dozens—hundreds and hundreds—of little, hungry and horny Unstoppable Soldiers.

"Holy shit," Rob said.

"Holy shit," I agreed.

We drove.

I lit another cigarette.

EPILOGUE:
LUCKY, A CIGARETTE RUN, AND THE BISON

I CALL THE boy *Lucky.*

It is only a nickname for the kid.

In the dead of a bitter Iowa winter when he was born, inside the same examination room where Wendy McKeon filled syringes with Robby Brees's blood, I gave him the name Arek Andrzej Szczerba.

I also reclaimed my stolen consonants.

I write in the library. The walls have been adorned with every imaginable beast and totem: a bison, a two-headed boy, an Unstoppable Soldier, a volcano in Guatemala, praying hands, a *Stanpreme* pizza, a sign that says Roof Access↑.

You know what I mean.

Today is March 29, but spring has not taken hold above us yet.

It is also Robby Brees's twenty-first birthday. We are going out on a cigarette run today.

I will explain.

Lucky—Arek—is four years old. We have been living in Eden for a long time. Wendy McKeon made rules about things like when boys and girls can take showers, and there is a new history. The new history is Eden's.

What I have written here is not the history of Eden. It is the history of the end of the world. All real histories will be about everything, and they will stretch to the end of the world.

The end of the world started when Andrzej Szczerba slid into the cold sea as his boy, Krzys, watched and wept and drifted closer and closer to the United States of America.

Nobody knew anything about it.

There are more of us now. The citizens of the New Universe include Robby Brees, Shann Collins, Johnny and Wendy McKeon, Connie Brees, Louis Ah Wong Sing, and my son, Arek. Connie Brees also gave birth to a baby—a girl named Amelie.

Amelie Sing Brees is a real dynamo of an Eden name.

We did what Dr. Grady McKeon told us we needed to do.

And Ingrid is here. She lies beneath my feet as I write.

I continue to be torn between my love for Shann Collins and Robby Brees. But I no longer care to ask the question, *What am I going to do?*

Sometimes it is perfectly acceptable to decide not to decide, to remain confused and wide-eyed about the next thing that will pop up in the road you build. Shann does not like it. Robby Brees asks me to live with him. I stay in my own room, which I share with my strong Polish son, Arek, and we are very happy.

Robby Brees and I ventured out into the world above during a snowstorm, in the first winter after the end of the world. We were correct in assuming the Unstoppable Soldiers would either leave Iowa or hibernate during wintertime.

We armed ourselves with the blood of God, in any event.

It was reckless and wild, going out with Robby. It was just like everything Robby Brees and I ever did together for our entire lives. Nobody else would come with us. We began to call these trips our *Cigarette Runs.*

Nobody knew anything about them.

Of course, we had enough cigarettes in Eden to last us for years and years.

We would be gone for days. It frightened the others, so we came back one time with battery-powered walkie-talkies that had a range of fifteen miles.

Robby and I always went much farther than fifteen miles.

One time, we'd gone all the way to Minneapolis.

Robby and I never found a single human being on the surface of the planet called Earth. I do not believe Robby and I *wanted* to find anyone else, but we never said that aloud. We did not need to say such things.

On our *Cigarette Runs*, we have killed a few Unstoppable Soldiers that stubbornly scavenged during wintertime, and Robby Brees and I always spend our nights together in the nicest abandoned hotels, penthouses, and mansions.

It is fun and daring.

It is on these *Cigarette Runs* that I have uncovered much of the history included in this book. It is the truth. It is my job. From hand-scrawled calendars, newspapers, appointment books, pocket-sized digital voice recorders, bones, cast-off clothing, and inflatable whales, I have put things together the best that I can, and I know that you trust me.

I have no reason to lie.

Animals have come back in tremendous numbers. On our last *Cigarette Run*, just after Arek's fourth birthday in February, Robby and I ran into a herd of deer standing across the I-35. There were thousands of them. The deer had already forgotten why they should be afraid of human beings. When we got out of the car we'd been driving, Robby and I could walk right up to the animals and pet them.

Robby Brees and I are the kings of the world when we are out on our runs.

When we come back to Eden, tired and exhilarated at the same time, Robby and I bring gifts home for the women and babies: new clothes and underwear, diapers, toys, food that does not come in army-issue cans, even sports cars and motor homes.

I always bring back books for the library. Books have everything in them. After the end of the world, you cannot learn a goddamned thing from a computer or a television screen.

Nobody ever thought about that—how humanity could only be preserved by paintings on cave walls, or books, and vinyl recordings. Robby Brees always brings vinyl records home to Eden.

I found an autographed copy of *The Chocolate War*.

We own everything in the world, and Robby and I stockpile whatever we might need if Eden breaks down. It is going to happen eventually. Things break down. History tells us that, even if we do not want to listen.

Shann is quietly pouting; no doubt hiding inside her bedroom. She does not like it when Robby and I go out on our runs. But it is Robby's birthday.

We need to do it.

There is something inside all boys that drives us to go away again and again and again.

Again is now.

We have not been out all month, and soon it will be too warm and too dangerous for Robby and me to leave. The Unstoppable Soldiers will come back. They always do.

Robby Brees and I found a two-man ultralight aircraft in the hangar at Cedar Falls airfield. Just like Orville and Wilbur Wright. Robby swears he is brave enough to try taking the thing up for a flight. We have checked the motor, and it runs fine. I think if I get drunk enough today, or shit like that, I will let Robby Brees talk me into sitting in that goddamned airplane with him and going up for his twenty-first birthday, as long as I can have a cigarette or two.

He promises we will fly over Grasshopper Jungle in our own airplane, and Robby will sing Rolling Stones songs and I will smoke cigarettes and spit on the planet called Earth and we will shout the names of our balls from the sky.

Johnny McKeon has never given up trying to contact other human beings. I believe there are others somewhere on the planet Earth. I cannot calculate how long an Unstoppable Diaspora could overrun every continent. I fantasize that my mother, father, and brother are all fat and speak German fluently.

Maybe Polish.

Johnny McKeon hooked up spools of flat, twin-channeled wires to the antenna posts on the television sets in the Brain Room. Every day he sits, watching nothing and listening to static, twisting and turning the knobs on the UHF and VHF adjustments. One morning, last summer, Johnny McKeon came running from the Brain Room, shouting, "I'll be danged! I'll be danged! I found someone!"

Naturally, we all ran to see what Johnny McKeon had found on the televisions in the Brain Room. When we got there, there was nothing. Johnny McKeon swore he'd seen a portion of an old episode of a program called *Gunsmoke*.

James Arness was the star of *Gunsmoke*.

Johnny McKeon has been losing his mind down here in Eden.

He watches the televisions every day.

Wendy McKeon makes rules. Robby and I do not follow Wendy McKeon's rules very well.

Ah Wong Sing cooks. He is a real dynamo at cooking.

Connie Brees has a 230 bowling average.

Before we leave, Robby, Arek, and I take a piss together in the giant Nightingale urinal. It is what we do. One day, I will tell Arek about Krzys Szczerba and Eva Nightingale, and all the rest of our history.

Arek is a good boy.

"I will look for a coonskin cap for you when Robby and I are out, Lucky," I say.

Arek looks up from where he is peeing and says, "What's that, Tata?"

Arek calls me *Tata*.

"You will see," I say.

Ingrid is up above, shitting in the snow.

Robby and I make several trips up and down, transporting things we want to take with us on our run. This trip we are driving a BMW X5. We took it, brand new, from a dealership in Peoria, Illinois, where if anybody was still alive, Robby Brees and I would be wanted outlaws.

Once the car is loaded, Robby and I say good-bye to the other New Humans.

Shann is tough. She kisses us both and tells Robby to be careful.

I still enjoy watching Shann kiss Robby Brees.

Robby tells her that he will bring her back a Rolex wristwatch.

Shann Collins has four Rolex wristwatches. It is a joke. I would have a difficult time imagining anything as useless in Eden as a Rolex wristwatch.

I say we will bring back cases of Cup-O-Noodles.

That makes everyone happy.

Cup-O-Noodles is Arek's favorite meal.

Arek gets to climb up the ladder with us. The boy has only been outside a handful of times in his entire life.

Robby is warming up the BMW. I still do not drive very well, although Robby has taught me how to do it.

Arek forms an icy snowball in his little pink hands. It is a game.

All boys do this, just as all boys build roads that crisscross and carry us away.

"Pow! Tata! You are dead!" Arek says.

Tata is Polish for Daddy.

The snowball hits my thigh and I feign injury. I scoop a handful of snow and return fire, purposely missing the boy.

The hatch is open. Louis and Shann poke their heads above the rim, like timid gophers.

I light a cigarette.

Robby gets out of the car and trudges across the snow to say a last good-bye to Arek. Like his father, Arek also loves Robby Brees very much.

In the swirling fog of smoke that rises in front of my face, I notice a large figure moving in the field beyond a row of parked motor homes and Cadillacs.

"Holy shit!" I say.

Robby has a paintball gun at his side. We never go out without one.

"Holy shit!" Robby says.

"Austin?" Shann calls nervously.

Shann cannot see what the three of us are looking at.

"What is that, Tata?" Arek, who I call *Lucky*, asks.

Across the field, I can see them. There are three of them, at first, and then I realize it is an entire herd: massive, dark, horned, and humpbacked. North American bison. The buffaloes have come to Iowa, to Eden.

"It is a big hairy thing," I say.

And that was our day.

You know what I mean.

ACKNOWLEDGMENTS

I have been writing all my life. I never for a moment considered the idea of publication until my dear friend, author Kelly Milner Halls, challenged me into doing it.

It was a good idea, even if I never actually wanted anyone to read what I wrote.

Thank you, Kelly.

About two years ago, I decided to stop writing. Well, to be honest, not *the verb* writing, but I decided to get out of the *business* aspect of it, for which I have absolutely no backbone. I never felt so free as when I wrote things that I believed nobody would ever see. *Grasshopper Jungle* was one of those things. It was more-or-less fortune, then, that I happened to show the first portion of the novel to my friend Michael Bourret. He talked me into not quitting. Michael is, after all, a magical agent. I think when he walks into offices and shit like that, people believe they are looking at a baby harp seal. Nobody says no to a baby harp seal. Michael wanted to represent me and this novel that nobody was supposed to see.

It was a good idea. Thank you, Michael.

We made a list: Who did I want to show *Grasshopper Jungle* to, well . . . besides nobody? And on that list was Julie Strauss-Gabel.

I never thought I'd hear from her, much less get the chance to work with her, but Julie gave me a phone call. We wanted to work together.

It was a good idea.

In fact, I have to say that working with Julie Strauss-Gabel as my editor and publisher on *Grasshopper Jungle* has been one of the most rewarding experiences in my writing career. Thank you, Julie.

Most writers never know the name of the person who copyedits their books. Copy editors are the people who tell writers they don't know the difference between restrictive and nonrestrictive clauses, or between Latin dance steps and dessert toppings.

I suppose it is a good idea to know these things.

My copy editor, museum date, and Hell's Kitchen dining partner whenever I go to New York, Anne Heausler, is simply the best; and she is so gentle when battering my self-esteem with her *Chicago Manual of Style* or *Webster's Dictionary*. Thank you, Anne.

And finally, I don't know if having a writer in the family is such a good idea. But I must give thanks and love to my wife, Jocelyn; my son, Trevin; and daughter, Chiara, for being such dynamos at putting up with me.